BURN MAN

SELECTED STORIES

MARK ANTHONY JARMAN

INTRODUCTION BY JOHN METCALF

BIBLIOASIS
WINDSOR, ONTARIO

FIRST EDITION
10 9 8 7 6 5 4 3 2

Library and Archives Canada Cataloguing in Publication

Title: Burn man : selected stories / Mark Anthony Jarman.
Other titles: Short stories. Selections
Names: Jarman, Mark Anthony, 1955 - author.
Identifiers: Canadiana (print) 2023015638X | Canadiana (ebook) 20230156460
ISBN 9781771965477 (softcover) | ISBN 9781771965484 (EPUB)
Classification: LCC PS8569.A6 A6 2023 | DDC C813/.54—dc23

Edited by John Metcalf
Copyedited by Emily Donaldson
Text designed by Gordon Robertson

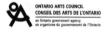

Published with the generous assistance of the Canada Council for the Arts, which last year invested $153 million to bring the arts to Canadians throughout the country, and the financial support of the Government of Canada. Biblioasis also acknowledges the support of the Ontario Arts Council (OAC), an agency of the Government of Ontario, which last year funded 1,709 individual artists and 1,078 organizations in 204 communities across Ontario, for a total of $52.1 million, and the contribution of the Government of Ontario through the Ontario Book Publishing Tax Credit and Ontario Creates.

PRINTED AND BOUND IN CANADA

MIX
Paper from
responsible sources
FSC® C004071

To John and Myrna with gratitude and affection,
and with love to Clarissa.

Yeats. Yeats. Yeats. Yeats. Yeats. Yeats. Yeats. Yeats.
Why wouldn't the man shut up?

— John Thompson, "Ghazal IX"

CONTENTS

WURLITZERS AND CHICKEN BONES

M ARK ANTHONY JARMAN's memoir writing and travel pieces are sharp with observation and hum with vibrant language. I was charmed by the beginning of the following memoir piece about an old-timers' hockey evening.

Drive the night, driving out to old-timer hockey in January in New Brunswick, new fallen snow and a full moon on Acadian and Loyalist fields, fields beautiful and ice-smooth and curved like old bathtubs. In this blue light Baptist churches and ordinary farms become cathode, hallucinatory. Old Indian islands in the wide river and trees up like fingers and the strange shape of the snowbanks.

It's not my country, but it is my country now. I'm a traveller in a foreign land and I relish that. The universe above my head may boast vast dragon-red galaxies and shimmering ribbons of green, and the merciless sun may be shining this moment somewhere in Asia, but tonight along the frozen moonlit St. John River the country is a lunatic lunar blue and the arena air smells like fried onions and chicken. We park by the door, play two 25 minute periods, shake hands, pay the refs, knock back a few in dressing room #5, and drift back from hockey pleasantly tired, silent as integers. And I am along for the ride.

Wind-carved snow drifts "curved like old bathtubs," Baptist churches and farm houses in the blue moonlight "become cathode, hallucinatory." How marvellously seen and captured! How essentially Jarman!

And here is Mark Jarman, tourist in Venice.

Walking the fondamenta on Venice's north lagoon, I see the snowy Dolomite Alps as if through a lens. This rare sight, such clear skies in February—a good omen, I decide. Somewhere out there in the bright lagoon is an island of bones, a mountain of skulls; *skools* says Antonello the bearded Italian archeologist. Plague victims from the 1300s to the 1600s and bodies exhumed from San Michele and moved by bone-barge to the *ossario*, thousands of nameless skeletons.

Antonello tells me he worked mapping the north lagoon and its many scattered islands. He tries to think of a word in English and I realize it is "drone." *Si, si,* his drone passing over a mountain of skulls, bones dumped over pestilent centuries. Antonello mentions the poet Joseph Brodsky buried on the cemetery island of San Michele close to Ezra Pound and Olga Budge and a few drowned sailors. Antonello likes Brodsky but says Ezra is problematic, *fascista*. Stravinsky lies there and Russian dancers and Doppler!

We drift to a bar on the canal, amber Nuda e Cruda beer and outside tables in the sunny afternoon. Winter, but we've had such good luck with the sun. A speedboat pulls up beside our table, at the wheel a man yelling wildly, "Ubriaconi! Molesto!"

Clarissa translates: "Drunkards! I molest you!"

Someone inside the bar waltzes out and bear-hugs the man beside the canal. I like a table where locals can roar up in speedboat-wash and shout such a line.

After reading several of these travel pieces, one begins to feel that wherever Jarman seats himself for a beer, surreal events will inevitably unfold; they are less dispatches from Venice or Oporto than serial reports from Jarman Country.

A recent report received, a summarizing postcard from Marseille:

Much dog crap, many rats.

Yet it is not the charm of such as the above that secured Mark Jarman's place among Canada's pre-eminent writers. Quintessential Jarman is suggested by the following quotation taken from near the beginning of a story entitled "Cowboys Incorporated," which appeared in his first collection, *Dancing Nightly in the Tavern* (1984).

The big country. Asleep. "Wake up, Wake up." Near Easter time too, the Lenten tornadoes touching down around the women in their gardens. "Wake up buddy." Jankovitch closes his eyes to rise from cancerous dreams of flooded towns dying in silt rivers, farm land leaching out, drifting away, Ironchild toying with his needles and grinding blue pills in the failing light. "Wake up." Jankovitch jerks forward: "What?" Saliva drying upturned in his stupid throat. Crows, nothing grows, gears gnash in testimony to bad driving and the Swedish car's endless capacity for punishment. This is the way they go: "We want you to drive again, okay?" Virginia in fedora and shades leaning over the seat to gently rouse Jankovitch who's down in shitkicker country again . . . as Carlene Carter said, *put the cunt back in country* . . . Johnny Cash's girl . . . the car swinging hard across the blue plains and raggedy-ass cottonwood, the endless flight through pale aspens and truck stop botulism, Kmart, snakeskin cowboy boots, cheating songs, box elders. This is just after the grain elevator blew over to Missouri burned for days and they couldn't get at the bodies. In the blind pigs and roadhouses, lizards cringe under the crashing rain of Wurlitzers and chicken bones. God and country are toasted. "Wake up buddy." Jankovitch supposed to be loyally prone and deceased in the smouldering ruin, not snuck off from work in the cross-tracks bar when the elevator spontaneously disintegrated, providing half-cut Jankovitch an all-too-neat opportunity to duck the warrant, the women and possible pregnancies, the big debts, the whole grieving family. Missouri: Show Me State, population 4,676,000. Capital Jefferson City. Best diner in Nine Eagles county. Hines Cedar Crest for Sunday brunch, fried chicken and eggs and thirty-one salads or Saturday night fishfry with their special recipe for carp and catfish. Jankovitch stares at the outlines of her breasts shifting in a soft halter top. "Yes yes, I'm awake now."

What approach can we make to this extraordinary piece of writing? I have long advocated that we should ask of a work of art not *What* does this mean, but *How* does this mean? This simple question *is* fairly simple but, because rarely asked, perhaps requires elucidation.

Quebec painter Claude Tousignant wrote: *What I advocate is the notion of paintings as beings, not representations.*

Lucien Freud wrote: *Leaning to paint is literally learning to use paint.*

Robert Motherwell wrote of ". . . the depth and the intimacy of the marriage between the artist and his *medium*. A painting is not a picture of something in front of your eyes— a model, say, primarily. *It is an attack on the medium which comes to 'mean' something."* [Italics added]

British art critic Roger Fry wrote as early as 1912 of paintings as "visual music."

Seamus Heaney wrote that poetry "must not submit to the intellect's eagerness to foreclose" but must wait "for a music to occur, an image to discover itself."

All these comments suggest that *What* is not the question to ask; they suggest that painters would wish us to look at paint, that writers would wish us to listen for "a music to occur, an image to discover itself."

(Heaney is using "discover" in the sense of "revealing" itself.)

Asking *What* of any "being" is already positioning the questioner intellectually and emotionally *outside* the thing being questioned. Current university jargon refers to asking *What* of a text as "interrogation," pompous tone-deaf cant with its unintended shadow-twin, "confession." To approach poetry or fiction asking *What* is putting the poem or story in the dock and casting the critic as prosecutor.

5

What possibly could be the charge?

If, on the other hand, we ask *How* we are inside the work, experiencing it, entering into an emotional relationship with it, in a sense submitting to it, though such submission does not, of course, preclude our reaching a negative conclusion. By asking *How*, we become not invading marauders but explorers with settlement in view.

Understanding the closeness of many of Jarman's stories to poetry and knowing that I was currently grappling with getting across to readers the *How* of Jarman's work, Alexander Monker, fellow Jarman fan, drew my attention to a passage in the Introduction by Dana Gioia to Aaron Poochigian's 2022 translation of Baudelaire's *Les Fleurs du Mal*:

Music was central to Baudelaire's method. He considered poetry an art of enchantment. A poem should cast a verbal spell that suspends the reader in a trance state of heightened attention and receptivity. That momentary enchantment allows the reader to experience contradictory thoughts and emotions, to feel hidden suggestions and connections that are never fully disclosed or resolved in the poem. *The reader interprets the poem—not as a deliberately constructed puzzle, but as a shared experience still in the process of being understood.* [Italics added]

Before all else, we should listen.

In an essay in *Canadian Notes & Queries*, Stephen Beattie, books columnist and reviewer, wrote of "Cowboys Incorporated"—"this early story—so assured, so fresh in its approach and execution—offers one of the first shouts from a voice that is *sui generis* in the annals of Canadian fiction."

We must listen to that voice.

But let me expand on the nature of that voice by quoting from another of Canada's finest short story writers, Douglas Glover, who suggests something of the tradition with which Jarman allies himself, and directs us brilliantly towards the heart of the stories.

Of course, what drives a writer's hand always remains secret, sometimes even from himself. We surge toward the shapes we love without knowing why we love them. Jarman's taste is rhetorical—not just because his narratives are monologues, speeches. He harks back to an ancient tradition of eloquent speaking much despised, as Marshall McLuhan pointed out, by Plato, the logician, who saw no place for poets in his republic. This tradition of literary revel has come down to us through the Elizabethans and thence to Joyce and the Irish and also, somehow, to the American South. But always it has been in conflict with a counter-tradition of the plain style, of pure representation, of telling a story the good old-fashioned way without the author drawing attention to himself and his oral pyrotechnics. Jarman doesn't care for the plain style. He's intoxicated with words and the playful ways they can be strung together using sound and rhythm and repetition. And the meaning he is after is not the meaning of the didact or some mirror of the world, but a meaning that murmurs through the words of a text like wind in leaves and reveals itself mysteriously in the play of language itself.

(From: "How to Read a Mark Jarman Story" in Glover's book of essays *Attack of the Copula Spiders,* which explores in searching detail Jarman's story, "Burn Man on a Texas Porch.")

Having in mind, then, that Jarman is, in essence, a language *performer*, a builder of rhetorical structures, a writer attacking his medium, let us go beyond conventional and perfunctory listening and let us hear, *really* hear, how the performance works. Let us imagine that you, as reader, are now called upon to deliver our excerpt from "Cowboys Incorporated" to a theatre audience. You must become a musician; your voice has to re-create the music of Jarman's score.

(In the opening section of the story preceding your excerpt, the fugitives Jankovitch and Ironchild are in the washroom of an Interstate rest area. Ironchild, in a cubicle, shooting up, overdoses, "buys the farm." Jankovitch bundles up the corpse, stuffing boots and ankles into the toilet bowl and, with a matchbook, wedges shut the cubicle door leaving on it a scrawled notice on a paper towel: Out of Order.)

Putting it very crudely, those three words resonate throughout the story.

Our excerpt starts with:

The big country. Asleep.

Are these the words of the narrator or are they the driver's thoughts? Jarman, intent on immediacy, goes out of his way

7

to disguise or magic away even the notion of an omniscient intelligence telling the story, so it is probably safest to consider the words as Virginia's summarizing thought.

In either case, the words need to be spoken slowly. A pause between them. A sort of, "Well! Here we are! We've reached the plains. And he's *still* asleep."

I think if I were in your shoes I'd give slight emphasis to "big."

"Wake up. Wake up." Obviously Virginia. And as she's described later as trying to "gently rouse" him (Jankovitch being possibly dangerous) the words should be an intense whisper, sibilant rather than commanding.

> The big country. Asleep. "Wake up. Wake up." Near Easter time too, the Lenten tornadoes touching down around the women in their gardens. "Wake up buddy." Jankovitch closes his eyes to rise from cancerous dreams of flooded towns dying in silt rivers, farm land leaching out, drifting away. Ironchild toying with his needles and grinding blue pills in the failing light. "Wake up." Jankovitch jerks forward. "What?" Saliva drying upturned in his stupid throat.

How to deliver this? Not loudly. Certainly, I'd think, slowly. Perhaps slightly slurred? It is a semi-dreamed vision of the physical world dying mixed in with their own complicity in that death in the person of Ironchild "toying" with needles and narcotics in the "failing light."

What rhythms, what stresses are demanded?

Notice the brilliance of the first sentence and the word "too," which needs a stress as it indicates that Jankovitch has been dreaming of other, probably violent events taking place around Easter time. It is also a deliberate echo of a Dylan lyric. The tornadoes themselves "touching down around the women in their gardens" continue a chain of surreal imagery that dominates the story.

That little word "too" combined with the rather peculiar word to be coming from a Jankovitch's dreaming mind—"Lenten"—reminds me of Dana Gioia's "enchantment" that allows the reader "to feel hidden suggestions and connections that are never fully disclosed or resolved . . ."

(Lent, I will remind readers, is the period of forty days devoted to fasting and penitence in commemoration of Jesus's fasting for forty days in the wilderness. Lent leads up to Easter Day, the festival celebrating Christ's rising from the dead. "Lenten" seems an odd word to crop up in Jankovitch's mind. Later in the story we read, "Jankovitch can still see the nuns and old school maps . . ." There seems to be in Jankovitch's thoughts and feelings a faint residue of Catholic instruction, a religious sense of the world, as if in an ancient church with whitewashed walls the faint colours from medieval frescoes are bleeding through. And the story does end with a resurrected figure, though not a saviour bringing the hope of salvation.

Readers may well sense in the work of Denis Johnson, a writer influential in the forming of Jarman's style, a similar faint residue of traditional teaching.

> Crows, nothing grows, gears gnash in testimony to bad driving and the Swedish car's endless capacity for punishment. This is the way they go: "We want you to drive again, okay?"

This brilliant hinge sentence records his hearing the cawing of crows; "nothing grows" is his slipping back again towards dream; "gears gnash," the violence of the sound before he sinks again back into the dream of their journey.

What follows next is a considerable challenge:

> Virginia in fedora and shades leaning over the seat to gently rouse Jankovitch who's down in shitkicker country again . . . as Carlene Carter said, *put the cunt back in*

country . . . Johnny Cash's girl . . . the car swinging hard across the blue plains and raggedy-ass cottonwood, the endless flight through pale aspens and truck stop botulism, Kmart snakeskin cowboy boots, cheating songs, box elders. This is just after the grain elevator blew over to Missouri: burned for days and they couldn't get at the bodies. In the blind pigs and roadhouses, lizards cringe under the crashing rain of Wurlitzers and chicken bones. God and country are toasted.

Starting at "swinging hard . . ." Jankovitch is capturing their flight in a collage of pictures and details. Before thinking of how to deliver the collage, it's essential to discover the dominant emotion of the details and pictures. That discovery will deliver to the performer the *tone* and the *speed* of delivery.

The collage rises towards the explosion. This is the rising tension of a blues harp solo, of a revival meeting, the eloquence of preacher or poet that the Welsh call *hwyl*.

The build towards the Wurlitzer sentence starts with:

This is just after the grain elevator blew over to Missouri: burned for days and they couldn't get at the bodies.

But how to make this seemingly flat sentence build. Does the rhetoric sag at this point?

I read it as being akin to colloquial speech, so read: emphasis on *blew*, slight pause, over to Missouri: burned for *days* and they couldn't get *at* the bodies.

Notice that the next sentence switches into the present tense and is very much *not* colloquial: it presents not so much the sight of the explosion as Jankovitch's imagining of its indescribable magnitude.

The passage ends abruptly with the seemingly flat, "God and country are toasted."

This seemed to me when I first read it as a limp letdown after the brilliantly hyperbolical "lizards cringe under the crashing ruin of Wurlitzers and chicken bones." But subsequent readings gave me a different take. I read "God and country" as the boastful patriotism of USA exceptionalism, followed by a pause, followed by "are toasted," a colloquial cliché that dismisses that assertion.

("Blind pigs," a term for lowlife illicit drinking establishments, is used here not only for its meaning but because the words, grotesque in themselves, reinforce the surreal aspects of the explosion. We might associate "chicken bones" with blind pigs, Wurlitzers with vulgarly "tony" roadhouses.)

The rhetoric of the story now changes again.

"Wake up buddy." Jankovitch supposed to be loyally ¹¹ prone and deceased in the smouldering ruin, not snuck off from work in the cross-tracks bar when the elevator spontaneously disintegrated, providing half-cut Jankovitch an all-too-neat opportunity to duck the warrant, the women and possible pregnancies, the big debts, the whole grieving family.

This paragraph poses a problem. It would seem on a first reading to be the words of the story's narrator but Jarman has avoided or disguised direct authorial intervention. So perhaps we are not reading with sufficient intensity?

The words "loyally prone" are funny and should alert us. It struck me that if we emphasized the words *supposed* and *not* in "*not* snuck off from work" and if we paid attention to "providing half-cut Jankovitch an all-too-neat opportunity to duck" we can read these words as the dozing Janovitch *thinking of himself in the third person,* as a character, a clever and wily man who has outsmarted the law, escaped from debt and pregnant women with their claims and "his whole grieving family." This is Jankovitch seeing himself as a Jack the Lad brilliantly escaping from the tedium of family life.

Such a reading chimes, of course, with God and country being "toasted," all constraints removed, all platitudinous expectations denied.

> Missouri: Show Me state, population 4,676,000. Capital: Jefferson City. Best diner in Nine Eagles county: Hines Cedar Crest for Sunday brunch, fried chicken and eggs and thirty-one salads or Saturday night fish fry with their special recipe for carp and catfish. Jankovitch stares at the outlines of her breasts shifting in a soft halter top. "Yes yes. I'm awake now."

Again we should read this not as authorial but as Jankovitch's thoughts. The "guide book" detail of population size and capital city, the detail of the menu of the best diner in Nine Eagles county, "thirty-one salads or Saturday night fish fry"—all this comically serious detail, plonkingly delivered, is Jankovitch's self-justification for his flight from the boredom of this life.

How to capture all this in your voice and delivery? I think I'd be trying different takes on the word "salads," food towards which I suspect Jankovitch would feel contempt. And the "special recipe" for carp and catfish—I think I'd play *up* on "special recipe" and *down* on those two bottom feeders.

The excerpt's final lines play with s-sounds.

The outlines of breasts shifting in a soft halter top. Yes yes. I'm awake now.

The yes yes sounds, (not separated by the conventional comma) suggest the slight slur of his still not fully awakened state and these and the other "s" sounds (which the reader might lightly emphasize) perhaps suggest what he is awakening *to*.

When readers-as-actors have won through to answers to these Hows, all the knots of Whats will have untangled themselves and now remains the task of putting all the paragraphs together to judge the rhetorical flow of the whole.

*

Where does all this consummate razzle-dazzle come from? The short answer is the Iowa Writers' Workshop.

In the *Salon des Refusés* issue of *CNQ* (No. 74), an issue of the journal that will live on in Canadian writing history, Mark Jarman wrote about our story:

> The story "Cowboys Inc." was a watershed for my approach to writing. There are stories in my first collection that I wrote before "Cowboys Inc.," and stories I wrote after "Cowboys Inc.," and I can tell which are which.
>
> I wrote "Cowboys Inc." while at the Iowa Writers' Workshop. I lived in a wrecked house that cost me $50 a month and I worked with Bharati Mukherjee, Clark Blaise, Barry Hannah, and the late poet Larry Levis, and in Iowa City I met Ray Carver. I had driven numerous road trips through the Dakotas and Colorado and Wyoming and Montana and Iowa en route to the west coast and Alberta, and back to Iowa and Chicago, and I had a shoebox of notes, matchbooks, cocktail napkins, maps, scraps, beer coasters, and postcards. I wanted to write a road piece. I wanted a triangle, and I wanted to make use of the guy I worked with as a janitor, a guy who popped speed and was always ready to punch someone. I also wanted a dead man as an ongoing character, and I wanted a sex scene on an ironing board (the ironing board was not biographical; I never iron).
>
> Usually I would try to make a story as smooth as possible, work on every word and segue. Some earlier stories took forty drafts. But "Cowboys Inc." quickly hit a point where I had an early draft, albeit a draft with jagged edges. The story wasn't easy to digest, was not A to B, and

not tied up with a pretty bow, but I realized I liked it that way. It had the power of pastiche or collage, a quality that was accidental and brutal, but attractive to my eye and ear.

I felt I had stumbled onto something evocative, broken through to a new way for me to smash together matters of head and heart. Not everyone agreed, some reviewers said to skip that story and read the others, but I was happy with it.

Jarman was much influenced by the Zeitgeist, by the matrix of the pulp and pulse of pop culture, by the *tone* of the times, by post-punk bands such as The Jesus and Mary Chain, Brian Eno, Talking Heads' "The Big Country," to Laurie Anderson's "Big Science," to Wall of Voodoo's "Call of the West," music of geography, maps and movement. When younger he was listening to urban blues from Chicago, Howlin' Wolf, Sonny Boy Williamson, and the harmonica legend Little Walter.

In his voracious reading there were probably faint echoes of Jack Kerouac and Ken Kesey—and he was reading Alice Munro—what Canadian writer wasn't?—but he was more in tune emotionally and technically with Flannery O'Connor's *Wise Blood, The Violent Bear It Away,* and *A Good Man Is Hard to Find,* with the Joan Didion of *Slouching Towards Bethlehem* and *The White Album,* with Renata Adler's short stories in *The New Yorker,* with Tom McGuane's *Panama,* a book that obsessed him.(I was rather surprised to learn that he *hadn't* been reading Harry Crews.)

When we were chatting one day about this mélange of influences, he said "It was fragmentation that interested me. Fragmentation as an end in itself. In some of Laurie Anderson's pieces there was a strange looping-in of fragments, sounds, pirated conversation, a sort of layering, other stuff, 'found material' I suppose you could call it . . . fragmentation as a way of feeling a way in deeper."

He paused.

"Of course," he said. "Eliot did all this so long ago."

Jarman's assaults on form, his attacking his medium, when seen in perspective, are simply new expressions of necessary assaults that have been going on for centuries, assaults to tear away the veil of language that covers everything with a false familiarity. Coleridge writes of Wordsworth stripping away the "film of familiarity." Wordsworth in his Preface to the second edition of *Lyrical Ballads* (1800) stated that he had repudiated "what is usually called poetic diction" and claimed that his poems were written "in the real language of men." Shelley wrote that "Poetry lifts the veil from the hidden beauty of the world." The Russian Formalists wrote of *ostranenie*—"making strange." Ezra Pound vigorously mucked-out the Augean Stables of Georgian prose, yelling "Make it new!" Samuel Beckett wrote in a 1937 letter to Axel Kaun:

> And more and more my own language appears to me like a veil that must be torn apart in order to get at the things (or the Nothingness) behind it. Grammar and Style. To me they seem to have become as irrelevant as a Victorian bathing suit or the imperturbability of a true gentleman. A mask.

Two major influences on Jarman's style and reach were Barry Hannah and Denis Johnson. In another *CNQ* article, Jarman wrote:

> The wild southern writer Barry Hannah was teaching at Iowa when I went to school there. His collection of stories, *Airships*, was a huge influence on me; it was liberating to see the way he'd mash up a sentence; he made me realize it didn't have to be noun verb, noun verb. And his language was a weird, risky, inspiring mix of Elizabethan and cracker. "Testimony of Pilot," from that book, is a great, great story.

Barry died of a heart attack in Oxford, Mississippi this past March and I saw his obituary in the *New York Times.* The obit spoke of his novels and his attempt at Hollywood screenplays, but he said he was a short story writer first, a fragmentist, with an imagination calibrated to the short burst. I like that idea. I think I'm calibrated that way and I'm going to keep living that line from a dead man.

The story does it for me. The short form has parameters and it works for me because of the parameters. Don't fence me in, the cowhands sing out west, but perhaps I like being confined. I think the story is the most natural form. The American writer Steven Millhauser has called it the realm of perfection and it can be that.

*

Steven Beattie wrote of the shape of Jarman's stories in the *CNQ Salon des Refusés* issue (No. 74).

> . . . no one would mistake his writing for the kind of kitchen-sink realism that still dominates the short story form at the beginning of the 21st Century. Stories in the Chekhovian mould, which Donald Barthelme once derisively suggested were "constructed mousetrap-like to supply, at the finish, a tiny insight typically having to do with innocence violated," are not Jarman's métier.

Douglas Glover wrote of Jarman plots:

> Though often rising out of situations that are violent or bizarre or both, Mark Jarman's storylines tend to be minimal, just enough plausible action to jump-start the engine of his verbal inventiveness. And this very inventiveness is somehow tied to voice—most of Jarman's stories are written in the first person, as monologues in the

point of view of characters under stress, their synapses sparking at high volume...

Glover wrote brilliantly of Jarman's meanings:

And the meaning he is after is not the meaning of the didact or some mirror of the world, but a meaning that murmurs through the words of the text like wind in leaves and reveals itself mysteriously in the play of language itself.

Clark Blaise said much the same kind of thing about his own stories as leaving "vapour trails, their slow dissolve into something more diffuse and nameless."

The stories Jarman was reading and beginning to be influenced by might best be described as voices talking randomly, at times incoherently, and from these foggy confessions, admissions, boasts, and complaints emerge into the light not conclusions, but a vivid sense of lives lived in the worlds their words create.

Typical Denis Johnson opening sentences from stories in *Jesus' Son*—

From: "Work"

I'd been staying at the Holiday Inn with my girlfriend, honestly the most beautiful woman I'd ever known, for three days under a phony name, shooting heroin.

From: "Steady Hands at Seattle General"

Inside of two days I was shaving myself, and I even shaved a couple of new arrivals, because the drugs they injected me with had an amazing effect.

And here the opening five sentences of "Dirty Wedding," an opening that Jarman absolutely *must* have loved:

I liked to sit up front and ride the fast ones all day long. I liked it when they brushed right up against the buildings north of the Loop and I especially liked it when the buildings dropped away into that bombed-out squalor a little farther north in which people (through windows you'd see a person in his dirty naked kitchen spooning soup toward his face, or twelve children on their bellies on the floor, watching television, but instantly they were gone, wiped away by a movie billboard of a woman winking and touching her upper lip deftly with her tongue, and she in turn erased by a—*wham*, the noise and dark dropped down around your head—tunnel) actually lived.

I was twenty-five, twenty-six, something like that. My fingertips were all yellow from smoking. My girlfriend was with child.

But years earlier than Johnson's stories, the opening of the story "Dancing Nightly in the Tavern." The features of Jarman's inheritance from Faulkner and Robert Stone are discernible but his rhythms are purely his own.

The horse surges sideways to fill Luke's vision. He feels the heat of its sides, reads the nicks in its winter coat, rolls from the hooves and fetlocks he had been checking, in the corner of his swimming eye sees Woody's skinny shadow climb the buckskin from the fence, sees as if from underwater, thinking, *no, ride the pinto, this fucker's not been rid all winter.*

Woody laughing: "He's a woolly sonuvabitch!"

"Crazy bastard," mutters Luke, Woody rocking above, the sky the colour of ice. Woody on the back, dark against the sky, strands of light, horsehair on the wire, Woody laughing like before the deaths, until his leg is raked down the barbwire tearing denim and skin, his face clenched, twisted mouth cursing, eyes furious. The gouged flesh open, visible, as the frayed white threads soak to pink.

"You hammer-headed cocksucker," hisses Woody, pounding the horse's big head, pulling the reins back until the buckskin's yellow-green teeth are bared to the slobbery bit.

The horse dances backwards, head erect, refusing to clear the fence, rump lowered, then hind hooves floating up in clods of wet ground and smashing back. The horse can smell him.

Luke pushes the wall of flesh, shoving it finally from the barbs, the shot strands of light and black hair caught, the buckskin rearing. Woody scrambling in the mane and hooves slam to earth, Woody's teeth clamping with a click, eyes closed and head rolling, snapping. The gelding contorts impossibly, heaving Woody off balance, one arm waving as if in greeting. The hind legs kick out, the back rises up, and Woody is free into the air over the Austin-Healey and flooded summerfallow.

Jarman was influenced first by Faulkner and Robert Stone's prose, and later by Johnson's poetry—its bleakness, its startling tone, was surely part of the attraction. The volume that particularly attracted Jarman was *The Incognito Lounge*, reprinted in *The Throne of the Third Heaven of the Nations Millennium General Assembly* (1995)

Here are the opening lines of "After Mayakovsky"

It's after one. You're probably alone.
All night the moon rings like a telephone
in an empty booth above our separateness.

And the opening lines of "The Spectacle"

In every house
a cigarette burns,

an ash descends.
In the ludicrous breeze
of an electric fan
the papers talk,
and little vague
things float over
The floor. When
you turn on the TV
it says, "Killed
by FBI sharpshooters ...

Or this opening to "Passengers"

The world will burst like an intestine in the sun,
the dark turn to granite and the granite to a name,
but there will always be somebody riding the bus
through these intersections strewn with broken glass
among speechless women beating their little ones ...

In 1986 Jarman published a poetry collection entitled *Killing the Swan*. The last stanza of the poem "Red Earth Broken" reads:

How many times will we waken
Staring down each bleached object:
sheet, leg, windowpane
Allegretto meadowlarks in air over a butchered hog
Head angled in heat as if on a rope
Eye swifts in silent inventory
Shuts

Eye swifts in silent inventory

When I first read "Eye swifts," his turning an adjective into a verb was discomforting, jarring, but rereadings soothed and justified it, made me realize it did perfectly what he wanted it to do. It was, I came to realize, wordplay that wasn't play. It was, I came to realize, a Jarmanism.

It's never safe to skim over words in Jarman's writing. Go back, for instance, to the opening quotation in this introduction, the quote about the old-timers' hockey evening.

"Drive the night, driving out to old-timer hockey in January in New Brunswick."

Drive the night, driving out.

Why is such a brilliant writer being repetitive?

But "Drive the night" does not mean "driving in the night," "at night," "through the night." It is quite distinct and different in meaning to "driving out to." It is not a command.

Such encounters with single words set me to thinking about the intense pleasures given me by the whole of Mark Anthony Jarman's creation to date. Set me thinking, too, about what must have been the loneliness of his creative life, his fortitude in the face of incomprehension.

Reading him is rather like listening to Thelonious Monk piano solos. It took us so long to *hear* Monk, but when we did, it was to hear that, far from being jangling and discordant, he was *gorgeously* inevitable.

John Metcalf
November 2022
Ottawa

BURN MAN
ON A TEXAS PORCH

Men who are unhappy, like men who sleep badly, are always proud of the fact.

– Bertrand Russell

At 50, everyone has the face they deserve.

– George Orwell

PROPANE slept in the tank and propane leaked while I slept, blew the camper door off and split the tin walls where they met like shy strangers kissing, blew the camper door like a safe and I sprang from sleep into my new life on my feet in front of a befuddled crowd, my new life on fire, waking to whoosh and tourists' dull teenagers staring at my bent form trotting noisily in the campground with flames living on my calves and flames gathering and glittering on my shoulders (*Cool*, the teens think secretly), smoke like nausea in my stomach and me brimming with Catholic guilt, thinking, Now I've done it, and then thinking Done what? What have I done?

Slept during the day with my face dreaming on a sudoral pillow near the end of the century and now my blue eyes are on fire.

I'm okay, okay, will be fine except I'm hoovering all the oxygen around me, and I'm burning like a circus poster, flames taking more and more of my shape—am I moving or are they? I am hooked into fire, I am hysterical light issuing beast noises in a world of smoke.

To run seems an answer. Wanting privacy, I run darkest dogbane and daisies and doom palms, hearing bagpipes and whistling in my head, my fat burning like red wax, fat in the fire now. Alone—I want to do this alone, get away from the others. I can't see, bounce off trees and parked cars, noise in my ears the whole time.

The other campers catch me and push me onto a tent the blue of a Chinese rug, try to smother me, but soon the tent is melting, merrily burning with me while everyone in the world throws picnic Kool-Aid and apple juice and Lucky Lager and Gatorade and ginger ale and ice cubes and ice water from the Styrofoam coolers. Tourists burn their hands trying to extinguish me.

My face feels like a million white hot rivets. I am yelling and writhing. One of my shoes burns happily by itself on the road.

Where does my skin end and the skin of their melted tourist tent begin?

At some point in this year of our Lord I began to refer to myself in third person, as a double: Burn Man enters the Royal Jubilee burn unit, Burn Man enters the saline painful sea. Burn Man reads every word of the local rag despite its numerous failings, listens to MC5 on vinyl, listens to Johnny Cash's best-known ballad.

I am not dealing with this well, the doctors tell me. I am not noble. They carried me in the burnt blue tent, a litter borne from battle, from defeat on the fields of fire and disassembly lines and into three months of shaking, bandaged pain. Your muscles go after you're burnt, but if you work out the skin grafts won't stretch over the larger muscles. Grafted skin is not as flexible as real skin. Skin is your cage.

Once straight, now I'm crooked. I lack a landscape that is mine. A doctor shone a light at the blood vessels living in the back of my retina. I saw there a trickle-down Mars in a map of my own blood: twin red planets lodged in my skull.

As a nerdy kid in horn-rimmed glasses, I haunted libraries, reading about doomed convoys in World War Two, Canadian sailors burnt in the North Atlantic or off icy Russia, Canadian sailors alive but charred by crude oil burning all around them after U-boats from sunny Bordeaux took down their tramp freighter or seasick corvette—circular scalp of sea on fire and flaming crude races right at them, so eager, enters them, fricassees their lungs and face and hands, the burning ring of fire come to life on the Murmansk run.

I can't recall what happened when the burnt sailors moved back into the non-burnt world, crawled back home above Halifax's black snowy harbour or the sombre river firs of Red Deer, the salt box houses of Esquimalt.

No war here; no peace either. Only the burn ward's manic protracted nurses sliding on waxed floors and the occasional distracted doctor with a crew of rookies whipping back the curtain, the gown, jabbing me to see if I'm done like dinner. Sell the sizzle. Door blows off the rented camper, spinning under sulphur sun, and I too am sent out into red rented sunlight, your basic moaning comet charging through a brilliantly petalled universe.

I was on a holiday in the sun, a rest from work, from tree spikers and salmon wars, from the acting deputy minister on the cellphone fuming about river rights, water divisions, and the botched contract with Alcan. I was getting away from it all, resting my eyes, my brain.

I had left the cellphone sitting like a plastic banana on the middle of my wide Spartan desk. I was working on my tan, had a little boat tied up dockside, plastic oars, nine h.p., runs on gas-and-oil mix. I rested my skin on the sand-and-cigarette-butt beach. I lay down on a pillow in a tin camper. I caught fire, ran the dusty levees of our campground, alchemy and congress weighing on my mind.

Back home in my basement, a 1950s toy train circles track, its fricative steam locomotive emitting the only light in the room, swinging past where a slight woman in a parody of a nurse's uniform does something for Burn Man, for Burn Man is not burnt everywhere, still has some desires, and the woman doesn't have to touch anything else, doesn't have to see me, has almost no contact, has a verbal contract, an oral contract, say.

"Cindi: Yes, that's me in the photo!" avows the ad in the weekly paper.

Cindi can't really see me, except for the toy-train light from my perfect childhood, can't make out my grave, jerry-built face. I can barely see her. She has short, dark, hennaed hair that used to be another colour. I imagine her monochrome high-school photo. Dollars to doughnuts she had long hair parted in the middle, a plain face, a trace of acne. No one sensed then that Cindi would become an escort pulled out of the paper at random and lit by a moving toy train and red-and-yellow poppies waving at a big basement window—mumbling to me, I have these nightmares, every night these nightmares.

I explain my delicate situation on the phone—what I wanted, didn't want.

Good morning, Cindi, I said. Here's my story, you let me know what you think.

She coughed. Uh, I'm cool with that.

So Cindi and I set up our first date.

My escort dresses as the nurse in white, her hands, her crisp uniform glowing in the rec room. All of us risk something, dress as something: ape, clown, worker, Cindi, citizen, *cool with that.*

Here's an ad in *Now* magazine I didn't call: "FIRE and DESIRE, Sensuous Centrefold Girls, HOT fall specials, $150 per hour." I didn't call that number. I don't live in the metro area. I'm not one of the chosen.

Once, maybe, I was chosen, necking on the Hopper porch, that stunning lean of a Texas woman into my arms, my innocent face, our mouths one. Perfect height for each other and I am pulled to another doomed enterprise.

The iron train never stops, lights up my decent little town, its toy workers frozen in place with grim happy faces, light opening and closing them, workers with tin shovels, forklifts, painted faces. God gives you one face and you make yourselves another. My nurse is too thin. I like a little more flesh. I wish she'd change just for me.

My slight Nurse Wretched carries my cash carelessly and heads out to buy flaps of coke, or maybe today it's points of junk, for twenty or thirty dollars (her version of the stock market), delving into different receptor sites, alternate brands of orgasmic freeze and frisson, and she forgets about carrot juice and health food, forgets about me, my eyes half-hooded like a grumpy cat's, eyes unfocused and my mouth turned down and our shared need for death without death, for petit mal, tender mercies.

Cindi is out this moment seeking a pharmacy's foreign voice and amnesiac hands and who can blame her?

Some people from my old school (*Be true to your school*) fried themselves over years and years, burned out over dissolute decades, creepy-crawling centuries.

Not me. Ten seconds and done, helter-skelter, hugger-mugger. Here's the new you handed to you in a campground like a plate of oysters. An "accelerant," as the firefighters enjoy saying, was used. Before I could change, had nine lives. Now I have one. O, I am ill at these numbers.

In the hospital not far from the campground I cracked jokes like delicate quail eggs: You can't fire me, I already quit. Then I quit cracking jokes. The skin grafts not what I had hoped for, didn't quite fit (*Why then we'll fit you*). The surgeons made me look like a wharf rat, a malformed Missouri turtle, a post-mortem mummy. Years and doubt clinging to her, the nurse with the honed Andalusian face tried not to touch me too hard.

At first how positive I was! Eagerly I awaited the tray with the Jell-O and soup and fruit flies, the nurse with the determined Spanish face carrying it to my mechanical bed. I overheard her say to another nurse, No, he's not a bigot, he's a bigamist! Who? I wonder. Me? My aloof doctor? Does he have a life? If only we could duplicate the best parts and delete the rest. A complicated bed and her arms on a tray and her serious expression and unfucked-up skin and my hunger and love for a porch, (*I spied a fair maiden*), for the latest version of my lunatic past.

I spill Swedish and Russian vodka into my morning coffee now (rocket fuel for Rocket Man) and, blue bubble helmet happily hiding my scarred face, fling my Burn Man motorcycle with the ape-hanger handlebars down the wet island highway, hoping for fractious fiction and the thrill of metal fatigue, hoping to meet someone traumatic, a ring of fire. I re-jetted the carburetor on my bike, went to Supertrapp pipes—wanting more horses and torque, wanting the machine to scream.

Before I became Burn Man, the Texas woman kissed me at the bottom of her lit yellow stairs, porch dark as tar, dark as sky, and her cozy form fast leaning against me, disturbing the hidden powers, ersatz cowboys upstairs drinking longnecks and blabbing over Gram Parsons and Emmylou (*One like you should be—miles and miles away from me*), impatient taxi waiting and waiting as we kissed. I had not expected her to kiss me, to teach me herself, her mouth and form, her warm image driven like a nail into my mind, her memory jammed on that loop of tape. (Such art of eyes I read in no books, my dark-star thoughts attending her day and night like a sacred priest with his relics.) In that instant I was changed.

Now I'm the clown outside Bed of Roses, the franchise flower shop beside the dentist's office on the road to Damascus, the road to Highway 61. On Saturdays I wave white gloves to passing cars—dark shark-like taxis, myopic headlights—and helium balloons with smiley faces bump my wrecked and now abandoned mouth. (*Where have all the old finned cars swum to?*)

Pedestrians hate me, fear me; pedestrians edge past the bus-stop bench where the sidewalk is too narrow; pedestrians avoid my eyes, my psychedelic fright-wig. I want to reassure them: Hey dudes, I'm not a mime. Different union.

At Easter I'm a giant grey rabbit but I can't do Santa. I could definitely use the do-re-mi but the beard isn't enough cover for my droopy right eye and melted cheek, the beard isn't enough to save face, and also I confess to trouble with the constant Ho Ho Ho.

Dignity is essential, I attempt to impart to a passing priest, but I start coughing like a moron. *Drugs too,* I finally sputter. *Essential!* He moves on. Brother, sister, I may appear in ape costume at your apartment door, will deliver a singing telegram in a serviceable tenor. My grey rabbit suit needs a little bleach. Dignity is essential.

Burn Man must have his face covered, bases covered. I'm different animals. In the winter nights I'm the mascot Mighty Moose for our junior hockey team down at Memorial Arena. You may recall TV heads and columnists frowning on my bloody fight with the other team's Raving Raven mascot. All the skaters were scrapping, Gary Glitter's "Rock & Roll Part

One" booming on the sound system and then both goalies started throwing haymakers. I thought the mascots should also duke it out—a sense of symmetry and loyalty. I banged at the Old World armour of that raven's narrow, serious face, snapped his head back. Hoofs were my advantage.

Later we went for a drink or three and laughed about our fight, Raven and Moose at a small bar table comparing notes and bloody abrasions, hoofs and talons around each other, shop talk at the gin bar.

Don't fuck with me, rummy beard-jammers and balls-up bean-counters snarl at every bar on the island, as if they alone decide when they get fucked over. I could advise them on that. I didn't decide to have the camper blow to shrapnel with me curled inside like a ball-turret gunner.

They hunker down at the Commercial Hotel or Blue Peter Marina or Beehive Tap or Luna Lounge thinking they're deep, thinking one ugly room is the universe's centre because they're there with flaming drinks by the lost highway, clouds hanging like clocks over the Japanese coal ships and the coast-guard chopper, and across the water a distant town glittering the green colours of wine and traffic.

I sit and listen to their hyena patter, their thin sipping and brooding and laughing. Sometimes I'm still wearing my clown outfit while drinking my face off. Why take it off?

Friday night a man was kicked to death in this bar. In that instant, like me, he was changed, his memory jammed on a loop in a jar of wind, living the blues, dying.

At my front door a rhododendron sheds its scarlet bells one by one. A dark blue teacup sits on the rainy steps, looking beautiful and lonely, and there's a bird in the woods that sounds like a car trying to start.

One Sunday session a man lifted his golf shirt to show me his bowel-obstruction-surgery scar. His navel shoved four inches to the left. He didn't mind getting fucked over—in fact he guffawed gruffly at his own wrecked gut. We're so pliant, I thought, prone to melt, to a change of heart, to lend our tongue vows.

I who loved the status quo, liked things to stay the same even when they were bad. I who didn't want to break up with Dolly Varden girlfriends when it was obvious to everyone that we should get it over with. Then the camper door flies off: Kablooie! Goodbye Louie! I who loved the status quo.

I'm different animals now. New careers in fire and oxygen, careering and hammering through the dolomite campground to fall on your tent, to fall on my sword. Home, I want to go home, darling. Take me back to Tulsa.

The skin is the largest organ; mine's a little out of tune. Your skin's square footage is—Jesus, how the hell should I know? Far more than your heart, which gets all the good press, attracts the spin doctors and diligent German scalpels.

Perhaps my Burn Man skin is more accurate now, what we all become after a certain age: parched animals, palimpsests in wrinkled uniforms, clowns hanging at the Pet Food Mart waving to the indifferent flow of traffic and shiny happy people.

I stare at a bottle of Ayinger German wheat beer, inhaling softest froth in my mouth, breathing in something good like a virus, like breathing oxygen and perfume with a woman's Norwegian hair all over your face.

I am The Way, I say to the drunken bottle, I am truth, heresy, *evidence* of what none of us wish to admit: that appearance is everything, that surface is God and God is surface.

Appearance: the white whale we chase every minute of every day. Looks and youth. We say this isn't so—Nay sir, No sir, No, No, No—we insist appearance counts for very little, but then I am walking at you, an ancient bog monster limping on the teensy sidewalk with my face like a TV jammed on the wrong channel, and at that sideways juncture ALL of us,

ME included, decide shallow is not that bad. Let us, we decide, worship and grovel at the church of shallow.

Only Tuesday but I need a drink, my teeth caught in my teeth. Down to the Starfish Room or Yukon Jack's, down to the sea in ships, hulls dragging on our city's concrete.

Flame created me with its sobering sound. Wake up, flame whispered in my ear, like a woman on a porch, like a muttering into cotton, a rush to action. It was ushering, acting on me, eating me. I'm its parent, I'm its home, and people worry they might catch it from me—catch ugliness, catch chaos theory, catch something catchy.

The baby doctor caught me when I came out in fluid, and my mother held me as a baby, such smooth baby skin, my skin dipped in baptismal water at St. John's, they washed away original sin, she held my perfect skin, my original skin. They lit fat candles in the cathedral and I came out in fluid in the university hospital.

The woman on the Texas porch said my skin was soft and that she loved my smell. No one ever said that before, and no one said it after. She created me.

As a kid I was burned by the summer sun in Penticton. My aunt from England peeled a section of skin from my back, and she still has that piece of my skin in a scrapbook in London.

Remember that map they torched at the beginning of each episode of *Bonanza*? I watched every week as a kid and when the flames came I thought, *neato-torpedo*, I thought, *cool*.

Where are my lost eyebrows? Did they fly up, up, up or drift down as delicate ash, floating like some unformed haiku on a winter lake? My eyebrows got the fuck out of Dodge. Flames went up and down me as they pleased; fire didn't have to obey pecking order or stop-work orders. Kids in pyjamas watched me burn like Guy Fawkes, watched me dwell in possibilities.

The doctor with zero bedside manner said the trick was simply to consider your face a convenience not an ornament.

Thanks for that, Doc. Maybe I could take a razor to him, see if he still debates function versus ornament after I've cut him a new face. Hate is everything they said it would be, and it waits for you like an airbag. You have to learn to deal with your anger, they said in the hospital. I am dealing with my anger, I'm dealing with my anger by hating people.

Here's a haiku I wrote in the hospital for the woman on the Hopper porch.

> Lawyers haunt my phosphorous forest
> I was bright paper burning in a glass gas-station ashtray
> Owning old cars is like phoning the dead

I might have to count the syllables on that baby—I believe haikus follow some Red Chinese system. The Texas woman plays a gold-top guitar, never played for me. She sings in a band doing Gram and Emmylou's heartbreaking harmonies. You narrow the universe to one person, knowing you cannot, knowing there's a price for that.

I want to be handsome more than anything else now that it's impossible, now that I'm impossibly unhandsome, and there is a certain hesitation to the nurse's step at my door, a gathering in of her courage, a white sun outside hitting her skin.

Before I caught fire in the campground I golfed with a smoke-eater from Oregon. Mopping up after a forest fire he told me he found a man in full scuba gear lying on the burnt forest floor. Crushed yellow tanks, mask, black wetsuit, the whole nine yards. At first he thought it was a UFO alien or something like that. Scuba guy was dead, recently dead.

They couldn't figure it out, how he got there. Finally some genius decided he must have been diving somewhere and a water bomber scooped him right out of the ocean and dumped startled scuba man onto the forest fire.

The smoke-eater from Oregon on the golf course swore this was a true story, but then I'm in England, a little seaside cottage in ugly Essex, my Thatcherite uncle snoring, and what starts off this American cop show on the telly? A TV detective talking about this scuba diver found in a forest fire. Then a month later a neighbour I bumped into at 7-Eleven insists it actually happened to him on Vancouver Island near Central Lake by Port Alberni. Water bomber scooped the diver out of the big lake, not the ocean. Now I don't know what to believe. Everyone keeps telling me the same false true stories.

The toy train runs and Cindi shows me a photo of herself as a little girl in a little bathing suit at the beach (*Yes, that's me in the photo!*).

Cindi cries, points at the photo: Look. I look so happy! Once she was happy. Now she has nightmares. Cindi lights a cigarette, says she wants to see real icebergs and lighthouses before she dies. Then she says, I dreamed the two of us travelled to Newfoundland together, and it was so nice and calm; not one of my nightmares. Cindi also dreamed I killed her. She says, When I die, no one will remember me, and tells me it must be her period coming on, makes her emotional. I decide mixed messages may be better than no messages at all, though I feel like the palace eunuch.

Cindi spends half her day looking for matches. Cindi struggles with her cigarette, as if it takes great planning to get face to end of cigarette; she seems to move her face rather than move the cigarette. Cindi says, Nothing attracts police like one headlight. *Do you know why I pulled you over?*

At the tavern by the rushing river, men said things to me in my clown suit, my eunuch suit, thinking they were funny. They were deep. The waitress knew me from my previous life, gave me red quarters for the jukebox. She trusted my taste, trusted me once at her apartment. She wore deliberately ugly plaid pants and her wise face looked just like the Statue of Liberty's. With the bar's red quarters I plugged honky-tonk and swing B-sides only. The B-sides rang out, sang their night code to me alone: Texas, kiss, lit stairs, a world changed.

The old boys in the Commercial Hotel had been drinking porch-climber, watered down shots of hooch, emptying their pants pockets, their bristle heads.

We watched a man kicked directly to death. Strangely, it was an off-duty police officer who had stopped another officer for drinking and driving and refused to let him off. The drunk driver was suspended from the force, from his life. Then guess who bumps into whom at the wrong bar?

The night alive with animals, the whole middle-class group taking some joy in the royal beating, displaying longing, bughouse excitement, wanting to get their feet in like mules kicking, believing in the right thing to do. He was struggling. I don't think they meant to kill the policeman with their feet, but it was a giddy murder, a toy in blood. They busted his head and eyes and busted his ribs and arms and kidney and returned to their drinks, expecting him to resurrect himself on his own power with his swollen brain and internal bleeding. Then the ambulance attempting to dispense miracles, a syringe quivering into muscle. It was fast. I stood fast. I stood shaking in my suffocating clown suit and they returned to their drinks and sweaty hyena hollering, their *Don't fuck with me, Jack*, their legions and lesions and lessons and their memories of twitching creations face down in the parking lots of our nation.

I can wait. Wait until they pass out, then punch a small hole in the drywall under the electrical panel and pour in kerosene, my accelerant du jour. I will run before the doors blow off. See how they like it. See how they like Cindi and the Spanish nurse's Flamazine lotion. It's basic psych. You want everyone else to have the same thing you caught.

Nothing happens, though, because I feel immediately moronic and melodramatic, dial 911 outside, and firefighters are on top of it lickety-split. The doors don't blow, their faces don't fry or turn to wax. I fly away on my rare Indian motorcycle with a transplanted shovelhead engine and Screamin' Eagle calibration kit. No one new joins my Burn Man club. Burn Man is alive and the unyielding moral policeman is dead, his family in dark glasses at the bright graveyard.

Oh, how our sun smiled on me, breezes blew softly in the dappled leaves over the low-rent beach and my head touching a cool pillow. I napped and the propane fire snapped my skin, remapped me. I twisted and travelled in beautiful lost towns and low registers of postmodern western wind from the Sand Hills of Saskatchewan.

I am a product of light, of hope.

I still have that shy desire for the right fire to twist me back just as easily to what was: to milky youth and a mysterious person falling toward me on a Texas porch with her tongue arranging hope in my mouth. Under oak trees by the river the Texas woman put words in my mouth, secret words pushed in my mouth like a harmonica. *Her temple fayre is built within my mind.* Perhaps God will have mercy on me in my new exile.

The right fire. Doesn't that make sense?

Like corny cartoons and television shows—amnesia victim loses memory from blow to head, but a second blow makes it right, fixes it all right up, no matter what.

I remember a relevant episode of *I Love Lucy*. Ricky Ricardo's memory pops back after Lucy hits him by the fireplace: Ricky comes swinging back, I come back, my old skin swims back from its minor shipwreck, from the singing sirens, the torpedo, finds the muscle memory held like a Rolodex in my new skin.

Doesn't seem to work. Can't buy pointed boots back from a swollen brain, can't drift again into your childhood face or her blue truck and blue eyes and blonde hair and stories of west Texas waltzes and Cotton-Eyed Joe. Can't saw sawdust.

Instead I rise Saturday a.m. with TV cartoons, set up a supper-time date with Cindi—God bless her, at least she takes me, takes me as I am (Yes, that's *not* me in the photo)—Burn Man climbs inside mask and clown suit like a scuba diver, like Iago on Prozac. For what seems a fucking century we wave white gloves at you (*Drowning not waving*), wave at blind drivers passing Bed of Roses and helium balloons—gorgeous ivory moons and red planets bump-bumping my skin, trying to enter the hide of Burn Man's teeming serious face, trying to push past something difficult and lewd.

Ours really is an amazing world. Tristan falls in love on a Hopper porch, but Isolde loses faith in a Safeway parking lot, Isolde takes the magic bell off the dog. And a famous scuba diver rockets like a lost dark god into smoking stands of Douglas fir, into black chimneys burning.

COWBOYS
INCORPORATED

Desire itself is movement
Not in itself desirable.

— T. S. Eliot

RUNK sheets of light, the ancient Volvo angle-parked in the Interstate rest area. Cooler inside: Jankovitch, slouched at the sink in shorts, a gaudy bowling shirt. A boy and a father yell at each other over the rush of hand dryers. BAM! Hot air whooshing loudly. "You warsh yer hands?" BAM! "Hahn?" yells the kid, two feet from his father. Ironchild cranking up on the government can, searching sideways for the mainline while Jankovitch fiddles impatiently with the button over the sink to get the weather radio. "YOU WARSH YER HANDS I SAID!!" The needle sinks into flesh, the father's new cowboy hat is blown from his small head. "YA!!" screams the kid in reply.

And Ironchild has bought the farm, the last shot too pure or maybe just a piece of talc jamming an artery and boom, lights out, works still jabbed teetering in his pocked arm. "YOU WARSH YER FACE?!" yells the father now, brushing dirty water from his felt hat. Jankovitch sees Ironchild, sees, closes the cubicle door behind him, grunting as he manoeuvres Ironchild's now heavy body, propping his paratrooper boots inside the toilet bowl, the dead man's armpits damp, his skinhead cut bristling at Jankovitch's face, breath gone, skin white, clammy, Jankovitch fumbling, grunting. "YOUR FACE. YOU WARSH YER FACE!" Jankovitch waits sweating: *Leave fuckheads.* The father and son finally exit. Jankovitch grabs the car keys, the German knife, wallet, cash and by reflex, the ziploc of powder; it has sentimental value. Jams the cubicle door shut with a matchbook wedge, scrawls *Out of Order* on a paper towel on the door. That should buy a few hours, hopes Jankovitch, maybe a day or two. With the warrant in Missouri there is little choice.

A State Trooper walks in leaning to the mirror to stare into his own red eyes, takes out a pink comb. "Comb the wind outta my hair," he says into the silence. He peers at the Out of Order sign, at Jankovitch's pen and heads for a further cubicle, undoing his big leather belt and pants. "Damn," he says. "Can put a man on the friggin' moon, what's it take to keep one of these shitters running?" "Yessir," speaks Jankovitch, sidling outside into yet another realm of meat. The sun makes him sneeze.

A legless cowboy sells pencils from a wheelchair, duded up for the tourist kingdoms of heat and light. Jankovitch peels a one from the dead man's cash, gives it to the legless cowboy, the sin eater. "Much obliged pardner." Buicks buzz in the sun like bluebottles. Jankovitch sneezes again. A mother: her child wants a drink. "Shut you up or I'll break your face." More sacred bonds, semi-trailers angled everywhere in the glint. "Where you headed?" she says. "West," Jankovitch says. "You have a good day now sir," she says. "I will try to," he says. He walks to the rusting Volvo. Lightnin' Hopkins is dead now. Murray the K. John Wayne with his Nevada cancers gutting him like a fish. Virginia has her feet up in the front seat perusing *Thin Thighs in 30 Days*. There is so much light around her, a haze of hooks, too private. She looks up at Jankovitch, at the book. "I used to have a fair vocabulary ... kind of quit 'bout the time I started selling lawnmowers." All Jankovitch can think of is the bald janitor at the party insisting to Ironchild that all dances evolved from the polka, saying it over and over with such seriousness that Ironchild hit him and now Ironchild in the cubicle for some janitor to find. Jankovitch stares up the road into the grasshoppers and hundreds of flattened jack-rabbits.

Why this worship of death and youth, of carelessness?

The big country. Asleep. "Wake up. Wake up." Near Easter time too, the Lenten tornadoes touching down around the women in their gardens. "Wake up buddy." Jankovitch closes his eyes to rise from cancerous dreams of flooded towns dying in silt rivers, farm land leaching out, drifting away, Ironchild toying with his needles and grinding blue pills in the failing light. "Wake up." Jankovitch jerks forward. "What?" Saliva drying upturned in his stupid throat. Crows, nothing grows, gears gnash in testimony to bad driving and the Swedish car's endless capacity for punishment. This is the way they go: "We want you to drive again, okay?" Virginia in fedora and shades leaning over the seat to gently rouse Jankovitch who's down in shitkicker country again ... as Carlene Carter said, *put the cunt back in country* ... Johnny Cash's girl ... the car swinging hard across the blue plains and raggedy-ass cottonwood, the endless flight through pale aspens and truck stop botulism, Kmart snakeskin cowboy boots, cheating songs, box elders. This is just after the grain elevator blew over to Missouri: burned for days and they couldn't get at the bodies. In the blind pigs and roadhouses, lizards cringe under the crashing rain of Wurlitzers and chicken bones. God and country are toasted. "Wake up buddy." Jankovitch supposed to be loyally prone and deceased in the smouldering ruin, not snuck

off from work in the cross-tracks bar when the elevator spontaneously disintegrated, providing half-cut Jankovitch an all-
too-neat opportunity to duck the warrant, the women and
possible pregnancies, the big debts, the whole grieving family.

Missouri: Show Me State, population 4,676,000. Capital:
Jefferson City. Best diner in Nine Eagles county: Hines Cedar
Crest for Sunday brunch, fried chicken and eggs and thirty-
one salads or Saturday night fishfry with their special recipe
for carp and catfish. Jankovitch stares at the outlines of her
breasts shifting in a soft halter top. "Yes yes, I'm awake now."

With darkness they are well west of the rivers, but still men
stand on backwater banks spearing huge fish with three-
tined pitchforks. Sand roads snake the steep hills, crossing
and recrossing the smaller brackish channels. The café menus
slowly lose fresh catfish and perch, buffalo fish. The Volvo zigzags north, west, past Indian paintbrush and stallions glowing
beside them, hooves sparking on bits of gravel, the four-
cylinder engine an absurd fire sucking air cool through two
carbs: night an azure tunnel. Loosening spring begins in mud,
ends in mud, calves on the ground or splaying forefeet, endless births and fecundity terrible at times and Jankovitch still
young, he thinks, pushing thirty but it seems he's always pushing thirty. He stares at Virginia once more, graceful in angora
and her hat, smells her perfume. Willows flank the dust, cold
beer and greased wheels carrying west over the big country,
west and then north up the clean coast, dark rocks in sand,
congealing circles slowing to the still point in the centre of
the wheel, the union of radii, like a Hollywood wagon wheel;
the Volvo's polished baby moon hubcap, a still blurred eye en
route to wherever, Eureka, the north Oregon coastline, maybe
Port Angeles and the Blackball ferry splitting the freezing
water. Always speeding, Jankovitch deliberately ignoring the
warning signs. Ironchild curled mumbling into his own world
in the dim backseat, hunkered with his cache and his vom-

iting paranoia and god knows what in his head and arms; "I need my muscatel so I can be well. . . " Virginia and Jankovitch drop into the golden bowl of earth. Green evenings, wind blowing the first warmth of the season.

The three of them stop in small towns to purchase fresh crusty rolls, bakery donuts, creamery butter, chicken fried steak and a huge block of Wisconsin cheese. In Rook River locals stare at Ironchild; shivering, a blanket wrapped like a cerement around his shoulders, his skinhead cut, tinted mod glasses, Union Jack t-shirt, zippered army pants and clunky paratrooper boots.

A woman is a support system for a cunt, he says and Virginia slaps him hard. Jankovitch bides his time, comforts Virginia. Trust now in Christ, yells Ironchild at the bar. This ain't no disco! Ironchild, I gave you my purse, says Virginia. Where did you put it? You gave me your purse, har har. Put money in thy purse. He lights a smoke, spreads slow large hands into a laugh. Har har, go dance. Trust now in Christ, go dance with Jankovitch, all this bullshit . . . SWAT squad could come in here . . . they get nothing from me. Hey listen, striking a fist down. This stuff's *good*. All you guys, ever been *busted?*

Busted? Gimme that damn cowboy hat, you ever ridden a horse, huh? Go dance you two, go dance. Virginia and Jankovitch are silent. Ironchild flicks ash, knocks over a chair, recounts a dispute over another chair, another bar, something about a door, it's hard to tell. So I went outside, he says, I was hammered but calm you know, came back in later and drank and they say I'm barred for life, eighty-sixed. They can't do that can they? Hell . . . can't go to prison for life. His sad puzzled look.

Plastic deer on the lawns and they drive, skies cleaned and deer on the lawns, police flashers bouncing on the grottoes to the Virgin Mary. Jankovitch throws away his wallet.

The Pom-Pom Girls has played all year at the local drive-in. The mechanical woodpeckers every dawn and in the mist cattle bellowing as if being gored or, as Ironchild allows, involved in some heavy fucking. Looking longingly at two horses by a rusting corncrib, neck to neck in the filtered light, Jankovitch envies their ease with one another (and he pressed the accelerator further to the wood, lighting for the territories cursing himself to *wait till this mythless century shuts down and my fucking hair falls out and what's it matter*, only wanting to be pure again, undiseased, to do it over again but this is not in the cards and then the merry-go-round of blue flashers, the man touching the night's perimeter, the grottoes, to tell of just what can and can't be done on this religious back road, in this century, the limits, the tickets Jankovitch can never hope to cover).

The two awkwardly switch seats so that Virginia, the ex-schoolteacher, the best driver, and not Jankovitch, hands a license to the police. A spiderweb over her face, the police a floating border astride the traveller's inarticulate hunger for happy trails, miles, women, to pay later. The dead man won't stop drinking or shooting and Virginia cries in the tent. She washes his needles dutifully. The year before nursed him from a yellow bed of hepatitis. Go dance! he yells. In October he locked her in the cold room afraid of losing her, knowing. She washes his needles. Just a little toot! he cries now, crashing into the undergrowth.

Glaucous gulls, polyglot. A tongue moves among lips. For Your Well-Being: We have provided electric hand dryers to protect you from disease. Stinking hands, cancer will be kind to me.

He took her by the wrists, the white hills where there were no trees because at first she laughed, a joke on Ironchild leaving him but, then realizing it is serious; yelling, yanking on the emergency brake until it reeked of smoke and friction.

Hitting Jankovitch. Pull over, pull over Jesus, where is Ironchild? And Jankovitch yelling back, look he's dead I can't stay, not with that warrant over my fucking head and me supposed to be dead in Missouri (realizing then he didn't even know who owned the car). If you want to stay (didn't want to know). If you want to stay. And there were no trees (took her by the wrists because . . .). Only boulders that looked to have fallen from another planet into the sculpted twisted badlands, her crying, crying, the paltry rivers, crossing and recrossing the same goddamn rivers all day (me supposed to be dead, not him), all day she wouldn't stop crying, no trees and always seeming to be a third with them. Her light eyes and dark eyebrows, brownish-blonde curls, bony cheeks and earrings giving her an older, lupine appearance. Both crying.

They washed and took some of the assortment of pills. She wore makeup now and in the new heat wore only panties and a bra, the white strap bisecting her sleek back. The vehicle, Yellowknife, velar voices sunk in throats, seats.

The plains fill with wind. The rattling seed-pod logic of cut fields, the plotted grid striped with ditches of purple weeds and prairie flowers: bluebells, black-eyed Susans, hawkweed. Wild sunflowers bend and bend. In the distance, beyond Virginia's freckled profile, rain slopes in indigo columns. "It will be rain tonight." A satellite dish perches over the cinder-block motel and rented roughneck trailers. Oil and cattle dividing the empty quarter. "Let it come down." The fine curves of her throat, wisps of loose hair about the schoolteacher's cheek, the back of her neck, her throat. Water hangs silver in mid-air. A razor. In the cinder-block rooms around them, the drugstore cowboys lie on narrow bunks as Jankovitch moves into her for the first time, as hard as he can, knows he will come too soon, but doesn't slow, resigned, the cheap bed shrieking, the bored cowhands around them sipping longnecks and gazing at *The Waltons* or fuckflicks from the satellite dish, the strange fruit of the space race; grainy breasts spread in blue windows, huge thighs kicking over the republic's dark fields, eyes always on the screen, uncapping mickeys or lighting Chesterfields by reflex, eyes locked blindly on the oval screens where a tearful John Boy won't shoot the doe or giant vaginas open in a red glistening. They leave their hats on indoors, not a movement is wasted. Jankovitch wears the dead man's hat for a while as he fucks her, his hat being shrunken and full of peanuts. "Goodnight John Boy," the cowboys murmur in unison or hum along to *The Ballad of Paladin* by Johnny Western, the ferret-like cowhands grasping wads of toilet paper, the lone couple coming, this, uh, can't, yes? Go, Jesus, go on. Is it safe? They age in his arms. Always.

"Be back shortly." The dead man jolts to a halt in one joyless burg, a county seat with Italian Gothic courthouse on the customary rise, to break into BigValu Pharmacy, the two, three, nervous, hurry hurry Christ hurry, sweat tingling in odd angles down the shirtback cotton, eyes up and down the spooked alley, the big metal doors creaking, Jesus H. Christ will you hurry, Ironchild? and he does, smooth, strangely efficient, escaping back into the anarchy of flight and vision splintered between coasts.

No wonder they hate the outsiders, thinks Jankovitch, no wonder the beatings in pool halls, the hair-trigger shooting over twenty cents of spilled popcorn. Where you from? they'll ask. Yazoo, he says giggling. Yazoo City. Fuck what a mouth. Going back soon too, love Yazoo and so on. He looked like a fag golfer in that purple shirt and he wouldn't leave it fuckin' alone. Yazoo! They took him. They're not from here. No one is from here.

Jankovitch wakes on the Interstate tense, nervous, unrested. Dreams of nothing, of close to nothing, of parallel nations of ropes and posses, the borders, the chases, cowboys crossing champaign and treed slopes, chase dreams, crossing ancient sea bottoms now in grain and being forced to face things at the fence, the tree. In nightmares begin responsibilities and Ironchild worries Jankovitch, doing more Talwin when he can, pacing it with the stolen Demerol, cans of Busch, chocolate bars, garbage collecting at his feet. Shadows under his bright eyes.

Ironchild grins, smelling of sweat and borax; he never changes his t-shirt. Virginia and Jankovitch change once or twice a day. In South Dakota, above a reservoir at sunset, they buy beer and a good hairbrush on the dead man's credit card. Jankovitch's scalp itching. Spring flooding, rivers twist into blue-red evening. Ironchild passed out again, breathing noisily. Virginia calmly signs, Jankovitch nervous, not wanting to leave his name. They wash up.

Passing the derelict feedlots at Ash Hollow and then the Cowboy Church of Christ, its sign in looping lariat script, a polished ochre cow horn over the doors. Every time they pass a church Jankovitch shudders at the sharp steeples, sees the works stuck in Ironchild's white fish flesh, teetering on the toilet, another dead country.

After showering at the YMCA: Ironchild in the stairwell, a wrestling mat hung. He pounds it fiercely, his fists blurred. Wouldn't want ten of those to the head would you? he says. Uh no.

Jankovitch is part of the car now, no longer stepping out to stretch or exercise, hands nailed to the wheel, staring ahead, smelling the gasoline fumes, the road everything; moving, random, sweet, his lost colours. Drive and drive until everything flies apart. Then breakfast. Worried, Virginia has to pry him from between the Volvo's rusting fenders. Inside, Ironchild turns at the table: "Got me a problem back in Missouri, people say this, people say that 'bout me. But I don't know who. Buddy, give me a name, I wanna be kissed when I get screwed." He takes a drink of lukewarm water, stares sadly over the white plains. Jankovitch buys a local paper: HE HUNTED DOWN 13 YOUNGSTERS WHILE DRIVING SHINY RENTAL CAR. The Red Brigade's Giovanni Ciucci confessed: "I could not succeed in seeing him as an enemy, but only as a man who was sleeping." Finds an article: Jehoshaphat Flats—An investigation is underway into a series of drug-related break-ins at medical offices in the northwest area of the state over a two day period this week....

"Y'all want coffee? Y'all want this on one ticket?" Jankovitch jumps. A huge waitress, wrinkles between blue earrings. They ask for tea, pigs in a blanket, *Huevos Rancheros*, chicken fingers, beans, unsweetened grapefruit juice, ambience, greasy ions. Jankovitch stares at a mass of eggs on the hot grill palpitating like a yellow heart. Ironchild eats in seconds; it is there, it is gone. A cockroach or something on Jankovitch's thigh. He flicks it down and stomps. After, he wonders if he was hallucinating and keeps lifting his foot to make sure it is there.

A local saunters in and the waitress pulls him a diet Pepsi before the man has spoken. The cook stands with a greasy spatula: "That be Pepsi and tenderloin or tenderloin and Pepsi?"

"Either way. Got any good numbers left?" He puts money on a football game.

"You wanna give me your tip now," says the cook, winking at the waitress. "I get off early." The cook laughs. "Last tip he gave me: Don't . . . eat . . . yellow . . . snow," drawing out each word slowly for effect. Outside there are apples and blood in the gutter. Jankovitch and Virginia and Ironchild stare. The floating wood of the storefronts. The primary colours surrounding the car, the food on their breath.

Nightcrawlers 90 cents. Jankovitch wipes the film of grease from his forehead, eases sweaty shirtback from the seat, reads the ads painted roughly on sagging white trash barns, reads them: Bull Durham, Mountain Dew, Do You Want Freedom *Joy* Heaven? Wrigley's Spearmint—Chew It After Every Meal, nodding he will, of course he will.

Ironchild out of it again in the backseat and she looks over with her cat-like eyes, the plains a bed, a white sea behind her head and she bends her long hair into his lap as he drives jolting, surprised, uh yeah, her bending into him and Ironchild stirs, wakes in the back seat: Where we now, buddy? asked sleepily. Near Red Mound, whispers Jankovitch, not knowing or caring where the hell they are. She's sleeping, he says, still whispering, lying. Ironchild rubbing his eyes like a child and Virginia calmly covers Jankovitch's unzipped lap with a jean jacket, feigns sleep. Jankovitch thinks of Ironchild's flailing fists in the green stairwell.

Wanna stop? You thirsty?

Not this cowboy, says the dead man.

Wash up? Maybe coffee to go?

Whatever, whatever, he says, sounding irritated now, staring out.

Gotta get gas. Ya.

Some fun now, thinks Jankovitch. Ironchild begins a groggy wash of talk about the last time he got busted, how two Blackfeet made the mistake of looking at him so he knocked out the closest with a flying kick, pounding the inert form on the sidewalk. The second man fled behind a Pontiac to draw a knife from his boot. He sliced Ironchild's arm and shoulder. (Ironchild stretches his t-shirt, points to the scars, the proud flesh knotted in lines.) Bleeding, Ironchild grabbed the long black hair, smashed the man's face into the hood over and over, face, metal, face mashed flat, bone, caved-in bone, a noise like a garbage can lid. A fat man intervened with a tire iron, complaining of the mess and dents in the hood. Yazoo City. With a reddening shirt Ironchild fled fuelled on adrenalin and diet pills until tackled by an off-duty cop in the alley behind the Army & Navy. Two male prostitutes were dragged into the same remand cell arguing, one bragging a john on The Hill had paid him fifty bucks. The second outraged, screaming "Ten! Ten dollars! No more, never." They fought and two older prisoners broke them apart then forced them to "give face" as Ironchild called it. "Better than my wife," growled one. "These guys know what they're doing."

Virginia rises. "So did you indulge?" she asks, sounding jealous.

"Not this cowboy," Ironchild says. "I told 'em I'd watch for the screws."

Jankovitch has the distinct feeling he should hop out and grab a Greyhound at the next town. Why do I stay? he wonders. This is what he thinks Ironchild has: Talwin, black beauties, NoDoz, an antihistamine that Jankovitch cannot pronounce, the Demerol, grinding teeth, a jumpy walk. Ironchild may have more, they cannot be sure. He slurs some words.

In Wyoming the three of them buy cowboy hats, one of those moments. A beautiful corner of the state, beef country, blue mountains in the distance. Inexplicable nostalgia, cattle and green cool hills shouldering up from each side of a hissing current, the spring prairie torrent deceptive, dangerous. Blue mountains in the distance.

Their three shadows lean and roll as if stranded in an open boat: he drove, she drove, then the other drove, and then she drove and he drove, they drove and they drove, climbing toward the higher passes and mining towns. Under red nimbo-stratus, black hulks staring at the soil, stoic, bovine, stray spears of grain confused in last year's stubble.

Speed, speed, the counties blurring two centuries past the cracked glass, the inevitable descent into fatigue and puzzlement, climbing, her stockings beside his leg and the giddy wonderment of these distances and her new body, the vast plateaus, the new comprehension of geography, the million schizoid nations of North America. His maps: Jankovitch can still see the nuns and old school maps, dusty Mexico, El Chichon pouring crud into the air to the south, sixty million tons of ash; sulphur dioxide gas, salt and dust in a cloud circling the earth every ten days, altering the weather over the crazy checkerboard squares of the Union and pink Canada almost tangible, breathing to the north. Jankovitch reaches a fevered hand out the window toward the sleeping cool light, another into her as she drives, the arbitrary borders, the blue silos of sweetgrass, Texas Playboys and Joy Division in an unlikely combination on the radio. The ash circles the alfalfa and red clover.

Jankovitch drives the peaks in his favourite red t-shirt, found on the ski hill after a knee-wrenching wipeout. The ligaments still sore. Virginia silent, thinking, watching Jankovitch's arm muscles in the bright shirt, leaning with the small car, physically forcing it stiff-armed through the mountain curves and hairpins, accelerating, always accelerating, whooping, swooping downhill until the red needle is buried, in the rearview the dead man floating up white-faced from his attempt at rest on the stiff back seat. Jankovitch laughing at his worried expression.

Hey buddy, you always drive this fast? asks the dead man. I'm getting rocked around a mite.

We're making good time, go crank some more shit.

You got a lot of class you know that do you buddy. Maybe you should try a little of this shit, cool your jets quick, I don't think it's ever been stepped on.

Me? I got enough problems without yours.

No buddy, I mean it.

The wind smells nice, she says. I feel sick, she says.

You been chippying too? asks the dead man.

Into Silver Valley. Wind off the hardpan plains shakes the saskatoon berries. Raybeats' *Piranha Salad* jangling the FM out of some Montana college town.

Have a line.

North, losing spring, all that. Winter wheat, the ancient pulls, secrets draining lives. The threat of rain at night, dependent on women and supermarkets. I'm dead, thinks Jankovitch. Night. Why does she stay? She blames my stupid brooding and outbursts on an Irish temper, ranting after a bad pool shot, a flat tire. Her thin form in the flawed mirrors and motels, bent in the modern dance: the bars neon atolls in the buffalo grass.

Her nostrils, her bare heel on a wooden floor tightening her calf and his groin, the way her legs run together against his throat. He wants her in the room where she stands, her brown back to him, ironing blouses in her underwear until he tears the panties from her, nuzzling her ass and climbs her spine to lean, a speck of caution crawling insect-like in the back of his mind, but body and cock push on until the ironing board crashes down and they're dazed reptiles scrabbling the floor's beer cans as the dead man comes out of the bathroom in torn Fruit of the Looms, haggard and silent behind yellow light, sniffs, moving each side of his mouth. Jankovitch waits for the punishment he has courted, the ten to the head or kicks along the rib cage, but Ironchild turns back to whatever, his constipation from Talwin or recalling which arm or leg is next.

Embarrassed, Jankovitch falls into the prickly armchair, sinking into dreams of curtains flashing on her metal skin, Ironchild in the tub, tides of highway traffic behind her shape and her shape, no longer pissed off, wakes him to move to the bed half asleep, dressing quietly and falling into each other's riddled karma, the big curves push-pull-pushing and everyone must know this bliss, cats falling in the air and gone into the rhythms of sleep.

The din of the roadside bar: horrible coughing through drooping moustaches, the suction sound of fridge doors, words sputtered out, boots slamming the rough wood. Nearly all the men have lost one thumb roping calves, the digit caught and ground away between the coarse rope and the hard leather saddle horn. Money changes hands at the pool tables.

Glasses smash. The men hang up yellow slickers, order a shot and chaser and squint and blink on the front stoop into the drunken light to the north, throats cleared of the railroad dust, spittle mixed with dust and hardened Montana mud; the payments waiting, going crazy in their thin grey skin, itching for some odd congress.

Sad bluegrass and cowboys jumping up and down, up and down, yahoo, on some poor clown in the parking lot, their playground. Lookit those sonsabitches, says Ironchild. They know how to live. Yippee Ti Yi Yo! White crosses in the ditch where the highway curves down from Canada.

Jankovitch fills his hat with beernuts and leaves it on the picnic table where they eat from it as they drain can after can of Foster's. Rain falls overnight. In the sere morning the hat is shrunken, bent, unrecognizable, sodden and floating with peanut skins and sugar. Virginia laughs, her kiss a hint of tongue between her lips. She's his only sure thing. Balling the jack across shale and limestones, the faulted anticlines and sawtoothed ridges, into the cirques. Jankovitch contemplates his fucked-up life: buzzing the awful country, drunken prairies and basement rock, evading responsibility and age, ignoring the mirrors, used clothes; *fuck it man*, never any money, never a car, renting rooms, alternately cultivating and blowing liaisons, wandering tired and staying with friends, lovers, bumming off relatives, in motel dives, on bus seats, couches; it gets old. No fatted calves left for this cowboy.

Hallway air, flies going crazy. She comes out of the shower. Jankovitch watches his cock disappear into her. Do you like to hike? Jesus yes, I like to. O God. You *like* to *hike*? Jankovitch thrusting on each verb. Fuck yes, love hiking, fuck. So. . . . His hand holding the back of her neck, closer and closer to her until he feels he will disappear, his heart beating through her into the mattress.

Roads slick, another white cross in the Montana ditch, another sign ignored. Rain soaks into the corrals and manure. Downhill to a curve at the bottom of the hill and the car is sliding sideways, just about through the curve and the rear left wheel catches the edge. Is it rolling Bob? Yes, rolling trees and horizon, roll and lay flat and spring up again spinning in the headlights, cans in the air, then stopped and steam from the radiator and tick-ticking from the dead Volvo dribbling out oil. Headlights still on, pointing. Jankovitch grins through splintered teeth because now, helpless, they await the ghouls from the prefabs, John Law with his flashing baubles and squeaking holster. Caught in the straps, the straps, his arm at an unnatural angle; now they are hung upside down miles past Little Big Horn and Virginia's face is a strange star, her ruined mouth leaking blood into a spreading stain over his clothes and though it may well mean she's still alive he wishes the dripping would cease because the car is on its roof and he can't stop puking up the last of the Wisconsin cheese. His one sure thing.

Border dreams, cuts himself from the wreck. Turn these fucking headlights off before the ghouls get wind. Finally. Staggers to the slick road and the next high plains cowtown, buys Levi's and a pearl-button shirt, tosses a bloody bundle in the weeds. He can't keep food down. Bruised ribs out like a dog's. He wants a bus to the clean coast, to start over, away from the binges of deceit and drinking, the trail of abortions and car washes, mescal and frozen grins, reckless driving, drinking. New Gleem! Fights The Enemies Of Your Mouth. He swears he's going to change. Starting Monday.

There is too much light at the border; at the stainless-steel table they appear ready to dine. These people dress and dream in uniform, dream of the fabled pipelines, mules and powder caches. This is their lair, try and tell them it is a false border, that none of it matters. Jankovitch imagines the sick line of questioning: anything to declare? Ha: where can you start. He remembers all the women, the grain elevator turning to atoms, maybe he's still there—but he recalls the great timbers and chunks splintering outside the neon bar. Ashes, water, the stench of grain burning the back of his nostrils. Fuck 'em, he's alive, in flight.

But there at the border with the guards at the ferry terminal is the dead man, in of all things, a fucking suit. Ironchild in a suit! Shaven with a tight white grin and waving a paper. Jankovitch does not have to read it to know his own scrawl: *Out of Order.*

All the women on the bus, there are only women on the bus, turn back to stare at Jankovitch in his sling. He wishes for Virginia now. Now he sees they are all pregnant and staring at him accusingly. A blade in his hands. With his good arm he presses it to his throat. The ziploc. He is washing, washing his hands in the can. Anything to declare? Jesus. He reads the green ticket: I Plead Guilty To The Offense As Charged And Will Pay The Penalty As Prescribed. *Terribilus est locus iste.*

Where is Virginia?

Did you eat the last of the cheese? Her soft drawl. Washing.
Yes, Virginia I confess, the last of the good Wisconsin cheese. El Chichon's ashes circle one more time. The strap keeps falling from her ivory shoulder. He replaces it but it keeps falling and falling from her ivory shoulder.

ASSINIBOIA
DEATH TRIP

Each man is fain to pluck his means, as it were, out of his neighbour's throat.

— Mourt's Relation: A Journal of the Pilgrims at Plymouth

S HE BUTTONS UP her tiny sweater, not knowing I study her. She is vanishing like a bridge in fog. Crow Jane is not a ghost, but I know now she will haunt me. I want to see her unbutton the same garment for me. Nothing stays the same in fashions.

The bridge vanishes in fog and I discover we are fretful devices wrapped in such thin skin. Or we are ghosts on river ice. What's the difference? Inside the erect palisades of Fort Robinson Crazy Horse sings his death song; Crazy Horse lies on his red blanket on the floor. *Have you met?*

My good friend Private Gentles runs Crazy Horse through with a bayonet and now ostrich feathers are in vogue on our ladies' hats.

To our hats we also add veilings, side combs, pompadour pins.

Her kind sad face by the icy shore, her long wrists. Does she have any feelings for me? I think she does, but I cannot be sure.

Did you see me in the bakery? she asks me.

I thought our paths would cross, she says.

Louis David Riel swings over the shop's mannequins. See the fine glass display cases, our high ceilings of slotted tongue and groove, see the snipers on the high ground, tied into trees like hanged men, and our poor young shop-girl run off her feet.

Hat boxes, invoices. *O Miss! O Miss!*

The bullet passes my head. *You missed!*

I like her silhouette down the block by the hat shop. I like her aqua eyes that open wide when she listens to you; I follow her like a dog, but on some profound level I know I am barking up the wrong tree.

I thought our paths would cross, she says. I like every single thing about her, the way she moves, everything. But I didn't see her by the bakery. A bad omen; I missed her.

Prices Right, Consistent with Good Workmanship.

Our beautiful proud horses gallop in the snow; in a blue uniform I ride with Three Fingers McKenzie; I am clean as an electrical storm. In the Moon of the Popping Trees we shoot into the skin lodges on the Marias River in Montana and we shoot anyone who comes crawling out. It's almost like war. We kill hundreds of Cheyenne horses.

And brave Mister Custer falls in his bloody village without walls, beside him a pasteboard box of cartridges, beside him Autie and Boston, Tom Custer's taffeta jacket, all dead, all the horses dead, and Brevet General Custer dies where his brother and nephew and hounds die on the hill above the river at

Greasy Grass, and fashionable women switch their hats from rolling brims to dropping brims.

Our buyers travel to European markets on an annual basis, we visit the renowned millinery emporiums of London, Paris, Glasgow, New York, Boston, and Montreal, bring the latest styles of hats back to our humble little town, our little piece of paradise.

As the pump organ plays to the choir, we patrol the earth for your Sunday best.

At the Battle of Grand Coteau the tiny circle of Métis hunters repulse two thousand Sioux, who leave behind one hundred dead.

Now the Métis and their screaming wagon axles and wheels are lords of the grand plains. The Métis are free to hunt in their scarlet sashes and beautiful buckskin jackets, they can roam like raptors. Now it's their new empire, their happy trails, their jail.

Thirty-four years later outside the Regina jail our hanged man swings; our government asks that Riel break his neck on the end of a scratchy rope made in Ontario. *Hangman oh hangman!* For two minutes Riel lives on, lives on the rope's intricate braid, but soon his little mutiny at the edge of the world is over, a brief empire dismantled.

And to our hats we add chiffons, tulles, fur, velvet wings, ribbon rosettes, lace, rhinestone buckles.

The black-haired captain loses his hat firing into the crowd, we are all face to face.

Who are we fighting? It doesn't matter a whit. I love her.

"Do it!" shooting metal into the close heads and shoulders until his weapon is empty as air. "See, see!" he shouts. See what unread vision?

A shell nearly cuts me in two, knocks me over.

Who is that who rolls back the stone?

His appearance like lightning, and his raiment white as snow.

I see a distant woman standing among the myrtle trees in the glen by the bridge.

I crave her and love her and I don't even know her. I feel stupid and pathetic and I'd rather not feel stupid and pathetic.

Pink light under the dark trees of the dooryard and what hat shall we don when snipers line the peach orchards and dusk-red ridges?

"Give me that gun, you bastard!" calls the choir, the converted, the café men, the crowd groaning and yelling as they fight under the low sky like carp, like eels.

We move, but no one moves far.

"I'm gonna die," insists the wounded man in my newly bloodied arms.

In this, I think, you are correct.

We walk the world's addled avenues, turn here, turn there, and various viruses meander toward us like zigzag butterflies. Your one-eyed teddy bear; where does it lie now? And the new diseases, the only child lost to diphtheria; all chance, a chance to walk.

"There they are, men!" shouts our captain.

Bodies held up by the close crowd, stabbings, brass horns, guns, shrieks.

The bodies can't even fall in the press. And I see my shop-girl with a full dance card.

Treachery! O Villainy! Her kind face; I want her like a child, I wander like a clod. Her attentive face, an image of her face stuck in my head. She has no time.

Mother! Who is she for? I can't tell. Long fingers buttoning her sweater, by her compact breasts the slimmest wrists I've ever seen. Gossip says Private Gentles and his bayonet have asked for her hand. Is she now sworn to another? We are induced to construct our own prisons—ropes, stone, bars, beams—we raise our own gibbets.

Sausage and honeycomb, her blossoms, corn cakes and rum, her bosom, potted meat, mouths open or grimacing like dancers, shouting and swearing, salt tongues stuck in babel and brothy breath, all the brains and bodies, in battle all of us pushing toward forest and fence, the flowers of the forest shredded under rounders and rowdymen, where are they, where, *see, see*, hundreds of voices becomes one foul full sound and we break rank, run like turkeys.

Walking the cedar bridge we can't stop talking, but at dinner with others she is so silent. I see different sides of her, like to brush her side when we stroll.

"Let us give thanks," says her father for grace. "Thanks you are back safely from the wars. Some don't come back, some come back and well, are altered."

She puts her eyes on me.

Her father asks me, "Do you believe in sin?"

"Yes, sir, sin is something I have seen in the world."

Leafy boughs breaking with shells, balls, the company settling into the earth, the captain shooting into the crowd of umbrellas and top hats and they absorb it and periwinkle shells decorate her new hat.

Ten ladies and ten gentlemen in a boat and one hundred Irish servant girls climb the back-stairs and scullery maids in long dresses on their knees scrubbing the flagstones outside the front door, a city of women on their knees, and the Nez Perce almost make it to the Canadian border.

Lord I wish I was a catfish.

The Nez Perce flee without even clothes, they are attacked and rousted again and again, some running naked, watery cells half-frozen, skin shot up, they've come so far, too far in fog and freezing mountain passes, tiny humans balancing on the ice of a tilting planet.

Cut off, the Nez Perce turn this way and turn that way and more horses again against them, always another blueshirt column, their old allies selling them out. Like me, they have no allies, no hats on their heads, and in every direction men in warm buffalo robes chase the naked ones on the snow.

Another night of doubt about her, though she is so good to me, too kind.

Why can I not stop thinking of her walking in the ice-fog off the river? There is a mechanism in my head that I hate. I think of her face when I go to sleep and I think of her face when I awake. Can I please have a five minute break?

I am becoming a lunatic who loves tragedy, punishing myself for something, some act that has no shape, doesn't exist.

Perhaps it is just winter destroying me, this most primitive of seasons in the river pines. Waiting at an iron pan, a convulsing kettle, and tears salt my eyes for no reason. My strange stumbling stupid blind libido. I would like just 19 seconds with her. Tormented, we are private and gentle, we try the new tricorne hat, the torpedo, the turban, the mushroom shape; in her shop downtown we must try the poke.

I am an optimist; I believe in so many possible worlds; yet really there is no evidence.

The Nez Pierce try so hard, almost make the border. That's the worst part of any thought: the word *almost*. Bullets faster in cold air, dragging their wounded, rearguard fighters protecting women and children from the ranchers and the soldiers' ammunition seems to distribute its own light.

Hurry, hurry, they flee naked in ice and snow, feet shredded, nostrils running with blood, chased by one-eyed teddy bears, in rocket's red glare, *oh, do hurry!*

Hurry for best choice. Our newest hats are selling out. A skating party on the ice! The trees frosted white as fish, and I find her friends know her as Crow Jane.

I want only to see my downtown shop-girl, want to live there under her sausage curls, her kind eyes.

Look at her wide brim, her wide peach shape in my arms, Crow Jane's winter coat so thick and warm. Is her derriere branded with a vivid red handprint?

But then whose hand?

Her white skates tapping the starry ice and what is it about hot broth that lifts the spirits *instantly?*

Those shadowed faces of our murdered brothers, our fallen soldiers in the great crooked ditch, their hats lost to them. Some men look asleep, but others look horrified, mouths wide as a river, eyebrows up as if seeing a spirit monster, as if seeing me.

My Dearest Love, as a souvenir I am sending you a sleeve patch from an enemy officer.

In ragged mismatch uniforms, some boys look so young, lost angels (once terrible), and some look hard in death, the blossomed godhead pushed up in their trousers; some were paid to be here as a substitute, part of a brokered transaction.

Ditches and bodies, ditches and bodies. I know we are all *ordinary,* but we don't want our faces rubbed in it.

These migrant loves; we are written on like toast.

Crow Jane shivers on the cedar bridge, her hat too thin in the harsh wind pushing the ice floes, her hat suddenly blown away, veering like a black bird over the ice.

"You're cold," I say stupidly.

"No, I'm fine."

Despite her protests, I insist she wears my fur hat.

I study the pale planes of her face, study her head. I am a student of her weather, her thoughts, her aquiline nose, I am a student of the several pretty triangles that form her face. How little I know, of anything. When my fox hat rests over her blue eyes, life seems richer, mysterious, variegate, full of traps.

"Unlike me, you're very nice," she says, bestowing both compliment and clear warning. We are inches from each other, inches from the bridge edge.

No one from our muddy village can spy us. Our eyes on our eyes. We know that neither of us is nice and we know that neither of us is not nice.

A Testimonial:

Dear Mesdames. Received my hat ordered by mail and I am greatly delighted; I consider it excellent value. You may in future number me among your regular customers, as I shall always feel perfectly safe ordering from your firm.

Some dead boys look so young, but other soldiers in the ditch look withered and aged; some fists clench at a chest, some with just one finger pointing, as if in stentorian debate. Some are unmarked, some bodies clean, and some in wool pants covered in blood that looks like black oil. Their one finger points at me, my eye.

Crow Jane sends me such wonderful letters, a secret thrill when I spy her name, her ink.

She writes, I enjoyed our chat today, she says, I dreamed of visiting you, I was on a bicycle and you had a house in the woods surrounded by flowers.

She asks, Are you happy, my charming one? I want you to be happy.

Pray, sir, Crow Jane whispers to me as my brotherhood of fingers travels the inside of her long leg. Not now, she says brightly, but not never. Her face glowing. I love her; it is the best night of my life. All these unknown parts hidden in the walls of our palisades, our forts. Can life be more lovely?

But how can I touch her again when we are always in our winter layers, bundled up like Egyptian mummies? I am wrapped, I am wrapped up in her, lost in the word *almost*.

In the darkened shop entrance my left hand explores between her buttons, Crow Jane's winter coat, such a dark sky and silver light rising from ice caked on streets where we linger as if in a living negative, and in the slabs and silver light of stone doorways where we hide it is always 3 a.m.

She is safe ordering from our firm, her grapefruit safely held to a starched blouse. She is a belle. Your firm cerebellum. My firm. Her mouth on me. Yet Crow Jane is promised to another. The Intended and my intent unclear.

We ate hotcakes with sprinkles of cinnamon.
  She sang a very pleasing selection.
    A man peeking through the window undoes trousers and troubles himself for a minute. The weight of fruit held in hand. Dip a sausage in the honeycomb bowl.
    All their Sioux arrows fell short. After the battle the Métis were masters of the plain.
  I do beg your pardon, she mutters to me with her tongue.

I held her long leg; such promise, but I was overconfident. I thought Crow Jane must be mine, that I was master of the plains and palisades. Tongue and hump a delicacy. Nothing will come of nothing. I wish I could forget everything, forgive everything.
    Her honeycomb and whose sausage?

These chemical weeks drive me crazy; such suspense must be destructive to my health, my being. Whose delightful peach in syrup?

I am shot down. And who shot Sitting Bull?

Do you think Bull Head pulled the trigger?

Sitting Bull sports the tiny sunglasses he affected while touring with Buffalo Bill's Wild West Show, just an ordinary superstar talking to journalists outside his rude cabin.

Come on in my kitchen, 'cause it's bound to be raining outside.

Give me that salt pork. Give me that gun, that old time, why the hell is Sitting Bull lying in a hump on the floor?

No, hold it, that's Crazy Horse dying on the post office floor on his red blanket, run through by Private Gentle's razor-sharp bayonet.

I get their deaths mixed up, their wooden hovels, their sudden exits off our stage.

Sitting Bull slumps by his little cabin, shot dead in the head by the tribal police, their big faces, their dark jerseys and gold buttons in light.

Now he is alive; now he is dead. The tribal police rode all this way in the middle of nowhere to shoot him for no reason at exactly five in the afternoon.

And Buffalo Bill shot down dead at his game of cards.

No, wait, that's Wild Bill, shot dead in the head at cards in Saloon #10.

Our vicious skills; I can't keep them straight.

Private Gentles stabs with a long bayonet: deep penetration.

A human's unknown parts and layers, so many unknown parts, private and gentle, a finely tuned machine until the introduction (*have you met?*), the opening, the insertion of your metal blade under the once familiar surface, you are inside, cut flesh, cut wires, now someone screaming at me, *what have you done to me?*

We sort through elixirs, our medicines: *Phoenix Bitters, Smith's Anti-Mercurial Syrup, Fowler's Solution of Arsenic, Bristol's Fluid of Sarsaparilla.*

We swim into brightness, salt, we love each other or we don't love each other and the blue pillow under her and goose-down floats over our bodies like snowflakes on a covered bridge.

Red sunsets, smoke and grey fire; we are remaking the world, scorching it, cooking it, burying our face in pillows.

Fucking Americans burnt the grass to drive the herd south.

Sitting Bull ran to Canada; those cusses want to keep the herd in the USA, starve him out. No more treats of tongue and hump.

They shoot all day, guns almost melting.

The buffalo stand still, even while others are shot all around them like trespassers, giant dark creatures dropping to earth off their skinny ankles.

Freebooters staked on a dead plain; your beatific rain-clouds that never arrive; crows yell RAW! RAW! Your raw deal, a dead man's hand: two pairs, aces and eights.

Engineer blows the whistle, fireman shovels coal!

In 1643, she, and all her servants and children, save one, were killed by Indians on Long Island. Some Puritans saw this as divine providence for her heretical preaching.

The pit of hell and the pit of my stomach. My face to Crow Jane's beautiful belly. Her mouth on my belly. *Yours*, she signs her letters.

This is off the record, off the clock. Why am I in the Regina jail?

Who is that bearded head trapped in a noose?
Have you met? Her lovely neck.

I love leaning into that narrow perfumed theatre, just there by her ear, where a hemp noose would catch her skin. We bring out some kind of kindness in each other.

I'm never quite sure what words you will utter next, she says happily. She writes, I hope to see you very soon. Crow Jane says, I wish I were tapping at your window.

A rope from the tree for the children to swing into the river. You lie, you lie beside her without touching. In the boarding house someone sings in a high country tenor, *Oh save me from the scaffold.* The voice sings, *Hang me oh hang me and I'll be dead and gone.*

In our layers we walk the snowy bridge to the other side, walk several charged universes. We chat and laugh, turning to another's eyes, and I wish to be free to feast on her skin. I don't know what she wishes, but I know we are not free.

Our desire to trespass and our desire to murder desire.

Crow Jane says laughing, After seeing you I can't concentrate on anything, I can't get any work done, I can't devote myself.

The Russian painter of religious icons notices us together on the snowy bridge; will he report us to the priest? The bearded man's face in the noose seems oddly familiar—as if I've seen him on a postage stamp.

At the banquet Crow Jane risks all on impulse as the band plays, excuses herself from her table to intercept me by the coatroom. She is suddenly there and I start, stunned, lifted from my depression. The light in our eyes, our glances up and down the narrow hall. We have invented love in this scullery passageway. I am so lucky to know her. But Private Gentles has become suspicious.

I wanted to see you alone for a moment, Crow Jane says touching my hand. Had to see you even for a moment. I write her that night: I am now officially your slave.

For you we travel to European markets, millinery emporiums.

The captain's gun must be empty by now, the ditches are full, but it never seems to stop. The dying recruits call out, *O My Dear Mother!* Their heartbreaking news. *If only I could see you again.* If only I could see her, touch for 19 seconds.

I feel hollow, Crow Jane says. I wish to open her, fill Crow Jane. I pocket the milky spoon she used at tea, keep it close to my leg.

I want to see you, she says, but Private Gentles has become suspicious. Private Gentles locks her in, won't let her go out the door.

She stands for something to me, but what? Some ideal or glowing promise, a change in the weather, a prison break. I wish her wrapped around me like a red blanket.

We murder opportunity like crows, murder each other at every opportunity and the baby's head is always too big and our dearest women die in childbirth over and over, yet we fill the planet and plains. How do we do it? We are murderers. How do we go on?

Some in eagle feather bonnets, some in crow feathers, some in shirts, some not. Some die and some escape. By the border twelve infants and several old people freeze to death.

Hullo, look what the cat dragged in. I fall for her like a knife to the floor. Unlike me, you're very nice.

After the war bricks are sorted and fences we burnt in our campfires are resurrected with rapture and silver nails—oh such bright fruit of the forge. The disappeared and dead too are repaired—they reappear happily at the piano—and our dear mothers linger at windows as river ice disappears like skin.

The same summer Custer kills himself at Greasy Grass, Wild Bill Hickok stares at the cards held between his thumb and fingers: what does he spy but two aces and two eights, his last cards, the famous dead man's hand.

In Saloon #10 Jack McCall's bullet tunnels through Wild Bill's interesting brain, blows out his cheek like a sneeze, and the well-travelled bullet bumps the arm of the river pilot who sits opposite. Aces are high. Buffalo Bill sends wildflowers to Wild Bill. The river pilot's grandchildren sell the spent bullet on eBay.

Here is my fall, my full loan of violence. I fall on the giant puny planet, fall on ice, break my hand, my big head dizzy for days.

There in town: my memories of Crow Jane and gaudy merchant walls walked by in rough sunlight, gaze held and returned or rickety gaze not returned (*Indian givers*).

And of course Crow Jane has flown from me—her beautiful handwritten ink on hotel stationary, her hand, her Louis Riel postage stamps (*Riel draws aces and eights*).

Goodbye, she said. And I feel very fine sandpaper applied agonizingly to my skin and brain and vanity.

Her promise, her promise to someone else, her sudden move to San Francisco with Private Gentles. *She moves through the fair*, sings the wild high voice in the hall.

I was the more deceived.

Oh, the scent of her milled hotel soap, my scratchy face in the scent of her warm head and neck where the noose would fit.

And in her buttoned buffalo coat she is seeing someone else, her cream-faced loon, her toad-spotted tallow-faced whoreson!

Traitorous whorish dissembler, goatish, clay-brained, malt-worm, spleeny canker.

Now it is alive; now it is dead. What is it?

Alone on the shaky cedar bridge I am a Banbury cheese, quailing, mammering, dizzy-eyed, beslubbering, betrayed, O I am aces and eights.

My hands were on her, Crow Jane ran to me in the lit hallway that one night, ran to me as the band played on; she wished she could tap on my window in the night. The birch forest seemed magic wherever we placed our feet. We drag our wounded far away and no bayonet can harm us (*I want you to be happy!*). Some drive keeps me going no matter what; I will never give up. At the same time I also give up.

All the bodies pressed together and our strange rules and rushes of ordinary sorrow.

Meant for each other, I believe this, but we can't talk, can't even fall together, not even for a few seconds. I disguise myself as a person and walk the shore, off the clock.

Slabs of river ice lie stranded on the slanted shore. The slabs of ice are several feet thick, ten to twenty feet long, the size of an oak wagon. Their sheer presence, forced into a dry new world, but their planes so clearly out of place.

Many slabs of ice are blue-green, but some slabs possess the fine blank colour of very thick glass, with perfect right angle edges, as if cut by a hard machine in a barn covered with dark shakes, acres of ice cut apart with industry and then fallen here on my shoreline.

This is my shore and it is sunny, but on the other side of the divide hang weird vertical clouds; long wisps droop down from them like grey ropes for children to hang on to and be taken away.

Climbing up the sloping riverbank I am hit by snow and wind; my body turns white, then the sun comes out again and melts me. This is my worm-screw weather.

A church bell gongs on the opposite side of the river, a thick cast bell ringing metal across the contorted ice field, a tolling bell's huge glottal voice, a sonic layer floating like a quilt over some stranger's wedding or funeral.

A big eagle hunkers on the ice while tiny delinquent crows deploy around the eagle, harassing it, crows lifting from the ice to lay talons on the eagle's white head. The eagle ignores the crows and little fish skeletons rest like delicate ivory combs under them on the ice. I wonder if the eagle is injured or simply inured to their talon and touch.

The eagle tolerates the taunts of the punk crows, then the regal form rises to swoop upriver, flying swiftly through the grey ropes, soundless sound, such a beautiful body vanishing in the veil of grey ropes.

At night the broken floes stand erect, an ice field held in moonlight's judgment, a field beautiful in its tincture, beautiful in its fracture.

The temperature and barometer rise all day; the temperature and barometer rising and women clutch their throbbing heads; women draw the blinds, lean on morphine.

Tomorrow the floes will vanish like a fashion, like our history, her sudden intimate absence more tangible than a presence. This document is my love song, my love letter to Crow Jane. She appeared in a cloud of light in the hallway and touched my hand and I was stunned. She runs to me and she moves away. We wear so many hats. Her magic trick; she appears and disappears. How did she do that?

In the river black salmon follow the ice out, a parade falling sleekly to the sea. We sing, *Hangman oh hangman!* The Sioux winter count reports this year as the hard winter many of the people broke their legs in the ice and snow; the winter count says this is the winter many of the people fell and hurt their heads badly.

19 KNIVES

He's pleased to meet you underneath the horse.

– Elliott Smith, "Speed Trials"

CAROL my caseworker vouched that I was reliable enough for carry privileges, so they let me have a week's worth of methadone to take home, instead of driving every day to the pharmacy across the island, especially since I had my boy to take care of. Carol knew I wouldn't sell the meth, knew those days were over.

Back in the days—way back—my buddies were salmon fishermen, buckets of money, growing on trees back then working mildew fishboats way up the rainy green coast. Lost cedar inlets with host springs and bleached totem poles. Too much cash flying like loose leaves through marina bars and government wharves, and the fish piled in dead heaps in the mist, in icy holds and bilgewater that smelled of money and diesel.

No needles at first. We only snorted heroin, a sport and a pastime, the conventional wisdom being that it's not addictive when just snorting. I planned to stop after a few lost weekends and get back to normal, but something failed me, old school words gave up the ghost, crackers in soup, and new vague words clouded through me like trained white mice.

Those Vietnamese boys in Nanaimo had that good pure stuff, stepped on with a little lidocaine to keep you lining up for more.

Just a taste, I insisted, that's all.

Those skinny Viet boys almost giving it away, points of China white going for ten or twenty bucks, deliver it by discreet courier, so the train kept arolling, and then a year or two later you're boiling up ammonia on the stovetop and the car has an expired temporary permit in the back window and your Swiss cheese brain is pawning your father's sax and you've spent enough to buy a space station.

Here's the funny thing: I always *despised* junkies, shunned their inhabited hectic arms, sleepy syllables, and sybarite synapses. Look at those bozos, I said, can't see a hole in a ladder. I thought I was smarter than the rest with my hornet-hive head. My earthly powers I believed to be manifold, special, hard as teeth on a chainsaw. I knew I could handle it, *knew*.

I mix my meth with the sweetest orange juice I can find, because the meth is so bitter. It's really gross. A strip of masking tape on my juice, where I wrote in big felt pen: DO NOT DRINK! I knew my boy loved OJ. I put it in the door away from the regular milk and juice and Kool-Aid containers.

I said, "The stuff in the door is my special medicine." I said, "Don't—touch—anything—in—the—door." I made it very clear. I could not have made it clearer.

My boy is a light sleeper. My boy wakes up in the middle of the night, our little house quiet. My boy loves orange juice, would say, "I need a dur-ink, Dad." He wakes up thirsty, a thirst like me, a night owl like me, like me his glasses folded on his nightstand, the night sky violet, quiet as a pyramid in the desert, no one up in our little house, kitchen clock ticking like an IV drip.

Maybe he's half asleep, floor cool, floating in pale pyjamas, ghostly, across our kitchen floor to the fridge, hesitates like a blank tape.

I couldn't inject myself at first. I needed help. Others helped, they fixed me, my costive pals summoned it up. Like a good Catholic I grew to love the ritual, admire the finely engineered syringe poised above like a needlenosed hummingbird waiting for you, so precisely tooled, the tiny opening rent, opening.

The door open, fridge light on the lino like blue light by the sea. The salmon are gone now and the boats are quiet and chained to the dock, and Carol and the College of Physicians knew I was OK to take a week's worth home.

The Nazis developed methadone in World War Two; but they called it Adolphine, thought it sweet enough to name after Adolph. Up to eighty mil a day. It's not the real thing. I tried to join the Pepsi generation, but they said I failed the physical. Outside in my yard is a pileated woodpecker, a baby. I don't know if it's going to make it through the night. Now I hear things at night, or when I'm down in the crawl space, hear my boy walking the floor to the white fridge: this is my new addiction, my crown of thorns, my Jones I can't kick. Like him, I wake up and need a drink.

Once I bought my boy a hot dog at the zoo and he dropped the hot dog on the ground and I hit him on the stomach and said, "What the hell are you doing?!" and now I wish I could tell him that it's OK to drop his hot dog, that there are worse things I know of now. I wish I could say to him admirable things, buy him that booster pack of Japanese Pokémon cards that he was always asking after or that full-colour book on Egyptian mummies, or take a spin at Island Go-Karts.

Start out chippying, but later you need three bags just to be barely all right. You just keep shooting it in, you give and you give, many hoofprints going in, but, none coming out. You think of the boy's blonde mother, a singer from Montana. She moves through the fair, moves through the airport with balloons of it hidden in her stomach, praying they don't burst.

I was waiting for her in the bar. Tight as the bark on a tree, I was waiting and waiting (but she didn't make it) at the ersatz Tudor pub by the piers. The inside décor was Mexican—an uneasy Tudor-Mexican alliance.

"The code is so brutal I can barely edit it," some tech said to a vibrating table of drinks.

Exactly, I thought. No more stuttering white thrill, no golden robot vibe, no leaping the garden wall. Instead you just want to *not* feel sick. That's what your meeting with God turns into. And you want to change before it's too late, want to change your outfit.

After he drank my orange juice he wouldn't wake up in his bed, open those eyelids, no longer a light sleeper. Meth is a slow-acting narcotic, shuts down the respiratory. I knew the symptoms. I called an ambulance to carry him to the hospital.

I knew the hospital because three years ago a policeman shot me in someone else's backyard. The intruder, locks on your backdoor, the tangled squares of night. One moment standing, next a flash, and it felt like a wheelbarrow hit me, knocked me down, but my hat staying on my head the whole time. I flipped to the ground in the rich careful houses (I found my boy crumpled), the sky on mute, hat still on my head.

The policeman claimed I pulled knife, so he shot me. I had no knife.

An ambulance came to visit my lamentations. The paramedics with their equipment ran bent over as if there were chopped blades cutting above us. I wanted to be witty, make a good impression, didn't want to be on someone's patio crying.

The police sealed off the yard so they could look for the knife in daylight. They needed that important evidence. Next morning nineteen knives lay in the grass of that small yard. Every cop in town must have driven by and flipped a knife over the fence.

I don't blame them for taking care of their own. I should have taken better care of my own. His sleepy eyes, spotting my OJ in the fridge door, forbidden fruit, my small boy in PJs, peering around with a ghost of a smile. We decide things lightly, pursue our pleasures.

At first the paramedics tried the kiss of life, tried driving in a needle of Narcan. How fine he looked in his pale pyjamas. His eyelids. The driver drove and I rode in the back of the familiar ambulance, thinking of that Neil Young line: *An ambulance can only go so fast.*

We got to the hospital but it was no good. Locks on the door, but I brought the intruder into our little two-bedroom bungalow. We decide things.

At first I just snorted. Nothing serious. A little pick me up, like ten-cent suicide wings, the good kind, dry as kindling. Now I hear him walking.

My boy was smart, loved yacking while I drove him around logging roads. He took first place in spelling bees at school, was fascinated by his library books on ancient Egyptians and their mummies and pyramids, their journeys to the underworld.

The embalmers pulled out internal organs but kept them in beautiful containers with lid handles the likeness of the pharaoh's head.

We drove around together, and I had a decent car. We were putting my life back together.

Egyptians washed the dead body with oil and spices, but they didn't keep the brain, didn't seem to value the brain. Why is that, he wondered.

We were driving in the Electra, flathatting it to a lake up in the clouds. My boy was in the backseat so he had room to play and read. He didn't get carsick reading there. From the backseat he told me all about the Egyptians preparing the body for safe passage to the afterlife, how the spirit was in two worlds—one world during the day, but at night, travelling back to the body. They worked over the body, made it hollow. With a long hook, they removed the brain through the nose.

BEAR ON A CHAIN

But it wasn't over yet, and now this valetudinarian native son stood in Monkey Park beside the locks shadowed with the autumn green of the banked earth and asked himself whether all this was a justified expense of his limited energy.

– Saul Bellow

If one defines the term dropout ... then every business office, government agency, golf club and university faculty would yield its quota.

– John Gardner

T HE IRON of the railroad bridge now allows happy pedestrians and cyclists across the big river. Train whistles and steam engines no longer echo up the valley, and the rails of Barrow steel have long melted. The hewn hemlock ties are torn away, but a cinder path still lingers behind pointed Queen Anne towers and *beaux arts* manses, a narrow shadow of a path behind turreted Second Empire carriage houses and Gothic wrought-iron widow walks.

Your eye knows the railroad formed that gently curving footpath, blue-grey gravel crushed by section gangs, tamped to last longer than a Roman road.

Your NEVER be forgoton

Walking over the railroad bridge I discover dozens of felt pen messages covering one section of the bridge's new wooden railings. *Trev RIP.* The notes to Trevor are all scrawled on the east railing, the side of the bridge he fell from and disappeared, drowned. The river flows east and south to the next bridge, flows to Indiantown, the pretty ridges and dairies of Belleisle, the polluted reversing falls, the Bay of Fundy's thirty-foot tides.

Man you were so cool to hang with that is what everybody told ME I wish I could of hung around you but noone ever told me about you until you died

This is my favourite felt pen note—it's somehow both comic and touching.

I'm curious why he was the coolest. Because he died young? Am I jealous that he's so cool? At first I wondered if it was a suicide.

I'll love ya 4 life & i'll never forget cha Trevor I don't know you I have heard you are the man and that you were everyone's best friend no one will forget you and when they die they will be with you

Trevor was a skateboarder—the rolling clatter and leap to get air. Was he stoned out of his gourd? He'd been drinking in Officer's Square. He was walking on the rail. Was he skating on the narrow bridge rail? I have that image fixed in my head, a bent-kneed elbows-out silhouette, his last evening buzzing like a gall wasp.

No one saw his long drop, no one saw him slip and fall from the narrow lip of the wooden rail, his friend just heard a splash at dusk.

Trev was from the north side of the river, by reputation the rougher side, working class, the hard tickets, Boss Gibson's side, Penniac, Marysville, the old cotton mill, Barker's Point, Hammertown, Rolling Town, Nigger Hill where last century a great black man had a house on a hill with a black bear chained to a rattling post—the other side, the other, the bridge a link between different shores.

Trev fell in the middle of the relentless river that is simply always there like a convenience store, river like an empty parking lot waiting, our eternal *Fleuve Saint-Jean* granting grace and bubbles.

Voices echoing on the bridge in the lobster-red sunset that night, waves radiating all points of the compass, the livid light going, and no islands close, no shore, no rescue.

As I walk on a nice day, golden sunlight smashes the river. At night city lights crawl the moving river, red spidery maps and blood orbits bending in the top of your head. Light ratchets through water, sways; light can bounce and return untouched to dry air.

Imagine coming to a body of water before there was such thing as swimming, and no lessons, just the primal fear of water—like the primal fear of a bear's big teeth, of a wolf's eye glowing, or river gods below you waiting, biding their time.

A cat will swim, a cow can swim, a moose, a dog swims innately, an eel. My kids take lessons and get nowhere and the instructors roll their eyes. Trev had no lessons. We are amazingly unequipped for this world, yet we've flourished to the point of ruining a world that tries so hard to ruin us.

TREVOR, ULIESE, TIMOTHY, HASHEY, b. Jan. 28, left us July 8

He flew: did he ever fly in a plane? Trevor went off the rail. I'm told it was an accident, not another teen suicide. The town worries of copycats. Trev, a dropout from Grade 11, dropped, dropped out of sight. The police put out a Marine Distress Call to boats on the river. The papers spell his name differently than those on the bridge.

In Orlando, Florida, a "drifter" drowns trying to ride bareback on Tillikum the killer whale. They find his naked body the same morning the divers find Trevor's body.

The famous conductor drops from his balcony, wants a way out from his cancer. Trev wants back up (rewind the film), arms flailing like a helicopter falling from the aircraft carrier, from a bridge, weightless again, a long lonely drop to wait for the world to kick in again, stop-time, stepped out of the office for a moment into the eels.

Someone on the bridge thought he seemed disoriented after he hit the water. Maybe he hurt his ribs, an arm, his back, was in shock. Someone on the bridge had a cell phone, called it in. But a teen I talk to says they had to run to houses, bang on doors for a phone. One newspaper claimed Trevor fell more than 100 feet, but the bridge deck is not that high.

My friend Jennifer drove by in her new Saturn and wondered what was up—police cruisers and lights by the bridge and river. Tales from the riverbank, a dark night, no moon, police cars parked on the grass generating as much white light as they can, and lights on the river from boats. They are looking on the bright side, but where is the coolest guy?

Cops hate the skaters and skateboarders hate the cops, but it's the cops who come looking, who probe the night, who dispatch the canine unit to the riverbank, transmit the Marine Distress Signal. They "secure" the bridge, vans at either end, and an RCMP helicopter buzzes the shore like a nose-heavy dragonfly.

YOUTH MISSING AFTER FALL

Fall weightless but become weighted: baggy gangsta pants heavy, shoes, weight like age on him. He'd been so light before, always got lots of air on his skateboard.

Make this your best trip

Beth, the same age as Trev, said he was swimming, but looked lower and lower in the water, then disappeared. Her friend Mark disagrees with Beth: Trev was trying, but he didn't know how to swim.

Another bridge's ethereal arches float to the south-east. His body fell from this bridge and passed under the exact middle of the second bridge, and when I look I feel I am looking down a gun-sight. Trev came from the north side, ended up on the south side, had no lessons. And the course is pass-fail. He dropped out, they lost him on the radar.

A north-sider tells me that your lungs fill up with river water and you sink down with the new weight, lower and lower and gone.

How stunningly simple to leave our corner of the world, how fast, how easy—*poof!* Blink and you miss it. I demand more time, complications, pomp and circumstance, demand more pay-dirt.

Walk along the river, drive in a car over the river, see it everyday for x number of years, mundane as an insurance office, an ordinary postcard, then one day you fall into the boring postcard and the boring postcard kills you.

Those on the bridge are dry, feet on wood boards. Do they laugh at first? Do they panic, run and yell? Nothing there to toss (I see an image of a lifebuoy tossed, of panties tossed at a bad concert). Running shoes on hollow sounding 2x6 boards.

High school girls weep by the river and walk the bridge, some possessing such tiny shoes, like feet bound by the Chinese, and a schoolgirl eye that shuns you, and tiny hips that don't seem capable of childbirth.

TREV: You were one of a kin a noone could ever replace you I remember all the times we got in shit with the cops. Well i'll always remember you and I hope that I c-ya again everynight I will think about you. until the day that I die I will LOVE you always. (Nathalie)

There is a small heart drawn to the left of Nathalie's name. The French spelling, perhaps Acadian. Nathalie has left the most messages on the bridge. Did Nathalie become a minor celebrity? The bereaved teen widow drawing felt pen hearts. In my mind she has dark eyes, speaks French, dark hair draping shoulders white as a statue.

This river used to be the only highway, wharves from Waterloo to Smythe. Now a boat ploughing the water is a rarity. Harleys with no mufflers roar over the new concrete bridge upstream. I'm told a boat tried to find Trevor, but ran out of gas. The papers do not mention this boat with no gasoline. KC Irving's giant white oil tanks squat on the north shore. Irving owns us.

I am new to this river town haunted by United Empire Loyalists who fled the Thirteen Colonies, fleeing liberty, some tar and feathering, a few shots, a little ethnic cleansing, the right to bear arms, to peruse automatic weapons at the gunshow.

The Old Loyalist Burial Ground: *Across This Flat Lyeth British Soldiers Who Died* (we'll never forget you). The military compound had a high wooden wall around it, not to keep an enemy out, but to keep deserters in.

This land seemed new back then. It's new to me.

The Irvings and several families, a family compact, have their hand in everything now, like a Central American oligarchy, a banana republic inside Canada, a banana republic tucked inside the skin of a banana republic.

The Junior High is beside the Old Loyalist Burial Ground and students smoke coffin nails in among the graves, trying to speed up the process. The rebels buy smokes from a machine, the rebels depend on a corporation. The wigger rebels are fed Hollywood ghetto lines, say, *Whassup guy?* as I pass.

Not much, I reply walking past, and then hear *whap whap whap*, wigger rebel hitting his palm with his fist.

EASTERN HEAT WAVE KILLS 71

And Zionville: Who would pour diesel into Anna Doiron's well? She had to drill a new well. I'm sweating in the humidity. On a country road two eastern lynx stand, necks out to sniff, ears rotating like radar, two lynx looking curious and alive. They're supposed to be extinct.

At the Sally Ann I buy five long-sleeved shirts all the same size and all with the mandarin collars I like and can never find—a dead man's shirts I decide, imagine his widow boxing them up for the thrift store.

Upstairs in The King's Shilling I look at the park where Trev drank. I drink, order a dark beer from Halifax called Black Pearl. The label shows what seems to be weir stakes in a river or ruins of a wharf in golden light, a dark moist pearl in the foreground, bigger than an eyeball, bigger than a clitoris, and under this compelling clitoris the words *Cream Ale*. The bottle sweats moisture.

Down the street stand stone barracks from the 1700s garrison, each stone a different size, high mansard windows, and behind it the sandstone and granite guard house and a row of cells with air vents and the trapdoor to the damp underground hole they threw you down for solitary for weeks and you came out and right to the hospital.

How you doing, I ask the stonecutter's ghost.

Functional, he replies.

The bartender intimates that the Hell's Angels own the massage parlour next door, recently charged by the city with being a common bawdy house. The judge fumes, *Nothing but a whorehouse*. The city trying to cut their power, their phone. Their pink and blue neon sign always says *OPEN* but I never see anyone slip in. Never. Ghosts.

The bartender with the paperback says they do a good business; sometimes they'll come to where you are. I never see anyone go in.

Why didn't someone go in and help the poor kid? asks a woman swimming at the YWCA. Why didn't someone jump in?

Currents too strong, says another woman.

Not that bad, argues the first, maybe ten miles per hour.

I wonder: Would I, would I jump?

Mark says he has jumped off the bridge to meet a motorboat, to swim and climb in, says he's in the river all the time and the current is no problem. Others talk of summers spent jumping from high bridges, or diving cliffs into quarry pools.

Tom sits behind me at the play. At the cast party he says the current is stronger on the south shore because that's the inside of the curve, and it tightens on the inside of the curve, speeds up. The newspaper, however, insists the current is strongest in the middle, right where Trevor fell.

A diver tells me he hates this river—too silty, can't see. Trevor must have had mud in his lungs, like Alden Pyle, the quiet American.

Tom tells me he didn't want to walk on the bridge after Trev drowned, then Tom felt better seeing the messages from the teens. That made him feel better.

I walk the sunny bridge unconsciously humming *Ode to Billy Joe* by Bobbie Gentry, her 1967 hit tune about a guy jumping from the Tallahatchie bridge.

I realize Trev's last name is pronounced the same way as Tallahatchie. T Hachey. That's an odd coincidence, me singing that old pop song, my brain dredging it up, a perverse, personal jukebox.

Families in the area spell their name Hashey or Hachey or Hache, an old Acadian name, Acadian families who shifted down from the north shore bays and woods to work in Boss Gibson's brick cotton mill and eat eels and crow stew, down from the Miramichi to work his Dye House, tannery, kiln, icehouse, grist mill, lath mill, shingle mill, double sawmill and gang saws and Nashwaak scows and booming grounds.

The grist-mill burnt in 1902. The saw-mills burnt in 1920, and the flames went higher, the flames took out houses on River Street.

Bobbie Gentry was a sultry woman clutching an acoustic guitar awkwardly, sexily, her big dark hair puffed up and falling down over her down-home Chickasaw County check shirt tucked into her tight pants, her tight pelvis, knees flexed—I would have been 11 or 12 and how I loved her and her sombre little ditty and her thick auburn hair, how she was packaged for my consumption by the Glen Campbell Show and Capital Records (*jumped off the Tallahatchie bridge*). I fell for her.

Trevor's fall reminds of a British Columbia man who fell off a ferry into Georgia Strait. His windbreaker trapped air, his jacket a lifejacket and he floated in warm water from the Fraser River, a toy bobbing out in the strait all night, gazing at cabin lanterns on the islands, but he can't thrash his way shoreward, the man held fast by the current moving him south to the American islands, floating alone and thinking all night of myriad food-chain creatures searching under his dangling legs.

American fishermen, out early, picked him up where the warmer river water is finally lost in the freezing ocean water, plucked him from the sea just in time.

The silty river water and his jacket full of air saved him. The river saved him. No such luck for Trev, though both are in the water the same amount of time.

Adam, you shouldn't only feel bad about Trev but good because you were the last person to be with him. If you need anything just call Sharon and get my number. I would really like to meet you if possible.

What sneakers did he wear? Did he demand cool-hunter name brands, curse his acne, his parents, and what favourite junk food and what fine music lived in Trevor's head? What music when it's 4:20, sparking up blunts in the railroad lands' ugly trees by James S. Neill & Sons Ltd yellow brick warehouse, the spray-painted warehouses at the wrong rusty end of Church Street and listening to the next shit, ugly urban missives on the headphones, not Bobbie Gentry's po down home girl, but on the bridge Trevor's brand new soundtrack is rudely interrupted, trouble in river city.

I haunt a strange town, move down streets named after dissolute princes and distant daughters and mad kings. Did Trev ever leave this town with its sidewalks shattered like crackers? Did he ever walk a beehive-buzz metropolis or burn out his shoes in foreign countries and flight paths?

A red kite stuck in a tree by the iron bridge, by the war memorial for the bloody salients, for Sanctuary Wood and Desire Trench, hard by the statue of Robbie Burns. A taxi cruises by slowly at night and a passenger yells at me, "Hey Skipper! Come here."

I've never been called Skipper before. I must purchase nautical outfits to match the new nickname.

"What?" I say finally.

"You know any other ma-ssage parlours around town?"

Trev you well always be the man
Love ya cutie
Every night I will think about you

How many girlfriends had he slept with? Everyone assumes teens today have sex early.

I hate to think of him going under in the cold not knowing what it's like to be so warm with a woman who likes you more than she lets on, to move in her (and not move in the river), move languidly, *there will be time*, a soft bed, old-fashioned, queen size, think and don't think, not furtive, not backseat.

Iago's supple beast with two smooth backs, the mystery dance in the city of elms, lost elms, the lost white music of her shoulders and skin planing south down two breasts pushing different ways, no one else home, the slight slight independent sway of each breast suspended in cotton ribbing, suspended in an afternoon above a summer belly that pulls a camera-eye down gold contours between the smooth hipbone's concave shadows, and farther down in silk where the silk road narrows to a fine line, a wispy line the width of a drowned teen's tiniest finger.

Lightest finger on that fine line, brushing just the surface of the closed garden, she pulls you, a home, none I think do there, current tighter, a warm world, she pulls you down and you pull her down.

She wants to push aside the silk, just the tip, but the river water pulls you down away from the bridge and none I think do there embrace, not fine and private, figures watching, they run, dial a number, watchers on the bridge, watches glowing, heads on the rail, dumb witnesses, running shoes to the shore, the riverbank, but no one saves you, and the black water is freezing, the shroud, sheets, and a silver van waits for you on the shore.

And then in daylight friends and strangers trek back with black magic markers, their *never forget you*.

And I'll go see if the hard October rains take the messages away, freezing rain into the river where the Star Line steamboats slid against the slip, paddle-wheelers *Antelope* (burnt for its iron fittings), *Aberdeen*, *Forest Queen* with a walking beam engine, *Reindeer* rocking at the Regent Street wharf 100 years ago, 200 years ago, and the rain brings up the bridge's creosote smell, the hewn railroad ties of last century's cedar and hemlock, sleepers a foot square hidden from us where we walk.

We *will* forget, is what they actually imply with the magic marker messages, what they struggle with, what they deny. In twenty years half of them will forget. What was that guy's name? You know. That guy.

Why do I insist they realize this, why do I want to rub their young faces in it? To me, high school is nothing, steam, a blip unrelated to what I now do, live, feel. I was that person, but not that person, cut off like the north side from the south side, a bridge attempting to join cleaved halves, weld old and young, iron and creosote.

Man you were so cool.

Remember me, asks the dead king from the clay world, the prisoner in the hole under the jail. The divers remember.

They find Trevor with his mouth open in four metres of water; they find the skateboarder resting with his head on the bottom, his parents standing only thirty metres away, all night his fingers drawing circles in cold mud, his brain gone still as wine in an old Dutch shipwreck.

TREV 4 LIFE
TREV KING OF KINGS

I see a negative: black lighthouse lifting from last century. The bridge's empty white girders up into empty blue sky. I wonder if the divers stepped on him in the silt, if that's how they find you.

There are dams upriver, the Saint John is not a free-flowing river anymore.

No cotton ribbing over a breast's slight sway and no underworld of underwear, no farmgirl leads me into the blueberry bogs or potato barn, and no Pollyanna pulls up in a 1940 Hudson that used to be the Marysville taxi, and no mermaids singing each to each. Is it purely egotistical to desire hands on you most minutes of the week? Yes, but there it is.

Trev 4 Ever
RIP Trev Ski it up bud

I fought with Trev's skateboarder friends down by Picaroon's doomed brewpub. His panhandling phyletic companions of King and Queen Streets harassing me as I walked past and I turned, swearing and shoving one in the chest, pushing him off his board, and I left in a rage (*dissed me*), weeks after still wanting to kill the skateboarder (*you the man your the coolest*). I now officially hate youth.

The brewpub closes doors soon after I arrive in town. The bookstore closes. The usual pattern: what I like goes under. The brick bar in the sun is a block from the river, but you don't know the river is there, the brick town turns its back on the river, like a relative you don't talk to. The town constructs windows and doors on the main street but turns blank red walls to the river.

To get to the river I dodge speeding cars, run lanes of traffic to walk the river's quiet banks, zooming cars noisier than the moving water.

These river towns flood every few years and burn down every few years, a river wandering into the church basement like a lost tourist, into the Bishop's mansion, the library, diocese archives lost in water, wharves submerged, the bottom bowl of the valley covered. The big flood of 1853, local roads eaten, and 1854 again, and riverboats lost in the Saxby Gale of 1869, a flood in 1902, and the dam smeared away in 1914, the big freshet of 1923, and 1936 the railroad bridge wrenched apart by ice and logs, and 1940 a farmer's beautiful barn floating whole until smashed to red splinters on a bridge pillar, and the freshet of 1961, and the big flood of 1973 still much discussed by shopkeepers on Queen Street, floodwater pouring into the town from all sides.

At the wharf in 1865 the steamer *Heather Bell* catches fire, burning its heavy hemp ropes until nothing holds it and the fire drifts on the water to shoals on the other side of the river, Trevor's side of town, and *The Royal* burning in her first year, or ships in mid-river and the boiler from Scotland explodes into a full ship, pilots killed, raftsmen killed, women in their long skirts swept away into the rocks and churning rapids.

And wooden towns on fire in 1825, the colony's forests all on fire, no more masts for the King's navy, families fleeing into the river in middle of the night, and fire in 1860, and fire in 1877, wooden shutters burning on their iron pintles, the sash and door factory on fire, the schoolhouse burning in 1895, this river's cool millions of gallons flowing inches from the silhouette of a flaming town's spires and mills.

Our river named for St John the Baptist by the explorer Champlain out of Dieppe. Some Canadians went back to Dieppe's stone beaches centuries later. Did Champlain name our river in 1604? Shakespeare was alive. I forget these dates, though I took it a million times in school, took the fur trade every year in history, social studies—*we'll never forget.*

Trev king of kings, his baptism, and Trevor's parents stand by, their separate lives entwined again in panic, disbelief. Does the father regret the fights now, the slammed doors?

"My kid," she moans by the bridge, and the boat flung back and forth, divers down, boat back and forth in its white wake trailing each time like a bridal gown.

September 1844: *The steamer will leave Indiantown on a pleasure trip to the Celestial City for the special behoof of our sequestered villagers, a rare chance to rub off the rust of our monotonous existance and expatiate ourselves with the aerial splendours of the great metropolis.*

Every lover of fine scenery, fresh air and good fellowship, and concord of sweet sounds should prepare for this excursion. What with the kindness of our friend the favourite Captain Wiley, our own steamer, our own Band, the aquatic amusements to which the dignified Cockneys of Saint John are to pull the lusty oar for our amusement, we are assured the liveliest expectations of pleasure.

Lightning and the river trees. This hot drought summer, he was the coolest. The river cooled Trevor, the river caught him, found him out, drew a crowd (with felt pens, his felt pen teen tragedy die young mythology—*love ya always, never forget*). No one was prepared for the excursion.

His parents waited all night by the river, the river low in summer, the canine unit there searching, his mother wanting to wade into the river, feeling she *must* find him, she's his mother, the policeman leading her back from the water's edge, but maybe they should have let her go in the river.

Trevor's father quiet, the two parents on shore all night wrapped in flannel sheets, *never forget*, bridge an iron giant above them, the dive-boat passing back and forth. *My kid.* Trying to be warmed by sheets and your boy cold in the river somewhere so close.

You were the best cousin to me. Even when you and Dad didn't get along it didn't bring us apart.

They pulled the divers from the river at 10 p.m., too dark, a safety issue.

The south shore: two giant weeping willows over the two parents, and a generous strip of tended grass sloping to a border of rougher scrub along the water's edge.

Dawn, bridge to the east becoming visible, river more visible, empty, can't see their son but he's there, Waterloo Row at dawn empty of people, copper steeples close by, my landlady's Anglican Cathedral where she sings in the angelic choir, sings *The race that pined in darkness,* sings *In the grave they laid him,* sings *Now the green blade rises.*

Divers back in the water at 8:30 a.m., and they find the body at 10:25 a.m. The river bottom, not far from the bridge. I thought a body would drift farther, miles and miles, like a piece of wood floating to the ocean. Trev stayed close to home, close to his parents. The silver van holds his young body. The TV commercials seem so far away. His mother steps to the rear doors of the silver van, the mother and child reunion, for his mother must ID her son's body in the silver van yards from where I will buy a house if I stay in this town. Its windows aimed at the bridge.

In the fall I walk the silver river, a solitary male, become my old uncle taking windy walks in a long coat, watching eastern birds, writing letters to the west. He never had a son. I have temporary work here, I am temporarily depressed here, and trying to decide whether I want to stay and whether anyone wants me to stay. I am skating a rail.

People jog by me on the river path, trying to live longer, eyes trapped in their face, working like a horse, eyes trapped in an old face (*So this is permanence, sings Joy Division*). I am temporary. We're all temporary.

Would my grey eyes stay open after drowning? The terrifying terrified Grand Guignol face someone must find or step on, try to hold an ankle, a forearm, a wet shirt. The search for the body and the body in its search.

In this town I met a blonde woman who searched for bodies at Peggy's Cove, for the tiniest parts of flesh, of someone's child, someone's parent, wondering about each pebble, each piece of glass, each person, what was a person, and I met a woman from Newfoundland who mapped the underwater crash site of Swissair 111, mapped a grid on the blurred stones and sand under the black sea. And the divers remember.

In Halifax a room full of dead passengers' suitcases, jackets, pens, passports, laptops, ballcaps, shoes, jewels, toys, dolls.

Military reservists expected to be tough, to take it, to just pick up the pieces of 229 humans at Peggy's Cove, bags and new Tupperware containers piled on shore, a Tupperware party combing the rocky shoreline, and they did it, walked the walk in their spit-polished boots, but the blonde woman emphatically does not want to talk about that scored shoreline. But they remember their mapped secrets.

He is my life. Asthon.

Asthon's name is encircled in a heart.

Is Asthon a rival to Nathalie? I see her as blonde. Like Veronica and Betty. Once I was Jughead stuffing my face. Now I am Mr. Weatherbee. *He is my life.*

The New England Journal of Medicine argues that roughly 10 percent of drownings have no explanation, that a genetic defect may disrupt the heart's electrical system, triggered by exertion or shock. Long QT syndrome. A daily dose of beta blockers can help prevent potentially fatal rhythm problems.

My mother always believed that when her father drowned in a canal outside Dublin it was because his heart stopped, wants to prevent it in me. In California a honeymoon couple is swept from shore at Lover's Point. The groom watches his bride pummelled by wave after wave. She weakens.

In Bible Hills, Nova Scotia, Nolan Ralph Cady beats his spouse with a stick on the front steps, breaking her ankle and several bones, and in Bible Hills she tries to get away and he attempts to strangle her and their two-year-old son, their bundle of joy. Perhaps a syndrome or such.

A steeple means nothing to some of us at Lover's Point, in Bible Hills, in Zealand, Zionville, in New Zion, a steeple no different than a telephone pole. Once it had such power, stared at you. Where did that power go? Down the well. What kind of stick did he beat her with, I wonder stupidly. Night after night the police climb down into their growling cruisers, prowl up and down King and Queen, and their weak light reflects on our dark river.

Trevor your the man. everyone that knows you will always love and remember you from now until the end. from somebody

The newspaper calls for lifeboats, lifebuoys, lifelines. A phonebooth is installed at the bridge's south end.

Ole Larsen took a beautiful black and white photo of the Edward Sinclair Lumber Company at the North West Bridge on the Miramichi River. Behind the mill you can see the masts of square-rigged sailing ship, and on the saw-mill's roof ridge you can see a line of wooden barrels: barrels of water kept on the roof in case of fire. A large wooden structure. Water held up top, just in case. But can you really hope to keep enough water above you, to take your beta blockers for your heart, that your tank will actually move on the stone beach at Dieppe, that your yacht won't blow up off the coast of Ireland? Can you always be ready?

No lifebuoys on the bridge. The day is gone you can leave a good lifeboat by the water. It'll get stolen or holes kicked in it or burnt. By the same skeletal skateboarders who knew Trev and spraypaint "Smoke Da Weed" and "4:20 All The Way" and burn the green vinyl sofa by the ruined warehouse. How original.

Citizens walk out on the iron bridge to watch the sunset upriver, eyeball the shooting stars, the Leonid storm of freak streaks and dashes, and the valley's stars are vowels you can't use, panels of pink light pinned in your head.

Adam you shouldn't only feel bad, but it's past 4:20 and our summer soundtrack goes on without Trev, the soundtrack goes on without me in a way too in my forties. On the oldies satellite channel *she is moving somewhere far away not slow* and *where have all the good times gone*?

My childhood music speaks in the greasy spoon over my 3 p.m. breakfast and lying on my bed at midnight Stereolab sing "Baudelaire" and I play Godspeed You! Black Emperor, play The Handsome Family (*and jump from the Golden Gate Bridge*), play Joy Division's "Love Will Tear Us Apart," play the fugue song over and over on my pawnshop headphones: the band's bass descends, notes down a ladder, a figure falling in air, and the band's suicide singer windmills his arms on stage, a slow riot for a New France, an Acadian boy falling from a high railroad bridge, weightless again, and a grey shadow in the best part of town, a perfectly engineered shadow, but that train don't stop here anymore.

As it gets colder I buy gloves and a black tuque (*prepare for the excursion*). The bass descends like winter. Signs on hundreds of houses in the Celestial City:

DANGER FALLING ICE.

Some signs show a concerned fellow with a giant icicle sticking out of his skull. With a black felt pen I alter the signs to read: **DANGER FALLING MICE.**

Summer humming when Trevor went underwater, but now this blue river is framed by yellow leaves. Worn hills, small trees travelling to the horizon. Snow soon.

In an autumn lens this pretty valley reminds me of river valleys in northern Montana or southern Alberta, the Elbow River, the Oldman, the Marias, the Missouri, the Milk River.

The mother waits, moans in her sheet like a ghost, chained to a bank like the bear on its post, any mother and son chained to each other, the boy pinned to the bottom (*so cool to hang with*), the long drop from the womb to the cold river.

Water beautiful and startling blue when I stand on a far hill, but up close it's different—green-purple water moving chocolate silt to the sad lowlands, the water impenetrable and my feeble eye can't push an inch into its mysteries.

I always loved his backflips. One of the best times with Trev was at Grand Lake.

Until the RCMP came

A year after he fell the felt pen messages are excised from the bridge rails, words on wood shaved by a city worker with a grinding sander, pressure-treated sawdust trailing lazily to the water where Trev last wandered.

But I still possess them, a stranger, a landlord holding a binder-twine suitcase in case the prodigal tenant returns to the chamber on Church Street.

I loved watching Trev skate,
he always had so much energy when he skateboarded
and lots of air.

DANGLE

The unharming sharks, they glided by as if with padlocks on their mouths

– Herman Melville

HIGH BEAMS, cursing, tailgating; I speed home in the powder-blue ¾ ton that's pretty well paid off and I crave the roughhouse with my kids. The RPM seems precisely right, perhaps a chemical thing. I've had a few and they're excited by my noisy re-entry into their space; they want me, they want airplane rides, they want to dangle over the big stairwell. I made the banister myself.

I dangle my favourite tiny son by his ankles over the stairwell. You let go of the pudgy ankles and clamp on again fast.

My kids all shriek. They love it.

Don't, she always says. She has no choice. Someone else wrote her lines. My mother said the same to my father. *Don't Jack.* The slight Scottish accent. The reaction is part of the ritual.

The kids go to bed; you stay up, an adult. Eventually you catch a few hours, but before you know it you're at work again, rich white dust in your hair, your hands tearing down recalcitrant pipe scaffolding as the blue crane swings tapered buckets of cement through space overhead, and then you're heading back home again, a muscled mystery really, but the kids always hyped to see you.

"Rides Dada," they call. "Rides Dada! Me first," they demand. Called. Demanded. Past Tense.

Past tense because one night I lost my youngest son's fleeced ankles. A mistake. He went straight down, a heavy blond bomb dropped in a blue sleeper. No laws were broken. My youngest son obeyed gravity.

Superman failed to fly under his path. Superman did not save me. You actually hope for something like that. Someone with ease and the power to bail you out. My son hit tiles I personally laid over the cement and his eyes rolled back. He didn't see me anymore. We ran down the corkscrewing stairs, the two of us actually fighting each other to get there first, a competition to show who cared more. Forever I'll run those black stairs. His perfect head and the great shroud of the sea closing over him.

In the Misericordia hospital I was crying, trying to process this shitty information. This never happened when my father dangled us by our ankles. Why did it happen to me?

My parents are deceased so they could not answer my textbook question. My parents' house was cut from blocks of pale stone; mine is made of white tin; take a can opener and you're in like Flynn.

Sorry, I said to her in the hospital, I screwed up, I said to her. I *always* screw up, I blubbered.

I admit I was hoping she'd tell me this was not so.

You wanted this, my wife said calmly.

I did not think that entirely fair. I think I could say I viewed a new side of her.

You don't exist for me, my wife declared. If my baby doesn't come out of this, my wife said, then you don't exist for me.

My blond son hasn't come out of it. He hasn't died, but he hasn't woken up either. My Goldilocks son lives on in limbo, machines telling him state secrets, his blue eyes refusing to aim. The doctors all say he could improve, but I no longer exist for my legal wedded wife. Pound of flesh, eye for an eye.

Look, I say. But she won't look. If his eyes won't look, then her eyes won't look. I willed it into being, she claims. I wanted this. I don't need to go home now. Not even a "Don't go." Not even nothing.

Time is some kind of invisible glue; you are stuck in your time, even after it's no longer there filling an iris. You're still young, but they knock your old school over. You remember her oval face staring out the window or a map with chocolate bars on it, or the smell of a green apple, an old crooked kind no-one grows anymore, or the stuttering janitor selling radishes. Then one day at the job site the new kid snickers at your time-warp fashions. It's a new era. The new kid lives to regret this.

I went to confession at the cathedral; I needed to confess.

As a kid at junior high school I always lied at confession: telling the priest made-up sins rather than telling the real ones.

"I lied twice; I disobeyed my mother." I said this over and over. I think most of us in that class at St. Vincent's did the same thing. What are we going to say? Forgive me for whacking off 800 times since I last spoke to you?

Anyway, I went to confession again and I lied again!

I found I could not force my mouth to say: Hi, I'm a fucking goof and I dropped my darling son on his fucking head. The priest behind the screen called me "son" just like when I was a schoolkid. And he gave me the exact same penance as when I was a kid: five Hail Marys and five Our Fathers. Maybe it was the same old priest.

I hope he knows we have other sins and forgives us for them. He's probably not even listening. He's probably thinking, *Hmm, gotta get the Nova tuned up before winter.* Jesus we must bore them. They must crave REAL sin, just once to hear utter depravity. Those hardcore ones probably never climb into their confessional. I tried to give him my real sin, but I could not. I failed to thrill him. I'm with my baby in limbo.

Since those trying times I've made certain subtle adjustments. That's me you run into at the Bruin Inn north of town or Curly Bob's Supper Club way down by the sweet-grass borderline. I get around now, do what I want now. The tanned blond guy in a sweaty tank top. Fu Manchu and the blue pickup truck with the high beams and much-squandered tread.

Used to be that every Friday after work my tiny blond boys gave me a hand spraying the construction crap out of the truck bed. The noise of the hose-water drumming the metal bed; the fine spray drifting back at us in rainbows; Friday nights I was free!

Now the garden hose hits the truck and I think of my lost boys: a reflex. Now we're in Dispute Mediation. I can smoke those tires at will. I've left a lot of them on our driveway, on my own tar. In reverse. Amazing torque. Makes the hippies across the street jump. I'm aware of my nervous neighbours. I believe there's talk of a court order.

Inside the rayless border bar I'm outside time's glue while Seattle's Blood of the Lamb Band rattles out "Muleskinner Blues" at 800 miles per hour. Almost as fast as my baby dropped, a glum plumbline down the corkscrew stairwell.

The music zines rave on about the new band, insist Sub-Pop's going to sign them to the hip label right soon. But hey. I've seen the hype before. I'm not a betting man. I'm a muscled bricklayer and I want to go, destroyed knuckles or no. It's a test and I'm a collector, taking it out in febrile flesh.

Smash your foreign bottle and let's do it because I adore shard sounds, that music that breaks something green, that melody of things twisting down fast and pyretic. I'm eager and Old Testament and I've got the bends. No feckless jabs or Marquis of Queensberry; just the routine roundhouse, the banal bodyslam, the pristine teeth to the curb.

I seek plain purchase and I win every time, but *that* takes its toll. The rest of my life dedicated precisely to my head and the stairs.

MY WHITE PLANET

Whether one marries or not, one lives to regret it.

– French proverb

HER enclosed boat a tiny orange orb among monstrous green icebergs, and I dream of her coming to me, waves like giant white gnashing horses, a female coming like a coma, a young woman staring at me from wild water spray, sliding in and out of sight, her little boat a dizzy dome with plastic windows, an offshore oil-rig's emergency lifeboat, an orange plastic cask bobbing and rolling at the same time.

I have a final golden vision of her at a microphone, many microphones aimed at her, rented jewels on her sunny neck.

I dream of her and then she is really here, inside a bubble boat, closer and closer to seven of us stumbling on the shingle beach (there used to be more of us, but the bears snatched one and the ice opened and took two), this garden of stone and ice abutting water's wind-wrenched green map, our world a snapping laundry line, her clothes stripped from her and floating in the corner and her marble white body washing and tossing inside an enclosed self-righting lifeboat, arms out, hair askew, awash in icy seawater, an orphan under glass.

Seven of us examine her. Seven men and our Snow White. Her palms turned out, shoulders back, wet dark hair over a freckled white face, and breasts that fit a teacup (we have no teacups here). We touch her neat ribs to hear a heart song, no heat there, navel like a slot for a dime, her thin legs in an elongated V. The first female for a long time, the first not on TV from the south, and so cold, yet clearly alive.

You imagine your hands moving up those ribs, pulled to teacup breasts, warming her, saving her, her dripping skin, our baggy pants, every man up straight as an icicle, not sure of her age, not sure what is allowed here.

We inhabit a line station secretly functioning after the accord, but something went dead after June 11. Our dishes and software seem without flaw, but our screens remain blank, thoughtless. No printouts. No officiant plies us with coded orders or fervent denials or demands our narrow, circumspect data. Is everyone erased in a war or did a budget-conscious computer take us out in a bureaucratic oversight? We are paid puppets, but no one is pulling the strings and no cheque is in the mail.

The freezing girl is alive but unconscious, and our ungenerous God has delivered a delirious female to our ice garden where we look at each other in wonder, wondering about things, about our farmgirl concubine with drained lips, our charcoal-eyed dreamgirl, our homage, our stockpiled ohmage.

Peter the Preacher pulls out his blue-grey Czech pistol, says he'll shoot us or kill her rather than let her be touched, and we know what he means, means our ugly paws on her lily-white flesh other than to save her, resurrect her, and I believe I once dreamed this part too, saw Peter the Preacher's fine skull and fine rhetoric and his fine Czech pistol at our nostril hairs.

Our long lost daughter, we decide, *yes*, our very sad orphan, why, our very own child, we all agree at gunpoint, no monkey business, the Greenland radio-man hard against her belly, me hard against the small of her back, our honeymoon, our blood raised, swollen cocks lifted on each side of her, raising her back to life one degree at a time with just our body heat, one cell at a time, hours at gunpoint, three crushed in one cot, Peter never sleeping, her eyes fluttering, legs relaxed, her hair soaked, mustached men in tears, in blanket memory of past and future sex, life or death, no monkey business, wanting her to live, and wanting to be in her, to slide in and out like a wave, the head so near to her, but instead a Czech pistol, a white towel drying her hair and shoulders and our two ungainly bodies clamped close until her body temperature climbs.

I agree with Peter the Preacher out of selfishness really; I want her for me or for no one, don't want all their chapped hands on her blue route-map of veins and fine skin. I choose no one on her, will take my lottery chances for later. Like our red barrels of fuel. They will run out someday, then we must find an alternative or freeze to death. Doc can calculate exactly how long the barrels will last, how long we will last, but as with long-range winter forecasts, some knowledge we'd rather avoid.

We carried her from the beach to shelter, my hand inside her senseless scentless thigh, happy to carry her; we were serious and happy, her skin ice-water tight, her hip, her perfect white shores, her ears seeming to listen to us grunting. Our duty, the feel of her leg in my hand, her ear by Rasmussen's hip, dead serious, and much later her dark Acadian eyes gleaming into life, taking in our world, two pin-stars of light suddenly alive in each chocolate-brown iris.

Now in the afternoons I read to her, our orphan, from old British picture books and periodicals. She is a blank slate for me to write on, to create.

> *These are farmkids chasing a greased pig.*
> *This is a bi-plane.*
> *This is a black bathing suit, a red guitar.*
> *This diamond ring.*

We used to explore on the yellow Ski-Doo, but a polar bear ate the fake leather seat (and ate Caird), and on the ice we ran out of oil and blew the whining engine. My hands black trying to find the problem, the carb in pieces, my fingers freezing and filthy. White polar bears after us all the time here—you have to keep an eye out or you're a dead man. Like Caird, pieces of him missing and pieces of him still there, life not the sharp apple it was yesterday.

We found a wooden ship on our lost satellite, stuck in ice, perhaps beached deliberately centuries before, lost men, food still on their table. Did the stiff-legged bears pick them off one by one, eating the years? Slopes of scree and ravens spying on us behind their formal wear, their Aztec razor faces.

I walk her to the wooden ship, as if we are courting, to show her the frozen Norwegian rat lying on ballast stones, stones and rats been there so long a time, born in Europe, Eurocentric rats, going nowhere now.

Have you been here almost as long? she wonders.

We keep the girl alive: she has no memory, learns the world from us, learns from me. A polar bear circles our camp, its feet huge and almost square, and I can't get over feeling it's a person in a costume. Two bears stalk us; we're bi-polar.

Preacher shot a bear last year and Gingras died after frying the liver with some wild bulbs. For the bears we have rubber bullets and cayenne and skunk spray and even angel dust. We're an experiment. Gingras taught us to not eat the liver.

Our pool table was shipped in, piece by piece, back when there was budget, someone cutting cheques. The way they carted beautiful mahogany bars and mirrors and billiard tables up the western rivers and over the badlands. Up the stone coast I discovered a U-boat weather signal left here during WWII and still transmitting, but our email is broken down. Your Reich takes a hike, your salad days turn Turk. You get depressed, run out of duct tape.

Nothing over satellite anymore, food stopped in our mouth as the satellite feed stopped: no death star, no blues channel, no idea what's out there still. May 1st brought brief pictures of Ho Chi Minh, stigmata, a Warhol banana, an AK-47. What is happening out there past the clouds of mosquitoes?

We play cards: Go Fish, War, Auction 45, High Chicago, Low Chicago, 5 card, 7 card. For exercise I jump on the tiny round trampoline. Run outside and the arthritic huskies attack you, though they're fine if you walk. Jog and they think they're supposed to kill you, some old animal instinct they won't let go. Jumping up and down seems good for your cells, plumps them up. You feel better, younger.

An electronic detection system warns us if bears are sneaking close while we're working outside the quonsets with our big hoods up, wind singing loud as jets.

We hear a real airplane—a beautiful engine's martial music with dynamic bass boost, silver fuselage, and no insignia, no pilot for all we know, or the pilot dead. A long jet stream heading to the north pole. The captain runs the rocky guano beach as if he can lasso that damn plane, catch its amplified buzz.

We keep shooting pool, running the table, though I play slop—just hit the balls and see what happens. The captain runs alone, comes back in with cold air hanging in his shirt. We give each other bad haircuts in our hours of darkness. On our beach we hold clear panes of ice overhead and smash them to the ground like breaking glass.

I read to her.

These are prickly hair curlers.
These are pink pedal pushers.
That's green grass.
That's the way a rich woman sits in an Adirondack chair.

Our VCR shows the old football and hockey games over and over, and we bet on them even though we've seen them a million times.

GO! GO! GO!
Blitz! Dog it up the middle.
Eat that blocker. Run!
Get rid of it! Shoot it!
Come to Daddy!
Top shelf!
Through the uprights.
Yes. No!

Or a history channel special on Dien Bien Phu, the bearded foreign legions, firebases named after a French officer's mistresses (Eliane, Beatrice, Isabelle, Claudine, Gabrielle . . .). How lucky the man was, until he shot himself in the bunker in Indochina.

Another dead pilot soars over us, their air gone, precision machine on auto, fly on until the fuel drains, flying on fumes, vapours wavering like ghosts inside steel rivets. And finally down, where no one witnesses, eight miles high and then that metal skin ripping down to the ice.

Some men in the group have each other; we don't discuss their arrangements, the *niceties*. You dream of rivers, riding elephants.

I remember childhood fields clad in yellow grain, and now they seem surreal. Did I really live there? Was the farm *real*? Such livid yellow blue red green and that Hutterite vibe. This ice the only real world, an afterlife, on ice, but the only world that counts.

In our afterlife she tries to sweep the rug wearing my white shirt, my shirt you can see through and her blue pedal pushers made of my cut-off long johns, shrunken from being washed, holding tighter and tighter, and she's bending at the gentle broom and I can't help but look on the cant and lexicon of her lovely lines and want to be all things to all people.

I am given to bad dreams, am the bearer of bad news, prophet of grim gesture.

I begin carving Rasmussen a Celtic Cross, his gravestone, his dark green-eyed soapstone rood.

> *These are bottles of stout.*
> *These are shopping malls.*
> *These are car dealers.*
> *Freeways and doom palms.*

Gambling is the only way we make our randomly picked taped football and hockey games more interesting, but then one fine Sunday our VCR breaks, movies flipping, eating game tapes.

Try tracking!

I tried it goddamit! You try fuckin tracking!

We clean the dirty VCR with virginal movies we never watch: Ma & Pa Kettle, Disney's *Snow White*, training films.

Our cranky VCR works for a while, we're happy again, then *nothing* again. Snow so industrious on the screen.

We look at each other, lost, no words, byzantine in ardour, drooping with anger. Time does not equal money.

Rasmussen's idea. The VCR dead. Everyone could have equal chits, Rassy says, have turns with her. And you can gamble your turn to be with her, lose or win, move a finger slowly, summon honey from her, and she can be Eve, create a new race.

Our faces change. I knew this was coming.

What's wrong with that? he protests. The old rules don't apply here. What if everyone is gone? You know, out there. Maybe she'll like it. You'd like it. You think anyone would do what we've done so far? We've been good. We've been stupid. Why can't we just do what we want?

We have all thought about trying it. I remember lying beside her at gunpoint to bring her to life, our orphan, our animal heat on both sides of her, my cock up against her white marble hip, its head also marble, a taut gleaming bulb, seeking my orphan, remembering her form, knowing her without knowing her. What I would pay to put it in, but we did not. Our daughter, our sister, the only woman we know. Who would be first? Who would explain? Me?

We were happier before Rasmussen brought this up again. We thought it had been decided that she didn't really exist. Instantly her hips and breasts suggest their shape to us through Gore-Tex or wool or cotton (*cotton kills*), suggest intriguing possibilities.

She brings us tea in the same battered tin pot but it is different now. We are secret czars of romance, closet Rasputins, long johns too small on her hips, clinging in pleasant lines that draw your eye down and in, show exact aspects of her female anatomy. Not every woman does that; she has that special look, that power. Sometimes she kisses us, sometimes she studies the seven of us, one after the other. What does she think?

Our radar spinning madly, the dish silent. We all know he's right. We are so alive. Fuck I hate Rassy.

Wear these snow pants, I say to her.
    They smell like diesel, she says.
    Wear them, I say.
    What's wrong with these? she asks.
    Wear these over them.

We shun Rasmussen for seven weeks; he slips and gets a concussion and can't get around, but still we won't speak to him.
    You know I'm only saying what you all thought.

    I think of her on her stomach, sunlight in her room, a liaison as if in a city, my fingers moving slowly up her legs, sunlight in her room, moving all around her middle, but waiting, moving up around her ribcage while cupping her in front, my dreamgirl waiting for me, open and smooth. I can't get her out of my head. We shun him.

We play music from the University of the Air tapes, the history of rock and roll, scribble extensive notes on Johnny Horton's blue period, Otis Blackwell doing "Pictures of Matchstick Men," Calexico's Spanish horn, Ray Price's crazy arms that long to hold somebody new, Jack Nitzsche's "The Lonely Surfer." Only I remember Jack's pistol pushing into the movie star, Jack's work with Neil Young, "Whiskey Boot Hill," and Graham Parker's best LP, *Squeezing Out Sparks*. Whatever happened to lucky Lene Lovitch? Our irritation.
    "Do you have to breathe so loudly?!"
    "Are we out of salt?!"
    No new music here, no murky swamp rock, no psychobilly, though a rich fantasy life. Where her legs meet, hidden

under the long johns. We are swathed always in layers, you get used to layers, masks for outside when it's bad, never completely warm.

Rasmussen says, *I may be gone some time*, edges out into the blizzard with his flowering concussion.

Our talks continue. She sits by me, her body so warm.

> *These are lawyers.*
> *These are debutantes.*
> *These are power lines.*
> *This is a sizzling steak.*

I find his frozen body, arm up with no glove.

We make brief contact with a woman in the Outback. She pedals a bike to power an old ham radio. She is never cold there, a woman's skin painted with sweat all day. We are connected, then lose her, but now we know the world is still out there.

Our two bears off somewhere hunting for tasty seals in slob ice and slush. We stand around the solar collector, drop our pants and show white asses, reflecting extra light into the panel. This display of white skin seems to make all the difference for our patched-up equipment.

First a video channel, then a shopping channel. Ads for heroic pickup trucks bashing and splashing through rivers, the mad colours of a lost world. When did I last drive anything with wheels and a heater? Did the world go away or did we? Its whisper-quiet ride, its no-money-down o.a.c.

The world seems ridiculous to me, but she watches the miraculous screen, fascinated. My old tracksuits seem to have surfaced on a movie set in Glasgow. She watches videos with tall models and turquoise swimming pools; she learns songs, takes on new moves, mannerisms, dances in her socks (my socks!). She is in love. After a while she doesn't really want to read books with me, *sorry*, doesn't really want to walk to our wooden ship, doesn't find our dead rat all that romantic.

A big boat with a stripe the red of lipstick used to call once a year. A mistake to mention it. A risk if the weather turns at all bad, in fact a dangerous journey even when conditions are perfect, and they have to be perfect, and they're never perfect. She says she's going to leave, go without me. Polar bears are worse than grizzlies, polar bears are meaner, and they like females. Bears like menstrual blood, are attracted, anarchists wanting under the underwear.

Wind up, forecast bad, we sneak away without word one to the others, knowing we might be dooming ourselves like Rassy, but life is losing, life is risk. She wants the world and I want her.

It's uphill and downhill, a plodding broken hike, and unreliable ice in the straits. The two of us follow the old stone cairns, dwarfs in the vast landscape, lunar explorers, endless lost horizon and cliffs like calipers, white mountains, wracked spiny shore, wind penetrating like a wish, but the sky clear and no bears taking a lively interest.

Binoculars and I spy nothing. Sit another day as if at a bus stop in the middle of nowhere wishing I had a cigarette, a rare steak sandwich with a martini, some Sernylan tranq in case we need to shoot a bear. Our backpacks as if at a sunny bus stop.

Then she says she sees its smokestack in the bright icebergs. I have my glacier glasses on for the glare. Where? I can't see anything. Are my eyes going? Is she seeing what she wants to see? Is she that lucky?

Bright daytime, but I fire the flare and half a day later the confident hull smashing black and white Dalmatian ice just for her, smokestack's lipstick-red stripe just for her, ice shot through with zigzags, shadow lines, the ice a white kitchen floor suddenly buckling up, a bright breaking world roaring below sous chefs grinning at the ship's rail and white-shag state-rooms where Brooklyn tourists bray *Hope we see a bear!!* Buffets, fresh Italian bread, pepper steak, blueberries, green eyes and the exact shadow of this ship laid on the ice.

Aren't I climbing aboard? she asks me. No.

What's wrong? she asks.

I give her my version of Nixon's Checkers speech; you won't have me to kick around anymore.

I'm mad at how happy she is to leave me in the leads, in the bright shadows of the ship, so white here, can't open both eyes. She tries to give me back my fur hat. No one will ever know me the way she could have—I'm a prince and a janitor both. We killed Rassy because of her.

Keep it, keep the hat.

Once she saw me about to have a shower. I staged it so she could see all of me, her eyes on me better than nothing on me. How strange it is to be alive. The men talk of tracing energy files, of molecular vibrations, molecular mechanics. Laughing, the men talk of the guy back home who could leap from inside one 45 gallon drum into another and do a flip without even a step and jumped right over a stock car to punch the driver, and Navvy was working the rock crusher and dropped a boulder on the roof of the guy's truck and he jumped out and hit Navvy and Navvy didn't know if it was Christmas or New Year, never been hit so hard, but laughing and proud to have been smacked by this backroader now dead of cancer.

On TV we see her on Infotainment Tonight. She is shacked up with one of Jack Nicholson's sons. They walk on the beach and Junior Jack smiles that rakish smile, light at that magic hour the Arriflex cameras love. The cameras love our dream-girl and Junior winks, their teeth white as bears on ice. In her new video she dances with tanned surfers. In late tropical light they all face us, scissor kicks, hair flying, sand flat as a gym floor from water lying over it, the sun going down in her video and she's wearing my white shirt. Water and western sky the colours of deep neon and she's in my shirt.

I remember the naked white body rolling in icy seawater, the window into the self-righting oil rig lifeboat, that window like a TV and we stared in like the bears stare in at us. Outside that window it's death. I thought I could teach her.

I feel everything is over now, I feel so ordinary without her. It's like missing yourself and maybe one thing waiting.

Her sodden hair and skin, that naked ass coming up into view like a frozen white planet, my lovely planet, never once touched save to save her, to carry her. Escaped—air we can't breathe. Would it have been so bad to breathe of her? Would the world have ended?

Once I looked at her in her sleep, half out of her army bag, that white hip, and I pulled her underwear down on one side just to see what she looked like. Shaking I was so tense and she was sleeping, dead to the world after walking with me all day. She lives because of us and even though she's gone I own her.

In the cold hangars and quonsets we're down to the last barrels of naphtha, diesel (someone is sniffing it), the last juice crystals while on the cruise ship they eat strawberries from Mexico. I could always fry up some liver I suppose, end it all with poisonous liver, but I like it here, these contorted icefields have become my vast home. Home is a strange pliable word, the world in a snapping laundry line, your mother a giant in blue sky, Adam and Eve now gone from the postwar suburb. Exactly how little you need—I'm still waiting to find that out.

After she gets out some of the others won't wait anymore. We argue about it. They're mad I left. They're even madder I came back. The Greenland radio-man and Doc the chess master-machinist decide on overland. Sayonara, adieu to you and you.

They're gone. They haven't made it, haven't made it on TV. Bad sign.

At the Emmys she gives us a message. Big hi to the seven dwarves if they're watching; they'll know who they are. A little laugh, her tiny dress taped to her skin to keep it on while we wear more layers to stretch the fuel. On screen she has so much presence, light, heat. She seemed smaller walking in this endless landscape. Her newest boyfriend wears my fur hat. It's trendy. People on the screen seem happy, coloured cars everywhere. What would I do in that world? Miss this one?

I jump on my tiny trampoline, do pushups, fat boiling on burners, eating shorebirds when I can catch them. We are alone up here, we're watching out for those two polar bears. They want us, they love us so much, and they do anything they want.

We make noise at the front door and the two bears run happily to catch us in their embrace and then one of us scoots out the back door to the next building. If they ever figure out the two doors we're dead. We have skunk spray, slink around, not sure how well it works.

I am proud of our frozen girl, in a way glad our starlet hasn't told, hasn't sent anyone to find our listening post where we don't listen.

The bears, when they stand erect, are tall enough to peer in any of our windows. White mountains far away, and dark lines of whalebone scrimshaw. Where are my hallucinatory fields of yellow and purple?

Sharpening a hacksaw in a vise grip, I look up and see the bear staring in at me, its long neck extended earnestly, black paw pads, black nose, squinty black eyes hiding in that expanse of white rug (*and I think of her naked on a fireside rug, bearskin, jealous of Malibu, the old highway*). A window ten feet off the ground and I am on display like a lobster in a restaurant.

The bear looks goofy standing up, a carnival act, arms out, a myopic giant trying to balance on two legs with this doofus expression: *Hey Ma, look at me!*

They know us, big carnal carnivores peeking in at our parts. It's love. They spy us in the window and are nostalgic for the happy future when they will have us in their arms.

KNIFE PARTY

CLOUDS pile high over the Vatican like horses biting each other, clouds rising over Rome's glowing peach walls and tiles and television antennae. One white gorgeous mushroom cumulus lifts higher and higher—I love looking at it, staring into the ruins of this God-like face.

The blue Italian night turns darker and darker and a stranger's ebony piano plays near my flowered terrace. Rome or Naples or Pompeii: a piano trills or a dog barks somewhere near me, perhaps the apartment across the way. A sense opens inside my brain or ear and needs to know where the sound is formed, to know more of this mysterious envoy from another home.

At home in Canada our household is divided, literally and figuratively.

Turns out I don't have room for the oak bookcases, my wife says on the phone, but I'd like to keep the big quilt.

Okay, I agree.

And the car.

Okay.

You can have the roll-top desk.

Okay.

I, the bad husband, find myself agreeing to anything. In Rome that divided home seems so far away.

South of Napoli our train speeds into the side of an Italian mountain and we have no eyesight, we knife noisily into black tunnels and then shoot out again, our new eyes viewing the patient volcano and ancient sea.

Our noisy engine halts its iron wheels at seaside towns where families alight with beach towels and fashionable sunglasses and sunburns that still have hours to flare into ripeness.

The train's exit doors have small windows, but they do not open and the cars are furnace-hot. Tough kids from the illegal burbs built on the slopes of the volcano stand in an alcove beside exit doors, where there are no seats.

Into light and out. In the confines of a dark tunnel something incredibly fractious and noisy grinds against our train and the tunnel walls that hug us. The windows are open to roaring air, open to relieve the incredible heat, and this new clamour makes all the passengers flinch and panic, metal debris bouncing and crashing and wrenching our heat-stroke dreams. What the hell is hitting the curved shell of our train?

In the alcove the sketchy teenagers are moving shadows and I make out one lithe shadow leap mightily to kick out a window in the train's exit door. The teens attack the door's sealed window when the train is in a tunnel; they think no one sees them in the blackness.

One kid swings nimbly on a high chrome bar, a true acrobat who, with both feet, hits the window hard, a human battering ram, and more fragments of glass and metal frame break away in the dark to clatter and bounce along the shell of the rocketing train.

Our train bursts out of the tunnel and they stop smashing the window and pose casually in mad light. In the next tunnel the kicking starts again.

Wives look to their husbands: Will you do something? Each husband shrugs. Polizia ride many trains, but not today. Where is the stoic conductor?

The Italian teens try to look cool in huge mirrored aviator shades, but their faces are so thin and the aviator glasses so large—the effect is of Clownish Child rather than Top Gun or Corrupt Saigon Major. I react primitively at times like this; I know they carry knives, but I'd like to trash *them* the way they trash their own train, our train, see how they like it. But I know we'll all be elsewhere soon if we just wait and do nothing.

I should just sit, but I walk to the alcove and stand beside the cretins so they will stop destroying the door. My move was not well thought out. There are more of them in the hormonal antechamber than I realized and sullen girls lean in the mix. I wish I was a more confident vigilante man with amazing eye-hand coordination and hidden weapons. They look to each other for guidance in child-thug matters. No one steps forward to test my skill set, my tennis elbow. Uncertain moments hang, served to us like writs.

The gang clambers off at the next stop, pushing and shoving each other out the doors with high spirits. *Ah youth; how I hate them.* The damaged doors open for the rabble, but then the doors won't close. Now the arthritic train can't move. The stoic conductor examines the doors, tries to heal them in the heat. He wears a dark blue uniform, but seems unaffected by the climate, while sweat falls from my sleeves. The conductor and another Italian man work to coax the doors to close.

On the station platform I see my cousin Eve and Tamika with the gang that smashed the doors. Why get off the train here? For pancakes and syrup? This is not our stop. I leap from the carriage just as the afflicted doors finally close and the train and conductor shunt away without me. The station sign and walls are covered with day-glo graffiti imitating American-style tags; a new empire paints over an old empire.

"Hey!" calls my cousin Eve. "I met these Italian guys at the beach. This is Giorgio and Peppino and Santino. They invited me to a party. For real. Want to come with?"

Tamika says, "Not me, I'm going back to the hotel." Tamika is shy and she is smart.

"Hey, you come with me." My cousin Eve takes my arm. "Please!"

I have a bad feeling; I don't want to go to this party, but I don't want Eve to go alone.

My cousin says, "We can buy cold beer here at the station."

"You will come?" says Santino from the beach. "It's a very nice apartment, a very nice freaking party. Yes, you may enjoy it."

In a line we pass the military base and pass rows of monochrome flats, pedestrians in a drab hidden Italy, party to an Italy that has little to do with tourist brochures and silk suits and genius marble. We walk inland away from the sea, around a hill and past a canal and cluster of Chinese factories and a military base with dark green tanks, World War Two vintage tanks hunched like guardians either side of the gate. A fat bee accompanies us for a few moments.

We hear the party before finding stairs like a ladder up into a crowd spilling into a dim hall and filling a living room and kitchen. In the living room leans a pole lamp with a blue light bulb, so we all look reasonably unhealthy, and every surface crammed with glasses, ashtrays, vats of red wine, cloudy Ouzo, grappa, tins of German lager, and green bottles of Italian beer.

Past the pink sofa hides an invisible but loud stereo: Jesus and Mary Chain ply distorted fuzz-box ditties. Are Jesus and Mary Chain still churning out discs? I liked them when I was younger; funny to hear them in this other world. A circle is smoking dope and a young woman is coughing up a lung. The fuming joint finds its way to us. I feel nothing at first.

A man flashes a glassine envelope of coke to the young woman. A neighbor, we are told, he lives across the hall, a party crasher attracted by the crowd, the women. The neighbour is not invited, he is not welcome, he does not carry himself well.

"Come stai?"

"You are from America?"

"I'm not from America."

"Yes, you are."

"No, Canada."

"That's much better culture."

"Bene."

"So, Mister Canada, do you like Napoli?"

"Si, Mister Italy, certo, very much, molto simpatico, it's amazing."

"Mister Canada calls me Mister Italy. Ha ha ha."

The unwelcome neighbour offers coke on his wrist to the younger woman, he says, "My coke is very fine. Just think, all the way from Equador to Napoli and to your pretty nose. Think of that. I bring it here in crates of bananas."

"Don't listen to his big talk," says Mister Italy. "He doesn't bring it."

"You should watch your fat mouth."

"Bananas!" says my cousin. "Bananas have big hairy spiders! I hate spiders!"

I know Eve's phobia, my cousin is very serious about this fear, as if spiders are hiding now in the small amount of coke. I wonder if I could get some of that product. I drink cold beer I bought at the train station. The party crasher neighbor with the coke is after the women. Like me.

Mister Italy tells him to leave. Mister Italy turns away, the neighbour sucker punches Mister Italy, and the young man drops, holding his face.

"Get out!" shout Santino and the others. They insult the neighbour, slap him, push him out the door to go back to his apartment. He crosses the narrow hall; all the doors are wide open.

My cousin looks at the table as if there might be spiders there.

"That cake," she asks me. "Is that icing or mold? It looks like mold."

"I'm going with icing," I say and take some.

"Eew, I can't believe you ate that."

"I'm starving."

A young man in a fetal position rocks in the corner, arms hugging his knees. Three women look bored. They are all younger than me, the new norm; now I am always the oldest person present as music plays loudly and the wild ones turn this way and that, shouting into songs and bright conversations.

One stoned woman walks past with a half-open blouse, breast curves greatly revealed. Rare once to see a lady's bare ankle. Blouses open wide and life goes on. A startling bright blue vein runs down one breast to disappear into her blouse. Bright as a streak of blue paint or a cobalt serpent and she is so happy to make public the blood pulsing in her vein.

My high school girlfriend worried about veins on her high school breasts. Your breasts are beautiful, I tried to reassure her, but she worried about a vein. And this Italian girl so happy to show off the bright vein on her breast, blood moving inside her breast. Blood is red as wine so why is a vein blue? Why am I blue? I wish to be captivating: is that too much to ask?

The neighbour motors back from his apartment carrying a staple gun, crosses the hall, crosses the room, and puts the staple gun to Mister Italy's thigh, driving in a heavy duty staple. Mister Italy leaps, tears springing out of his eyes, Mister Italy flees the room yelling and cursing.

"I'm worried about him."

"Is he all right?"

"Does he even know his way?"

"To what?"

The stoned woman disappears down the hall of muffled echoes. Later she comes back to the sofa and says to my cousin, "Don't worry."

I try to not study her sea-blue vein, though I find it fascinating and would pay money to look carefully and touch it, but I do not believe she would be interested in such an examination.

The neighbour wanders into the kitchen, still wielding the staple gun. Everyone in the kitchen is shouting normally. I stand up. The party in the living room rages on around me, roller coaster voices, the droning fuzz-tone of Jesus and Mary Chain picking up speed and slowing down. I sit down.

The stoned young woman with the cobalt vein on her breast dances jerkily in the living room, blouse now completely asunder, her skin taking in the air, the last button no longer intimate with eyelet, free. I assume Cobalt Girl is aware of her blouse and breasts out there like vivid menus, though who knows. Above her neck hovers her very own brain, choreographing her dance in our music and shouting.

My cousin pins her mouth to my ear. I enjoy her mouth at my ear.

"What?" I whisper into her warm ear.

"Have you noticed?" My cousin directs my gaze with her eyes.

This young woman's brown nipples are extremely thin and long, like tiny twigs, where a bird might perch. Now, would milk squirt a greater distance farther from such narrow nipples? A question of physics, pressure. And my cousin's nipples so tiny and pale pink glimpsed once in a hotel room, in repressed memory. Forget that image.

Cobalt Girl dances with Santino, dances with elbows close to her waist, hands and wrists outward as she shimmies, almost The Twist. I would like to start a new dance craze. Do the Mashed Potato. Do the Staple Gun, do The Lazy Lawyer, do the Dee-vor-cee dividing his assets.

Santino grins at me, Santino whispers in her ear and they dance some more and then they stop.

"You must watch, my new friends," says Santino. "In an American movie we saw a dancer do this."

The other, is his name Pepini? Penino? My brain is not to be relied on. Where is my drink.

Santino takes one paper match and splits the middle of the match so that there is an opening. Cobalt Girl takes the match from Santino and carefully places the opening of the one match to her breast so that the match grips her long nipple. Santino hands her another such match.

She lights both matches, pointing the head up and away from her skin, then Cobalt Girl dances proudly in front of us, shifting her hips and smiling at her party trick.

She says something in Italian.

"Do you see this in Canada?" Santino translates.

"No."

"No, I thought not. Not in Canada, eh."

Is that an Italian eh or a Canadian eh?

The stoned woman dances and moves her head side to side, she's seen this sultry style of dancing on videos, moves so that her hair swings about like a star on celluloid. I was worried about the small flames hurting the skin of her breasts, but instead the burning matches cause her swinging hair to catch on fire, perhaps a tad too much flammable hairspray or some weird gel.

My cousin Eve says, That isn't good, and she points a finger like a gun.

Santino looks from us to Cobalt Girl, stops grinning and calmly throws his drink on her, so I pour the remainder of my beer over her burning hair and others add their drinks. It is as if we are allowed to urinate on her. Cobalt Girl is crying, tears and drinks tracking down over her breasts and snuffed black matches, Cobalt Girl runs to the bathroom, hair smoking like a volcano. It's kind of sexy. Where is the volcano, I mean the washroom? Where am I?

Sometimes when traveling I must look about and remind myself where I am, what country I gaze at. I like that feeling of being momentarily lost, of a brief gap, of having different eyes, new eyes upon old trees and the brightest scooter. I am near Napoli on a scratchy pink couch and I am opening a beer that is now warm. Sometimes I feel like that dead Roman rat I saw beneath the trees. Sometimes I feel like a chocolate bar with too many bite marks. Sometimes I feel the world is a very beautiful white t-shirt.

Another giant joint makes the rounds, strong and harsh behind my teeth. I feel instantly stoned or re-stoned, I'm not sure, not used to this quality. Eve says that Mister Italy is back. By the door a teenager from the train is showing Santino and Mister Italy a knife with a beautiful handle the shade of dark honey, as if an ancient insect might be trapped there in amber. They admire the knife.

The woman with hair once on fire is laughing, though her hair looks frizzily fucked up: she moves room to room laughing, smoking up from a tiny bag of weed.

She says to me in Italian, "After that ordeal I am thirsty, tell me, do you have birra?"

"Si. Yes. I'm happy to share."

"That's good you are happy with me." Cobalt Girl smiles, puts on a porkpie hat, just a girl who likes the traditional drugs. It may be the fine dope, but her laughing makes me laugh.

I'm not happy, but I know I can be happy again. I know it is there, but what port of call, what passport, what bright map on my wall, what coast and sea? I know a port exists, know it is close. When I find it I will write a book called Duct Tape for the Soul and it will sell millions.

"Thank you for the birra."

"Prego. De nada." Or is that Spanish? I get them mixed up, think I'm back in Spain. I wonder if Cobalt Girl was with the group kicking out the train window. She mimes tossing beer on her hair. Si. She mimes a moonwalk. Michael Jackson! Yes! I get it now. His hair burnt too!

The kitchen group fights as if one pulsating organism. Perche vendichi su di me l'offesa che ti ha fatto un altro? Why are you taking revenge on me for someone else's offense? It sounds too Sicilian for words. Why are they all so fucking loud?

The white doorway pours noise into the living room; young males run out and males run into the kitchen talking in tongues, raucous Italian voices producing a rapid clatter of words, like a rock beach rolling in brisk surf.

Mamma mia, che rabbia mi fai! How you enrage me!

Mi trattengo dal dire quello che penso solo per buona educazione. I refrain from saying what I think only because of my good upbringing.

Santino has a silver pen, or is it the knife? What is he saying to Mister Italy?

I will kill him. Hands waving. To give a lesson.

In the kitchen dozens are shoving each other, pushing and fighting, two sides, three sides, one room of the party becoming a minor brawl.

A young woman says something and is knocked over and kicked by the older neighbor and she crawls the floor like a shouting crocodile. Maybe this is normal, I can't tell as there is so much noise in Italy, so much life, so many scooter horns beeping threats and throats calling out la dolce vita, vim and vengeance, someone shouting *dare una lezione*, give him a lesson, a leg for a leg.

During the day they shout at me at the grocery, at the cashier, at the café, in the street, from the kitchen; it's almost comic to be shouted at so much. What leg? Mister Italy's leg?

I start to stand up, but the stoned woman laughs and pushes me down into someone's lap. From my odd perspective I have a sideways view of the crowded kitchen.

Santino bends low, his face looking so sleepy, swings his arm low in a resigned arc that ends with a knife driven into the older man's thigh. Blood gushes immediately at the base of the knife, as if Santino struck an oil well and in the room a general hiss of understanding and pity and then more voices, more shouting, more gesturing. His leg, his blood splattered denim, blood falls from him, blood on the floor, smeared on the white fridge.

Santino runs out of the crowd like a hunched assassin. Mister Italy and others follow him out the door in a more assured manner. Staple Gun Guy looks at his liquid leg. The knife is gone from his leg. Who took the knife?

Maybe the assailant thought a jab to the leg was not dangerous, but the blood wells, pours from him, blood born in the kitchen, he can't stop the blood freed from culverts and tunnels. The blood is dark, but glistening at the same time. Blood polka dots around the kitchen, dots the size of coins, red coins painted everywhere so quickly. How can there be so much blood draining from one cut? The eye can't understand the image it seizes (*I smote him thus*).

He stares at his leg, nature staring back at you. The stoned woman holds a tea towel to the gushing leg. "It won't stop!"

The long knife must have met an artery, severed an artery, we meet in a rented room of blood, blood so scarlet on their white floor and dark rug and a trail as he heads to the door, to another country. The neighbour wishes to go home with his staple gun. It's my party and I'll die if I want to.

He passes and my cousin and I stare as if a monster is walking past on a moor (*amore!*). The monster passes the armchair the shape and colour of an ancient tombstone and the coffee table with my bottles and the small baggy of cocaine under the blue light bulb. My cousin says he shouldn't walk if he's bleeding like that.

The neighbour makes it to the door, but in the hall falls like a Doric column. He has bled out. Now the kitchen empties, groups pushing and shoving, not to fight, but to exit. Party-goers nimbly leap his body blocking the doorway and flee like goats down the long hall. An older woman opens her apartment door to peer out at the raucous stampede, the mad stomping hurdle race. Spying blood and a body, the woman dials her small silver phone, whispers, *Madonna save us.*

A few stay in the room; either they didn't do it or they live here; I hadn't thought of someone living here. One well-dressed man stops, calmly checks the body on the carpet.

"E morto!" he states as if saying the weather is fine.

The stoned woman with burnt hair takes the staple gun.

My cousin says, "They called the police. Let's go, okay?"

"What about an ambulance?"

"Someone said polizia. We have to leave."

"My beer."

"Forget your fucking beer!"

I grab the tiny bag of coke and step over the stained carpet and body in the liminal doorway. Why did I ever walk up this narrow hall? Morto, blood flees the body so quickly and all of us drain the rooms so quickly and down the crowded stairs, slim bodies draped in black suits and pants, knees and arms moving jerkily in black crow angles against sharp white stucco, stucco where you cut your elbow if you touch the wall.

On the street we run past the World War Two tanks again, run like pale ghosts past the Chinese factory and canal water and a distant figure throwing something, a tiny splash in the silver canal, perhaps a stolen phone or the knife.

Men in soccer shirts outside a social club watch my cousin and me come up the sidewalk. They can't know anything. We try to stay calm.

"Scusi," says my cousin. "Train? Trena? Stazione?" Her Italian is better than mine.

They point down the boulevard toward the sea. "Giri a sinistra."

"Left," I say. I know that sinister means left. The left hand is unlucky.

"Si. Sinistra. Andate avanti per due minuti."

"Grazie," says my cousin, "grazie."

"First you come drink with us," the man says.

"Sorry, we must go."

"One drink! To life!"

"Numero di telefono?" another asks hopefully.

"No, no," says my pretty cousin, "I have no phone."

"Sieta a piedi?"

"Si, we're walking."

They grab her ass. "If that was my wife ..."

"That's my ass!" I yell. Why did I say that?

"Fuck off," she yells.

"To life!" they yell. I think that's what they yell.

We're walking, now we're running, we run blocks to the train station and I'm gasping; I can ride a bike all day, but I'm not used to running. The station ticket window is empty, no one there, which is fine by me. I've been travelling on an expired pass that also allows one into art galleries and museums around Napoli. I'll pay a fine, I'm just glad to be on board. Now if we will just move. I can't sit. *Move, move.*

I don't care where the train goes, I just don't want to be around if the polizia are looking for witnesses or a scapegoat, don't want to be a person of interest. Our art school is not officially recognized in Italy.

"Are we supposed to carry our passports? Mine's at the hotel."

"Any blood on us?"

"No one knows we were there."

We check our clothes for blood splatters anyway, check the bottom of our shoes. Did I walk through the dead man's blood? And that blood-sodden tea towel.

"Maybe the guy's ok."

"I'd say he was pretty well gone." Gone west. We sit for what seems like humming hours, then our train betrays that buzzy feeling just before movement begins, that pre-coital imminence, and we sail forward in a silent sway of deliverance.

I remember a funeral for a good friend on the west coast, a lively giant of a man, very well liked. I've never heard so many people say, *He was my best friend.* At the open-coffin funeral we sat in solemn pews waiting for the sad service to start, then the Steppenwolf song "Born to be Wild" roared to life, loud as hell.

Everyone in the chapel laughed; he would have liked that; he laughed a lot. But I saw his big face blank in the coffin and thought yes, he is spent, he is dead, missing. Some force that was him is no longer there (Elvis has left the apartment building). Maybe that's why they have open-casket funerals or a wake with the body right in your parlour, so you *know*, really feel the knowledge physically and don't wait for him to show up at your door or expect to see your old friend for a pint in Swan's pub. E morto. You must know.

Our night train will swallow us, will travel all the way to Sorrento. The swallows return. Now, is that Sorrento or Capistrano? A leg with a knife severing a major artery. No more stoned young women for the neighbour with the staple gun. The dead hand, like the men groping women on the subway, *mortua manus.* See the wonders of the ancient world!

"Did you even see who stabbed him?"

"No, no, I just saw legs and a blade swinging." All that blood that should stay inside.

"I just want to be back at the hotel. Be back in Texas."

"We'll be back soon enough."

I show my cousin the stolen baggy.

"You took that from the dead guy? Why?"

"I had some years ago and really liked it, but I could never afford it."

"Fuck, what if we get stopped?"

"I'll get rid of it."

"They'd see you tossing it."

"I don't know. I want to keep it, I want to try some again."

The familiar seats will deliver us back to chapels and chipped frescos and Fabergé eggs and our whining art group. The aged conductor so calm in the heat and sweat of day and the ennui of night. Our conductor possesses natural dignity. He does not bring up the idea of tickets. I am glad he runs the train. His childhood bride waits at home; this I am sure of. She is plumper than when they met at the dance and the world was shot in black and white.

The calm conductor and his bride make me think more about marriage. Marriage is success, marriage is failure, marriage is music, a ride, marriage is a train with windows. Every job is a train with windows, everything in the world is a train with windows.

The question is, Do you kick out the windows or do you sit politely and hope for the uniformed conductor? Does our conductor live with his wife in the city of Naples or out in a suburb under the volcano?

A man on the train answers his phone: "Pronto!?" His voice sounds so hopeful. The dead man went pale as we watched. In the mountain tunnels this time no one kicks out the glass. There is no one Italy, there is a collection of Italys, but this Italy is somber, in black, this Italy is sixteen coaches long, our train moving beside the sea, on top of the sea, dories on painters bobbing between the stars, white moving lights and the words of the sea, the church, City Hall.

Ah, I recognize where we are now. I'm becoming an old hand, an expert.

Prossima fermata, I say very slowly to my cousin, my best singsong Italian accent, drawing out the pleasing words as I try them. "Next stop is ours. How are you doing?"

"Rock and roll," she says weakly.

We stop and start, lean into each other, her head fitting under my jaw. I like my cousin's warm form against me.

Eve lies on my hotel bed stripped down to a t-shirt and small white panties. She says, "You don't need to sleep on the floor because of me. But I'm afraid to go to my room. You still have the dead guy's dope?"

"You don't want that now."

Her clean leg by my eye. She says we can share the bed. The unstabbed skin of my cousin's fine thigh leading my eye up to her hips and her secrets, where I want to touch, the tension vibrating in the air like silver wires, I will explode if I don't touch, but I don't touch her. *Mortua manus*, the dead hand. She is restless, but there is no knife in her leg.

"At the topless beach today I was so happy," Eve whispers as she drops into sleep. "I met those Italian boys. We'll pray for him. In a real church. That one with the amazing Caravaggio. Promise?" She is drifting off in my bed and I stay on the sea-coloured tiles the Croatian woman cleans every morning.

Yes, I promise. In my head for some reason an old Blondie tune, "Fade Away and Radiate"; those NYC junkies, how do they hang on? My cousin's face looked so pale reflected in the train window, inside tunnels, inside a dark mountain as if something pushed into a body.

Later that week I see that my souvenir of Naples is gone, my baggy with the dead guy's cocaine is gone. Maybe Naples is also gone, buried once more by the volcano.

Could my cousin have taken the baggy? Certainly not clean-living Tamika or the conductor who loves his wife. The pretty Croatian woman who cleans my room? Or did I consume all the stolen cocaine during a deranged night and also consume the memory? That has happened before.

Around this same time our aged Director misplaces his fat envelope full of so many Euro notes and now our group is bereft, now we are bankrupt. Is our Dauphin getting dotty or was the cash nicked by the rooftop cat-burglar who plucked an American's Rolex and camera from an open third-floor window? The hand coming in the liminal space.

Our director wears a hound's-tooth jacket draped upon his shoulders like a cape, hoping for that continental La Dolce Vita matador look. How will we survive when he has lost all our money? How to pay for meals, for months at the hotel? How will we get home? Perhaps our future holds a giant dine & dash with luggage. Can we sneak our backpacks past the grumpy French woman who never leaves the front desk?

And what happens after you feel the sly knife penetrate your thigh and you die in a kitchen across the hall from your home? Can you bring a staple gun to heaven? His daughter was there at the party, saw her father die. I don't know how I missed that, but my cousin says it was so. In the hall the weeping daughter held her father in her arms as we left, as he left the country.

The stoned girl with the volcanic hair: I threw my drink on her to help her, I feel we had some link, some strange chemistry. So many things you will never know, so many naked legs you will never touch. But if you do make it to heaven, these matters may seem less important.

Some nights she can't sleep and takes tiny blue pills; my pretty cousin says she remembers the knife, like me she remembers waiting on a train and willing the monster to move. But time passes and we forget. I love time. Time gives me everything, time cracks me up, time kills me.

SONG FROM UNDER THE FLOORBOARDS

GO about 190. I'm down in the pit and you drive over me, wait for me to do it. I'm broadminded, but sometimes my head just hurts and hurts. I hope it's not the years living with hydrocarbons and monoxide.

I hope it's not anything serious (meaning I hope it's *comic?*). In high school I was thirty pounds less but who wasn't? Toting our thirty-pound sack: now that alone should be dandy exercise. Logically, you think, flesh should defeat itself just from lugging it about a decade or two.

There is no convincing logic in my life. In high school I am shy and they decide I am stuck-up. I got in a little trouble, hated the sabre-rattling coaches, though they were just humans trying to get the job done with a herd of hormonal cutups.

As running back or wide-out I couldn't make a first string, but an assistant coach with a cueball head and a Texas-Saskatchewan accent converted me into a deadly defensive back. Found my niche. Big white numbers painted into the grass under our cleats, rows of zeroes and our uniforms glowing like phosphorous, like pillars of salt, and I liked how I looked in shoulder pads at night, my long hair sticking out of the helmet, gold bolts of neon lightning licking our midnight-blue helmets.

How I loved to submarine someone cocky from a rich school in the west end, take out their knees and flip them onto the rock-hard earth behind our purple-brick school, flip them like a burger and make them mortal.

The big lights painful to stare into, the wider black sky and six white suns set on each stanchion, shifting halos and coronas and sunspot flares. So much bleached light pouring down on our playground, our lonely glowing squad.

God I could run and cut like a damned cat and I didn't need to catch a thing: just bat the ball down or torpedo them exactly as the pigskin arrived.

Some voice in my ear like Captain Beefheart singing "Willie the Pimp" and the voice always right.

He's going long, it's obvious.
Buttonhook this time, watch out for the mondo fake.
Fast slant, QB thinks he's Tom Wilkinson, trying to munch
*   us a few yards at a time.*

I was no star and I dated no cheerleaders but I danced backwards with a voice there like a dog at a gramophone, like a microphone screwed in my skull; plant a cleat and change and charge, polished helmet lowered smack into the receiver's floating thighs and he cartwheels, pigskin flying loose into space in slow motion, and now down in a pit I do lube and oil and differential and I slap econo mufflers onto econo cars with a little greasecap on my head like a miniature fez and that speedy special voice gone AWOL, lost in the stars, no more Captain Beefheart voice telling me what to watch for in my econo life, just the sign STOP Please Wait for Attendant and a trouble light hanging.

White smoking klieg lights hung over the high school field; red and green strobes washing the blues band on the high school stage. We smoked up walking to the winter dance, laughing in the snowy laneway, jostling, pay the cover, big Har

Har Har at the milling steamy entrance, but on the gymnasium dancefloor I felt less sure, a child bride of sorts, prepared to dwell in possibilities but suddenly sure that females sensed unknown failings in me. Paula looked so pessimistic and fetching that one winter dance, but I could not put a sentence together.

She was serious, brainy, disapproved of me not being able to put a sentence together. I knew she knew the word hippocampus. On the dancefloor I seized up, stopped dancing completely and she stared at my paralysis, and I fled out the alarmed doors, red bells and hammers smashing, crowd panic, and then the girls definitely sensed some failing in me. My high school years breathed disappointment, fear, white noise. One thing did not lead to another.

Everyman's Tonto or Alice B. Toklas or Angus Park Blues Band grinding it out onstage, distorted psychedelic bands I loved, but the *voice* failed me on the dancefloor, the voice didn't tell me how to move at the stoned Sadie Hawkins dance. I always did the wrong thing, uttered the wrong syllables, and these wrong things blew my chances. Why do very tiny events make me question organized religion or the actual width of a wonky life? Still, I never pulled a trigger. I'm waiting, waiting for the attendant.

I try to be smarter as an older person, try to make up for how stupid I was, try to stay awake after sex, that beautiful performance, to stay awake whispering sweet nothings as a sensitive Redford might in a putrid romance flick, but God or some very convincing authority figure hits a switch that basically says, Slim, your current onboard DNA and sorry salt of the earth brainstem inclinations really lean toward deep primitive sleep now. I do apologize about that.

Hating school I stayed another year just to play ball in that phosphorous uniform the colour of some trendy cocktail. Hated school and stayed extra. I'm a fool for ball though I haven't played now for, oh, several years.

Two friends, guys I liked, killed themselves while attending my purple high school. I was surprised by the suicides, saw no "signs," though it's safe to say I was too wrapped up in my own complaints to be aware of anyone else's obtuse smoke signals. Both friends liked smoking dope. Jack Gaines in my biology class has long hair like me, acne riding his face, and a big calm grin like a wolf, a stoned wolf. Twenty years ago. Does anyone else remember Jack and his wolf grin? I can't remember much else but at least I remember something (I remember that we smoked a lot of dope before I quit because of the paranoia that sent me running from parties).

Jack Gaines and I joked around a lot in Biology 20, gabbing, not really paying attention, though we liked the biology teacher who drove a cool Mercury from a year like 1947 or 1953. I didn't see Jack much outside of that biology class. The teacher we liked was fired. If we thought the teacher was good, then the school board thought he was bad.

Hey I could make a whack of dough just betting against myself.

This McLube must sit on the tiniest piece of real estate downtown, corner of two main drags, world spins by and tiny dust devils in the parking lot, like the dust devils in the old playground, dust devils in the schoolyard. Memories move across your head like headlice did in that childhood classroom (thought Miss Sampson said someone had *headlights*).

Two suicides but I don't remember two funerals. Suicides were hush-hush then. The papers would say, Joe Blow died *suddenly*. I bet they both thought the world would be sorry, the world would miss them now. Does the world miss them? Is the world sorry? Do those naked bald mannequins in the store window sense the streamlined future first? Mannequins already live there with their unblinking marble eyes and lack of high school blemishes, mannequins like suicides, alone in the many blue futures.

Was Jack's acne a factor, a reason to snuff yourself? In high school acne walked over my back and chest, but my acne was secret acne and Jack's acne was public acne, his acne was testifying, out in the open, his red flag. He saw skin doctors, he ruined pores on his face dabbing on too much drugstore alcohol.

Jack Gaines sat in a Pontiac with another guy listening to radio music as the Detroit engine purred in a closed garage, sleepy, you're getting sleepy, carbon monoxide changing their skin to a healthy reddish-pink, tiny new riders kicking into their crowded bloodstream.

Cars pull in over my pit and they shut the motor down, try to spare me from monoxide. I wonder if the car radio played crap or something good like Cream or Tull, some good wah-wah pedals and Leslie speakers. I wondered why Jack was sitting with another guy. Did that mean something, dying with a guy? Not exactly Romeo and Juliet. Maybe it was a stoned error; maybe Jack just turns over the Pontiac's Slant-6 mill so he doesn't wear down his dad's battery, so the 'rents don't yell at him, the parents who will find them, engine warmed up, bodies going cool. Carboxyhemoglobin concentration of 91 percent in blood, the post-mortem pathology report tells the parents.

Down in my pit I open four litres of 10-30 and oil flows like beautiful honey while women drivers linger in cars above me, long legs and my sure hands calling forth slick fluids. My face and fingers so close to their legs, their warm *loins*. They come and go. Women pay. The car shudders like a live animal. A game of inches but they might as well pass miles overhead in a supersonic jet. I'm groundcrew in a high-tech tomb, voice muffled in a muffler shop. They shut off their motor.

I put my head back on my neck and stare straight up through steel floorboards at woman nestled (the cozy nest they carry about themselves) up there breathing on milky coffee and a complimentary copy of the *Globe*.

Women worry about their car. Their white blouses are so clean. My hands are filthy. They're always buying impressive underwear and chairs. They pay. Customers turn into pieces of paper; blow away like a voice. Women wonder if their boyfriends love them, they're sure the Atlas moving men with panther tattoos stole something. I'm deep under their blue Polaroid city, the virtual reality village we stroll through in our head, our hippocampus route map.

I knew a woman who moved to this city from the Badlands and she couldn't believe how white all the men's hands were. She was used to coyotes and miles of fissured land, hands with dark oil and grease ground into lines and under and around the nails, hands working over truck and tractor engines, grime never coming out. At the farm and at the tiny Badlands school house these altered hands moved around her, moved over her clean blouses and impressive underwear like magpie shadows, travelled inside her, altered her.

My hands are a crosshatched mess; I check your transaxle level, your U-joints and PCV, I'm your underground greasemonkey in a boiler suit, your monkey man doing the same task over and over. Crazy crows look identical in every city. I know the smell of new cardboard boxes and rubber mats. When was the last time I saw a bluebird roving a skeleton forest? Let's just say on occasion the bluebird of happiness morphs into a heat-seeking missile and you're trying to stay one step ahead, keep it from zooming up your exhaust pipe.

Gram Vincent, suicide #2 from my class, had wit and charm to spare and black hair in a nice Beach Boy cut; he had a lopsided sarcastic smile and an elegant shotgun in his parents' basement. Why attack the head, attack yourself? His ornate shotgun looked like it might utter witty Ivy League bons mots, but it clawed a section of his head away lickety-split. Gram always seemed to be laughing at some private joke while talking with you about mundane things. Gram and I never talked shotguns. Of course we never talked mufflers or crappy jobs either. What did we talk about?

Gram was an interesting guy but the shell's lead pellets expanded outward in a cone shape and cut that exact shape out of the front of his face, and at that point Gram was no longer an interesting guy. Do you change your mind at the last second, when the lead pellets are already released?

Grim Gram was down in the basement mixing up the medicine: Gram became a song from under the floorboards, a message waiting for his mother trotting down the stairs to find, to see some of his brain stuck on the wood panelling. The gun in your hand rattling like a seedpod and the head with the Beach Boys haircut waiting.

I don't get sentimental about Gram's suicide yet I do about Jack Gaines's. What's the difference? I can't figure it out. Gram's death with a shotgun took more courage. Your trigger finger versus a familiar key turning in the ignition. A car key is easier, more gradual than a shotgun's exact trigger, but that doesn't sway me, doesn't cut the mustard now twenty years later. I think about Jack Gaines in his car.

I stuck around. Hated school but stayed where I was. Now I'm down in the snakepit trying to make sense of things. You drive in over top. I'm the person under you. *Wait for the Attendant*, the sign says.

You're in a hurry, you're on top, you're glad you're not going down in the hole. I remember Jack and Gram in the hall grinning, laughing, joking.

Playing ball I could run, run amok, run smack into any guy in the field, but we guys never asked each other anything that was important. Guys find about two things safe to talk about. No one talks shotgun itch or sincere worries or mystery grievances. Maybe Jack and the mystery guy in the car talked.

The muffler shop radio serves up classic rock: Aerosmith, Petty, the Stones. All *lame*. Why play the Stones and their prepackaged predictable version of sin and death? The second album with "Down Home Girl" and Little Red Rooster," okay; 1965, okay. But now the Stones put their teeth in and flog fake sin like a shoddy wristwatch in a Woolco parking lot and everyone shells out for nosebleed seats in then arena. The haunted Louvin Brothers or any owly 1950's bluegrass band knew more about sin and death.

I didn't go to your school. I went to that school across town with the weird name and purple bricks and new design with no windows. They filled in the yellow swamp, the cattails and hidden birds, the pasture at the edge of town, the horse with cow sense, and the calves with screwworms.

You knew no one from that school, but your coach said, Keep your head up boyos. Your coach said, Watch that sumbitch defensive back with the faggy long hair submarines my best goddam receivers.

In memory Jack Gaines's garage becomes our garage; I see Dad's car purring, our family's wooden toboggan hanging in the rafters; I hear a good car radio playing, notes hanging in the exhaust, radio playing on, but no one listening after a while.

Outside the garage winter stars and northern lights crackle over tapered snowdrifts in the backyard. As kids we blasted through icy crust to crawl inside those soft snowbanks. Our old cat tried to walk across the crust and fell into a different world.

Jar those pretty boys from the other side of town and they think twice before drifting across the middle, before taking flight like an angel in Sport Chek cleats. Horses and calves stood here. Crimson players scramble swiftly off the line, a herd rumbling on hard ground, trying a pick play, but they don't fool me.

Over and over a football leaves the quarterback's hand. Gangly receivers crisscross, look back for a ball. We float in night sky to meet, strangers under stanchions of blinding lights, and I hit like a mock sparrow-hawk, knock them out of *my* sky, down into the pit.

Your coach put a $50 bounty on my head, but that made me play better. He was giving me valuable coupons, put methanol in me, rocket fuel.

1973. I float, a low SAM missile set loose by the Viet Cong, miles to roam and no one can touch me. I'm not even twenty-one. I am what, maybe seventeen, eighteen. . . . For a while I am free, that voice jammed in my head like a high heel on a dancefloor.

FLAT-OUT
EARTH MOVING

Thoughts black, hands apt, drugs fit, and time agreeing;
Confederate season, else no creature seeing.

– Lucianus, nephew to the king

THE STOLEN VAN was home to one thousand donuts, some laced with crimson jelly; some lacking. My sister and I peppered our puzzled metabolisms, worked our jaws scarfing the contents of said donut van, spilt pounds of sugar dust in our laps. Any pilgrim or fellow travellers we gave them some, jetting gifts at any mouths that murmured. We had baking-sugar epiphanies and we employed retro rockets; fly and crash, fly and crash.

A rich person, a smarter person, might decide not to eat an Econoline full of someone else's jelly donuts. Is this solemn choice one part wisdom or two parts repression? As when love, jealousy and hate break themselves over your head: Can you read the true ratio of each? So. Can you cease consuming yourself like a cruller, cease being the less than exemplary creature you are? Whose life is fuller? Whose belly?

Often police are associated with donuts in a comic manner. Not this time. Well, later they were, later the RCMP were involved. But we finished the donuts days before they found the van abandoned in the Okanagan hills where I picked cherries and apricots and peaches so many years ago. The RCMP nailed us, but they got not a single donut.

They did find the $10 receipt from the tollbooth. A tiny white receipt lost on the slushy floor of the abandoned van and THEN they had the papers on us. The Bauhaus tollbooth with its video-cameras killed us. Evidence, dates, video-tape, lenses, Desdemona's handkerchief. My sister borrowed money from the woman at the tollbooth and then later I paid the woman back. Paying the money back was what actually sunk us. My brilliant idea. My brief stab at honesty, trying to be *good* just once. Jails are stuffed full of people who have not thought things through, folks who are not clear on the concept. This is no state secret.

Recounting my tale in Remand I saw others at the long steel table rub chins and say, I believe I have heard of your exploits, how you were caught. These learned fuckwads chuckle into their dun sleeves and I know most of what that chuckle means. They are in the same boat as me, exact same—Remand, Corrections, a bit less a day or the Feds if the judge is pissed off and adds a day or two and then you're working toward Club Fed—but my snickering protégés have a need to feel superior to someone, to an idiotic other. I'm their man, their buffoon. I keep my mouth shut. This much I know.

In the spring before this soap opera unfolded I had a pretty great job running a backhoe, a blade-runner working a sharp point of land, a tiny peninsula jabbing its nose into tricky ocean currents and sparkling riptides and shaking planes of light that moved me to sneezing fits if I did not avert my pale eyes.

The blandest of mornings demanded excellent sunglasses so first chance I steered my trusty prune-coloured Rambler under dusty trees and Tarzan ivy vines to the tiny drugstore to purchase a pair of Ray-Bans and inhalers. Extremely fine real estate. Gaze each way and step into another staggering view: sheets of hazy ocean sailing off toward Seattle that direction and China many leagues that way and six sea lions following each other in a line like precise bulky Rockettes just past my backhoe's knobby back wheels. Your skin warm, eyes pierced.

A cancer doctor I know in Alberta froze his eyeballs climbing mountains: brutish pain for hours when the ice in his eyes melted but he could still see, his eyes still worked.

Twelve killer whales cruised by my backhoe one sleepy afternoon, a pod blowing water like steam trains and rolling their long black fins like nightsticks in the waves, harassed the entire time by whale-watching Zodiacs and sundry small craft and even a red and white floatplane carving circles above us. A dog swam in the cove and I wondered would an Orca swallow a giant poodle.

My backhoe drove sharp shores, shovelled purple and orange boulders while crabshells and bivalves were dropped and broken by gulls and shearwaters for their delight, for their seafood buffet.

Seals eyed me with professional interest and paranoid herons (they flee from me) hiding around corners in orange poppies and east of these wild poppies a snowcone sits on a volcano and to the south-west glaciers spread spectral light on a range of American mountains rising straight out of the water that divides my two countries, snow glowing up there all summer in strange light like goldbeater's skin and ocean all around us in a whispered charm and I worked the haul road listening to FM radio thinking of blue money and raising-Cain taverns in smoky American milltowns huddled under that washed India wall of mountains where the jukebox played Johnny Cash and Merle Haggard singing songs about life in prison.

William Head medium-security prison, where I am incarcerated, looks out on the same view. Club Fed, the taxpayers call it. William Head has a floating pier where we are allowed hooks and glow hoochies to fish for chinook and coho and pinks and sockeye, where the Kokanee Bandit can't find a choice spot to fish and goes nuts, yelling and pushing skinners and rats off their side of the wharf and into the freezing sea. Cobalt seas moving on three sides and turkey vultures hanging overhead waiting for a good draft to help them cross the Strait of Juan de Fuca to another country. He shoves hard at the skinners, nervous guests of the nation yelling and flailing like hopeless Morris dancers, then the Kokanee Bandit plunges in himself, feet-first and sloppy, swimming with a little kid's thrashing stroke far out into Quarantine Cove, into the tugs and log booms and gloomy Indian burial islands and colonial leper colonies and American submarines hiding under the freighters in the strait. Staff gallop excitedly past the Buddhist shrine and the native sweat-lodge and vandalized Wicca altar, confer at the wharf that lifts on wash: now what? This is a new one for most of them. The bullhorn lifted to lips, Excuse me, you'd better hightail it back in here right now!

"Cold day in hell when I come back to that goofjoint," he yells over the water, breathing hard, hanging onto a log as if waiting for a Haida war canoe to zip by like an Uplands bus, spiky islands ranged behind him in an infinite granite archipelago. Swimming is harder than he thought. We laugh, egg him on, but I also wonder what the staff will do

A guard produces a trim little shotgun and jams in two shells. What would that baby bring in a pawnshop, we think collectively, and all of us jump as he fires one loud shot at the Kokanee Bandit. A tuft of wadding flows out from the shotgun as we jump and water flies up beside the Kokanee Bandit. He lets go of the deadhead log to swim like a sullen dog back to shore. Okay people, party's over. How depressing

Our friend has been dubbed the Kokanee Bandit because he lifted a case of Kokanee beer on the way out of the 27 beer and wine stores he robbed. His signature act, his claim to fame. He could do a very convincing Kokanee beer commercial when he leaves prison if they wish to employ him.

You better wake up, he yelled at us on the shoreline, a sodden seedy moralist, and he yelled the same in court. People on this island better wake up! Bunch of pervs here! This is the animal kingdom gone bad. I'll take Kent over all these fucking skinhounds. I'll take maximum security. I like Kent, I love Kent! In Kent I can think straight.

He waded shivering surf, chattering, hardly able to ambulate, yet our sky open and warm, weird birds in it pushing where they wish to push. He's right: there are too many sex offenders here now; it creates some tension.

The William Head prisoners staged a vampire play years back and at night a convict escaped on a coffin, floating rough seas like Ishmael on a stage prop coffin. I don't know if the screws ever found this cowboy. You could be drowning and you're all alone and pulled eight directions in razor-rock channels. Maybe the guy with the coffin got away. Just this month an inmate with one leg tried to swim out through the riptides off the maintenance shop. The amputee was in the fifth year of a fifteen-year bit. Ten more years. He could not wait. He didn't have a coffin to cling to.

Walking along the foggy shore at daylight I thought I saw plastic bags floating toward me, but it was our amputee, something syphoned from him, neck limp, his face down in the misty sea, white hands brushing the rocky shores of our very private peninsula. Peninsulas that taper and distant peninsulas that end in a pencil line and sink under the waves with seabirds squabbling and whistling, grebes with their skinny necks and beady eyes diving under the amputee, and white-noise waves that drive us to this shore, waves in my ears rhythmic and endless—don't hear them after a while. A tug in the distance yanking a barge, seeming to get nowhere. The amputee went away briefly, but he came right back to our bored arms, his brain put on hold (we value your call), no pulse, no red flash. What exactly was inside that head that has left the building? Where did it go? Where did *he* go? Escaped: here but not here. I found what was left to float like a jellyfish, dead man float we used to do at the city pool. The sun feels kind, but freezing seawater seizes your buffed-out muscles. You try to move but your limbs are jelly, torn sails, a jail.

People from the city drive out to the jail to stare at plays we perform; cling to the Kangaroo Road, purchase a ticket at the country store, and an affable prisoner chauffeurs you the last stretch in a green Corrections schoolbus. Past the conjugal trailers, under the towers and videocams. The old driver sells his cedar cigar boxes and native carvings to the visitors. He's become a good carver since he's been inside. Inside we favour Beckett, Sartre, Greek tragedies. Our prison productions are festive and paranoid at the same time.

At William Head we live in housekeeping units with four bedrooms and dishes and chores and forks and steak knives. It's a new approach in Corrections, preparation for life in the world. We have to take turns cooking, though one guy refuses and gets someone else to cook his day, exchanges some favour. Some of these men do not know how to open a can or turn on a vacuum. We are being taught how to turn on a vacuum.

However, two tough older cons in our common-room, fuelled on homebrew, start arguing over which TV channel to watch (I kid you not) and out come the rolling pin and steak knives supplied care of the Feds. First it's the rolling pin to the teeth, and that old guy drops with splintered molars, he's gone, he's history, but then, to my amazement, he springs back up, mad and fast with a flashing steak knife. Now Rolling Pin Guy crashes and hinges down on the new broadloom and Smashed Teeth Guy cuts the writhing man's throat open, slashes this giant new mouth on the front of his gargling neck, then starts slowly sawing Rolling Pin Guy's head off while he's still alive, cutting in a bloody methodical rage through the man's voicebox, cutting and cutting at the knuckled links in the man's spinal column like it's a hard corn cob.

The bloody beheading takes some time, some diligence to draw toward an end for you, sir. Smashed Teeth Guy's applying himself, he's mad, but knows a hawk from a handsaw, knows he's never going free now. Covered in blood, head bowed as if in prayer, fight suddenly gone from him. There goes the new broadloom (Shout it out), there goes the new approach, the Alternative to Violence workshops. Back to the drawing-board, back to maximum security, back to the hold for No Teeth Guy, and no more pastel condo by the ocean. *Location location location!* Just when he was getting healthy, his teeth filled, his shit together. Several of us roomies stare at him in shock, the half-severed head drooling blood at his knees, then we silently slide (wanting to vomit vaporous chunks) over to the next building with the pool table and telephone and mortified red mailbox; pretend we've been hanging there the whole time.

One traumatized roomie immediately transferred out to another prison; he couldn't deal with it. I have had technicolor nightmares about this murder. In one version I'm being beheaded. In the other version I'm doing the beheading. Don't know which I like least.

You know what is a pain about prison? No-one cares about your beef but they all assume you'd love to hear theirs. Everyone beefs all day long: at the meals, at the pool table, watching TV, writing puzzled letters, washing the steak knives, feeding the resident raccoons and cats and deer under the coils of razor wire, bitching about case managers or useless city lawyers or bragging about women (*slept with Tina Turner I did*) or how much smack they've beaten through their bent liver or protesting their innocence (*wasn't me what pushed her off the balcony*). Standing around at lockdown, our brains of pink coral breathing like tongues, you hear the crackling walkie-talkies and older guards' voices calling out in the dusk over the concertina wire and you think of people downtown at Swan's pub lifting a cool pint of Bavarian with art on the walls and women walking between oak tables in light bouncing from the harbour and no jukebox songs about life in prison and on this shore our collection of brains under the rain clouds, the cloud factory behind the American mountains, our addled brains, our puzzled brains: *How'd I end up here?*

Doubtless I will find trouble at the border from now on; men and women in uniform, and me blinking on their baby computers. Our summer camp that never ends.

From the seat of my Case 580 backhoe our city seemed small and harmless in the distance, a puppet city hovering over water with angelic seaplanes riding high past hills, log booms and tugboats, sawdust barges and sailboats pulling splashing dinghies, flat-bottomed Zodiacs zipping fast as coffee through tricky channels, ripping through rocky islands right offshore and me swivelling neatly to and fro in my yellow backhoe.

A million views: one person cannot take them all in. And when his house sits on the earth, one man will own each view I knew. Property—the first hard division of the mantle of earth. Will we be invited, industrious citizens that measured and made the mansion, those that swore and dug and hammered full of grim percussion? Will we be invited back to the house we built? Don't hold your breath. And if it was my house, would I do any different?

One morning on that backhoe job the water was so low—a negative tide—that I walked to an island, scrambled slippery rocks in my city shoes, climbed a cliff and on top of the steep chimneyed island a windy complaining rookery.

This is my island now, I yelled at the wheeling birds. Pay me rent! I'm your new landlord! The warden! I'm your puppet.

I made bird faces and stomped about but was secretly careful not to disturb any nests in the tall yellow grass. For seagulls I was considerate! Is there any shortage of gulls? No. What a fool. This island trek, this parting of the water made me happy.

In this negative tide I saw a sailboat strike an underwater rock with its keel. They swore mightily, late for their regatta and drinks. They couldn't back off and sat to wait grumpily for the tide to lift them, give them freedom. They were not there fifteen years.

On the haul road rock trucks came and rock trucks went, doing rounders, and neighbours in sun hats grumbled and stared, but often I worked by myself. No one on my case. The grader broke down and the clay punched out of the haul road, leaving holes that break your back, drive your spine into your skull, but that was a decent job.

In the rock we drilled holes the width of hot dogs and blasted and split and scratched to find the T-shaped foundation drawn on the blueprints.

An old Newfoundland dog wandered down each morning to stand in deep water, to ease his sore bones amid the sea sorting and cooling its gravel and glass on the sloping beach and trees blossoming like Salish sweaters.

Occasionally the land owner drove out to watch, climbing out of his V-12 Mercedes with a childlike smile, his white Scottish face flushing with pleasure. From the Old French *plaisir: to please.* He waited years to knock down his farmhouse. Now he's a laird lifting up a glass pyramid full of native art and star blankets. A chain crossing the driveway with fluorescent ribbons whipping in the sea breeze. Private Property. He owns private property all over this city, a hotel and pub, a bakery, nightclubs, gentrified apartments. No flies on this silver-haired boy. He has no wife, no family, no tollbooths. He has real estate and dotted lines and silver glasses and serial lawsuits.

My machine touched each of his stones lightly, convincing each block of the glacier's rock where it must now live in the

159

seawall. I was like a mother with a precious infant child. That light a touch.

Children on the beach imitated me, digging with plastic dump-trucks and tin excavators. Three boys studied me, my yellow backhoe, read out CASE 580K from the shovel of my machine. Three children studied me and I studied the rich man, as if he was a blueprint you could read.

When I have monied moments with monied people I study the trim words living in their symmetrical mouths and I try to think as they think, be like they might be, but in the flesh I can't pin down what transpires, what exactly they prove, moment to buzzing moment, to claim and deserve it.

Perhaps this is like trying to watch someone pray.

The guards (*the furniture* we call them) confiscated my cat, trucked it to the SPCA. I trained it to hide under the bed during inspections but someone reported it and they raided. Sometimes the female guards are the hardest cases, which you don't expect. But I have made my peace with lowered expectations. Often I am happy as a clam just to tag along for the ride, a passive passenger, mobile in terms of miles put on, but stretched out lazily in back of a roomy American-made car, say early Paul Butterfield Blues Band on the tape deck, Mike Bloomfield on lead guitar, Butterfield and Bloomfield both on heroin, both dead now from their smack, all of our heads empty of maps, empty of nitpicking neurons or knowledge, head empty of destinations or covered granite islands. I leave that responsibility, THAT, to someone else.

I am a fast form flitting under cool underpasses and gliding finely engineered shoulders and curves, these nearly perfect roads, these garden paths. I am a savage luge rider rocketing through the amazing system but I'm not entirely engaged, not actually plugged in so to speak. What is peripheral is pointed and pleasant.

I am not a wheelman, not a triggerman, just a passenger glancing up past hills of ponderosa pine to appreciate fully, to murmur in a stoned voice, *Cool cloud*. Data and stardust up there in files, possibilities. Sky is the best blue. Is there a better blue?

Not a wheelman, I insisted to the court-appointed lawyer. A *passenger*.

The Crown hoped to prove I was a wheelman in the Penticton and Kelowna robberies where the Chinese kid got shot in the ass or the one where Werner claimed fruit punch in a syringe was AIDS blood.

I thought Werner's prank with the syringe showed imagination. The legal question: Does fruit punch constitute theatre or indictable weaponry? Imagine it's your parents' store and the silver needle with the tiniest eye is aimed at you. The eye never closed and the Crown wants federal time for provincial transgressions.

Sea otters close their eyes clutching onto kelp; they tie themselves to kelp and sleep. I saw several otters while working by the ocean. I thought of them sleeping peacefully in the coast's swaying kelp while we were on edge in the mountain blizzard or knocking over nervous drugstores in the Interior, our heads full of snow, mouths full of powdered donuts. The pharmacies wait for you now, resigned, stoic; you are part of the equation, you are overhead, a business expense they would love to deduct.

My pale sister and her boyfriend Werner boosted a white van full of donuts and the three of us rolled happily toward Hope and the expensive hot springs and the sudden sullen mountains.

My sister didn't know about the tollbooth at the top of the pass. I was not thinking clearly; clearly I was a passenger. I liken myself to Switzerland in the war.

We climbed straight into blizzard echelons in a van from Van with skinny summer tires that made us feel hardly conjoined to the icy hills and climbs and tense tunnels and curves. We were lunar, on some frozen bulbous moon, on a lightbulb.

Cars down the ditches and every car in the ditch looking like it had flown off sideways in a big swath that the snow
and light started filling in immediately, leaving the fine sedan
stranded, a melancholy nervous vista.

My sister failed to read the fine print on the tires before
she boosted the van. You wish the murderous journey had no
corners, you could just go straight with some dignity.

With ice, contact is erased, the contract changed. You're
alone, abandoned, out of real time; it can't help but seem a
warning. Your stomach drops from your abdomen but it's also
fun.

It wasn't snowing in Vancouver; why on earth is it snowing
up here?

The snowy tollbooth looms above us like a bleak wind-
mill, an icy guard tower in dark glass and concrete and coffee
breaks, lemon lights and wheeling whipping gusts testing the
smoked windows.

At William Head the guards hate pulling time in the tower;
the furniture get so bored watching over us pilgrims, watching the mindless waves and the empty parking-lot.

Why is the tollbooth leaning up here in the middle of
nowhere stormy mountains? The government must have its
reasons. Likely this was the first part of the highway com-
pleted before Expo 86. They put the tollbooth here to start
collecting revenue, some dinero. The staff drives hours to get
to work, to stand guard where sharp fir and dark unfocused
mountains dwarf our paltry line of vehicles huddled in snow
and exhaust vapour and tail-lights, cars stopping as if at a
Cold War checkpoint and a camera hanging above, giving us
the lubricated eyeball.

Werner! You have any money for the tollbooth? Nope.

Three losers who can't come up with ten bucks between
us. What are we going to do?

My sister was amazing talking to the woman working the
tollbooth. My sister rolled down her window, drew in breath,

and soon she had ME believing that my mother was dead, that we were speeding to the funeral in Jasper, beside ourselves, no time to think, no time to stop by our bank, stunned by the terrible news, our loss, upset, grieving, moping misty-eyed at the thought of our sad bereavement. Werner's face beside me was both red and white like some European flag.

My sister was unnaturally good. Our loss started to be real, and I began to pine for this imaginary mother whom I imagined resembling an older Betty Crocker.

Hang on Ma! We're coming Ma!

My sister should be in Hollywood, she's wasting her life (unlike the rest of us). Depths and tempting green hallways in her eyes and a golden sensual tongue. Definitely Oscar material. The camera likes her, but it can't catch her.

The woman working the tollbooth listened and considered, a tight mailbox of a mouth, then she paid our $10 toll out of her own pocket. She handed my sister an empty brown envelope. The clerk had written her name and clerk number on the empty envelope.

On the way back drop off this envelope with the $10, okay?

The woman at the tollbooth (You're a lifesaver!) also gave us a tiny receipt which my sister let flutter to the floor of the stolen van where it would be discovered later, after the robberies, by the RCMP who always get their man and where women and minorities are especially encouraged to apply.

In Remand my mind went back to my lazy excavation work, running the backhoe by the ocean with rusty Russian freighters and seals drifting past me. Sailboats with the jib and mainsail down, a little toy engine pushing, tall naked masts moving the way giraffes on television move their long lonely necks, masts moving awkwardly past on slow rhythmic waves, and I'd be hitting a midden pile, crunching into the past, shells and bones and carbon stripes, my bucket grinding into some Songhees tribe with the white sea in their head, the white sea in my head.

My strawboss made it clear: you hit any middens or dead and gone tribes or skulls or bones or graves or native artifacts you keep digging. Don't tell a soul.

I dream of running the backhoe in sunlight off the sea, but I want to make this clear. I don't pity myself now. I pity myself back then, whistling and working happily, not knowing that I was going to jail and fingered for a rat, that I'd come out of court and find a dead rat in a plastic bag on the front seat of my Rambler. I was working on that seawall just as innocent as a baby with building blocks and the fact is no baby knows a thing worth a tinker's damn, that's how I feel right now.

The RCMP find the receipt. They talk to the tollbooth staff. We're all there still on snowy video, every car rolling through like smoke is recorded on video. They watch the clerk hand us a brown envelope, back it up, watch her hand it over again.

Why sure, she remembers, I lent them $10. They gave me donuts for the whole staff. And me trying to slim down. A few days later they came through again going south and dropped off my $10. Paid me back.

They paid you back?! Brought back the $10?! The RCMP are in shock.

The RCMP go back to the video, fast forward to the right day and see the taxi we took from Kamloops en route back to Vancouver, the taxi with the plush purple upholstery and the East Indian driver who leased it. I like cruising in those big V-8 American numbers: *Rollin rollin rollin, keep those dawgies rollin.* On the video they can make out the cab's number and company logo. They call up the driver in Kamloops.

Yes yes, says the driver, yes I remember them: I always insist on cash on the dash, pay up front and they did. Much cash. They were drinking alcohol, they were gunned, they were testing the portal vein.

— Mr. Driver? You having fun?

— Oh yes. I am having fun.

— We're fun people!

— Leave him be.

— I want to talk to our *chauffeur*. I want to make sure everyone's happy.

— Yeah yeah right. Good road. Why is it here?

— It's easier than the Hell's Canyon route.

— And because the suntanned Premier and his suntanned friends bought a bunch of real estate up this way.

Here's the address in Vancouver, the taxi driver tells the police. One guy got out by himself near the Sky Train, but the couple I dropped off at this address.

They gave their own address! Why didn't Werner and my sister get out down the block? Why give your own address? Retards.

Everyone concerned remembers us. They must all be taking those Dale Carnegie lessons.

If I hadn't insisted on stopping to pay back the $10, we would not have been picked up. I thought it would be a classy touch to pay the clerk back. Bonnie and Clyde.

The SWAT crew put on their strangest black and yellow costumes and, hyped for door-wrecking, drove straight to my sister's address in Kitsilano, knew exactly where to find them, so Werner and my sister become convinced I ratted on them, cut a deal with the narc squad. All because we paid the woman in the tollbooth her $10.

The Crown decided I'm the wheelman, and not just a passenger. As they say in the darkest fields of Texas, if you hang long enough you get used to hanging.

Werner tried to explain his idea to me by the orchard the bank had repossessed: A thief steals something it's because he put a value on it, but now a fascist takes something because *you* put a value on it. Of course the net result is the same, he giggles.

Oh, thanks for clearing that up, Weiner.

In the backhoe's worn-out seat, I alone controlled the levers, pushed hydraulics like blood in an artery wall, I had power and vision, my back like teeth on a string. I pretended I was a Pharaoh's architect piecing together a new tomb in the Valley of the Kings. That time on the beach working for a rich man seems like someone else's time now. I was a puppy, a chicken; now I'm a new fish.

Pre-fish. Trying to decide who to rob. You assume the mellow neighbourhood grocery keeps a whack of dough around; they must be flogging hundreds of Lotto tickets when the jackpot climbs up near $17 million. But the whole Chinese family comes running out to defend their stash, lay some chopsocky karate moves on Werner and my stunned sister.

Werner went down like a tree under this crazy family, his finger on the slim silver gun and his gun popped, action, reaction, and there's a stray cap embedded in this teenage kid's skinny ass and he's okay, but mama-san is freaking, ends up down writhing on the floor. She has a bad heart. The store has it on video. Smile. Cameras everywhere now.

Werner and sister exit stage left. Obviously the kid's not totally happy getting shot in the ass but it's nothing serious. The mother, however, decides on a heart attack and in the *voir dire* the lawyers say this doesn't look so good, they're implying her heart attack is our fault, that her heart attack opens yet another can of worms. $650 Werner paid for a clean gun. Weapons charges carry a minimum four-year bit under the new laws.

While they were shooting this skinny kid in his skinny bullet-prone ass I was in the Toyota riceburner waiting, parked by a school (grocery stores always by a school). Toyotas are easy to get into. I guess in Japan they don't steal.

The donut van already history; we ditched it by an orchard near Naramata on that windy road by the repossessed orchard. Werner and my sister thought it wise to change vehicles, take the Toyota, lose the van, get rid of evidence, links. They thought they were using their brain.

When my day in court came I admit I was graceless trash, was less than articulate. The Xerox in pieces on the floor and nowhere lawyers sweating and popping Rolaids by slabs of marble and coffee tasting like a foreign language. Not my world. I am not a rat, I decided looking around the court-house. I decided to say nothing in this world.

Clerk: You have to stand up to be sworn. Please take the Bible in your right hand. Please state your full name for the court.

Me: I'm not testifying.

Judge: I'm sorry, I didn't hear you.

Clerk: Spell your last name.

Me: I'm not testifying.

Clerk: You have to stand up.

Me: Charge me. Whatever you want.

Judge: I find you guilty of contempt in the face of this court.

Me: Up yours.

Judge: I sentence you to a period of incarceration of six months consecutive to any—

Me: Fuck you, you goof.

Judge: —time now being served or assigned.

Me: Goof.

Judge: Get him out of here.

Crown: I think the case has not been advanced by that witness' attendance.

Judge: That would seem to be the case.

Crown: No further evidence to call.

I tried to demonstrate to an invisible audience that I am not a rat, not a performing seal, not a killer whale jumping through a hoop (jumping the waves that drive us to this shore).

The children play with plastic bulldozers and the children's mother finds the dead otter on the beach and throws the otter's limp carcass in the bushes so the kids won't see something like that. Her children play with bulldozers in the sand. Why can't you share? she asks in tense falsetto. Why can't you share? A blond boy hammers together a raft from long driftwood logs, wanting to strike out, *escape*.

Some predator found the otter while it was dreaming tied into the kelp, tied up, while Werner's arm was tied off, while we were driving the donut van in the Interior.

In the Interior we entered towns that consisted of FOR SALE signs where it seemed entire populations were herniated. There were sun-wrinkled dwarves in those orchard towns. Repo men and tow trucks and bailiffs took away their most valued pieces. There were sun-wrinkled dwarves in those orchard towns offered extended warranties, new roofs, earthquake insurance, Lotto tickets. And we were the same, took from them just a little more. How do you like them apples?

I picked apples here in these hot spicy valleys. Plums too. Peaches full of beetles, but beautiful plump cherries, if the rain didn't split them. The Bank of Montreal owned the orchard on the hilly meadows that slanted down to the cliff above the lake.

Alive in aluminum, we shall gather by the trailer park, by the river, or we'll sleep on the grass strip beside the beach until the programmed sprinklers come on in the middle of the night to soak us and keep us moving, keep us away from the beach, keep the tourists from seeing our bent figures dragging sodden U.S. Army sleeping bags.

The man with property wanted a channel carved, wanted real seawater to cut right under his palace of iron girder and glass so his suspect men friends inside the house will be suitably impressed gazing at a piece of ocean brought inside or maybe they'll drop their sore ugly feet in the saltwater and wait for some rough-trade equivalent of Mary Magdalene with her long convenient hair and questionable heritage.

I wondered if this channel idea was legal. The rich man did not hold a gun to my head. The children play, do not want to share. The children's paths are faint in the sawgrass and wildflowers. The man's property is above the high-water mark. Below that is public land. Below that belongs to all of us.

At the tollbooth I tried to do the right thing, pay the $10 back my sister conned, pay back the woman, and that $10 was the only link to us, the only evidence, and it sunk us, sunk me. I did it and someday they'll try to get me, maybe sink a sharpened toothbrush into my kidney. That would be original.

I have my Class 1 with Air, my Dangerous Goods Certificate, my WHMIS card; I've built and destroyed, rattled up and down punched-out haul roads with my sore back like a pinched-nerve concertina, climbed into black halls of mountains and into eye-piercing points of television light. I've been an incoherent passenger lying over the gnashing gears and I've been a wheelman working rented reptile sides of my brain. But I am not a rat. I refuse to sit on the rat side of the pier. I won't fish on that goof-ghetto side of the pier. I don't want to be shoved in freezing Quarantine Cove or feel a sharpened toothbrush ratchet and maneuver between my ribs. But really, who does?

Should I have dug that channel on the shore? I wore cool sunglasses and ingested inhalers, a village idiot bombing my own larder, a shovel with hands crunching madly in middens, a stuttering machine with sugar and sand swimming in the gas tank.

The rich man does not own the shoreline. I own the shore if you want to get technical.

SKIN A FLEA
FOR HIDE
AND TALLOW

I never want to leave this country;
all my relatives are lying here in the ground,
and when I fall to pieces I am going to fall to pieces here.

– Shunkaha Napin (Wolf Necklace)

SCHULTZ and the drunken Orangemen chased me out of Fort Garry with horsewhips and bayonets. I lit out for Pembina and St Joseph, worked as a scarecrow gravedigger down around Fort Snelling and Sacred Heart Settlement.

Dig graves or starve. I could have eaten a folded tarp. I dug dirt for six years and now six seasons later I'm in a blue uniform riding into Montana Territory with that horse's ass Custer and a thousand arrows coming at me. Men I ate pork with last night twitch strangely on the ground and Brûlé children try to kill me in a thicket, laughing at me. More damn graves for someone to dig. Flint arrowheads and cut-tin arrowheads break bones, open in you like a flower. Tin arrowheads are the worst.

After the bitter bad Sioux raids we moved warily on the troubled road between pillars of smoke to bury anyone we stumbled on. Could not tell sometimes if they were white or otherwise, bodies stripped and heads mangled or cut off or eyes scooped out with horn spoons. It takes a long time to bury a dozen or two dozen bodies, to dig holes for whole German or Norwegian families. Their pets or animals we threw into the high grass or into lakes with weights.

None of us on the side of angels. Both sides plunder and rape and both sides kill children (nits make lice). Both sides scalp, especially the escaped convicts and Missouri bushwhackers and veterans of the war between the States; they are tough old dogs with knives hidden and nothing in life spooks them anymore.

The hangman was happy to hang dozens of Indians, charcoal and pigment still smeared on their faces; happy to hang almost anyone since Sioux had recently killed all of his children and his young wife.

I saw the merchant John Bozeman and his freighters and scouts killed by strange roving Blackfeet on his own road to Virginia City, the Powder River trail, the Bozeman trail, John Bozeman killed on the trail named after him, killed by his prosperity and industry in fur and gold. Sioux and Blackfeet didn't want him barging through the choicest parts of their beautiful country. They'd already seen it happen.

I could tell John Bozeman something about that, about losing my country.

The Orangemen with bayonets and horsewhips made me flee Fort Garry up in Canada, made me leave my family behind. The Ontario volunteers and the Schultz faction tried to kill me in the river with rocks. Goulet was murdered, murdered as if we were the intruders.

They chased Fenians and Métis and hillsiders, chased anyone they didn't like the look of. Guilmette was murdered, they shot a priest, bayoneted Nault. They drank the country dry looking for wagon men to stab or shoot or beat or turn in for a reward, bothering poor Louis Riel's mother, turning her little house upside down every few days, in case her son was hiding there in a kitchen drawer.

A man back in Toronto was offering $5,000 for Riel's head in a sack and any number of Christian razors wanted to collect.

I lived in Minnesota for about three years, then drifted west to Nebraska, along the shores of the Platte, and up to Deadwood with a shifty outfit of wolfers and reeking hide and bone men, teamsters and whiskey-traders following more rumours of gold and all of us hungry men, all of us hungry. The government was about to open up the Indian Territory, so let's get there first, right?

In talk by the tents and night firelight it comes out that I am a gravedigger by trade, and then the look in a fire-lit eye changes, every time, as if I am sizing them up for a coffin or a shroud, which I am not.

Now Indians in broken eyeglasses and with buffalo blood streaked on their cheeks are sizing me up, trying to provide me with a military funeral in the valley dust and sage and wild rose and crabapple. Is this my grave? Why then I'll fit ye, they seem to say. All this coming down on my skull because there were no jobs after the Panic of '73. I was skint, clawing wild bulbs and turnips out of the ground, scrounging coal left along the railroad. I was lousy, starving; but to think I asked to do this, to ride with Iron Butt Custer.

My cavalry horse was hungry and half dead when I finally shot the nag so I could burrow behind the hot belly and shoot savage nations and Jackie Lyons beside me doing the same behind his horse.

In the morning we rode down the ridge, down the slanting earth, and dismounted briefly, but Dreamers and dog soldiers roared at us like a threshing machine and we mounted again and climbed back up the ridge in a mad race, there to dismount once more. A cursed place to make a stand, no cover at all. What was Iron Butt thinking? Goes to West Point and all he knows how to do is charge and chase women, white or red. Damn your eyes, I swore, knowing my luck was running muddy, knowing we were bogged to our saddle skirts, Christ to be dead, and to know that, brain before the body.

One young soldier couldn't stop his spooked horse and it took him into the Indians, his horse's head out low and his head leaning back trying to turn the plug. How do you hide from five thousand Indians? Their tiny wild horses snapping like ugly dogs, savages lining up in the dust to get a chance at us, taking turns, more of them than there are fiddlers in hell. You'd need wings to get away.

I joined the U.S. Army with a false name because in 1875 they were taking anyone who could walk and chew gum. They didn't give a hoot. March green recruits around a sunny parade ground for a few days and issue rifles and let us hunt after Lo the Indian. Immigrants with no words of English, and ragtag ne'er do wells like me, seeking an army blanket and maggoty crackers and pocket money, though they never pay us when we're near a town with a bottle of tonsil varnish or a whore to lie with. I know how to ride and shoot from summers hunting bison with Gabriel Dumont, but many recruits do not know a muzzle from a pizzle. I wish Gabriel and some others were riding with me.

Iron Butt Custer is supposed to be a sharpshooter but Bloody Knife joked that he couldn't hit the inside of a tent. I saw Custer shooting chukar in the Black Hills, though, and he looked a good shot. We were not supposed to be in the Black Hills. Looking for gold. This was asking for it. We found human skulls and a Canadian penny and cave drawings of strange animals and ships.

Custer cut off all his long hair for the summer heat and dirt and vermin; Custer took metal horse clippers to his head; maybe Iron Butt cut into his good luck when he cut his hair.

Hurrah, we've got them, the jackass Iron Butt said in the morning when he saw the circles of the huge village through the Austrian field glasses. Painted Nakota, Santee, Cheyenne, Blackfeet, Oglalas, Unkpapas in their peltry lodges, singing like dry axles. Custer scribbles a message and gives it to the Italian, Martini.

Is the man blind or poxy in the head, Jackie Lyons sputters. He'll have us all killed! Does he not see this coming on us and does he not care?

The papists and ex-papists among us crossing themselves, smelling brimstone and buck-horn-handled knives.

Three Crow scouts melted away after they noted the brevet general wanted to attack. No one can call what we did an attack. Rifles jamming from dirty ammunition and arrows rattling down and I am thinking, Blast me, if these savages don't kill the ghostly blond fop I swear I will. Thinks he's so lucky that he can do anything, ride into hell's half acre with a few fop cousins and his pretty gilt hairbrush.

I'll crawl over F Company on my belly with a hatchet and kill Custer if the Indians haven't. Put a window in his skull. That would be a good trick: kill Custer and not be able to tell anyone I was the murderer.

Minutes or hours I have been lying on my stomach with five others in a circle, our heels touching. Marched half of the fecking night for this, no sleep, bloodshot half-blind eyes, grumbling at each other on our dog-tired nags, nags hungry and trying to eat grass right until we shot them behind the soft ear.

Some lost their horses, and I still see the men trying to hold their horses' reins, boots wide, arms out and pulled, twisted, unable to stand and hold their reins in the mayhem.

I wanted to run when my companion Jackie Lyons took an arrow exactly in the spine—it sounded like it hit brick or wood and lodged there as he screamed out, as he reached around and touched the shaft and tried to yank it out of his backbone. Legs dead, face not his face at all, grey as his shirt.

Jackie's screaming does not aid my nerves.

A 16-shot Henry rifle and a Spencer carbine are firing to the north of us and I shoot over my poor skewbald horse until my rifle jams. I hit one savage with a shot right in the mouth and a goodly portion of his lower jaw flies away. He is wearing porcupine quills and a weasel tail. He has smallpox scars. This particular cut-throat does not fall but walks away from me without a chin, walks away as if he just recalled an appointment elsewhere. I don't know if I have killed any of the pirates. We seem to have little effect and they are merry as crickets.

Every few moments I look back at Jackie Lyons but I can't help him now, I have to watch the slope below us.

I tried to pull the arrow's shaft but the tendon tied at the top of the shaft gave way and the arrowhead remained driven into poor Jackie's back in sweat and blood. I get my knife out, not for his back, but to clear my jammed rifle. Something wrong with the ammunition or rifles. Spent shells won't pop out, making it hard to shoot more than once. These cursed Yankee rifles. I want to scream. We had better weapons with Riel in Fort Garry six years ago.

I'm sputtering and crawling around for another rifle when Connell and Howard make some agreement with their eyes, count out loud 1—2—3 (*Why are they counting?*) as I'm crawling past and with Colt pistols shoot each other. God blind me, scares the hell out of me. Two shots and two heads half-destroyed. Couldn't the double-cunted arseholes shoot a few more dog soldiers before leaving the rest of us short of good men?

Arrows fly up in awful flocks. You do not know what arrows are like pulled back by strong men, by devils, and drawn in by us *wasichu*. A good bow can drill an arrow through rock or an army wagon. A storm lifts with its weird whizzing sound and drifts down in our legs and backs, pinning us to yellow prairie, snowflake horses and red speckled horses stepping through slim chokecherry shafts. Hundreds of arrows rattle and hum and I can't even see who is shooting them.

We were touching heels, but finally no one else is left alive but Jackie Lyons and his fecking arrow in his spine and me using someone else's Lancaster rifle behind someone else's horseflesh, in yellow land by a liver chestnut horse that could have been good, silver river looping below like an earring, wrinkled bluffs above my eyes.

We've got them, boys, the blond ass said when first on the high ridge. We came here looking for trouble.

Jackie with his arrowhead is still screaming for Doctor Jesu and I tell him to be of good cheer and then I run away from yellow-eyed Jackie and the other, bolt like a coward from the bleeding bodies of my companions, run low toward a ravine that is already a graveyard for Smith's E Company.

My bootsteps seem so loud, everything noisy and slow, sliding into willow thickets and wild roses. My skin torn, lightning flashing up my elbow where it hits rock. Maybe I can hide in river thickets until dark, find the drunkard Reno's men.

An Indian in a sailor's monkey jacket and a red woollen shirt dances, lifting a long sabre, but it cannot be one of ours; we left our sabres packed in wooden boxes at Powder River. Indians in bear coats wave shiny government axes they were given as gifts at some peace parley. Thoughtful of the politicians to arm both sides in the fracas.

On the slope I see women using axes and knives and stone hammers on our fallen soldiers, see the women pull off the young soldiers' pants and slice at what is between their legs. Some men, pretending to be dead, jump up at that news, at that knife nudging their nethers. Some men jump up and the women and boys fall away from them, terrified of spirits back from the place. Some men jump up, then are hammered back down into the new world, the spirit world. No longer pretending. Shots ring out, hoarse voices call names. *John! John! Oh mother!* We fly and we crawl and we bleed. Horses flattened and gloves and hats and carbines around bloody pale bodies.

It is June, summer in Montana Territory. I don't know how Major Reno is doing, where he is, how many of us are left.

I delve deeper into the draw's modest scrub willow, clamber on hands and knees in the red branches, shifting my hiding spot; young boys fire arrows into my thicket and the young devils laugh when I am hit in the calf and cannot help but yelp. Blood running in my hair and blood dripping from my leg and I am going to be killed by children with shining eyes. They find me amusing. They cannot see me, but I lack dignity, an adult crawling back and forth like a clumsy blue lizard.

Children with smallpox scars laugh at me and try to murder me as boys will with a frog or a snake in a bush, as I used to do with my cousins along the Red River, as the Orangemen did with poor Goulet.

I am panicking as I crawl about on hands and knees like a cur, not staying long in one spot, arrows and rocks crashing knobby branches. They toy with me, their laughter ringing my small refuge, and I am primed to give up hiding and run again when a green recruit from E Company, naked and bleeding from eyes and crotch, staggers past. He escaped the women with stone hammers, but now my young boys chase after him with a whoop and a holler. Dripping with blood he looks so richly white, as if bleached by the diseased laundry girls that follow the 7th. We are rich in princes. A new victim is always more intriguing than the familiar victim. The poor bleeding recruit saves me for a few seconds.

I fall down in a flowered rocky draw, banging both kneepans; crawl right into the rock, into a long crack that might protect me from the flint and gold arrowheads. Pushing willow back, I lie in the crevasse and let the ugly bush bounce back to cover my grave, and I shove flat pieces of sandstone and fistfuls of dust over my feet and legs and chest until only my French nose stands up to betray me. I am dead in the ground.

My knees and elbow and head throb and the whole glinting river valley lit by low billows of dust and smoke. In the sky several suns drift; sundogs swim around them. I knew we should have stayed away from this country.

Riders with bloody masks and wolf voices and stolen blue uniforms sweep one way and others sweep back down until they hit a high riverbank or a coulee or a ridge and turn again, riders perched lightly on their mustangs as if playing on a piano stool. One horse drags the remains of some recruit. See what the ground does to you, the smallest bump or boulder. When that boy of ours falls to pieces the noble savages tie up another boy for their amusement and then that young boy falls to pieces on the bloody end of the hemp while his mother sits talking to a parson in a parlour in Ohio. This I watch from my grave of slatey stone and wildflowers, watch my friends torn apart, seeing too much, an underground man, knee high to a June bug, limp as a neck-wrung rooster.

Horses with red hands and suns painted on their flanks stumble over bodies or shy away with crazy eyes as the 7th Cavalry's paper money blows around, hundreds of bloodied dollars decorating our bone orchard. The Indians like silver, don't know paper money. Christ's foot I am thirsty and would give any amount of that bloody money for a cup of river-water or malt beer or even bluestone gin. We were paid day before the march, paid in the middle of nowhere so we couldn't run off. All this money useless to us here, useless to dead men. If I get out of here I'll hang onto a dollar, I'll squeeze it until that eagle grins. Or I'll spend it fast as I can, go on a jag of ribsteak and blue potatoes and growlers of Leinenkugel's ale every damn day and night till I die of a knife and fork, put down my knife and fork and big clay mug and lie on goosedown. Christ on a crutch I am thirsty. I slip grass and pebbles into my mouth. Thirsty! Past sweat, my throat made of timber. I don't want a knife to my privates. I want a tumble down the sink. Why on earth do people want to cut up other people? I have seen too much of it on both sides. Why do the women like it so? I believe some of these Indian women would skin a flea for hide and tallow.

Our brevet general lived for a long time with a very young Indian woman, was sharing blanket duty with his brother Tom. I don't know if his wife Elizabeth knew; she may have. Lo the Indian, say the popular verses. Many of us, including Iron Butt himself, had to get the mercury treatment for the clap. Calamity Jane followed us wearing lice and the clothes of a man. Our deadbeat outfit was often drunk as lords, drunk as a boiled owl, trading coffin-varnish whiskey to the Sioux for buffalo tongues and onions, or *grosse bosse*, the big hump those animals ferry for us like camels, or tender *dépouilles*, that tasty soft flesh under the ribs.

From inside my grave I watch as men I'd drank pine-top barleycorn with and ate bison tongue with and marched with wearing creased American boots have their private skulls broken into, like a head is a Chinese box, and their tongues and live brains pulled out and set up on rocks in some kind of display. Howdy James, Hello Will. The boys' arms are broken, feet cut right off, teeth chopped out with axes, and eyes turned into tiny tomatoes placed carefully on whited ledges. Our daubed and greased enemies don't want us to see or dance in the afterlife. I see Adam's apples cut from men's throats. They don't want us to have throats in the next world; no more crackers and whiskey, songs and cursing. No Latin prayers or laughing drabble-tail whores. They want us to have nothing there in the afterlife, not a thing, not even a voice singing ballads about Garry Owen or a brain recalling the Panic of '73 that pushed me here in '76.

All those boyos who deserted over the months, got sick of army life and took the Grand Bounce, took French Leave, gone hunting for Montana Territory gold or hiring with the railroad or shooting buffalo for 40¢ a hide, Wellsir now I think them smart for clearing out, avoiding this, although many of those deserters may be long dead in other spectral greedy ambushes, boots yanked off their corpses and cut into pieces for the soft sweaty leather.

I think of my cousins up in Pembina and Batoche and St. Laurent and Duck Lake, running a flat-bottom ferry (*Best Scow on the River* says the poster on a poplar) and hunting and farming strips of land to the mahogany river's edge. A peaceful cabin with a lantern glowing yellow and blue in a parchment window. Batoche is not that far north of where I hide in this ravine. In a week or two I could walk there, call out from the yard. Remember me? The one who left? Show them my wounds.

I wait some time and the warriors seem to shift south to a copse of timber above the river, perhaps pulled to Reno's men or Benteen or to flummox themselves, and when they're gone a bit I rise from my grave and crawl north to where I started, where my dead horse lies, where I lost track of time, of early light and late light.

Jackie Lyons has dozens of arrows in him how. The arrow is gone from the hole in my calf though I don't remember pulling it. The Indians set up Jackie on his hands and knees and then shot arrows at his back end for sport. By running like a coward I missed that.

Pieces of bodies at my feet. Three heads cut off and arranged in a circle, staring sternly past each other, as if just finished arguing. Three heads and I know them. One bearded head used to play hornpipes on a cracked fiddle: Johnny Reb, the ex-Confederate Irish Volunteer, why is your head bleeding red and black pitch on the dusty prairie? Laughing boys come to kill. Can I patch you boyos back together? You salty pilgrims squeezed through so many skirmishes and lung wounds and border wars, then Custer forced us in here. The bugle sounded for a while on this hill and then it stopped.

George Armstrong Custer is wounded, but still alive just north of the three severed heads, Iron Butt Custer with blood coming out of his girlish mouth, Custer still alive with four dead officers sitting in a circle around him as if having China tea, and not with their men, their own companies. Why aren't they with their men? It is a strange scene, swallowtailed silk guidons fallen on the ground, the blond devil alive, and the dead circle of sycophants still trying to listen to him under clouds like ripped stunsails and golden light on the river and treed islands below.

When we first snuck in here I saw an Indian man peacefully washing a horse in the river—that seems so long ago.

Custer is shot in the side, just one wound that I can see. Custer's eyes are intense, one side in shadow, and he seems to be thinking hard, looking around but seeing God knows what. This vain man, famous for a handsome countenance, now looks like he'd been weaned on a pickle.

My skin is darker and coloured with blood and earth, my hair black, and I'm out of uniform, half-naked, a grimy wildman, but Custer calls as if we're old friends, as if we often shared lemonade and ginger-cakes in his tent with the cast-iron stove that was so heavy to haul about.

Trooper, he says to me, waving his pistol. We've driven them off. Custer, at this moment, strikes me as someone who gets out of bed to turn over so his blankets last longer.

Custer cut his hair short before we left Dakota Territory and wrecked our luck, but *his* damn luck has held. He's had yet another horse shot out from underneath him, but he's survived. Bodies bristling with arrows, but not his body. Others have their entrails slip out and their entrails tied up with other men's entrails, but Custer's white skin is almost pristine. Custer's famous luck.

I pick up his hat from the dust and skewed legs of the dead officers. I'm going to keep the brevet general's hat.

Tom, Custer calls. Tom, are you there? Boston? We must get back to Elizabeth. Autie, are you holding on? Where are my greyhounds?

He is alive and mad in all this carnage. George Armstrong Iron Butt Custer looks very old. It's almost supper, I'd guess, and I'm very hungry and my eyes are sore. I need to take care of a small detail. He's still waving his pistol.

I move my hand slowly. With his own pistol and squeezing his own finger on the trigger I shoot George Custer in the temple and George Custer topples against one of the four men lying around him like a crib, smiling as he leaves a world. He looks happier. I expect more gore after what I have seen on this hellish hillside but the tiny hold in his balding blond head hardly shows. I assume there is more of a mess just inside that private place, inside his version of the Chinese box puzzle.

I help George Custer shoot George Custer and begin a long trip with a step, another step, limping north wrapped in lice, wrapped in a dead Indian's twenty-dollar blanket and wearing Custer's floppy hat, my bloody head where his bloody head was.

I dodge down into the next dip after our gory ridge, and what do I spy but a murder of crows and a spooked U.S. 7th mare with the reins dragging and a picket stake bouncing behind on a hemp rope. Close by in the grass is a dead soldier with a hole in his face and his pistol lying by him and crows looking him over. I believe the crazy cuss got free of the aborigines, but shot himself, expecting a wave of them over the smoky ridge, believing himself doomed surely.

I pick up the suicide's pistol, catch his spooked horse, and coax it toward Rupert's Land, toward Canada, coax my wrecked knee-pans, sky going crimson and yellow over the benchlands. I have some hardtack. I lost all my sugar and coffee and bacon back there, my letters and my crackers and molasses. I used to have anything I wanted when I was younger, anything, and it meant nothing at the time.

Nights I hobble the horse, trying to sleep before the hard-mouthed mare gets too far away, riding and walking on my sore legs, my bashed knees, the two of us fording or swimming the Yellowstone and the Redwater and the Missouri and Poplar Creek, drinking from a river and waiting for the next stream or lake to drink, crossing squatting hills of creeping purple lizards and red rattlesnakes and roses and berries that haven't ripened yet, watching redtail hawks and buffalo wolves and the poisoned carcasses, walking the suicide's tired horse toward Montagne de Cyprès and Batoche and peace with my uncle and Dufresne and Father André. Keeping grassfire smoke to the south of me, pushing north, sun burning me badly despite Custer's hat.

Beside a small creek I drink and then attempt sign language with three Indians in the skins of beasts who talk of the crazy whites shooting each other or cowards who threw their weapons away weeping, and I think of my rifle jamming and I want to weep and curse again. They all know within hours what has happened, pluck the news from the air. Their scalp-locks stick up. Like a dream they surprised me at the stream. Are they Crow? Cree? I hope so. The stream likely has no name. The three men examine me and my horse with suspicion, mumble about my suicide's pistol and my knife, an old Arkansas toothpick. My blanket is full of lice. My skin is burnt black, blisters and pustules rising on my nose, my lips swollen. I listen to them and keep my burnt mouth closed.

Sioux did not kill Custer, I want to say. Lakota, no. Cheyenne did not kill Custer. Rain in the Face did not kill Custer. White Bull or Wooden Leg did not kill Custer. Hump did not kill Custer. Crazy Horse or Spotted Eagle did not kill Custer. Tatanka Yatanka and the Dreamers did not kill Custer. I killed Iron Butt. I want to steal it from them, own it like a seized pocket-watch.

I have Irish blood, Scottish blood, Cree blood, and French blood. I wish to keep that mixed blood safe inside me, keep it apart from the dust of this destroyed summer where grasshoppers replace buffalo.

I still have my hands and feet. No one has chopped them off. No one has hammered my teeth out with a rock or set up my brain or eyes on a rock table.

Iskotawapoo, they wonder: fire liquid, blind tiger. No, I insist, No, for these three will kill me if they think I'm a whiskey trader and I'm alone. I could use a drink of blind tiger. I don't want my face to betray that the suicide's pistol has no bullets left. If it enters my mind it may enter their mind.

If I can get back over the border, I'll settle down near Batoche, a gentleman farmer playing a cracked fiddle like Johnny Reb. Wolfskins stretched and lantern glowing yellow and blue in a tiny window and no more stone hammers to the brains, no more Orangeman horsewhips or bayonets at my backside. No more hacking and reeking trouble. I am from north of Assiniboine and I can keep my mouth shut, not like some of these Texans in the 7th.

The lice in my blanket trouble me. I see an anthill. I stir the anthill with a willow branch, churning deep, irritating them, and then I lay my blanket down on the dirt as the three watch my naked back. Frenzied red ants, streaming out to defend their ruined home, pick the lice clean from my borrowed blanket.

They'll leave us be in Batoche. Isidore and Jean and all my uncles and aunts and cousins dancing in my poplar cabin so snug you can't curse the dog without getting fur in your teeth.

Railroads gone broke and ants picking off lice and these three with greased scalp-locks looking at my naked back and wondering whether to kill me or let me cross.

NIGHT MARCH
IN THE TERRITORY

Be good and you will be lonesome.

– Mark Twain

OST-BATTLE MARCH, stormy sky, no light. The weary surgeon pores over our bloody wounds, pours himself another drink. We hear our orders travel down the slope: *Bury the officers, but not the enlisted men.* A blunt message to us peons.

In this Territory there is too much light, then there is absolutely no light. The surgeon hides crates of brandy in his white tent. I would take a drink, some corn. We are bloodied and splayed like egrets on the oatgrass.

Where's old Crabtree? I ask.

Stay here and you're dead.

They shot Crabtree. They shot all of us.

Dead?

No answer from the yarb-doctor.

We're moving out right away. Stay here and you're dead.

You have to carry Crabtree.

Crabtree's still alive, says Navvy.

I can't carry anyone. Where's James the Lion, where's Pinky? Dead?

In a better place, Navvy says. Navigator is a cream-face loon.

No, I say, just dead.

I just know you have to carry Crabtree, he says.

How to carry the men? We possess no stretchers, didn't plan on getting killed. Somehow we must carry the mammering wounded men to the honey-coloured river where the hissing boat awaits us, awaits our bad news.

With bayonets we scissor strips of skin from the ribs of our dead horses (*that sound!*), flensing their pale liquid flesh, and for poles we tear what we can from the hostiles' lodges and we also chop green cottonwood trees. Hides cut open and guts wandering out and flies on us immediately—how do the flies *know* so quickly?

With such improvised litters we lug the wounded through a wash and climb a bit, but we all have to stop, we have to rest after about thirty steps.

We're getting nowhere, says Navvy.

We walk and stop, walk and stop, our wounded men screaming like fishwives each time we let their bloody stretchers hit the ground.

This is fucked. Call that clay-brained horse-faced lieutenant.

The pale officer assigns more men to each litter, but still we keep tripping and dropping the litters and the men keep screaming.

Can't leave them here.

Well what the fuck we going to do then.

We'll try the pack mules, cut new litters to fit the mules.

They hang stretchers between two mules, the front mule led by a trooper or a teamster. Now some of us are free to take turns lugging the last few stretchers the mules don't haul. It's better. The sky blackens, lower and lower, pressing down and I still have Crabtree on my aching shoulder, but the mules work far better than we did (I hate mules), the wounded are more comfortable, and this is something good to hold to.

Prickly pear in the dark, though, is hellish to march through, spikes catching our skin and why is there goddam prickly pear this far north?

They're gonna kill us.

Shut up.

No path for our way, our way is dark, stumble into cactus in the dark, drop our wounded.

What is that? Jesus, there. What's that fucking light?

Words move down: scouts ahead are lighting our route, fires winking under black clouds, flashes of silver ice in the low clouds, some eerie animal sound raised to our left.

What's that noise?

We are convinced these demons can hide anywhere, in the ground even, bury and rise up, attack us again, the skill bringing a brisk kind of terror in the brain and nerves. You can't help some admiration with the hatred, but I don't want to live through this, last this long, and then be one of those with a blade to my parts or hair sawn from my skull or decapitated head rolling downhill. We've all seen it now; it's exactly what we're running from.

That's coyotes or wolves.

No, that's them. Their signals. Wolves'd be back with the bodies, back there.

None of us liked to think on it, wolves at them. Friends with no intestines, no ears, snouts into their organs.

Think so? I said to Navvy.

At the bodies? They'll be there.

We pinned canvas and rocks over some of the fellows' bodies.

What the hell's that going to do? says Navvy. He is mad.

We had to do something, but he's right. Animals are going to scatter our friends' bones all over hell. Savages will dig them up too, tear them up for fun, they're worse than the packs of wolves. Our lost bones and marrow, our dead feeding unknown graves. They can't defend themselves, I can't help them. No feeling that death is natural, inevitable. Can't happen to me, I think, though I know it can and may any second. The earth can't take us all in.

Earlier this summer I dug a hole and buried four of our soldiers in the one opening and that night I picketed our horses over top, their hooves moving all night on the yellow dirt disguising the recent burial so no savages would discover the grave and have their way with our poor fellows. My dusty boots the same yellow colour as the four men's grave. I will raise them. I put them in the hole and I will lift them up. I'll go back.

I want to leave, but can't desert now, a wee bit too dangerous out here. I remember the man drowning beside me in the river up north in Assiniboia over the line. Orangemen chased the two of us into the water with rocks. Only one got out. Here swimming in cactus I think of that river in the earth. That water. My wife loves to swim.

The size of those fucking wolves, says Crabtree. I guess he's awake. Big as tigers. Those brutes feed up on buffalo meat. It is terrifying when night falls.

They'll be at 'em.

Bury only the officers, they said.

Our wounded yell; their slow dive into laudanum and later their driving return to us as the metal kicks in again and their tongues start up, and Crabtree says to me, Need a swallop of brandy to wash that laudanum down and keep it in my guts. We move, gradual as gangrene in a leg.

A line of fires in the distance guides us to the steamer, push on soldier, push on dead man, watch for spikes, watch where your boots go, our legs cut and bleeding, and bull bats, their little squished faces bouncing off our greasy faces, my spine wrecked from riding with Iron Butt and always the weight of litters on our aching shoulder and neck.

At each fire our column travels out of the dark, we trade blackness for flames and light, flames rising on our faces, our dead dirty faces pushed forward, a brief gleam of skin and eyes and buttons and badges and weapons and then we disappear back into darkness, night-blind after the firelight. I roll up an extra shirt as a cushion on my shoulder, our blouses shoddy, made by some crooked contractor in Philadelphia.

Who lit them?

The captain's boys. Came off the boat.

Mighty white of them.

March and march, again and again we see ourselves coming into light, flames on our faces and then firelight on our backs, trick knees and cracked watch-faces, what a heteroclite spectacle, all this racket, our failed circus troupe cursing like drunks, a perverse chivaree bouncing through cactus and hoodoos, married to each other, our bonds, our matrimony, sign on the line, our line of fires delivering us to the line of the river.

Thousands of invisible savages trot nearby, happy to kill us; we feel surrounded, unsure of what's there. How did this mess start? How did we end up in the unmapped Territory? A motive somewhere, but I can't really recall.

Think the devils can't see these fires?

Maybe they went north yesterday, get away.

All this noise, they're gonna kill us sure as well as the others.

Shut up both of you.

I don't want to get killed out here.

You prefer being murdered somewhere nicer?

Shut your fucking face. Navvy argues with Crabtree while I remember the man's body on the hill with grass in his mouth.

Eat grass, Krisak said to them when they were hungry and begging and they remembered him, now they're saying it, grass in his mouth, getting him back for his insult. I still see the other body, Manning, with his cock and balls stuffed in mouth, no loving up anyone in the next world. No more riding. Manning is cut off. Man, men, our myriad gifts, our qualities, but still the stamp of our animal heart, our flawed causes.

God knows everything, Navvy says, that happens to us in the world.

So what the feck was on his mind this time?

I potted a few, but my rifle kept jamming.

Your shells are dirty. You got to keep your shells clean.

I potted a few of them anyway.

Can't keep anything clean out here. Their rifles are newer than ours. Those pelican politicians, hope they're happy.

They were using goddam Henry repeaters on us.

Next they'll have cannons.

Repeaters. They'll give the damn devils artillery next at some government pow wow. Wish those Indian lovers back east were riding with us now.

We have been carrying heavy litters since well after supper, stopping and starting, someone else's blood running and then caking on our shoulders. Eight of us take turns, stumble, wamble, trip over feet, over damn prickly pear, can't see a thing.

Remember when that cannon ploughed into us by mistake?

Crabtree's belt buckle driven into a tree, but he survived. A woman in a long skirt brought us donuts at the fort one Christmas. When was that? I stagger and dream of that woman's fried Christmas donuts.

The plateau we have to cross is high, the night settled far under us in broad alluvial valleys. These skins holding the wounded were live flesh-and-blood horses today. Horses ran or stopped to eat—then they had no skin. Now they're razored in strips and Crabtree bleeds on their hide, leg touched by fracture, Crabtree and a bloody horse-skin on a litter rubbing my sore shoulder and dreaming of fried donuts.

I try to get up again. Get up, says Navvy. Can't. Get up, says Crabtree. It's dark. The idea of someone fishing in a sunny river seems very funny to me. We take turns, we walk—walk and we live—simple. *Get up.* My campaign hat is wrecked, doesn't even look like a hat. I can't walk. I push on, I hum when I'm nervous, songs laying in wait in my head, horses in my head: *all our fine horses frying in the sun, how we gonna get any riding done.* Wrecked my back riding those skinned horses left curled like commas on bloody grass, that bulk of their meat, all the pale naked bodies on a slope, all the kids killed. My humming drove my wife batty. We cake-walk; somehow we are still in our smooth bodies for a while, glad it's not us dead, not yet anyway, if we can follow the light, arrive at the river, guilty to be glad, but glad enough anyway, alive a few more moments.

Navvy humming: *Were you there when they crucified my lord.*

No, sorry, I wasn't there, I missed that.

We're dead.

Do you worry over your soul? I ask this of Navvy and Crabtree both. The things you've done, the stains?

Do you mean am I afraid to die? I think we'll get out of this, if I keep my skin in one piece my soul'll be all right. Who lives forever?

Just yesterday Crabtree said this to me: "My horse is yawning. Horse yawning means it'll rain soon," he said to me.

Now his yawning horse is white naked wolf-bait and Crabtree is all fecked up and being carried by me and the others with their turns. It is stormy tonight—his stupid yawning horse may have been right about the weather. My feet sore, my back bad, my head sore, my nose a broken pot full of clotted blood. Thank God for the pack mules and the bloody horse-skin.

Spent, can't spit if I want to. None of us stop to piss or wander off to shit, no need, nothing left inside us now. An act of sex seems like another planet, to love her up, to be clean, tender, sane. Never happen. I remember a Minnesota woman where the devils took turns with her. We found her on the road by the lake. But I can't see her face.

Stumble along, her face on the ground, no, recall that stunning woman at a costume dance, an officer's wife, blooming, lit with her own glow.

Why does a body seem to lift, to rise above us all, above an event, a masque's music, talk and small lamps lit by blood-red wallpaper, and long bloodless gowns and white cuffs and clean faces with no stains or grime or punctured organs, no Henry repeaters or metal arrowheads or clubs made from rocks in the riverbed. Which is the world? Can't be both. She was glowing above us.

That dance lit in my head seems unreal. Not so this chaparro plateau, this nightmare music from mules and wounded, this fracture and fracas, this morbid chatter of broken skulls and skeletons we abandoned, the dance we left, our comforting wet stench of raw horse-skins and fear, mules marching into spines and darkness, craving the water's eaten bank, the bubbling edge.

We're still alive, night's murderous miracles, but so tired, tired. My thirst. If Crabtree dies will I still have to hold him? What is sleep like? Maybe we're all dead. This place is unnamed and unmapped to us, though Herendeen knows the country, Crows know it, this blank place, this blank face. Nothing grows here, we fight shadows, fight over a half acre—for what I can't recall. They want us to milk pigeons. I just want milk, to sleep, will never sleep again. As they tell you, one's thoughts, one's desires become wonderfully clarified in such straits, in another country.

I sleep, but jerk awake over and over, expecting the rock hammer to my head, the wooden handle tethered to hold the big round rock like a cobblestone pulled from our river. A war-club on the ground with flesh on it: someone's brains. I have seen the crushed heads and brains, the hags running through us with knives and hammers. The officer with a pair of red sideburns and they plucked just one, scalped one side of his face. Went back later and his arms black. No one will want this country the dead fight over.

The next day we wake to view the peaceful river in sun, silver light flashing like fish-scales on a vibrating surface. My eye perceives a triangle of light, a trick of perspective. The narrow arrow of the triangle is closest to me, flashes of light scattered on the near side of the river. But at the far side the light is wide and solid, at the far bank a shimmering band of silver, the wide end of a triangle that my eye interprets. Just sun on a river, no triangle really if you move your eye a different way, a different angle or perspective, and when the sun rises higher the triangle is gone. What you see may not exist, but it's there anyway for a while. The eye processes the day, illusions enter your head, but you can't explain them to the others.

Some of our men in the company are altered now.

"Unfit for field service," says the old surgeon. The men are declared insane after our very brief campaign against hostiles.

They are to be returned home by steamer to their families in the rooms, in the soot-dark east. Who knows what awaits these newly created people. What a mad thing a mind is, a humming miracle, a thin baked cracker that can snap, a horse still standing with seven wounds.

On deck I lay cushions of grass for the badly wounded. A huge horse steps on a sleeping man's skull, his brain pushed, moves, alters shape, and he's jerking like he's trying to kick in a new door.

The whistle blows at first light and the steamer swings away from shore, the steamer turns and drifts sideways like a leaf, a life. We tried to wave goodbye to a few of them, but who saw. I'll never see them again, they disappear into the reaches, their journey, they go back, the other side of big rivers, back to correct flatlands, their quieted world where there are fields fallen to plows, elms in planted rows along brick banks and twin parlours and twirling parasols.

Replacements arrive, green and worried, new recruits walk west to replace the new versions of people we're shipping east, our product, our traffic in souls, the soldiers made insane, the asylum's new recruits. Tit for tat. They stare at us like we're carnival geeks and we laugh at them, spook them a little.

Out here in the Territory there is nothing and everything, what you see is what is here, and what you can't see. But no fields, no parasols, no mercantile banks.

Scouts drink stone wine at Fort Supply, the scouts good and corned, Custer feeding meat to his posse of dogs. *Aren't you a good boyo, yes you're a good boyo.* Dogs grinning. His staghounds eat better than us.

Give us a gun, a scout says, joking of eating dog instead of hardtack. I patch my pants with pieces of a grain bag. No blacking left on my boots.

Can you scale heaven? *You. Climb,* an officer says to me, walk over there and climb, see if any hostiles can be spied from above. A small gold telescope, the tiniest eye. The heavens are entered, mountains transformed. No hostiles nearby, but views revealed from these heights stun me: snowy mountains mass to the west, big ranges where rivers and light plunge through western walls and tiny mountain goats under clouds like bright wooden blinds. I am of the heights. I have to trek sometime to those snowy mountains west of our riverbank camp, I must desert sometime soon.

One summer day she went away. Who aims at me? Who adores me now? No one and no one. I have become an attic with no light. Your second morning in the new world, too many years in the new world. I can't forget her on me, on my legs like a tourniquet, hand at my backside, a radiant life, her mouth down on me like a butterfly lighting. Her head in light. Now I am an attic lit by shadows and cracks in the beams, now she's gone and I don't worry.

Our second morning waking at the river. Sunrise: green and blue water perfectly still, but tiny wisps of mists run sideways across the glass surface, as if hurrying, a journey in glassy sunlight. We look at the river as if we've never seen one before. We've never seen sunrise on water, an invention, a new world, an invasion of pure light.

Always these invasions. Both in battle and in courting, court and spark, a body's endocrine secrets revealed, your body opened like a tin, revealed, laid bare like a country, country breasts the bright colour of milk, the tiniest pink nipples, skin and blood bare under the nervous birds of God.

What an eiderdown tells you, or ammunition crates broken open in the weeds, heads open in the grass. I can read the trail of spent shells up the grassy rise, like crumbs left in the forest. Try to hold the heights, try to stay alive. Where are our bearded fathers? Were they alive a thousand years ago? Did they toil and die or laugh, build wooden boats without nails or screws, till the loam, strip the trees, the oaks tipped in sunlight's red henna, fight and fornicate, climb each height to see the next ripe valley? I believe I am the same basic collection of mix-and-match cells. And now to this decline, now to be stopped, now to die on a slope.

That night we marched in the dark and waited for dawn, for heaven's hour, blood on my shoulder, heaven's golden shoulder finally appearing, our world come back, my throat so dry marching, no milk pails and how I miss it. The beautiful words unsaid, the flowers unsent. March in the dark and crave white milk. Why didn't I appreciate it before? My guts cry cupboard, how I want milk frothing in my mouth.

One foot forward, the next foot, night follows the day, day follows the night, and then we are in a town of crooked brick and wood, too much food in our throats and corn whiskey and porter and the good wine-room girls in the private boxes and old Crabtree alive and singing and his crutches tapping planks in the skinny saloon of the Palace Hotel, and we walk and we pay money and I see women in long skirts, people walking pleasant river paths, *strolling* for God's sake, no one ordering them to march and no assassins and in that city I can't exactly sleep.

I carried him on me and now Crabtree and I talk and we walk hilly streets, round boulders for cobbles, we walk past iron gazebos and wooden bandstands where formal little boys and girls waltz clumsily, arms about each other while a young boy saws a fiddle for them.

Crabtree says, You know they came back and they dug them four poor fellows up and cut them to bits.

And grey horses pulling black Concord coaches up the hills (*our poor flensed horses—their skin stolen from them, I still hear that sound*).

I always imagined travelling back to the prickly-pear haunt and my thirst. I locked those four men in the ground and I'd dig them up. Dusty, they'd rise grinning, whacking soil off their clothes, all a joke. I put them in there and I will raise them up. But the others got them, desecrated them just to taunt us, to bother my years of sleep. That I understand, we do the same to them all the time, cut up their women and display the trophies on our saddle horns. But this is what drives me crazy: how did they know where I had hidden my friends?

They just know, says Crabtree.

I thought I tricked them, but they drew out my friends and ripped them up with war-clubs and singing knives. I feel like I was the one buried and dug up, that it's *my* maimed rites, not theirs. Fuck them all. They can't forgive us coming in and we can't forgive them for being there.

Wagons float past the town's busy shops with heaped oranges and pretty signs and carcasses hanging in the Belfast butcher's windows and money in our pockets and money in the till and women walking in swaying skirts and beautiful words and white blouses and milk again in my mouth and I find now I don't care all that much for it.

THE SCOUT'S LAMENT

Y OU'RE the GM, you bring in sixty bodies. But only twenty you want to see, I mean really look at.

The next twenty have a chance. Say you show them something they like. Say you're drilling holes in goalies. Knocking them down, a hot streak.

Then there are the last twenty. The last twenty are filler, warm bodies, keep a scrimmage going.

Now, do you know which twenty you are? You've *GOT* to find out.

Say the coach comes to your house, or a scout. Or maybe they don't come to your house. Get a feel. Phone them up. They treat you rotten, you know that's how they'll treat your kid. You want your kid there? No you don't want your kid there.

Ask them what your kid should do for conditioning over the summer. *One*, this shows interest. *Two*, you see how they react. Whether they could give a hoot. It's important. *Three*. I forget three. Go with your instincts.

And *Politics*. It's brutal. Some kid will make the team and you'll say WHAT THE HELL!? Whoa, whose nephew is that? It's really bad. And remember, they get money for a draft choice from the NHL, so they're always looking at that. Factors. Certain traits they want, right or wrong. Some get pushed into steroids, get out the needles, bulk up, get in a 'roid rage, screw up their kidneys. They think it's their only chance at a barrel of cash and a hot car with local tarts climbing on it. Guys can't see past the end of their dick so they find someone at the gym can get 'roids and hypos. Backroom deals and politics like crazy. Not everyone's a star or a rocket scientist. Not everyone has a million choices.

Go to Portland, you walk in you're handed clean sweats, towel, the whole nine yards. You feel like a human. They phone, you listen. They got money and they'll spend it. Good food, good hotel.

The Cougars are a different can of worms. Cougars: bad food, bad rink, bad cans, housed poorly. Last year half of them got mono. No leadership. Coach of the Week club.

They screwed kids on eligibility. Traded their best players to Kamloops.

No, forget the Cougars. Go down to Cornell or Harvard, Notre Dame, Ivy League, or NCAA, do a degree, good degree, use your brain, play some hockey at the same time. It's impressive. You'll get invited anywhere after. Like Manderville with the Leafs.

You have to teach them something. Not just to brawl. Some of these guys, they are not kings and counsellors. Three-time losers in nylon jackets. Gumchewers, can't organize a lay in a whorehouse with free labour. That coach we had here was too hard on them, knocking heads for no reason, pointless drills where they're getting injured, killing them, demolishing them; jeez they hated him.

Kent Manderville is a funny case. Told—not tough enough, kid. His ma pulled him out. His ma. Now look, toughest on the team. Well maybe second or third toughest. College kid, Cornell, Ivy League, good degree, nice kid from Victoria, and now he's bashing and crashing with the Leafs. They want a berserker, make him into Curt Brackenbury. If he wants to stick. Same choice as when he was a kid. But he's not really like that. More a finesse guy. Maybe you get to like being a berserker. Never can tell. I still haven't learned to read minds. I tried though, tried to learn. I tried to read minds.

Some of those coaches got their certificate out of a Crackerjack box. You have to teach kids *something*. You have to deal with kids' *heads*. Million miles from home, from their families. Fifteen, sixteen, they're *babies*, really. Long road trips. Junk food. Blizzards, whiteouts, black ice all over the roads. Fall off the team bus with no legs and that instant you have to play some humongous farmboys waiting to knock your frigging block off. Things not going well. Bunch of strangers giving each other the greasy eyeball. Buses breaking down or going in the ditch on their side, like those Swift Current kids that died. Collecting stitches, broken noses, broken hands. The Philly flu. Psychology is a big thing. Some kids party like there's no tomorrow, go out and drink right after practice, boozehounds pissing it all away, soup to nuts. Or doing coke. They get a rep that's hard to ditch. And some kids just never fit in. What if your kid gets traded to Fernie, Podunk, Nowheresville? His best buddy gets cut from the club? What if your kid gets cut? They're out there, they're out there on their own, hung out to dry. It's hard on the kids. *Really* hard. You have to deal with kids' heads.

Lot of jerks out there too. Believe me. Lots of jerks. Guy here ran minor hockey and now in jail for molestation. I tried to punch his lights out in '69. I tried to take him out. Know what I mean? Guy hangs around injuries, all concerned. "Need sharper skates," he says to the kid. "Let me do them," he says. Bring them to your house. *Jeez*. Good service. Molesting eight- or nine-year-old boys on the hockey teams. Imagine what that did to their game, their love of the game.

You're asking. You're worried about your kid. It's *good* you're asking about this. Go with your instincts. There'll be tough times. I tell you no one but no one knows how hard it is to make it. Even to the minors or Europe. No one knows. We just see the guys that make it so we think no prob. Watch TV and think, I could do that. It's a long shot for anyone, no matter how good. I remember going through this. You're the skinny rookie, you're the new guy at camp they say to a veteran, *Run him*. See what you're made of. Tell the vet: Run the new guy. Maybe the new guy makes the team the vet doesn't. Blindside you in a scrimmage, cheap shot to the face. Try to get up he knocks you down. Creams you, you spear him back, slit open his face, chop him upside the head—hey no ref at camp. No penalties. Other guy'll be pissed bigtime, but coach'll be happy. He sees what you're made of. You go after the other guy no matter he's the size of a fucking ape. You can't back down. You must *retaliate*. Helluva thing but there you go. Carve him a new asshole need be. Dig down, find that old time religion.

I can give you a name—Tommy Black. Your kid'll have to join the Y. Tommy won't show him how to fight but how to defend himself. Nice guy. How to defend himself. Can't get away from it. Your skinny kid here goes into the corners, he needs to worry about the puck, not the other guy. He needs to know he can take care of himself. Confidence is important to any athlete. Call Tommy Black. Firefighter, in great shape. Fifty-five and he looks half that. Friends with the Courtnall boys, coached them when they were kids. Went down to Los Angeles when the younger one married that movie star.

I've never been to Los Angeles. I've scouted for the Montreal Canadiens and the Whalers and some ragtag WHA outfits along the way. I knew Rocket Richard and Gordie Howe and his sons. I almost got on the same plane with Bill Barilko, yeah that one that crashed, and I've caught a lot of salmon over the years up in Campbell River. I shot a moose in Newfoundland and I've been treed by a grizzly in the Rockies. But I've never been to L.A. Seems kind of scary to me actually. I know some tough young players in L.A. and they got mugged at a Wendy's. Knife to the heart. Maybe someday I'll get down see a game at the Duck Pond.

My boy was about twelve, small for his age. Gets levelled by a guy way bigger, knocked right on his can. But he springs right up and BAM BAM BAM! All over the guy. I was surprised, I didn't know he was like that. Little Tasmanian devil. You never really know.

Four years later some gorilla charges in full steam from the blue line—running him. My kid comes around the net with the puck, fast, BAM!! Into the boards. Then gloves off and drills my boy in the face going down. Brutal. Face a fucking mess. This time he didn't spring right up.

The needle moving through his cheek. I could read his mind this time.

My boy says to me while they're sewing up his face, "This isn't worth it. I don't like this game anymore."

He works with numbers now, an accountant. Handles money. Not a puck. He won't even watch hockey on TV anymore.

I watch. My job is to watch. I see a prospect I put in a word. Hope the big club will listen. Hope I'm right. I've sent them some good ones.

My boy had wheels too. Afterburners. And hands; make that puck get up and talk. Deke you in a phone booth. I still remember that needle moving through his cheek. I don't like this game anymore, he says. And I still love it. Helluva thing.

But like I say, twenty get a legit look-see, twenty have an out-side chance, and twenty are filler, nothing, losers.

Which are you? Which twenty are you right this moment? Do you ever know? Do you ever *really* know for sure? All my life. All my life I wonder this.

POMPEII BOOK
OF THE DEAD

MY WIFE is from Florida and is moving out of my house while I am in Italy. She takes the dog down to the river and hits a ball into the water with a tennis racket. The moving van comes and the moving van goes. The faithful dog swims to retrieve the ball again and again. Again and again I climb the stairs to my room to pack my bags.

The city in ruins seems to go on forever. Pompeii is so many worlds, so many levels, a strange village below, families caught like an underground zoo, mothers and children frozen in their poses, then a breathing world built just above their heads, busy footsteps on the dead's ceiling, roads and tracks and our slum train's noisy motion just one level above the digs, above their heads, wheels and engines rolling over graves.

It must be odd to live in Pompeii right now and have this shadow city below and to one side, this destroyed duplicate in the basement. Like Las Vegas, like New Orleans, no visitor cares a whit about the real city. In Pompeii we want the roof-less ruins, those ancient bedrooms and brothels and shops broken open to the sun. The excavations are fantastic, but locals must resent this favoured twin, this magnet shadow so close to them.

And we are the same, that other place shadowing us here, the lost place we left and must return to, return to a face and cheques to be written at the kitchen table and deep leaves to be raked past the backyard swing, a return to winter and shoveling a driveway and a new battery and heavy-duty wipers, a return to providing and caring and staying put. Will that cooler world stay put while I am gone from it?

Outside under the latest model of the sun I try to stay in shade, creep close to a building, veer under pine trees and cypress. Pack on my back, I walk to the ruins, excavations at my feet, dead conversations with that woman in Canada in my head.

Did I say I am fascinated by Pliny and his demise in Pompeii? I travelled to Pompeii because of Vesuvius the volcano and the excavated ruins, but also because Pliny sailed there. In Pompeii the sky grew dark after the eruption and the sun stood still under the volcano.

On a morning just like this the volcano woke over the vineyards and all of this city was buried deep, left to sleep so long; amphitheatre and villas and cobbled lanes and cowering families covered over. Children and babies hold each other and suffocate in seconds, then discovered by chance, dug out and exposed once more to the harsh sun and to tourists like me, the sun inching forward a crimson ribbon at a time, their ancient roof peeled back and the living come to visit the long sunlit avenues of the dead.

At the station I bump into Ray Ray and Tamika from our group in Rome. As we chat on an outdoor platform, a high-speed train pulls in for a brief stop.

A stray Jack Russell terrier trots around full of pep, the stray dog wants to cross the tracks from our platform to see who is at the station, but the streamlined train blocks the dog's path. The diesel will leave any second, we know; these high-speed trains never stop for long. The little dog peers this way and that for a way to cross the track. The dog places his head between wheels of the idling train. We all groan when he does this.

"Don't."

We see his quick terrier eyes and brain working in tandem: *Can I sneak through the iron wheels?* The crowd tenses as if the curious dog awaits a guillotine, the lull between beheadings.

"No," I say out loud, "come back." But the dog does not know English. Tamika turns away, she can't watch.

"Here!" The dog turns, runs back to our platform, the train shrieks and wheels scythe where his head had been a moment before.

"Good boy!" He has bright eyes and soft brown ears. I saved him, I am Pliny the Elder. I must have a treat in my backpack. It's a Jack; it doesn't want to be petted; it wants to run, it wants to run until it dies. I know this dog will die. It has no one.

Tamika and Ray Ray ask me to hike with them up the slopes of the volcano. Only days, weeks ago, Ray Ray hung out in the Hong Kong meatpacking district; he tells us of suitcases full of gifts in China.

"Shoes, electronics, they cost nothing there! The Customs people wouldn't believe me when I declared the total value, they thought I was lying. They held me for hours."

For hours we climb the side of the volcano, sweating like mules in the sun and rock, the drugging sun. In the scrub brush we halt, knowing we're not going to make the peak, the Gran Cono. I've seen satellite photos from directly above the cone, this strange opening, this gash, a black hole in the planet. Pliny died doing this, he stopped and didn't get up, covered in ash and molten lava. Shelley burns on the beach, I burn in Pompeii. My scalp is toast, my head hurting.

Below the mountain, African men sell new sunglasses to an ancient nation; the tall men set up tiny tables on the street or a cloth spread on the sidewalk outside the church. Southern Italy so warm, a boot aimed at Africa, a long fashionable boot, so close to Tunisia, to Cleopatra's Egypt and golden breast, artifacts taken from Nubian locales scattered everywhere in Italy. North Africa was part of Caesar's empire, and Mussolini's empire, Africa is so close, yet black people seem like strangers in the living room.

"Italians treat you like family," says Father Kelly at the restaurant. "Italians are wonderful, so warm."

This is not always so for African street vendors or those in our group with darker skin like Tamika from Philly or Ray Ray from Nigeria. My old uncle used to say, We are made of the same dough, but we are baked in different ovens.

In a café a woman beside me is talking of money. Is this what it seems? Non ho capito, my Italian is very poor, I lack language, the secret code.

Thirty euro, thirty pieces of silver. The possibility should not be a surprise. A few blocks from our table are frescos of Roman orgies and ancient delights, and shop entrances boasted their good luck charms of erect penises, and pictures of Priapus, the god of gardens and fertility, Priapus proudly weighing his giant cock on a scale, his cock out in front of him like the neck of a goose.

A few blocks away in the ruins are faded frescos of cunnilingus. But what if I am misunderstanding her? Is that her man there at the curb? I could be beaten or killed over an insult, over a woman's honour.

The woman with curly hair speaks to me again. It sounds like quindici, or is it dieci? 15, or perhaps 10, or is it 19? Why would she say an odd number like 19? I wish I knew for sure what was happening. She seems to be bargaining, dropping the price rapidly. Did she take "For you" as a ploy, an insult? I don't want to insult anyone, I just arrived, I want to wait a few days before insulting anyone.

No, I say, No, grazie. I say it several times, trying to be polite, that I am grateful for something, her attention, not wanting to insult her. Grazie.

Across the bay at the naval base at Misenum, Pliny the Elder saw the massive cloud the shape of a tree. Pliny took swift galleys to Pompeii to help old friends stranded on the shore of the bay, to help them escape. He died near this spot, a hero, gave himself right here.

The café woman walks away from me, walks away looking hard at her phone, leaning forward toward the square eye of the screen. Her eyes are changed, her face no longer friendly. I've seen that look before, that sea change.

A man sits down to show me his mangled hands, a refugee from Tunisia, he crossed the desert then he floated in a boat to the island of Lampedusa. In Italy he has tried to remove his own fingerprints, he has burnt his hands, afraid the police will send him back. They have his fingerprints registered.

Will I give him five euro?

No.

I no longer want my place at the table, I want to walk too, a street walker, I walk the city, walk and turn into an alley as a shortcut to the basilica and central piazza. I think I know my direction, my landmarks, but the alley turns the wrong way, turns away from the centre and keeps going and going and I'm alone and start to get jumpy, paranoid, I've made a bad move, entered a box canyon. This encounter with this woman and then the man with the burnt hands, this has thrown me, I was so happy to arrive here, but I am edgy now walking around waiting for lurking strumpets and robbers to jump me. Perhaps the guidebook is right about Pompeii: the world is full of foul deeds and sneaking mischief, a mousetrap, miching mallecho, a cold beer and a knife between the ribs.

All around the bay the Nuvoletta-Polverino cartels open suitcases and sell groceries, garlic, and leather, hash and high-fashion gowns, ecstasy and cocaine in the northern suburbs, stolen antiquities and jewels in the narrow lanes and the train moves past ruins, a uniformed man calling for tickets, tickets. And yet I ride the train for free most days, my pass expired, a Unico Campania Three Day Travel Ticket. I am rarely asked, trusted or I am invisible, of a certain age, so no one checks my fingerprints to see if I should be deported. I don't have to burn my hands.

Circumvesuviana, the local train, circles the mountain, the violent mountain held over us no matter where we go until I feel it has always been there, looming over me all my life. The ancient vineyards rise in long perfect lines to the volcano, a series of triangles and convergences and my eye follows eagerly, pleased by the sightline.

The area around the Bay of Naples is so fertile, crops in sun and soil enriched by the repeated ash eruptions, grapes and arbours and orchards and flowers, and all this beautiful coastline, this sea stretching away in the sun, all these islands, all this potential, so I wonder: Why does it seem so fucked up? Grapes and blossoms, but also trash piled in cul-de-sacs and vandalism and graffiti like ugly tattoos and larceny and no work and graft and gangs and payoffs and homicide. In suburbs of Naples men cut packages into vials, kilos roll in and the kilos roll out. And the money? Where does it go? Like water, it has to go somewhere.

Ray Ray and Tamika catch a milk train to Sorrento, but I travel the other way to a smaller excavation site. Coming back I find a seat in a compartment with two men and an elderly woman. Two seats left. I sense each passenger's unspoken hope that no one else comes into our compartment. Then a young woman struggling with a heavy case. I jump up and I help lift her suitcase up on the high rack above our seats.

She sits beside me, flushed in the face from exertion and heat, introduces herself. Abby, an American, she has been teaching in Istanbul, but her contract is done.

I'd love to see Istanbul, I say.

She is travelling for a month and will meet her parents in Venice; next year she will teach in Asia. She asks if I can translate a sign for her.

The older man in our compartment says, You come to Italy and can't speak Italian? He has a dark upswept pompadour and leans forward, head deep between his shoulders, like Elvis with osteoporosis.

So all travellers must speak his language? Then how would I ever see Russia or China?

You must be very careful in Napoli, he says to Abby.

He points to his eyes. At first I thought he meant they'll go for your eyes, but then I realize he is demonstrating that he has seen of what he speaks with his own eyes.

"This is not a normal country. Here up is down, down is up. Here everyone wants a share off the top and a share off the bottom and a share off the side and then what is left? Since the war? A new government every nine months, as if having a baby. But what is the result? When the Americani voted for that fool Bush I laughed. But now we have elected a buffone, a clown. Now I can't laugh. And the criminals. Even the football matches are fixed, it's all contaminated. In the old days Mussolini would take care of them. If you stepped out of line back then, this is what happened to you." He makes a motion of slitting his own throat.

I have my hand on her neck, it seems so intimate. Abby and I walk the Naples train station together. *Attenzione Ai Borseggiatori*—Beware of Pickpocket! We sit for a drink at the station. Vore una birra, per favore. Vore many beer, per favore.

She asks me if I have been to the Gaspé; she went as a child and still remembers.

Yes, it's beautiful, gannets and whales and so much light. Her head is there and I can see down her top and spy what is hidden, her black bra and small breasts nestled there. I am allowed to touch her shoulders and neck. Yes, the Gaspé is beautiful.

I know it's impossible, but I want to skip the awkward courtship steps, the phone calls, restaurant candles watching scallops shuck their bacon wraps. Can't we simply look at each other once and know and walk by the sea and lie down. Can't I just say, *You and me.* And we would both somehow know it's right.

"Email me," I say to Abby, worried about cementing things before I leave for Pompeii. "I'll check at the internet café."

"No need to check, I'll see you in Pompeii soon."

When she says this to me I adore our world. Abby walks into Naples and I take another slow train south, the right side unspooling views of the aqua sea and up lift the tribal cameras and always a church up like a narrow knife, the body heat increasing markedly inside the cars as the train travels along the bay to Pompeii. Canada's snow or ice seems impossible in this drugging heat.

In train tunnels we travel in and out of light, in and out of mountains, pupils dilating, pores sweating. In Pompeii's raw ruins I enter another tunnel on foot, down into the forum, the amphitheatre, this place where they died. A dark passage leads down at an angle, into the ground, I follow the tunnel to get out of the relentless sun and down into the lower level of the forum, the Teatro, down into shade, hiding from the sun, even for a few rare moments.

Tamika and Ray Ray spot me from afar; they cross the dust and pigeons and follow me into the underworld. The dark tunnel passage is cool, shade is so lovely, so good to be briefly out of the sun under the forum complex; the burnt skin of my forehead hurts so much it worries me.

They found a horse when digging under this forum, torches once burned in these haunted underground halls, animals and men waiting, waiting, sweating, then your turn, it's time, pushed out into the harsh sun, live or die.

From the level forum floor we raise our eyes to the rising rows of stone seats heaped above us.

"I suspect this was a very bad view for most who saw it."

The majority of people would be above looking down. This minority on the floor of the forum standing where we stand breathing at the bright bottom of the stone walls—slaves, foreign exiles, prisoners of war, gladiators, *infamia* pushed out into the sun—well, in a few moments most would be killed.

Trident pitchforks to the skull, Roman stabbing swords, curved Bulgarian swords, chains and nets and shields, starved African lions with their ribs showing and a chanting mob overhead (do you feel lucky, punk) and, at the end, dragged bleeding across the sand by Juno in his mask, dragged behind the walls by masked Juno who swings his square hammer into the private curve of your porcelain head.

In the ruins I see a dog running and jumping in the distance. The dog runs over lava and candy wrappers and king's tombs. It's the same Jack Russell terrier I saw at the train station with its head in the diesel's wheels. In this heat the crazy dog chases pigeons in the grassy ruins of the Grande Palace, the dog galloping by ancient Corinthian pillars lined up in rows, pillars or stumps left to hint of the space where emperors and nobles roamed vast gardens and pools.

The running dog cares not a whit about gardens or hidden history or the future or the heat, the dog cares only for the moment and the nearest pigeon. The dog is running full speed in the heat when I arrive and is running full speed when

I leave. Its pink tongue hangs and I hear the creature pant, a clicking sound.

"How does a dog find water here?" The sandy ground is like a desert.

The terrier turns to me and speaks with its beautiful brown eyes: Yes, I am the same dog you saw at the railroad track. I appreciate your concern, but you can do nothing for me. You are visiting here briefly, a stranger, a foreigner, while this is my life, short as it may be. You are used to one way, I am used to another.

An Irish boy jumps away nervously as the mad dog rockets past running down a pigeon he will never catch. The dog turns and runs again, over and over. That woman in Canada, I must change her mind, I must swim with her again.

And I must tell my cousin Eve of the dog; she'd understand, Eve is my new confessor. Does the dog bark at Italian pigeons in Italian? It has no owner. The terrier is a stranger. The terrier is me.

We stagger in the heat, we must leave the dog, leave these ruins for a drink, leave this skin that feels so sore from the merciless sun. We tromp the same Italian dust that slaves and emperors and gladiators ate. Place this ancient soil in your mouth like a thick piece of pizza pie. Eat the rich past. Dig in the ground anywhere in Italy and you find the past, you can't escape your past.

In the family hotel the staff and family members eat after we have been fed and our plates cleared. The mother with dyed blonde hair and the tired father with his neck brace—once so handsome in the old black and white photos decorating the lobby and halls, posing with movie stars and soccer players, but now he spends the day in the lobby with a tiny TV set and a neck brace. Now they are aged parents, watching Euro Cup on a tiny TV.

Big Pico, my favourite waiter, sits with the family, and beside him sits a skinny cook; they lean together at the same table in mid-afternoon, huge man and thin man leaning toward each other over delicious plates and much wine. This is their time, not ours, an intimate inner circle, relaxed and pleasantly tired from waiting on us, serving the guests breakfast and lunch.

The German man in the café says to me, Italians all lie, they promise you something and don't deliver, they laze about, nothing on time or when promised. I'll never come back, he says. A horrible place.

He hates it here, yet I love it so, the same place. I love Italy.

The German claims that southern Italians are lazy, but Pico in Pompeii works so very hard for us. My hotel room has no clock and I travel light, no watch, no cell phone, no laptop.

My glazed window does not reveal if it is 5 a.m. or 9 a.m. So down to the lobby to spy a clock, and I glimpse Pico bent in the kitchen creating his raw pastry, no one else about at this hour. He is here at dawn, he is here at night: when does he live, when does he sleep? I worry whether he has a life outside this hotel, whether he is lonely, whether will die from work. He is not lazy.

After another luscious dinner at the hotel, Pico brings me a simple repast, a lone superb pear with a knife and fork.

Okay? Pico asks me.

Si, si!

Did he read my mind? The single pear is exactly what I need after all these rich dishes, such beautiful texture and sweet taste.

Prego, Pico says so kindly every night, his hand and arm out like a silent film actor directing me to my lonely table, welcoming me to the table for one, the one solitary place setting among the hotel's couples and families and singing nuns. I am in my place.

Abby, the woman from the train, said she'd meet me here today at four or she'd call the hotel. The phone rings at the front desk; I strain to listen. Is it her? No call, no email. The sirens do not call to me from the blue grotto.

The dog runs past. I sit outside the hotel at a wobbly wicker table with a huge cold bottle (*grande per favore*), waiting for her. I keep buying more big bottles in the lobby and the old man does not approve.

Trying to seduce a young American woman on the train to Naples is somehow more honourable than paying a prostitute in Pompeii. Where lies the logic? We were walking and kissing after the train, strangers on a train; I was allowed a view under her blouse, but I will never quite get under that enticing black bra. She decides I must wait.

I can't live like this much longer. I thought she'd make me whole somehow, keep the pieces together, would be my duct tape. All these people in the street, at the store: how do they do it? They move directly, they know what they want! They function as if they designed themselves and no need for duct tape.

"What's up, fool?" Ray Ray and Tamika join me at my table.

"Look what the cat dragged in. Pull up a chair." I buy them anything they want, happy to see them, to break my funk, my lowered mood, happy to have company at my lonely table in Fortress Europe.

Stucco walls line the road. A yellow sky smeared like oilpaint and above that yellow streak perches a dark mumbling thunderstorm. No rain in weeks and now we drink in a giant jagged tunnel, light waning after a bright boiling day. The new weather alters the air's colour, the street in front of the hotel moves many shades of mauve, and finally it rains, canarycoloured plaster darkens in rain, welcome rain.

Thunder and lightning reverberate over the ruins of Pompeii; our nervous hotel dog opens his jaws and speaks to the sparking sky, loose dogs loping everywhere. We sit in wicker chairs and watch the sky and the street and the dogs.

The wild dogs running free make Tamika jumpy. We walk to the central piazza and dogs trot out of nowhere, surrounding us while we look for a bank machine.

"Damn! That's not right!" she exclaims, looking all around. "Where are they coming from? I don't like them running free."

Ray Ray stops to talk with any other blacks he sees in Italy. He grabs my arm, asks me, "Where is *nowhere?*"

"What do you mean?"

"Those guys I just talked to say they live in nowhere."

"They're homeless? They live on the street?"

"No! A real place, man, they said they live in nowhere."

A place called nowhere; I have to think about this one.

"It's way up north, man, they said it's a good place, I should come visit."

219

"It's a country up north?"

"Yeah, man, way up there."

"Norway?"

"Yes, man! Nowhere! It's a good place. I should go up and see Nowhere, I don't dig it here in Italy." He lowers his voice. "In fact, I think I'll leave tomorrow," Ray Ray tells me in a confidential tone.

"Give it a chance."

"Man, they liked me way more in China. They bow to you! In China they treated me like a king. They don't like me here in Italy."

In Italy we walk such crowded cities and underground grottos stuffed with grinning skeletons crowded in bunks and deep hallways like mineshafts and then on trains I see so much empty countryside between the cities. Millions crammed close into projects and slums and yet so much wide open country just out the door, just down the road. The same is true in Canada, the same all around the world.

We don't want lebensraum, we shun the orchard above the stream. No, we love cement curbs and peeling walls, if we are not born inside the city we move there as soon as we can, we follow our bliss, our desire for hustle and excitement and dumpsters and rats in stairwells and staple guns and opiates, to hang out on a concrete corner or line up for a bonehead job and pick each other's pocket and scent doorways with the ammonia of our urine and exist without leafy trees or pink blossoms, our desire to avoid God and nature, to take elevators, to ride machines climbing toward boxes set atop boxes like bone ossuaries set in the sky, our manic desire to stand on each other's head to the soundtrack of machines on the walls and machines past the window circling the sky and machines rumbling the ground under our feet.

Ray Ray said yesterday that he felt sick; maybe he caught something in China.

I ask, "How you doing today?" I shouldn't have said that they spit in our food.

"Man, thank you for asking. I could be dying and that dude running this show doesn't care." Ray Ray says, "I've had it, man, I'm leaving tomorrow." He says this to me every day.

All the trains in the gloaming and buses beneath olive valleys and aqueducts and trefoil arches in plumes of diesel. Our group always on the move like vapour, up and down, back and forth over roses and skeletons, changing towns and minds, changing trains and tunnels, crowded platforms and subterranean stairs and no seats on the trains and such sweaty carriages under the looming volcano and cactus and lava fields and burning rock once taken for portals to hell.

A shantytown burns below a freeway (is it a Roma enclave?) and I know I could drip my endless sweat over the class-war conflagration and easily extinguish the flames. I have never sweated like this, I'm sure our collective sweat will pool on the floor of the train until our ankles are deep in sweat, in aqua vitae, the saltwater of life.

The city streets at night—ah I can still conjure the scent of crazed Vespas in the heaped garbage and brilliantined pickpockets—then to pull ourselves from a mattress at dawn for another woozy train to Pompeii's sun-bright ruin, and a milk-train back again to Naples in sore shoes to climb a narrow 13th-century alley of cobbles and scooters and skewback abutments and we dodge the Vespas and wolf down the best food ever laid against my tongue.

The Napoli station, where I last saw Abby, makes me feel like a loser, the Napoli station a sad axis. I buy a ticket at a machine. All the redolent names, Pompeii, Herculaneum, Sorrento, Amalfi, Positano, and soon we will be back in the bosom of peach-coloured Rome.

We climb on the last train and down the aisle. I take a seat on the right. Ray Ray takes a seat on the left of the aisle. Ray Ray tells me he is the second son of second wife, he says this is lower status than the eldest son. This was years back in Nigeria. I never know what to believe, what is real.

Ray Ray says to me, "Bet you five euro no one will sit by me."

I've gotten to know Ray Ray in Italy; he chases all the Croatian chambermaids and is a bit of a con man, but he is a creampuff at heart; at a party he worried I hadn't eaten and deftly cooked me a seafood stir-fry. But he is so tall and black; the Italians fear him.

"Will you take my bet?" Ray Ray asks me. "Five euro."

Sure, why not. Someone will sit by him. The seats around me fill up. The rest of the train fills. The feeling of pure will as the train shunts out of the station, every seat taken except for three blue seats around Ray Ray.

To my surprise, Rome's rouge walls seem calmly familiar and pleasing to the eye after Napoli's grey forms and volcanic dust and volcanic drugs and jackal bedlam and mountains of aromatic refuse and a knife steering its calm way through the air of a kitchen party. Naples is more compelling, stranger and wilder than Rome, a fascinating paella, the true capital of Italy, but now as I walk Rome it seems almost a home, as if I know it well and have spent some worthy part of my life here, which may not be true, but is a comforting feeling since I seem to have lost my sense of home.

We leave the train station and subway and stumble up into ground-level sunlight and a tiny corridor of mirrors that passes for a hotel lobby, so many puzzled versions of me. This narrow hallway seemed lunatic the first time I saw it and now seems so normal. The French woman at the desk hasn't moved all her life and sends me to my same room, the same terrace waiting at the top of the same stairs, which pleases me. See, I am not always morbid. It's as if the French woman and the American intern kept the room empty just for me.

My cousin Eve finds me for a drink and chat on my high terrace. I'm living near the top of a tree; I stare out at Rome and the green parrot in the tall trees pleases me; trees sway in green hours and I water my flowers again. They survived my absence. No sign of the smoking Spanish woman in the atrium, but my orphans and nuns below make me happy.

My cousin agrees. "It's so beautiful here; it makes me happy. That sun every morning. Italy makes me happy. But I have trouble with happiness; I'm suspicious of it. My mother always said I was a very serious child. I should eat something. You're always laughing at me, mocking me."

"I am not mocking you." (I am more mocked than mocking.)

A light dusting of freckles on my cousin's lovely skin, like an animal imprint. I like them. She hates the freckles, uses lemon juice to fade them. My cousin tells me she has had two periods in one month. Short cycles, she says, and lots of blood. One day I saw her wince from a cramp and gave her some of my painkillers. She washes her sheets in her shower and dries them on my terrace, which has more room and sun. I give her raisins for iron, give her a cold German beer. "Did you know," she says, "that the beer bottle was invented in 1850?"

"I did not know that." We drink, eat apples from Afghanistan, dates from the Euphrates.

At the café at night she orders a dish called strangled priests and observes that I am like her mother putting butter on everything. It is odd to consider how much butter I have swallowed in my life, how many gallons, barrels, trucks, ocean-going tankers.

My cousin Eve tells us of the time she entered a tiny taverna deep in the south of Italy, asked a man for directions and an ancient woman spit on my cousin's bare arm.

"She spit on you for real?" asks Ray Ray.

My cousin says amiably, "I was wearing a top that showed too much skin."

Usually she carried two shawls: one for her shoulders and one for her head, in case she was going into a church or formal event, but she didn't think she needed a shawl in this shop.

"Man, no one spit on me in China," says Ray Ray. "Seriously."

We eat and drink and walk and I realize I missed the streets and lovely murky rivers to the sea, what is borne by the chartered river past the red palaces, the peach-coloured walls and cheetah shadows and forlorn Italian faces and frank sexual fashions. And I missed my cousin. I tell her of the angry prostitute in Pompeii and of Abbey's no-show.

She says, You are such a fool with women, but she laughs at my tales.

On my terrace I stand and survey my kingdoms, my holy Roman empires, another Pope, a new King of Rome! I am a spy in a tower and who are these statues I spy? If I stand on a chair on my terrace and look several blocks east I can see a glass and brass cupola and a group of polished white statues in situ on one corner of a building high above the huge Vatican walls.

My statues are not near the giant violet Basilica, they are far from the centres of power; my statues inhabit a lost corner above the Vatican's north wall, isolated in some plaintive ex-Catholic exile, their perch high with the birds and helicopters.

Perhaps the statues are from the list of murdered popes, or pretenders or disbarred lawyers or weird patron saints, set off on their own cliff edge.

Here is the odd thing: I search the street directly under the wall, but I can never spot this mysterious group from below. I zigzag my neighbourhood crossroads and avenues, and follow the huge wall, which should lead me right to them, but there is never any sight of them. My statues only exist when I see them from my rooftop terrace, they are simply not visible from ground level. Am I the only one who sees them? Look, there they are, looking out over the city, but if I run down the stairs they do not exist.

I become more and more fascinated by this lonely lovely group of statues. They seem thuggish, hip. Why can I not find them? Do I need to sneak inside the Vatican walls? The Mexican rock climber from our group went over the wall for a lark and was caught by the Pope's Swiss Guard and put on the next flight to Mexico and the rest of us were nearly kicked out of the country.

My cousin and others in the group make a day trip to the beach at Ostia. Such heat, not used to it, air wavering in heat, like fumes dancing over a nozzle at a gas pump. My cousin's sun-burnt shoulders are so red and tender, and in the evening we are altered, groggy, as if felled by sunstroke, *coup de soleil.*

I have a round plastic container from the discount store, soothing cold cream, *crema corpo*, for her tender shoulders. She opens her blouse in my hotel room. It's better if I don't know such things, if I am not allowed to see.

In the amazing ruins we eat apples, in the amazing ruins of the temples, of marriage. There stands my cousin and her legs and lingering glances. Do not go near there, do not follow her frock in the frescoes as wild dogs run past, *mondo cane*, a dog's world.

Man is his dizzy desire and I desire knowledge of her bare shoulders, that curved planet, that new home. Her neck part of a naked crescent, a lovely curve from naked earlobe to naked shoulder. Why do I love her neck so, that nexus of delicate ear and fine hair and shampoo scent, the shoulders, the skin, the jaw and cheek, the shadows and perfume; it has everything, right there. I can hide my face there; what a world exists just there!

She asks for lotion for her skin. I approach my cousin with a round container of lotion from an Italian shop, approach a planet, once distant, now in view in Rome, a room with a view. Her shoulders glow in the spacecraft window, closer, closer to touch, a new looming planet, the lightest touch, my fingers like landing craft and her intake of breath.

Crema corpo, revitalizzanta aloe vera. Rubbing her tender shoulders and her neck, her back, lightly down her spine to her round hips. I worry she'll get mad, but I can feel her body move nicely to my touch. She stretches her neck and shoulders, murmuring pleasant sounds, moves into my pressure as a cat will.

I will not lie with her, but I keep rubbing more lotion, her shoulders and back and lower and lower down her back, on the sides of her hips and brief forays near her belly and a bit lower below her navel, teasing, testing, lower and lower, circling closer and closer, so close, but never all the way.

My cousin says, "You have such a calming effect on me."

"Me?" My mind is always racing and my life is chaos.

"You seem very calm." An East German woman travelling in the west of Ireland said the same thing to me, used a German word for calm.

My hands wander, my mind wanders, catacombs and tunnels and travel, planes, airports and tunnels, my mind inside her, the lines where her strap was in the sun, the lines and borders, the line and colour of her face, the lineament of her eye and cheekbone skin. I think of the old woman in the south of this country spitting on Eve's skin. Country matters.

My cousin gasps when my fingers stray and find where she is wet, my fingers connect with her brain, a direct tendril, another hidden passageway, her breath quiet as the mountain town that makes you sing.

My hand wrecked a marriage, wrecked unions, and I killed the beautiful scooter couple, and I listen to the Fleshtones, their best album, *Roman Gods*. At night when I get under the covers my cousin seems awake, but she mutters a language I can't understand.

What did you say?

She kicks my shin or calf. Is she being impish? She pulls at my hair. How to interpret this? She goes back to sleep, breathing rhythmically.

The next day she laughs with joy at my account. I kicked you? I spoke gibberish? She recalls none of it. She leaves my room like a sleepwalker. Soon we will all leave Rome. We move, we sin, we confess, we fly to and fro, we are on earth, then we are in the heavens, then we are not, we are on earth, then we are flung through the heavens, then we are not in the heavens.

And she loves me, then she loves me not, she becomes another woman who says in a doorway or in an airport, says I'd hate to lose touch with you, you know I love you in so many ways. Another one who says, It's been wonderful, as did Nata-sha, Natasha my buried past, another quiet buried city.

"Don't be depressed," my cousin says, "I know you'll be depressed." Or did Natasha in Canada say that? All these peo-ple living in your past as if in a nearby apartment building and waiting for you to get there. The anatomy of desire and the anatomy of loss—I have them mixed up in my depressed, sun-burnt head.

My cousin looks pale in the train window. My cousin is in my room, no, she is gone, she is walking a narrow lane miles away, she is coming downhill in another country, she walks a line between whitewashed homes that have been there for-ever, a lane curving this way and that and quiet as a suture. She leaves my room, leaves the station, leaves the airport and somewhere a waitress carries a big curved glass just for me.

In Pompeii last week the hunched train lurched forward and the steel wheels did not slice off the dog's head. Perhaps like the dog I'll persist, survive. Perhaps the terrier did hear and heed me, perhaps the terrier knows many languages, will travel to Russia and China, will visit the chambermaids in Croatia. The sunny peak and the valley depth so close together. The scooter couple is so beautiful, yet they die high above the charming sea, the shallow coast, they fall from the ledge, the ledger.

In my last days in Rome I grow obsessed by my group of stat-ues peopling a ledge, I stare out from my terrace and I pace back and forth on blisters under the Vatican's high walls; I must find where they live high above us. I borrow binoculars from the American intern.

As I focus the binocs on the statues they turn their heads to look at me, lean to speak with each other, as if posing for an album cover, say early Blues Magoos or Velvet Underground. One statue wears Bob Dylan sunglasses, resembles Lou Reed.

Another pats his perfectly curled hair. They whisper to each other and one statue turns his hips, wags a pale erection at me, his Roman good luck charm, a large statue gripping his generous phallus with two large hands high above the milling streets crowded with tourists all dressed in motley.

We meet in the street and my new gang of ghostly statues brings me along on a mission. They are not murdered popes, they are not exiled saints. No, their ambitions are far simpler, for they are lard thieves, they steal used grease, fryer oil. The statue with Lou Reed ringlets is the ringleader. We gather in the alley behind the famous restaurant, for money is to be had in rancid lard and biodiesel, the price climbs daily and they know someone who knows someone who can move grease, who takes this filth off our hands.

Cats rub our legs in the long alley. Wild cats roam Rome's ancient sunken ruins while dogs run free in Pompeii's train station, and this speaks to something about each city: Rome is feline and Pompeii is canine.

In June my cousin sang songs while we kayaked and her lovely voice carried and she rose from the sea with jellyfish stings like red scratches or burns. Swim into jellyfish and recoil and try to escape their touch, and the next day small red whip-lashes on her right shoulder and breast. She put toothpaste on the stings to soothe them. My cousin Eve is afraid to go into the sea again.

My cousin leaves me over and over, on a bicycle, in a kayak, but she comes back over and over, vague as Janus, divided as Janus. I have such faith in the future. I love the future just because it is so nicely vague; the future's so vague I have to wear shades.

In the alley of grease we have our duties. If anyone stops us, my role is to pretend to be a lost tourist and speak English only, though the statues insist to me that police have their hands full with murders and the mob and the ultras and can't be bothered with small transgressions regarding fryer oil. The grease in the alley reeks. Lewd Priapus is with us, but he is not popular, his huge phallus gets in the way of lugging the sloppy plastic drums.

"Clearly he is of little use in enterprises such as these."

Pliny the Elder died rescuing people from the volcano and here I am stealing lard. Pliny was noble, took a fast cutter to the shore. "Fortune goes to the brave!" Pliny shouted into the wind. Now there was a man! I must make some changes in my life.

No, you are wrong, says Priapus beside me in the alley. No, I knew Pliny well and he had grown quite corpulent, he died sitting down and his friends abandoned him in the pumice. He was no admiral, he was given the post as a patronage appointment. He sailed across the bay, but wind pinned his cutter to the shore and there was no rescue so they waited and feasted and drank and slept until the volcano drove them from the dwelling, pillows tied to their heads as helmets. Out on the burning pumice Pliny collapsed, he asked a slave to kill him.

That can't be true, I insist.

Yes, he couldn't breathe, he sat down and couldn't stand up and the party was afraid of being covered in ash and lava. His friends left him, left him lying on one of his sails for a bed. They are as bad as we are, sinners all of us.

Near the Vatican a tall American man glares at our procession of pale talking statues dragging big drums of grease. He turns to his wife.

"When we get back home, at church?" His Dockers are creased beautifully, his posture erect; at some point he commanded aircraft carriers in the Pacific.

"Yes, honey?" she says to him.

"I'm not giving another cent."

His wife lingers, her wistful eyes linger on Priapus's dangling gifts. Can this elephant trunk be real?

A man lies face down on the sidewalk outside the Vatican walls; he twitches, but he does not look up at the passing crowd, as if the sidewalk is a movie screen he is studying. Are the dark lumps pushing from his scalp sign of a true disease? They look like small wooden knobs, knobs fashioned from dark-grained wood. In Rome we are learning about craft, art, faith. Can we have confidence, can we believe in this affliction of the head?

The swarthy man lies begging face down on a wide sidewalk below the Vatican walls, one of his hands reaching straight out for alms. Tourists are forced to step around his twitching form. They cross the street to join a lineup at the bustling gelato shop, choose gelato the colour of tulips.

Is the man prone on the sidewalk a Gypsy or Roma? A Turk? Croatian? Albanian? We tiptoe around him, around his flat arm, wondering whether the lumps on his head are real or a con job to elicit sympathy and more coins.

Before she left, my cousin lay pale as a statue under my hand, my white body cream spread over her back, and this swarthy man lying on the sidewalk, one arm out to beg, dark as a collier. Doves gather around us like doubts. Have confidence, have faith, believe in the man with his arm outstretched.

We move on to our reward, our cash, we move on with our drums of grease. The statues have a gig tonight playing Flesh-tones covers, a café near Via Cola di Rienzo; maybe I'll sit in on harmonica, try out my new silver chromatic. The other statues are resentful of Priapus and his weighty phallus, the way he smiles to show it off.

"Last time we bring him along," mutters one.

"He's going to ruin my fifty-dollar buzz."

"I get tired of looking at it," adds another.

"Yeah guys, I think I'm gonna jet."

We resent Priapus, yet we have a strange pride in knowing him. You should see this thing! We tell our wives and girlfriends about his gifts, which might be dangerous if they become curious to know more, to become intimately acquainted with such a formidable phallus.

On my terrace I hear splashing sounds and gleeful voices; I peer over the edge. My orphans: in this insane heat someone has given my orphans a wading pool! This makes me very happy. The nuns and orphans will never know that I care, that I watch from above like a powerless God, that I look out and I am happy for them and their little wading pool. We are all playful orphans seeking to splash each other. Our needs are simple.

Now I need to call a taxi. This final steadfast servant outside the hotel door, the most silent man in Italy, perhaps the only silent man in Italy, and to this driver I gladly hand over my gold and last coins and folded bills of colour, the last of my amusing euros, and the quiet Italian steers me to the portals of an airport named after the genius Leonardo da Vinci, west of Rome (in my head the suicide Vic Chesnutt sings sadly).

I'm not happy to leave, but I am happy I came, I saw, I want to come back, *vorrei un biglietto e ritorno. Ritorno*: that sounds so nice, return to the light dusting of freckles on my cousin's lovely skin. Under the volcano she orders a dish called strangled priests, mutters a language I can't understand, kisses me, kicks me. In Napoli or Pompeii, what were they eating, what were they saying, who were they kissing and kicking when the volcano hit and buried them? The coast so beautiful there below the volcano.

Pliny couldn't walk and was buried in ash, they came back to find his body in the cremated world, the buried world, and the beautiful scooter couple dies on the narrow Amalfi coast road, so narrow, a wall to one side and empty sea air on the other side. Such fine views and the musical bus horn like a pleasing trumpet flourish at each corner and tunnel.

Vespa means wasp. The red scooter weaves quickly through cars, streaks through a galaxy of colours, roars inside a brief noisy tunnel and exits the tunnel and in the next sunny curve an oncoming bus strays over the line and a scooter bounces off the non-committal front of the bus and breaks into many pieces, the scooter breaks into one wheel and side mirrors and the bright plastic orbs of signal lights.

The boyfriend's helmet stays on his head, but the young woman's helmet flies away and the crushed scooter and the young woman skids across the road, bare legs, no helmet, the ruin of her dress and skin, and she tumbles past the cliff edge like a scrap from a plate, like luggage tossed from a balcony.

She falls past the cliff turning in air, her legs up behind her and spinning down toward the green sea and her green eyes aim up at the clouds. And the boy sits on the road far above, helmet on like a diver, his suit torn like sausage casing; the injured boy studies his broken legs and lives to know that he killed the girl on his scooter. An idea blooming in his head, quiet as the white towel that once fell from her hip. He crawls toward the edge.

Many Greeks sailed these seas before Christ did, before Christ became a fisher of men, pirate kings ran this coast and invasion fleets waited, nervous men in rows, planes filling a sky overhead with silk. So many voices calling, but the bus driver can't open the bus door, bent by the impact to the front of the bus. We can't get off the bus to stop him.

The young man in the torn black suit glances around our narrow arena, wall to one side, empty air on the other. The young man stares once more at us, at the bus that hit him, the bus that hit her. He raises himself on one good arm, pushes with his good arm, and like a crow he drops over into space to follow his girlfriend.

And at that moment I begin to understand the language of race and age and grief, that you can have everything at once and suddenly nothing at once, like an orange bullet train screaming past your platform in Dublin, blurred windows there in a streak you can touch and then just air ringing above the tracks, the train vanished, but that echo of reverb still hanging.

Both of them fly into space and both fall into the sea, Icarus and his pretty girlfriend hanging over the sea's glare and boats with white scar wakes and lean sails and the sea's ancient beaches pinned at the base of these stunning cliffs.

The beautiful couple falls into new worlds and now our giant plane rises toward another world, now I fly to the far west, we have liftoff, hundreds of rows of passengers thrust west in the night, air clubbing through the gnashing turbines and giant black wheels spinning as they tuck themselves up into the Boeing undercarriage, tires and turbines and rows of seated travellers strapped into a dome of stars and jet contrails and blinking lights that betray our route in the sky to those citizens who might watch below.

Our plane's route takes us high under a ghostly cupola, our plane moves inside the jet-blue ceiling of a vast starry chapel, but are we amazed?

Instead of being amazed, most of us choose to close our eyes, to drift into a preliminary form of vibrating sleep.

While held like a brain inside our plane's strange roiling motion I remember Pico toiling endlessly to serve us in the family hotel and I remember those workers digging out a cellar by hand and bucket and families unloading crates of fruit and peppers and loaves in the tin-roof market at dawn and O my love, will you and this Decembrists song always make me sad?

I remember the young woman washing the aqua tiles of my room with her hair (how I wanted her in my bed, the giant white bed floating in my tiny room, but I knew it would never happen) and in Rome they allow no highrises and my floor tiles mimic peacock colours of the sea, mirror the collapsing wave's complex codes and syne curve and the sea's secret inhabitants.

Luke the Apostle asks us, *Who is better, the one who sits or the one who serves?* Every day we take what they offer to us, the cabin crew, the maid, the baker, the waiter, every day we take what they give us, what they serve, muttering *grazie, grazie*, as they bend to our needs, our care, our eternal care.

High above that charmed parish of villas lit by milky Italian moonlight, high above our planet, we simply sit. We do not swoon or high five. We sit and we hold serviettes to our thin lips listening to George Jones (*put your sweet lips*) or Radiohead and at our plane's tiny windows our tiny eyes swivel in the crowded heavens above that turbulent benevolent boot of a peninsula (*a little closer to the clyster pipes*), above Mediterranean waters and above Spain and we devour our last spicy repast and we turn our heads to those serving and we wonder and hope, if we ask, meek as orphans, Might there be a little more.

And then we travel back to sleep and we travel back to the New World with ancient dreams of Rome's glory and our lack of glory and Janus giving you the eye in Trastevere and the black shamrock sprayed on a wall by my hotel and under the Vatican that naked woman showering on a rooftop and the Pope blessing her sunlit form.

Rome so beautiful, Italy so beautiful, the lunatic world so beautiful; we must embrace it purely, wantonly, for we are alive, we are free. Here is the plain truth: We are not dead at the bottom of a cliff, we are not suffocated by the volcano, no showers of stones and hot cinders fall on our heads, no knife is driven in our leg.

So why are we so sleepy? In the name of heaven, why do we not swoon, why do we orphans not high five over and over, why do we not dance and laugh every moment of each living day and night? I can't dance, but you know, just a suggestion.

JESUS MADE
SEATTLE
UNDER PROTEST

Sᴇᴠᴇɴᴛᴇᴇɴ rides, seventeen rivers. They drive tilted streets past OK Loans, Cinema X, the tunnels of exhaust. The left lane closes and no one will let you in. "Where'd you learn to drive, Sesame Street!?" Ray Savitch senses a lesson: punish the slow, the ugly, those from out of town.

At sea level, Ray climbs from the snake-coloured Galaxie, thanks the driver. "Good luck," says the driver. Ray brushes his teeth in a Union '76 and spits blood with toothpaste, sink speckled, striking. Some days it gets hard to drag yourself from the puzzle of sheets.

Ray stands above a shore; ceaseless ferries bisecting the bay, wakes like scar tissue, Warrior Peaks looming as salt heaps across blue chop.

Yachts heel, sails brushing sea. Port-holed shanties perch a line between eelgrass and air. Pink boathouses yaw in sunlight, emitting snatches of hillbilly fiddle, the aroma of coho. A day that makes it worth the mildew.

Beneath sooty Alaskan Way a man strangles another. The man stops and the two converse. He begins strangling him again. Then the rock to the head. The rising tide does not lift all boats.

This spring things fell apart on the oil fields; a glut, the energy policy, shit and fan. They broke down the drilling derricks and trucked them south of the border to the Over-thrust Belt of Wyoming and Montana, Ray given his pink slip, every guy and his dog given his pink slip. "That's all she wrote," the last driver slamming the Kenworth's black door in disgust.

Leases expire and are not renewed. Stepping from a Bauhaus highrise, Ray holds aloft his hand on the Yellowhead highway, to roll through magpies and mustard and silver poplar, to wend his way south and west from the oil-patch boomtowns, from home and the thought of a winter without work, rising and falling across cordillera and glacial rivers and jackleg fences holding dreamy-eyed cattle.

Like a shutter, clouds close for the rains of winter. Ray figures it out: his savings from roughnecking are gone, cash from picking apples and peaches in the hot valley gone, the pittance from working the cattle ranch in the Cariboo gone. It is Halloween, it is the sea, the sun and moon pulling tides in brainpan and vein, cock rising to ask what day and what month, seeking solace in red hearts, in the distance to her navel, in going home. Toothless men swing off the Burlington Northern freights and ask for the on-ramp to Portland. Cherry Street. Studying women's shoes and hips.

Ray paid for his last woman at the Calgary Stampede, through the nose, an eventuality his immigrant parents failed to foresee in his Bible Belt youth. Wearing silver shades, oilworker Ray Savitch put his cock to the planet and the planet rolled and opened under him, hinging to take the stove-hot idol within, working Ray into sleep after sleep, an anvil off a cliff, but still this business of price is like hairs in your peach cobbler.

Time was Ray strummed a Spanish guitar, had a nice two-bedroom with a view of the river, had a thirty-year-old Buick, two-door, red with a white roof. En route to the Ma-Me-O dance, Ray rolled the Buick in the fields of spring. Sneeze and it's laid it in a corner of green oats, whitewalls spinning. The apartment and Spanish guitar fell away similarly, the Sunday brunch with mimosas. Now what? is his question. According to Immigration he is an alien. The unions have the Seattle docks; any way in there?

On Occidental, a man stops Ray.

"My name is Howard T. Melville from Chicago, Illinois." He speaks very quickly, lifting a long brown finger to Ray's chest. "I need to call my mama. Can you hep me please with a single dollar?"

Ray laughs at him. "You're asking me?" There are scars at the man's eyes, his voice is soft. He wears white cowboy boots with zippers up the back. A Panama hat with a feather. Here he is swept west of the mountain chains, a foggy corner of this nervous republic, and asking me? "Call your damn mama collect!" Ray wishes to shout. Instead he mutters, "I'm not working."

"Neither am I brother!" Howard T. Melville exclaims in a happy falsetto.

"I'm not your brother."

Ray remembers the hustlers hanging out in the Chicago depot, middle of a winter night; men glaring, rolling coin at his feet. Does Howard know the gang that hassled him for money and smokes? "Gotta Kool my man, gotta Kool?" The freezing lakefront, the men busted at the urinals, the trench coats dealing dope from an alligator attaché in the ugly Burger King, while Ray waits and waits on the Greyhound to deliver him *please* to the ordered fields of the west.

"Man can you hep me please!" Howard begging now, uncool. The scars put Ray in mind of Little Walter, blowing genius blues harp, but killed in a southside bar brawl, laid low, head kicked in. Reminds Ray of the young ancient faces, the black and white photos on the Chess records. Howard and Ray move uncertainly under the brick of old bordellos and card rooms, posters for the Violent Femmes flapping everywhere. Gun Club is playing Norway Centre. Howard points to the stadium: "Seahawks in there this Sunday or they in

Los Angeles?" Now Howard stretches each syllable like rubber, searching for common ground, to be more than a faceless beggar, or a body found rolled in a carpet. "Los Anguh-leez?"

"Hell if I know," says Ray, preferring the man stays faceless so Ray is free to loathe him. Howard looks pissed off. Ray worries about offending panhandlers in these times; they're dangerous, shaky about their new calling. You see them hang in doorways, surf music loud as rain on the box, women friends with tracks between toes, under the tongue. How to find that big vein, Ray wonders, I could not put a needle in my mouth, does someone else help you?

Ray craves some eggs *sonora*. What he would give for a hissing T-bone, something with life in it. "Aw hell. Let's go for a drink."

"Now you're talking," nods Howard under his Panama. He begins singing. *Kansas City. Going to. Kansas City.* They take stairs down to a table of thick cedar.

"Your health." Ray drinks Rainier. Vitamin R.

"Uh huh," Howard having a glass of harder stuff.

A burly bearded man joins them. He wears denim, and a red bandana over the top of his head, pirate style. Sunglasses. Ray cannot see his eyes. Keeps trying to.

"Gentlemen," the pirate man says. "I don't take my shirt off in here out of respect for this place, don't show tattoos, I'm an Angel: Oakland, California. Can't show my colours or hundreds of brothers would be here and I'm not talking Gypsy Jokers. Angels! I tell them not to hang around and it hurts me. Jack lets me stow my stuff here, I respect that, but outside on the benches that's my turf, my people, understand and I think you do gentlemen, I'm Eye-talian Irish Indian."

Howard and Ray don't say a word. They drink quickly. The pirate's denim is immaculate. His sheepskin collar is white. His cheeks are smooth, tanned deeply under the sunglasses.

"Millionaires lock up the washrooms, where you supposed to go? Remember Jack, lights go down and they're gone we're still down here. This is the four corners, a mission on each street, the centre see, the web starts here …"

The pirate struggles for words, points to his palm as a map of the streets around them. His index finger is gone, reminding Ray of the rigs, bits given to the machine.

"Like a black widow sending lines all over the city from right here! Know what I mean and I think you do, gentlemen."

"Yeah," say Howard and Ray uneasily. They drink even faster and eye the exit.

"I have seven, hey I have women, but this is different, the brotherhood, the *brotherhood*, IT'S IN THE BLOOD SEE, I'm a Hell's Angel!" The pirate shouts. "I'm Eye-talian Irish Indian! Joliet! Ten years seven months four days. Joliet! Q. Folsom. Nineteen years!"

Tense, Ray studies the bulky man's build and boots, in case he must fight him. It has gone ugly over nothing. Big dark boots. Howard irritated, his long-awaited drink turned evil.

"See this is the black window, uh, widow, web, fuck …" The pirate believes he is being deep, but is losing the words. Ray stands to leave.

"You want to lay some money down, man?"

"I'm stony," answers Ray.

The ex-con glares with his glasses. "Get away, get outta here!" The pirate stands menacingly. "You people. You see brothers on the road—leave them alone!" he shouts as if Howard and Ray had approached him, and not the opposite.

"Sure thing," says Ray. They take their empty glasses to the bar and go up some stairs.

"Thought that sucker was going to beat on us," says Howard.

"Nice quiet drink. Wish Joliet would take him back."

"Got to go see a man about a dog." Tide beats in flooded chambers beneath the low streets. Clouds the colour of herons, black evergreens, Scandinavian gloom.

"We see you."

Ray hasn't eaten, has a vision of himself being rolled somewhere, caught with others in the Depression, a post office mural, a Hopper painting, in the USA. *Think positively,* Ray counsels himself. *As what we came for eludes us, so we will replace it. At the food bank there is cheese. Hot coffee and three-bean salad in those cheery church basements!*

Someone passes and Ray sniffs rich weed. Sensimilla? Maui? Ray peers to the cupped hand, the Pierre Cardins and V12 Jaguars bought with cocaine, Quaaludes, methamphet-amines, methaqualone and real estate, cash in shoeboxes, sultry women waiting in Italian restaurants. A blonde! Kissing a neck. This is not the fucking Depression. I will not line up for handouts, gnaw the bureaucrats' cheddar. There is a bone stuck in my throat. I want, I don't know, something.

By brick missions, Chinese grocers, the Merchant's Café, taverns of pickled eggs and yellowed popcorn, Ray walks briskly. A town within a town, copses of bums talking privately, voodoo harmonics. Men with coughs shove at tavern doors; stevedores and loggers and Alaskan fishermen with eye patches and beards, bright socks and metal crutches. No more handouts, vows Ray. He turns twice to see if anyone follows, turns by the South End Steam Baths, drawn to the long piers' cadence of whitecaps and wood pilings, the cranes, trucks' airhorns bleating and men living under the Interstate in a tangle of bottles and sodomy, strangling each other and Ray backs up slowly, the wind cold off the water, backs up to the totem and the souls huddled under the dripping pergola.

Mountains hang in the clouds, pale split ranges each side of the horseshoe inlet, snow dropping this instant into the passes, the white volcano floating at his back, climbers lost up there now as he stares, hidden to each other. At this spot in July 1897, $964,000 in raw gold landed from the north. This must have looked pretty to them, filled with promise. Safe harbour.

Men at the piers plumb the depths for yellowtail, squid. They pass sea-green bottles along the rail. Eagle scouts keep turning up bodies in the riverbank brush. Cormorants hunch like old men on logs broken loose from the booms, moving on winter tides and November storms. A man plays violin expecting change, a hubcap on the walk.

At 4 p.m. the girder crews descend, head home in their helmets, warming Ray with the thought of money made by balancing like gods over the citizens. Ray made as much with the diamond drills and thirty-foot pipe, working the grave-yard tower, twenty-one days on, fifty-six hours off. Ray misses the tumult of the drilling floor, pipe hooked on the catline and coming in the V-door, spinning chain, wracking the the Kelly back, mud and mosquitos and black flies, the sweetness of double-overtime, of all-night poker. Ray misses the red Buick. A real cock-coach, a leasehand called it. Ray wishes he had his Buick, or even a skeletal moped, streaked with oil. Anything from 1955.

Guitars in a warehouse, the Ramones's "I Wanna Be Sedated." People in costume cross the square, devils kick pumpkins apart, a weird mist hasn't burnt off all day.

One head bowed while a hand fondles it. Looking for lice? Ray approaches and hears Saved, Jesus, Amen—words like that. The men draw smirks from those passing in London Fog and Old Spice. The head lifts and it is Howard T. Melville, try-ing Jesus on the mainline. His slight grin says I'll try anything once brother. You know it. What do I know?

Ray in a room with her in the American Hotel, the view of chimney-pots and roofs and misty mountains reminding him of northern Europe. She works at the theatre part-time. The patchwork quilt falls to bits under them. Traffic flies past the curtains, lifted on Railroad Way. A glance at sixty-five, her face at the glass. Men fall in the square below as if hit by wind.

"I picked up a lot of mushrooms last week. Fell asleep in mushrooms, dreamt of mushrooms." She smiles. "Not those kind of mushrooms." Green eyes. She tries to erase the mist on the window. They are uncomfortable.

"I remember on Halloween, when I was little. My ma always dressed me as a clown. What am I doing down here? Any idiot can do this. I'm pure sick."

She has a small dresser, mirror etched with flowers and tendrils. Walls decorated with pictures of horses and on her nightstand a photo of her father, *The Complete Poems of Thomas Hardy* and an empty can of Coors. On the door a typed list of places to look for work. A Mexican throw rug on the wooden floor, dried flowers standing in a clay vase.

They are dragging Howard from the Whistling Oyster Tavern. Jesus didn't take.

"What's the charge! What's the charge!"

"No charge. This one's on us."

"Do you mind?" Shoelaces tied to the headboard and footboard.

"Not at all," says Ray. He ties her wrists and ankles. She is naked, face down in the bed, hair at neck, tapering back under his fingers, spine in shadow, skin surrounded by gold and white light, an arm in a shaft of light by the flowers.

"Too tight?"

"No."

The first feel of heat and skin.

"This is a new one to me."

"I need to be touched a while first."

Ray tracing with fingers, his hands around front, learning her long waist, hips flaring, arms and legs to the edge of her bed and then his weight on her lifting.

"That hurt?"

"No, that's nice." Boxcars stumble below, her hard breath driven into the pillow, cock and fingers in her, ear wet in his mouth, biting, the trill in her throat and to Ray a blow, the top seems to explode and he jerks like a fish on a barb, her wet scent and small sparks jumping in hair and nerves. Freed, she raises herself on both arms and takes a long look at him, then drops to the sheets exhausted. Drifting in and out of sleep, Ray half-awake with her breathing on his skin, the small bed, drifting, Ray remembers. Worked this week clearing land on the island, ferry across in the morning, chopping cord after cord of alder, now feeling every muscle in her bed, unable to bend his back, stretching, tiny bites on his forearms from underbrush insects, scratches from blackberry thorns. Money to drink with, day and night coming through like big tides. That last flophouse in Spokane, top drawer, seventy per, the manager Air Force Retired, still going on about the Warren Commission. The grassy knoll, Ray. There had to be another shooter. The manager neglected to introduce his young wife. "Never mind her, breech birth."

"I am not," she said, looking at Ray. He asked Ray to sign papers stating alcoholics belong in hospitals, not his hotel. Across from the depot: The Dead End Tavern. Ray thumbed to the coast. To this. Man, I never thought it would be ... this.

They try to sleep but freeway traffic keeps him awake.

"You eat?" she asks. No.

"I had creamed chicken and rice at the mission. You better take care of yourself," she says. "Have some cranberry juice. Vitamin C."

"I take care of myself. I'm down here, but I'm not like the others. I made damn good money on the rigs."

"That's nothing special. I got your number. People don't do this for the fun of it. That Reagan man going on about it, ticks me off something fierce. What is happening to my skin?"

Ray glances at the clock.

"Computers," she says. "That's what I have to get into. Computers are what's what now. My sister in the valley makes thirty-five thousand. What a mess I've made of my life," she says beside him.

There are distant bells and Ray feels steady regret. "Let's go for a walk," he says. No steeples visible, but bells. Rain on the ocean like flung coins.

"You bet," she says. "Been on all the other rides."

Ray leaves his duffle bag and bedroll in her room.

Under the bridge. "What's wrong with him?" A head anointed with flies. Newspapers. Pigeons cooing.

"Dead," answers a man over the body, making the word two syllables: "Day-id."

"I have phoned the police," he adds and a number of onlookers disperse. Ray sees Howard T. Melville on the dirt with his head stoved in. His zippered white cowboy boots are gone. The rock by the head. Humming Kansas City.

"You know him," she says. Ray understands. It happens fast and you're alone.

"A drink."

The authorities decide Howard has fallen on the rock.

She kicks through maple leaves and looks at Ray. The clerks sweep the sodden leaves from the walk but next morning there they are, huge wet hands on the pavement, a smell like sardine oil and booze working the neighbourhood. Ray imagines he has children and they are dead. He wants a tribute to what can be hidden, to the sweet conjunction of legs, an Iowa nursing student in sensible white shoes, Rene, stuffed animals, hammer and tongs, mean head unlocking his jaws and allowing sleep, dreams.

"Old Ed in there will give you a very fine cut for three."

She walks to her theatre job and Ray gets his thinning hair cut by Ed. In Pioneer Square the upwardly mobile mix with the palsied heads and the dead-in-the-water. The rich rattle on in the EBCO bookstore: "Herb's flying to DC. The Cultural Committee does not want him to go, his emotional situation is a total mess. We all had sushi, everything was real strange, oh look at those darling futons!" Art galleries open and close around their whims. Their feet are killing them.

A tall merchant marine pokes his head in the door: "Say, do you know the way to the shipyard? This way?" The man drops hash on the barber's floor, a piece from his palm the size and shape of a hockey puck, now rolling on the floor collecting hair. "Going cheap," the man says, chasing it, and he and Ray laugh. "What the hell is that?" asks Ed the barber. The strange Asian green, soft as spring fields. Scissors stopped.

From the square's wet stones a child stares, rock doves crawling his lap in a purple-grey mass, as if feeding from him. His eyes stare from a shirt of birds.

Elsewhere tonight, thinks Ray, kids are getting their good things; Milky Ways and caramels tossed in pillowcases for Halloween. At The Bread of Life Mission men and women line up early, sheepish. *Come Unto Me* spills the neon, like a bar sign. Some lean by the bookstore awnings, pretending they are not poised hungrily for the instant those doors swing at six. They doff hats passing through the door, as if into a country church.

Ray cannot take the thought of joining the crowd, entering that narrow portal, mouthing words at the piano.

Ray walks by and she is with someone else. Ray worries he is drinking too much.

"I can control it," the guys say. "Some can't don't you know." They pour another shot down their throat.

Ray sees her at breakfast with a younger guy, joking and whispering over the table. Some older women look at Ray but it is early and he doesn't know what to do; he hasn't brushed his teeth or put on underwear. They stare brazenly at the outline in his cotton trousers. A new age.

Where the Wobblies were shot, where the old sawmill was below the original Skid Road, where the statue of the Indian chief stands by the streets that don't meet.

He reads the paper alone, killing time, drinks Irish Breakfast tea, wishing he could think of a way to talk to the women at another table, instead of waiting for night to start again in darkness, reeling in the gulf of green liquor and the taste of that woman denied to him, mumbling into the cold pay-phone, the goddess of thin dimes. Is this the one? How will he know? Breathing slowly and cursing.

"Got enough?" asked Howard at the time. "Let's get the juice. What you want for drinking?"

"I used to bring her chink food," the other man said. "You know those little containers. I was driving with the others you know, man I had a red canoe, prettiest little bird dog, things come and go big fuckin' deal right, but you know what I've got, you know what I've got and if you don't mister I feel sorry for you."

"Man you got dick you ain't got dick. What a day."

"What are you saying to me?"

"You and me, us and them, what a circus, how much we got man is what I'm saying. Been one hard hard day."

"Don't get my dander. Now is now right, a chance comes by you take it or leave it right? I don't know frankly. Day comes chink food don't cut it and you're drinking with some spade. Did you know her? Where she went? No. You don't."

"Hey I don't know her from Adam, you're not from Chicago, just count up the change and let's get it and get under The Way and kill it alright?"

"Don't patronize me," the man said to Howard. "Here, we got enough coin to do it right. We'll get it done just don't get my fuckin' dander or I'll brain you so help me. Have your guts for garters."

"Ya ya, big talker," said Howard.

Ray is walking. A sidewalk creature, yellow-eyed, hirsute, rises as if from the dead.

"I gave at the office," says Ray.

"You and me," it whispers, "we go way back." It comes on, a partner in a weird contra dance. Ray pushes at it. Don't come unto me, Jack. Ray kicks at the advancing creature. The sole of Ray's Raichle boot splits under the toe. Things are being unglued, now the rain will get in. This places Ray near tears. The thin edge of the wedge.

"Trick or treat," rasps the creature, rolling, tasting pavement block. "Halloween apples," clutching his ragged groin.

Ray runs guiltily. They have forced my hand. Lungs pushing hard. They have driven me around the corner, Ray bounding marble steps to the gas jets and the waitresses' bone structure, the brass breath of the oyster bar, laddered walls of Irish whiskey.

Ray, in a maze of marble, procures New Zealand lager, platters of bay shrimp and salmon on a bed of greens, mussels and clams with julienne vegetables simmered in dry Chablis, butter, garlic and thyme leaves. Fat loaves that scald the tongue.

"How is everything?" his waitress asks.

"Delicious," he replies, both of them smiling. Ray likes her and he is lonely. This is her first week. Last spring she was Miss Missoula. Antelope ate in her yard. Now barristers pinch her, leaving tips and room numbers. Howard T. Melville's ghost and his gang pass outside in their costumes. There is a quarter inch of glass. I know which fork to use, I eat slowly and consider each dish lovingly, I am a real sucker for waitresses. Ray decides he has fallen for Miss Missoula and when he is solvent, when say his blood count is more impressive, he will return to woo her and walk at sunset, comforting each other with tales of their honesty and past suffering and in the flat fields she'll pull him down to snap the stalks, mingling his blood with her honeyed skin of apples, her naked ribs floating from the long rope of her backbone. Ray knows he is not being realistic. He pulls the fire alarm.

A golden fat bouncer appears and growls tersely over the shock of bells: "You're a funny kind of duck."

Ray recalls the oilpatch paycheques squandered in places like this, paying these big men's salaries. "Correct," he replies and a crowd flies conveniently between them. Ray makes his way to the golden doors, some of the well-heeled stumbling at the steps. A hand at his arm and Ray swings an elbow, feels a tiny nose give way and she drops to the floor, her legs spread wide, ice-blue underthings peeping and blood pouring in ugly syrup from her nose to her lacy blouse.

"Oh no," Ray says, not believing. She peers at the tiles between her stockinged thighs. Jesus now I have hit a woman I have struck a girl, Ray thinks, and the crowd, whitefaced as Herefords, pushes him through the gold doors, firebells clanging above.

In the narrow street the patrons mesh with a larger crowd moving to the stadium with basketball tickets and pennants and children in Halloween masks.

Ray strains to peer over heads and sees the fat man lift Miss Missoula from the French tiles, her black skirt high off her legs and his hand pressing her bosom. *Get away from her*, Ray thinks. Her face bleeds crimson into his shoulder. The bouncer glares from left to right and Ray struggles to turn back, to wrest the woman from this lout, from the rainforests and mildew benches, to go home with her to the heartland, cruising close together in a high Chevy Powerglide, a yard of sweet ozone shaking under the engine on a Great Plains backroad, to eat game hens and steelhead and Saskatoon berries under skies not cloudy all day, to jump in an iron bed at sunset, but no cigar, Ray is accepted by the fat-bellied fans and taken. Another is lost to him. They press like range cattle before a winter storm to the whiskey-coloured dome, the cement breast, the here and now of the sellout crowd, the broker training field glasses on a corn-blonde cheerleader, bleacher and hawker, pale mother, lit portal. One is tempted to just keep moving, to drift with the feel of earth underfoot.

Hi will have to collect his bag and bedroll.

The streets that lead from the harbour: Jefferson, James, Cherry, Columbia, Marion, Madison, Spring, Seneca, University, Union, Pike, and Pine. JCMSUP: Jesus Christ Made Seattle Under Protest.

Geese go south, salmon move on autumn instinct into tributaries. Men and women wander a shore of rubble, lie on seats staring sideways at the blood-black inlet, separate islands, dreaming of an ocean's riches, of Alaska and Asia, sailors' payrolls, trawlers, treasure. Above in the rain and oxygen, sedans blow past without beginning or end.

Ray studies the passengers, balanced on their splashing radials, as if they are from another land. Rosaries knotted around rearviews, staring straight ahead at the river of tin, the rose constellations of tail lights. They lean on fast food, on the Bible, on the horn, burn the fossil fuels Ray drew from the earth. There is no brotherhood. You walk the planet and hammers dance off heads and the women try to cure us at home. *I'm gone motherfucker, you killed me.* Everyone with the same thoughts. *I'm gone sister, I'm gone dinkeyes, I'm gone daddy gone.*

"I'm gone," Ray says, "I'm nowhere."

The road lifts him over the mills and steeples of a Lutheran city, over mouths open in lost hotels of crucifixes and radio tubes glowing like morning planets, over the wild ferns and roses and whores of Pike St. Market.

Night's traffic crosses the roofs, the continent, the century, again and again, on a journey home. No one uses signal lights, they change lanes without warning.

DANCING NIGHTLY IN THE TAVERN

THE HORSE surges sideways to fill Luke's vision. He feels the heat of its sides, reads the nicks in its winter coat, rolls from the hooves and fetlocks he had been checking, in the corner of his swimming eye sees Woody's skinny shadow climb the buckskin from the fence, sees as if from underwater, thinking, *No, ride the pinto, this fucker's not been rid all winter.*

Woody laughing: "He's a woolly sonuvabitch!"

"Crazy bastard," mutters Luke, Woody rocking above, sky the colour of ice, Woody on the back, dark against the sky, strands of light, horsehair on the wire, Woody laughing like before the deaths, until his leg is raked down the barbwire tearing denim and skin, his face clenched, twisted mouth cursing, eyes furious. The gouged flesh open, visible, as the frayed white threads soak to pink.

"You hammer-headed cocksucker," hisses Woody, pounding the horse's big head, pulling the reins back until the buckskin's yellow-green teeth are bared to the slobbery bit.

The horse dances backwards, head erect, refusing to clear the fence, rump lowered, then hind hooves floating up in clods of wet ground and smashing back. The horse can smell him.

Luke pushes the wall of flesh, shoving it finally from the barbs, the shot strands of light and black hair caught, the buckskin rearing. Woody scrambling in the mane and hooves slam to earth, Woody's teeth clamping with a click, eyes closed and head rolling, snapping. The gelding contorts impossibly, heaving Woody off balance, one arm waving as if in greeting. The hind legs kick out, the back rises up, and Woody is free into the air over the Austin-Healey and flooded summerfallow.

Luke picks up the hat, hands it to Woody. The horse smells it on Woody, Luke knows.

Woody limping to the car, his bottle. "You ever want to de-nut that fucker let me know," he says, taking a swig.

"It's a gelding." The buckskin tongues the blue salt lick innocently, but a glare in the eye betrays it.

Why would anyone put a well in such low ground, wonders Luke. The bucket drags up streaming water, full of bottles of Calgary Export, his hand cold tugging the rope, the freezing metal handle. Luke pours water into the claw-foot bathtub that serves as a trough for the horses. The water is dirty with spring runoff. Woody hugs the beaded bottles to his chest, limps uphill to the crooked cabin with Luke trailing, shoves his shoulder into the door, swearing as it scrapes over the crooked wooden floor, a blond arc cut in the dirt-coloured planks.

Woody paws a pack of matches, lights up, coughs the first jawful into his closed fist. Leans back in the wooden chair, smoke shrouding his face, thuds his cowboy boots on the sill of dead flies.

Luke finds the Mercurochrome and Woody winces even before it is applied to the wound. A torn shirt for wrapping. Woody's head twists in the jacket's sheepskin, checking out the tiny cabin and, through the grimy window, the yard; the mess of the flooded drive, the pickup with glass kicked in by a stallion, the rusting tractor and harrow. The stands of tamarack he knew are gone, cut into fenceposts.

His mickey of five-star whisky is finished now, the sardine can crammed with butts, no filters, smoked to the ends. Luke fries eggs and beans on top of the wood stove, iron clanging loudly against iron. Woody swallows his food noisily, nearly choking, broken yolks running into the beans' brown sauce, a bead of yellow caught on his chin. With both hands he grips the emptied plate like a steering wheel and licks a pale tongue over the grooved surface.

"How are the oil rigs?" asks Luke.

Woody thrusts up a hand missing two fingers in answer. The hand stained the shade of the gelding's teeth. The fire snaps as they feed planks into the stove's belly.

"Money's good." He sucks his smoke. "I could get you on. You want to get on? I could get you on."

"Save much?" asks Luke.

Woody shakes his head with a bit of a snort, laughing smoke from his nostrils. "Spend exactly what I clear. Hit town with a grand and leave without a pot to piss in." He leans back. "You get hooked," he says, peering around as if for someone else, dragging dirty fingers through his curly hair.

"Didn't you have a job?" he asks Luke.

"I had a job." Working the summer and sere fall fighting fires with the Indians on the eastern slopes. When it got colder, the Indians stopped setting the fires and Luke was out of work. Woody opens another bottle.

Luke steps outside to the horses, the silhouette of the barn-shaped cabin leaning starkly in last light. A red-tailed hawk spirals the burnt stubble south of the cabin. Blackbirds harass the hawk, forcing it to the ground. Luke stares at the red-tail, the horse, its winter fat. Should be more fun trying to get a saddle on that broom-tail, he thinks.

"Long time since I've been on a horse," says Woody inside. "Bad winter. Damn near froze my ass off this winter."

"Same as always," says Luke.

"I don't know, seemed colder."

In the flat light Woody's flesh resembles dead wood. "Swear I'm going to quit these damn things."

At midnight Luke scrapes the chair back to stand.

"Stay up a while," says Woody, his eyes unfocused. "Come on. Stay a bit." The cabin creaks around them. Under the imitation grey-brick siding are the original logs, contracting, settling into the clay. The cabin is over one hundred years old, the cellar once used by rustlers to hide beef, a dirty rug now over the trap door.

Luke lays a mattress on the living room floor for Woody. Two blankets. As Luke lies in his loft he can hear bats scrabble in the rafters and walls.

A loud thump. Light glows from the kitchen. Woody, pitched from the rocker, lies on the floor, mouth parted a fraction, breath whistling in his nostrils. Cigarette burns scar the white table and floorboards around him. He takes a vague swing at Luke as he tries to rouse him. His lined face as grey as the tamarack posts they dragged in and burned. Luke attempts to drag him under the arms to the mattress. Scythes of sweat soak the armpits of Woody's jean shirt.

"Christ you weigh a ton." Luke gives up, wraps the cowhide around him where he lies.

Later Luke wakes in the darkness, a cowboy boot cuffing his face, the close smell of roughout suede. Woody rolling into the bed. Woody's head at Luke's feet, Woody's belt and pants bunched at his ankles, caught there by his boots.

"For Christ's sake, Woody. Sleep on the fucking mattress!"

Woody grunts, swears in reply. Luke moves against the cold wall as far as he can. Later Woody falls from the cot. The shirt-strip bandage tinged red. Again Luke swathes him in the cowhide, adding a striped Hudson's Bay blanket around his shoulders. "You sorry bugger."

Luke wakes after dawn, Woody is up already, perched coughing on the purple couch. He wears only a shirt, unbuttoned, his eyes squeezed shut, head and chest shaking, a fist clenched to his lips, rocking as if still on the buckskin. Between coughing fits he gazes blankly into corners, white skinny legs apart, the one bandaged, the shadow of hair under the shirttails, his cock shrunken.

It is too cold to get up, decides Luke in his blankets. He hears the truck start up, but sinks back into sleep.

Slashed plastic beats at the glass. Using the dipper, Luke drinks from the water bucket, then fills the washbasin. Half-stunned flies buzz in the soapy water, graze the dirty plates and silver. Luke rubs cold water into his face, fingers his hair back.

Shadowed with several nights' beard, Woody's face glares from the doorway; dark and white skin puffy, the inexact shade of the cloud cover.

"How'd ya sleep?" Luke asks, bending to peer in the tiny cracked mirror.

"Bad. Wake up sick and can't get back to sleep. Lie there waiting." He sits, then gets up, paces. "The guy at the camp did some tests." He picks up a *Western Horseman*, glances at the blue cover and then chucks it. "I'm supposed to be in Charles Camsell right now but fuck if I'm going to lay round some friggin' hospital and get poked at ..." Woody walks to the cold stove, arms tight around his chest.

"Cold?" asks Luke. Camsell is the TB hospital in the city, he thinks, Indians mainly. Fifteen to a smoky shack; them and TB are like that.

"Fucking freezing," says Woody, wiping his nose on his sleeve, trailing a dark stripe on the denim cuff. The air pink under the clouds in the distance. "Just might clear up."

Down past the well the horses scratch at a last bit of snow. Woody cradles a half gallon from the Austin-Healey, pours wine in two teacups.

Luke wanders onto the porch, a breeze in his damp hair. His pickup is backed up to the porch, a small freezer in the back. Woody walks out, a grin cut ear to ear.

"Stole it, off a stoop. Some mobile home other side of Max Solbrekken's Bible Camp." He chuckles, but it foams into a cough somewhere between his throat and mouth.

"Well kid, you said . . . you said you like your beer nearly froze."

Hands in his pockets, Woody spits into the hedge, leaning on one wall as Luke opens the freezer. Inside are frozen loaves of homemade bread, whitefish from Pigeon Lake, packages of moose, beef and venison—their brown wrapping labelled with felt pen. A woman's handwriting. Luke thinks of her detailed work, her time, the pen and butcher paper. He climbs behind the freezer and pushes it easily from the truck to the porch wall.

Woody plucks two T-bones from the freezer. "Dinner," he announces formally, holding the meat aloft like a trophy, his chest shaking in his shirt.

Cloud banks bulge, porcelain. A slate-blue goshawk, male, clings to a dead willow. A rank of aspens and willows shake in a windbreak around three sides of the Conjuring Creek Cemetery, bark on the trunks cropped by deer. Branches form cracks in the sky, reminding Luke of the inside of his parents' china teapot. Woody drinks wine. Magpie and hawk nests hang in the higher boughs.

Luke points out the truck window to the back of the grave-yard.

"Saw a lynx in there Christmas day."

"That a fact."

"Lot of deer this winter."

Tiny white fences hug some of the graves. Flowers sprawl on two recent Cree suicides. Crooked and chipped stones are scattered like broken teeth across the clearing. Most have simple crosses.

"You got a lady?" Woody asks, scratching his chest between buttons. Where one pearl button is gone, a safety pin hooks his shirt together.

"No. They all get knocked up by high school. Or they fuck off to the city."

Condensation beads on the insides of the cracked glass, shivers down the window in rivulets. Woody traces his name with a yellow finger, then rubs it out.

"I always meant to put flowers on theirs," Luke says, nodding into the graveyard. "Seemed like the thing to do."

"I guess."

"Never knew where to get any though."

Smoke from Woody's cigarette drifts into Luke's nostrils. Clouds wreathe Woody, reminding Luke of the bushfires fought in the hills above Brule.

"Yablonski's burnt. Watched all that booze go up."

"Where's he now?"

"Motel."

"You drink all those?" Woody pointing to the plastic stars taken from Five Star bottles and pasted on the dash. "You drink those?"

"Nah. Took them off old bottles in the yard. I liked the way they looked on your dashboard."

"Yeah, but . . . that's not the point. You drink them and then you can put the star up."

"Okay, I'll take them off."

"Don't bother now. Hey, leave them, kid leave them."

Luke peels the gold plastic stars and hurls them into the ditch, leaves the window down and stares out, breathing in cold solid air. Woody finishes the wine, then brings beer up from the back of the truck. He opens two on his belt buckle and hands one to Luke as a peace offering.

"You wanna look at the graves or anything?"

"Nah, let's just sit."

They sit. The windshield is spidered with cracks spread to all corners of the glass by gravel back roads and long freezes. Things get brittle, shook up. Things fall apart, thinks Luke.

Dusk falls and they stare into the dark windshield. Luke counts the bumps on the bottle, noting how many times it has been shipped back to the brewery in Edmonton. Five and they smash it, he is told. Hank wonders who else has emptied this bottle.

Headlights flare in the rear-view and Woody turns, the seat creaking beneath him.

"Head her out. Might be my friends the Mounties." Woody rolls his window down quickly and throws the bottle over the top of the cab toward the opposite ditch. The bottle shatters against the wooden stock racks, raining glass in the headlights. "Damn, forgot the stock racks."

Luke drives down the All-Weather Road, past the old creamery and turns off overlooking Empty Creek. After the truck is shut off, the engine chugs violently. Luke keeps a boot hard on the brake pedal and lets the clutch out. The motor stops with a jerk.

"You did some time?" Luke asks.

"In the Fort. Got picked up running smoke from Vancouver." He sits staring straight ahead. "Fuckers must've set me up." His mouth a level slit, a crack in dry kindling.

"What's it like?"

"The Fort? Fuck. Like anywhere else, its own little world. Fun if you like guys and tattoos. Hey kid, is that town cop, what's-his-face, still around?"

"No. RCMP took over all the smaller places. They cruise by every Thursday. We all behave on Thursday." Luke carries more beer up to the cab. "Want to check out town?"

"Just sit," Woody mumbles, a smoke between wooden lips.

After the case is gone they decide to go in after all, to pick up more beer at the hotel.

Moths spit lazily into the lure of their headlights as the pickup rumbles down the Correction Line, the moon steaming from a cloud, shining, a chrome hubcap rolling from a car wash. The marquee on the hotel states: Black Stallion Hotel— Dancing Nitely in Tavren.

"Learn to fuckin' spell," comments Woody. "Hey, I didn't tell you about my new gun. Guy in Oregon made it for me. Does nice work."

They tramp across the ugly tavern to buy a cold case, staring into the noisy farmers and Indians, into the dusty mirrors. Woody forces money on Luke for the beer. The touch of the barmaid's hand giving Luke the change. Luke looking back at her as they leave.

A crowd is circled in the gravel. Walking by they hear breathing, blows and grunts, someone's heavy fall and the dance going on; drunk boots kicking the gut, the head, *pock-pock* like blows on a rotten melon. Three older farmers pull the big guy away and a skinny kid lies face up in a pool of yellowish puke with swirls of blood in it. One eye looks broken open.

Woody yanks Luke's arm hard, drags him to the truck, the rough edge of the beer case banging Luke's thigh. They hear the skinny kid is up from Ontario. Looking for work on the oil patch.

"Stupid fuckers." The moon wobbles in the clouds, a vacant socket.

"You used to fight a lot," Luke says. Woody is small but tough, what is called wiry.

"Used to," cracking open the fresh case. Hunches in the cab fuming smoke and sweat, inhaling half a bottle in a swallow, half a cigarette with a furious drag. "Get me out of here."

Woody breaks Luke's favourite chair. They are Indian leg wrestling on the floor of the cabin, lying flat, head to feet, raising one straightened leg once, twice, a third time and locking it around the opponent's thigh. Luke slips him over to win and stands, off guard.

Woody punches him. Luke lands hard on the chair and the legs splay, collapse, both of them yelling like idiots, mouths open without a bottle. Luke stands shouting and Woody shoves him once more and Luke's boot breaks through his father's old gut-string guitar, Woody stomping out to the car with Luke after him trying to shake the splintered guitar from his foot.

Outside the rising sun is crooked and red and Woody's Austin-Healey revs and shakes free of the mudhole where the driveway was last fall.

Luke watches the slate-blue car disappear. He blinks into the new sun, his cats chasing cabbage moths that flutter between their paws from the dew-damp clover. Tosses the guitar on the porch roof, hearing the engine for a minute after the sports car has slipped from view.

After the ground has thawed and the transmission gone Luke rides the gelding into town; pays some bills, pick up a few things at the Co-op and Wilson's IGA. Luke had hired on at the gravel pit, running the crusher for two weeks, but the truck's tranny seized and he had no wheels. Had to quit. There was a promise of overtime. Dumb luck, he thinks.

The gelding is no problem; it knows Luke, the sure smell. His legs.

The store is dim, low ceiling and pine floorboards. Wilson thinks Luke has to know already, fills in a crony, an insurance man in a hunting jacket.

"Two bouncers up there in Grande Cache. Kicked the shit out of him and threw him through a couple picture windows they got in the new mall there."

Luke moves in the aisle as if hit with a rope. Turns to listen. The insurance man shakes his head, places a pinch of Red

Chief in his jaw. The grocer's soft hands tally the sales, ring up the measly cans of tuna, the Kraft Dinner.

"Kid, I'm real sorry," he says.

Luke bites from a stale Oh Henry!, looks around. There is no taste to the chocolate. The store smells of aged wood, polish, Ukrainian sausage.

"Those two fellows been up before the judge before," Wilson continues. "Mark my words, if they don't get it good this time." The grocer looks up from behind his apron at Luke walking outside into the light. "Don't you worry," the grocer calls, still sticking Luke's order in a cardboard box.

Luke buys a sealer jar of homebrew from Yablonski, the displaced bootlegger, at his new quarters in the Sail-Inn Motel. Room zero. They sit drinking as the town's clapboard streets ease into streaked darkness.

Luke steals into one of the grocer's cars after midnight, a repossessed Chev. The ignition protrudes and can be turned by hand without a key. Off you go. Yablonski promises to take the gelding back to Luke's corral in his GMC. Driving north Luke leaves the last farms, enters scrub pine.

By dawn Luke wheels into Woody's last camp, an ugly clearing of trailers and 4 X 4 crewcabs. Roughnecks wander muskeg in crusted jackets, clutching gloves and hard hats, looking too tired to stare, coveralls blotched in slime blown from the drill's shaft.

A foreman is in a tiny office drinking coffee. He gives Luke a final pay slip, some cash and letters, and a battered horsehide grip, bound by binder twine. Wind rocks the panelled trailer. Luke drinks black coffee, signs the papers for the paymaster, gives away the Chev.

The Austin-Healey is stalled in gumbo to the axles and oil pan. The foreman waves a D-9 over to haul the car to solid ground. The bulldozer clanks over the muskeg, blue-black

smoke jetting from twin stacks above the earmuffed opera-
tor. The exhaust system tears away as the car is dragged.

"Woody worked for me for years!" shouts a toolpush, leaning over Luke in the Healey's low driver's seat. The engine idles
high, deafening without a muffler. "He was a good worker," the
toolpush shouts. Some words are lost. "Fell off a triple rig onto
his head. Sonuvabitch walked away! You want on the oil patch,
no sweat. Ask for Carl!" he finally yells, slapping the muscled
fender. The name RUDY is taped on the front of his hard hat.

Luke cannot keep his eyes open. "What about these bouncers?" Luke asks. The wind everywhere, another season imposed
over the muddy muskeg.

"Legal channels, let's say." The man leans. "Son, I know
you're itching. One question: you going to fuck over yourself
because of this? It'll be taken care of." He leans even closer,
stubble nearly brushing Luke's face. "You should've been here
few nights back. Woody's Newfie buddies had one of their
wakes. Man oh man. Sat up all night drinking Screech and tore
up the bunkhouse so bad we had to haul the thing right the
fuck out." His eyes look sad, crazed, but Luke cannot decide
if the man is affected by the loss of Woody or the trailer. Luke
stomps the gas to the floor.

It is cold and loud driving the Healey. Luke kills a mickey
of Five Star he finds in the suitcase. The horsehide reminds
Luke of Woody struggling to stay on the gelding. There is also
the heavy pistol Woody spoke of, a .45 bored out to take a .410
shotgun shell. With some flame and smoke it can punch eighteen holes in a door or fender. An illegal gun and Luke doesn't
much like it; it affects the balance of things. It could be handy,
he thinks. The radio plays Lawrence Welk crooning *Life is a
holiday on Primrose Lane.*

"Like fuck it is," the bottle thrown against the dials. The
radio quits with snapping sounds, broken glass littering the
dash, the seats, Luke's lap. He laughs. "Cracking up," he says.

Steering with one hand he leans to retrieve the gold star, accidentally cutting his index finger on the chunk of glass it is attached to. The car veers from side to side between the ditches, drifts as he peels the star from the shard of glass, sticks the star on the dashboard, a bubble of blood on one point.

Looking at the star, the road, Luke realizes he has Woody's bottle, his car, his pistol; he glances in the mirror expecting Woody's face. The same blue eyes. Legal channels! Jesus. Who will take care of it if not me?

Luke drives fast thinking, I don't know that I can kill some joker even with what they have done to someone close, family, but there is a clear need to get even, eye for a fucking eye. He has never felt what it is to be a coward. He tries hard to imagine what Woody would have done back before he was sick or what he would have Luke do now, and Luke doubts they are one and the same thing.

It is some miles to the T intersection where Luke must turn one way or the other. He wants to stop in a bar for coffee, a beer, pick a fight, pick up a woman, anything, but there's nothing here. Except for a pull to the side, Woody's Austin-Healey seems to pilot itself, the slate-blue machine unmuffled and powerful around the heir. Lobstick pines loom green-yellow, the same shade as the horses' teeth, as Woody's fist. The blurred trees line the only road cut over ridges of lodgepole and tamarack; the scaly conifers climbing right back up with the purple fireweed after each cyclic stripping by winter or seasons of fire.

GOOSE, DOG,
FISH, STARS

HERE are black antlers, cashews, a clock made of pool balls. "You should meet Olofson," the young bartender says after a while. His eyes dark, the skin around them unmarked.

"Why not," says Hank.

Olofson wears a bleached work shirt, has a bit of a beard, weather-beaten cheeks. He looks to Hank like a longshoreman, maybe a sailor. Second generation Swede, raised by the docks of dark Ballard. "Give me something that will sneak up on me," calls Olofson. "Leave me handicapped." He waves a muscular arm around.

The bartender pulls down a bottle of bourbon: Fighting Cock, the label says. "This is basically nutritious," he offers solemnly.

Olofson nods, pale eyes closed, head moving like a blind man's. Behind them the coast guard pilots shoot eightball.

"Don't I know you from somewhere?" speaks someone.

"I don't know," Hank says softly.

"This tastes terrible!" Olofson the sailor cries, eyes still closed, drinking it anyway. "Well, how do you like it here?"

"It's interesting," Hank says. Locals seem disappointed by his replies. Is he to kiss the ground every ten minutes? Hank thinks of the frigates that once called here, holds heavy with stone ballast, timber, or the silk trade. He wonders if Virginia is sleeping. They had argued earlier about a guy she had slept with in Wyoming.

"She's bummed," grumbles one of the pilots at the tables. "Hasn't talked to me since I had that Cat run into the side of her trailer."

"Never did find that marriage certificate. Got the dee-vorce papers though. Those I need!"

At 2 a.m. the doors are locked, but Hank and Olofson drink on, the bartender drawing them Red Hook gratis. The bartender reaches in a yellow box of Hav-A-Tampa jewels, lights up a bomber and passes it across the bar to Hank. "What the hell," Hank says, and has a toke. He imagines telling Virginia about it in their motel room.

"No clams this year," says the bartender in his smoke.

"Dead as doornails," says Olofson the sailor. "Took a backhoe to the beach. Zero. Nada."

"Oh," says Hank, feeling somehow to blame.

"Are you working right now?" they ask. The lights are dim, Los Lobos plays manic Tex-Mex accordion on the cassette deck.

"No. Not working." What had he been thinking of? Virginia. He feels sudden affection for her.

"It's bad right now."

"What is this stuff? Paint thinner?" asks Olofson, examining the bottle of Fighting Cock. "I think I've been damaged," he says holding his chest. He stares sadly at Hank.

"But you, you're both working?" asks Hank.

"Well, you know." They glance at each other. "This and that."

The joint is strong. It is cut with something, it makes itself known. Olofson lectures on about loss of the clamming season to the peninsula, about blackmouth salmon, about money or *chickie-pull* as he terms it, and about his dogpack theory of human behaviour.

"Think about it," Olofson the sailor says. "Like dogs. It explains everything. Even the clams."

Dogpack theory, I'll have to remember this, thinks Hank. The bartender touches his dark moustache.

"This one knows what we're talking about," Olofson says, nodding sagely. "Right? We're not rabble. Not everyone knows what we know." They study Hank.

It seems profound. Hank comes to believe that Olofson is the devil, in Port Angeles to talk personally with Hank about his dogpack theories. Hank is laughing and there are arrows in him: he is pinned to the bar at the knees and elbows. He is Saint Sebastian. Deer and antelope play. He is in his white pants. They keep staring.

"He liked that joint now, didn't he?" says Olofson the sailor. "I'm getting definite vibes from this one. He knows what's what." The accordion wheezes to a halt, pale air hanging.

Hank realizes they are after his ass. The handsome bartender and the grizzled sailor. They have the wrong man, he tells them. He can't stop laughing, but the boys don't find it so funny. "Why me," asks Hank. There was another, a dull servant with a broom. He pointed out Hank as sympathetic, likely, alone. And Hank stayed late with them, taking their drinks and smoke. Olofson flexes his biceps.

"Did you hear the one about the goose?" Olofson asks the bartender, pointedly not looking at Hank. "Seems there was two guys, want this same goose. In the tussle the goose got its head smashed in." His voice has anger in its edges.

"Gotta go," Hank says. "Don't like the parable," Hank says.

"He's gotta go," says the grizzled sailor to the bartender. "I guess he's not going to get physical." He seems disappointed. Hank finds the door.

"Watch yourself," says the bartender at the top of the iron stairs. "And whatever you do, don't say you're sorry. They all do."

Hank descends into the black alley. The door closes above. He walks warily to the front of the building, expecting cocks and knives under the skein of stars. He climbs up and crosses at the sidewalk. A dog howls by the quiet mill.

A black and white pulls out of the darkness of Front Street. For a moment Hank is relieved to see it. ID, says the policeman. Hank has none. "If you'll take me by my motel, I can show you ID."

The policeman runs his fingers over Hank's legs and torso. Hank gets in the back. He thinks about police shows on TV. This is not really happening. The plexiglass slams into place between them.

"Can we talk through this," Hank pointing at the plexiglass, an odd echo with his words now.

"Yes, go ahead." Hank realizes the cop feels a confession is forthcoming.

"No, just wondering, you know." Hank has been drinking since the afternoon. It is now 3 a.m. Plus the joint. Things go around but he gets hold of it. The cop mutters at his hand. The radio crackles a reply.

"Why are you interested in me?"

"Burglary. Not ten minutes ago. You fit the bill. Where you been?" The spine of the road bends.

"That bar."

"Closed an hour ago," counters the cop. Hank is wary of mentioning the two in the bar. Some alibi. He wonders about the two men: did they want to fuck him, or want him to fuck them? Just what is the etiquette?

"I know you from somewhere. Any record?"

"Speeding tickets, you know."

The tires hum uphill. The officer wears no hat. Hank studies the back of his head, his ears. Off in the distance squares change to triangles; the pull of perspective. Gravity pulls at Hank's face.

At the Flagstone, Hank steps inside to find the wallet in his other pants. Cheap Eddie is asleep in his bed. Virginia is awake, hugs Hank.

"Where were you?" she asks. "I was about to call the police." Hank laughs at this, tries to explain what has happened. He cannot stop laughing or slow his babble. He feels basically he is crashing wings, bull in china.

Outside with the police, Hank articulates slowly, politely. Like two different people, Virginia tells him later. In the light of the parking lot Hank shows his Canadian passport, driver's license.

"You smoke?" they ask.

"What, marijuana?" Hank asks, trying to sound innocent. Is this a set-up engineered in revenge by the sailor and bartender?

"Come on. Tobacco."

"No. No. I don't smoke," relieved it is not about dope. A second patrol car bumps into the lot, carrying a woman and a man in the backseat. Their apartment had been broken into. They woke to see the burglar. A Black policeman walks them past as Hank speaks with the first officer.

"Yes, that's him," they say.

The officers inform Hank that his age, build, beard and dark t-shirt all match the description. "You have the wrong man," Hank insists, as he had to the men in the tavern. This is getting old. Hank talks and talks with them, giving them Virginia's California plate numbers, their IDs, various numbers, names, addresses, cities.

"I'm convinced," says one uniform finally, the Black man. Which way? wonders Hank, what does that mean? And then they leave, leave him to go inside the room with Virginia. Cheap-Eddie has slept through it, dreaming of pieces of silver.

"I'll never sleep after that," Hank groans, lying beside Virginia.

"Talk to me," she says.

"What about?" Hank says.

"Talk to me," she says.

Hank passes out. She lifts and drops his arm several times but he is gone into whatever it is.

There is banging. "What the hell?" mutters Cheap-Eddie, blinking like a mole in his blankets. Hank opens the door. Two badges are held up. The older detective in a shiny suit that's hard on the eyes this early. "You want to get dressed and we'll talk," they say. The mountains look pretty behind them.

Hank pulls on loose pants and a shirt, talks with them on the hood of Virginia's MG. Sunlight glares off every plane. Hank feels at a disadvantage; he is pale, shaky, unrested. The detectives have showered, had their coffee and breakfast.

"I know you from somewhere," one says. "You play ball?" Virginia brings a glass of water. Hank is touched.

"I talked with the police last night. You have the wrong guy."

"We'd like to hear it again."

The plainclothes seems to look down on the uniforms. The B & E artist has done any number of jobs and they want to nail him so badly you can smell it. Hank will do in a pinch. They want him downtown.

The older one in the golden suit tries to come on tough. They have probable cause he says. He has a lot of laugh lines and his hair is greased straight back. He reminds Hank of a TV preacher. Or he played surf guitar in, say, The Ventures. The younger detective is blown dry, in a tasteful sienna suit. He seems apologetic and looks like someone Hank used to know. It will come to him. Hank's head feels a turn too tight. And what will the neighbours think?

"Can we see that purse," the older one pointing inside the MG. Of course it matches the one stolen, down to a lipstick smudge.

"Been in Port Angeles before, Hank?"

Now Hank feels the MG's California plates seem suspicious, as does the heavy flashlight given Virginia by a worried brother in San Diego. As do the tools in the trunk, ditto the tire iron, Hank's socks, anything. They get to you, thinks Hank. They say you did it, then you did it.

The detective rifles the purse, inspects Virginia's bank book. The gold suit shimmers.

"They can't do that," she says to Hank. They do what they want, thinks Hank. The veils drop lickety-split. Things become evident.

"Are you working, Hank?"

"No sir."

"Not working huh."

They take Hank to the ghost car. "Call my brother," Hank says to Virginia. Cheap-Eddie has not shown his face for fear it may cost him. "Call my brother in Victoria."

Hank is in the front seat this trip. They back onto the highway, the older detective at the wheel. How easily it happens, and what the hell is probable cause, wonders Hank. I was weaned in the suburbs: aren't I exempt from all of this?

"You keep your mouth shut some of the time. I like that a real lot," the older detective says, as if reading Hank's mind.

Farther west the street is blocked off for the annual salmon derby parade. There is a naked woman at a window. There are barricades and bowlegged Kwakiutl and Quillayute wander booths of beargrass baskets. Dogs run in circles.

"You smoke, Hank?"

"No. You have the wrong guy."

"They all say that. No offense or anything. Last week it was a woodcutter slit a hobo's throat along the river. Same deal."

The ghost car pulls in an alley and Hank assumes he's going to get roughed up. The older one walks with his head bowed to a dumpster, peers in it, spits or tosses something, Hank cannot tell. Looking for evidence? Planting it?

"What's he doing?" asks the younger detective from the back.

"You're asking me?"

"This'll get him." He slips his pistol from a shoulder holster, levels the gun at the window and shoots at the older detective. Hank jumps, his stomach paining him.

"Goddamit," yells the older man, "you firing off those blanks again? You didn't shoot it at him, did you? Jesus Christ!"

"I was just showing him," says the younger detective sheepishly.

"Well we have to account for every goddamn shell or the chief will have our ass in a sling. Every shell!" The older man fumbles in a small box, then throws the box at the man in the back seat. "The numbers better be kosher my man, or your ass is grass." He slams the car into gear, mumbling.

They back out of the alley fast and drive the one-way downtown. Snow-touched mountains move behind the brick buildings, reminding Hank of Wyoming, of infidelity. He can imagine the face she would make when he put it to her. Some stranger.

"Been fingerprinted before, Hank?"

"Yessir, with the railroad. You have a computer, right? Can't you feed me in and see if I'm clean?

"Only works if what you're giving us is straight."

"Did you know this is the world's largest fishing derby?" asks the younger detective. "Really super prizes."

"Whatever happened with that big blonde tart?" the other asks.

"Oh her. She discredited her testimony, no one believed a word. But I got a great deal on her Nova. With the divorce she's selling everything, going to Alaska, get away from it all."

"Well I tell you Anchorage is dog meat," says the older man. "Bumper to bumper with all the new cars and money, but nowhere to go. Terrible place for the family. Dog eat dog I tell you."

This can't be happening, decides Hank. He begins a gloomy meditation on chance, the greased passage from wrong place, wrong time, to shit creek and lack of paddle. If only he'd left the bar five minutes earlier, if only Virginia hadn't gone back to the Flagstone in a huff, if only he'd quit school in grade eight and gone into real estate. The real felon is likely in a sunny kitchen nook, forking up scrambled eggs and reading of his latest exploits. Hank feels peckish.

"I should at least get a breakfast voucher or something out of all this."

"Not from us," says the older man, grave as a fish.

Hank turns his eyes from the men and the mountains to the Strait of Juan de Fuca, past the tottering canneries and coast guard buildings, hears the thumping of a freighter clearing Ediz Hook, watches oystercatchers and curlews trot in the surf. Slime-green waves run in one after the other. One sneaks farther; the others follow. Dogpack theory. A heron seizes something in its dagger bill.

Hank understands this beautiful country has been made ugly for him.

He thinks of the couples moving on the sunburnt tides off Tongue Point, Cape Flattery; with their hooks and coolers of ice, searching for the main chance, the trophy salmon, the happy coincidence of bait to unsuspecting prey.

He thinks of the mix of currents and creatures, the pieces of the food chain. And over that sparkling blue stripe is Canada, the leafed islands just out of reach. Hank wishes to climb in a sloop with Virginia, drop the keel and become a dot on the horizon.

They lead him from the ghost car and he may as well be guilty for the way it looks. Tongues rattle, daughters drawn to fat mothers. A murmur of drums; the Port Angeles Rough Riders Marching Band and Color Guard bleats, prances in the parking lot, warming up for the big parade. Dragoon hats, tiny fishscale skirts in light and legs, bosoms and thighs lifting to the sun. Batons hang forever. Much of life here seems to involve parking lots, understands Hank.

Flags full of stars droop everywhere. *I hate marching bands*, Hank realizes.

Inside the building few uniforms lift their heads. Another wayward one, no big deal. They talk, laugh at a joke about Dolly Parton.

"I'm cutting out for coffee," says the older one to the younger detective. "You finish up here, alright Jimbo?"

Hank is fingerprinted in the hall. A man brushes his teeth at the water fountain.

"Sorry if my hands are cold," says the little woman in a uniform of blouse and skirt. "Some of them say my hands are cold."

She rolls black ink on a glass surface, takes Hank's hand in hers. Each finger and thumb is rolled in ink and pressed to the paper forms, to the squares.

"Sorry dear, let's try your thumbs again. I can't seem to get them right. See?" She shows him the flawed impressions.

"Sweaty palms?" says the young detective. He rubs his palms together, then holds out a trembling hand, in imitation of a nervous prisoner. The detective is grinning. *A joke*, realizes Hank, *a joke*.

"Let's try again dear." She grabs his thumb.

Beyond the walls the band begins its anthem. Tuneless horns blat obscenely and drumbeats push hard through the blond wood of the hallway. Now the thing is starting.

RIGHTEOUS
SPEEDBOAT

For no animal admires another animal.

– Blaise Pascal

VEN NOW the vibrating screen maims the very molecules of my eyes but how I have to gaze. How many bent berserkers, how many peckerwood imposters will they call to the silver microphone before they call to me, here with my nigh-on ruined vision? No finish at the net and hands of stone, but I can read a play, backcheck like a madman and I move malevolently inside a snarling wind. Pins go down.

That ought to be worth *something*, a few paydays, a winning smile from the bank teller. Tampa could take me down there with their palmetto bugs. Need be I'll go to the moon, I'll skate on Mars.

Maybe a scrounging team will grab me in a late round. Scrounging is okay, late round is okay. I could help a club in the Colonial League, work my way up. Just give me a contract. Or else I'm toast. I'm overage. I can't go back to my junior team. I burnt a few bridges there, pissed off the scunt-eyed coach. I caught an elbow in the nose and saw visions of gasping lightning while the guy with said elbow slid away like a pulse to score the winning goal, to bury it top shelf. All season who had the best plus-minus on the club? *Moi.* I repeat: I had the best plus-minus on the team. Yet in front of everyone the coach really reamed me out. Up and down, went to town. He had no need to do that, to humiliate me.

Elbowed nose still throbbing, I moved in close to the coach, paused to get him wondering, feinted, then I gave his nose a shot; I clocked the coach. Nothing really. They want you to hit everyone else; *Him*, they say in Spokane, and you know what they mean. Bing bang bong. Do it to *them* though, touch *them* and it's the end of the fucking world. They tell the reporters you're "difficult," you're a cancer on the team. Control-freak wimps. Blue-legged fops. Pukely ticket-punchers. I say this much is obvious: the "difficult" players are the real action, living it. Lean as whippets; they throb, eat at the air like engines.

I call my agent long-distance and he allows, *This is he.*

Doesn't look good, he says. Our noisy years are moments, he says.

I call my mother and she sighs, "You had so much potential."

I'd call my friend from Salmon Arm, but Ryan's lost his head. The bloody trail across the gravel road I still dream of, and the green radiator water burning my hair. Ryan's head rolling.

Once upon a time this was a happening bar but now it's a loser bar. The bar has no view at all, a pocked pallid concrete bunker, which is good. Night for day, no trees and no sky. You pay extra for trees and sky, the darkening harbour. You need no view. You need to hear your name echoing in that distant subsidized convention centre; those two sweet words in that room of tasteful blurred suits. Your name.

I like loser bars. They're quiet and I can think.

I think there is always some injustice. We depend on tales of injustice. At the small curved bar an intense young man is telling a dark-eyed woman his specific story of injustice. He's well dressed: black custom-cut pants and a beautiful shirt that is white and tapered. Gel gleams evenly in his hair. I decide his name is Laszlo. Someone looks after Laszlo's cuticles. Laszlo smokes. He collects things: plenitude, kudos, ivory elephants. The young woman is listening, yet she is clearly fidgety, restless. Her dark eyes move in a sad poised face. I watch her dark eyes shiver. Her lipstick is almost black. She shows her teeth in a sad brief smile and it is everything. You learn everything. I can't stand the idea that it's all random.

Here's a guy, Laszlo says leaning right at her, real good guy, he says. Here's a guy, I don't know, so-called best friend.

Laszlo lowers his voice, but I can still hear him. He's too
close to her.

This is a guy that. Feed him breakfast. Pick him up, take him to work. Give him a job and uh, *float* him. And uh, my mom has his cheque, some deductions of course, he looks at it, something wrong, he says.

The young woman asks Laszlo a question.

Yeah, my mom, she had it. And he stole! He stole from us! Laszlo cuts the air with a flat hand. I went by the next day. This is not the agreed ... What is this—this, this holding company? None of your business. Well, I said. I was ready to kill—

The dark-eyed woman breaks into his story.

Sorry, she says, I *really* have to run. Give me a call, she says. Gotta go!

Oh, he says. A-O-KAY! he says brightly. Laszlo tries to get funnier after the serious story. He needs a fast transition. He picks up her key ring, a tiny flashlight hooked on it, and he sings into the tiny flashlight as if it's a microphone: I DID IT MY WAY! he belts out.

"My Funny Valentine," he croons softly, eyebrows up like Elvis Costello.

They both try to laugh, but still she takes her keys back, plunging them deep within her Peruvian satchel.

The young woman leaves briskly, outside to oaks, oaks up like oars in a spooky sky, and Laszlo glances around, ill at ease now, alone, no longer singing. Now he has to adjust himself, recast the last moments, her exit. His status has changed here. He peers around at the subterranean concrete tomb as if for the first time, at the monotonous hockey draft unscrolling on the monster TV screen. It's a crapshoot. Some of us are wanted in the first or second round. Some players wait all day and no one calls. I'm not flying down east for nothing, for crocodile tears in the arena seats and maybe your parents phoning your hotel room, telling you there's next year, or you could play in Italy or Blackpool. Everyone will lie to you at some point. They decide they know best. Some are allowed dignity; others scramble. I will scramble if necessary. I'm not 6'5", but I'll run my cranium into the Zamboni if that's what they desire. They can croon my name, tap me on the shoulder, and I'll get it done. Only connect. Call my name. I'm shallow. I want to hear my muddled name run through a silver microphone, to shake hands with a million people I don't know.

Laszlo shows the red-haired bartender something from his wallet. A sunlit photo, waterfront property, a speedboat docked. The speedboat has a blue canopy and a blue racing stripe.

Looksee, he says. Is that a nice place or is that a nice place? Just up island. Hey, tell you what. You want to go there, let me know. I'm driving up there practically every week.

All the goddam time.

He carries a photo of property in his wallet. Now: would I be any different? I'd probably carry a photo too.

Laszlo scribbles a note left-handed, passes it over. The bartender does not read the note.

I order a Greyhound, bite from the small onion I always carry in my coat. I'd like some chowder or chili, some good cornbread or sweet potato. Carb-loading just in case I get picked.

Laszlo points with his sterling silver pen at the bartender's red hair.

You must be Irish, eh?

No, says the red-haired bartender, looking irritated.

Our place up island: we've got ten acres, two hundred grand. Bay goes in like this—we own from this peak to here. Goes back, big trees. Ten acres.

Laszlo keeps smoking. He opens his wallet again. He likes to open his wallet.

The ferry system, this is how . . . The Schedule. Thursday. No, hold that. Tuesday. Right. You know why Tuesday?

He lights another smoke. Dull Clapton plays: post-heroin Clapton, post-lobotomy Clapton. A much more popular model; his *Unplugged* CD under all the Christmas trees. I'm truly sorry his little kid fell out of the highrise, but I don't like 279 the tape. I like *Disraeli Gears*. I like Nirvana, Lyres, Ramones, Art Bergmann, the crown prince of detox. I like Art Bergmann's new single: *create a monster, something something, we got a contract, contract, who's using who?* His sneering lines seem pertinent to me at this moment. The hockey draft is still on the screen. My draft. I'm so close to a contract, to treasure. Mr. Eric Clapton sells a billion boring records and no-one wants me. The bartender doesn't ask why Tuesday.

On TV men in suits argue and wave clean hands en route to the silver microphone; they must speak their pick, announce who will skate, who will consider a million-seven, who will buy a sleek growling speedboat. Something is wrong though; men in suits argue like they're chewing a mouthful of bees. They act as if they don't know their pick.

I'm available! I shoot out mental telepathy messages from this edge of the country. Me! I have a head on my shoulders.

The erudite GM bends over; he seeks the ear of the frowning coach. The GM straightens, walks to talk with the worried head scout, then puts glasses on the end of his nose, peers over some papers. A weird delay of some kind, a plot complication at the meat market. Just past the media tables I can see the cackling old owner who was jailed for fraud and mob connections, for taking the Fifth, for taking the assets, for chortling. Well, no one figured he was a choirboy.

They'll take a d-man, says one customer.

No, they need a centre. Definitely a centre, says another

The GM at the mike finally mouths the name of the anointed, the chosen. A goalie! Takes a goalie! They have goalies in the system. They have goalies coming out the yin yang. Trade bait, but who? Trade the young guy? The backup goalie? Trade the older goalie, the former cokehead?

They screwed up, someone in the bar says. They screwed up. He says this four times in a row.

They've been tricked. They traded up to get the franchise bruiser they wanted; they made a deal, and all parties agreed to square dance, to give and take. They agreed what bodies would be available when they got to the microphone but at the last second another team, a team without scruples, traded draft choices and future considerations, snatching the franchise bruiser out from under their red noses. Stole from them. Their *property*.

We've been snookered, states the GM, we've been submarined. The GM's byzantine manoeuvres and agreements are useless. I traded up for nothing, he thinks, all that trouble for another goalie. The troubled scout tears the bruiser's name off his jersey, his sweater waiting at their table. How sure they were. They don't have my name on a jersey. They have different tables for each team, like it's the United Nations, like it's the fate of the free world. Then there are prickly pears and sea lions, sooty terns and albatrosses and California sea lions dripping in the sun on the colour TV. Another highly illogical car commercial that seems to be flogging some product other than cars. What exactly is it they are hawking? Vermilion and sienna sunsets? Oceanfront? Does it work? Do these ads actually move their lipstick-colour cars to the tire-kickers and lot lizards and lay downs and strokers?

Insects crash at the screen, hearkening tragically into their multi-hued harbour. They want to eat the TV light, the only game in town. I keep studying the draft, but Laszlo studies two women who seat themselves at the bar. The first woman keeps her sunglasses on. She is taller than me. I see her and think *stature, presence.* Her friend is shorter, with lighter hair and the small peaceful face of a follower.

The woman in the dark glasses inhales hugely, exhales: Well, we broke up. Went pretty well considering

Woman #2: No sobbing?

Woman #1: A little. (She pauses.) Him. Not me.

Woman #2: Let's go prowling!

Woman #1: No thanks.

Woman #2: Oh yeah. You're in THAT phase. Wait two weeks and you'll be crawling the walls.

Woman #1: No. I don't think so.

I realize she has someone lusty waiting, someone already drafted, but she hasn't told her friend. She broke it off with one guy to move to another. She possesses a five-year plan.

Woman #2 complains. My roommates are doing it all the time and I have to sit and listen. I mean I can't help but hear it. I can't afford my own place. And he has to end up with *her.* I had such a crush on him. It was supposed to be *me.* I had hopes. Now I'm going nuts. Why do I have such bad luck with guys I like?

They sip their drink specials.

Woman #1 says, This older guy took me to an Icelandic film festival. The movies were like, what the fuck!?

AHA! I think. An older guy is chosen.

For me the charm of hockey was always its lack of charm. It wasn't hip. My agent says he'll call me back. He's busy with his "real" clients. I walk to the washroom and see a nickel gleaming at the bottom of the porcelain urinal. I do not pick it up. I look out at my nation. I have no nation. Okay—I have a wormwood nation.

Laszlo is talking to the two women: We'll take my dad's speedboat across. If you don't have tackle we can get you some. Waterfront. On the water. Everyone said we paid too much. Local yokels laughing. Day later, twenty grand more. Who's laughing now? Very rare find. Very rare. Nice beach. Arbutus and oak. Beautiful property. We'll get some people. We'll go up there. Road trip! Road trip!

Well now isn't waterfront always on the water? Woman #2 wonders.

What's the catch? I wonder. Why does Laszlo have to cajole people to go to this Shangri-La?

Doesn't it come stocked with beautiful people? The way they stock a fish farm? A fat farm?

I realize Laszlo is talking to a different bartender. Bartender #2.

Bob Hope, Laszlo exclaims. Bob Hope's been there. We'd just fumigated so he wasn't too happy. Log cabin, some bugs. Ants I guess. Cedar. Wouldn't think so. Puzzling.

That loser shirt, Laszlo says laughing at the bartender.

Hey sport. Hey pal. This is my brother's shirt. My brother who died in an accident. A *fatal* accident.

Oh. Sorry.

Laszlo lights another smoke, looks around. On TV a GM slides right by a team's table, a team he used to coach. He jumped ship. He doesn't look and they don't look at him. He found the loophole he needed to break his contract, to dance with another party, a party other than the one that "brung" him.

Bob Hope's a card. Bob Hope says, Any chance of anything here? Something other than pinochle and Ovaltine? Nyuck. Know what I mean? Country girls, nice country girls.

He wanted some action. Horny old bugger. We caught a cod. Engine broke down, going slow, get a blueback, keeper, three-pounder, eat salmon that night. But I'd rather catch one big one. One big chinook, a tyee, a king. Bob Hope bitching at me all day in that irritating voice. I'm looking for this ledge, I'm looking for this ledge with a depth finder. Jigged, buzz bombed, mooched, nothing. Tried a new lure, a silver one I found in Dad's tacklebox.

(Now it's Bartender #3 half-listening, a guy in a muscle shirt. I think the bartenders must take shifts with Laszlo, then go hide back in the cooler.)

ZING! GOT IT! Laszlo mimics a fishing rod and a sudden strike on the line. ZING!

He doesn't finish the fishing story. He smokes non-stop. I have another Greyhound. Maybe they don't draft players who punch their coaches. Maybe there's a secret agreement, rules they don't tell you about. I'm bitter (wormwood, wormwood). I'm starting to feel like saussurite, like schist, like stone.

A stoned voice bellows in the direction of the jukebox: "PLAY SOMETHING BY SOMEBODY . . . WHO KILLED THEMSELVES!"

This desire to be fucked up, and think it something special, or something to be attained. That's rich. Ask my friend Ryan about dead guys. Ask a dead guy about getting fucked up. Ask if they're really happy.

All my friends are lawyers, Laszlo says. And the women are incredible! They work so hard they don't have time to meet anyone else. You want to meet great women hang out with lawyers.

Yeah. Like I really want to hang out with lawyers, Bartender #3 growls.

On TV the GM in the suit is helping the young hockey player pull on his new team sweater. It's too intimate. There is some awkward tugging at clothes, then embarrassed smiles and camera flashes for the sports cards.

Who's this clown they pick? Who's this sack of hammers? Some Swede faggot. A *foreigner.*

You on a team? Laszlo asks the muscled bartender.

Used to be. Same old used to be.

Now I recognize Bartender #3: a fantastically shifty forward with Tri-Cities. He had moves like a humpback salmon, and Pittsburgh was after him until he was submarined, blew out both knees big time. Good old Tom What's-his-name. They said he'd never walk again. Huge writhing scars each side of his knees. Twins. A suicide pass. Skate into the middle and CRANG!, you flip over with a quicksilver crunching, then they carry you off, a sudden screeching pauper. Wheelbarrows of cash will alter anyone, but he's been changed by the cash he never got, by what could have been that draft year. He could have been the one under the blinding television lights, the one getting offered a million-seven. Instead. Well instead he watches with me. Now Tom What's-his-name is a major drunk with rehab muscles. I'm not as shifty, but at least my knees are okay. My knees are not too shabby. I cast a shadow, I get my back up, show up for every game. Buffalo could take me. The Jets. There's that windy corner. The Sharks. This sounds like West Side Story.

I'm going to drive up there to the property tomorrow. Come on along. Pick up my cousin and bullshit. Deli grub, some Heineken. Greenies. You like Heineken? No? The airport and take the speedboat across.

Laszlo has told three different bartenders about the speedboat.

Laszlo asks, How does that bear joke go again? Let's see. Bartender tells the bear he can't serve him because he's on drugs. This part. I can never remember. Drugs. What drugs. You help me yeah. Oh, the *barbiturate. The* bar-bitch-you-ate! Ya ya. Ha ha. That's a good one.

The two women do not share Laszlo's love of the bear joke.

We're lucky you know, Laszlo says to the women, that place up island. Played our cards right. Cheap locals can go jump in a lake. If they knew anything they'd be somewhere else, right? Road goes around pretty little bay. Speedboat. No waiting. Catch a big one. No tackle we'll take care of you. Little general store not far. Good beef jerky. If we don't have it you don't need it. That what they say on their sign. They don't have it you don't need it. That's their hick philosophy, their London School of Economics approach to local yokel marketing. Road goes around nice little bay. See the smooth golden stones at the bottom. A beautiful place. We own it. It's ours.

Lizard King Jim Morrison says Hello. Jim Morrison says he loves me. Jim Morrison says he wants to know my name. The jukebox decides what to play. And the big screen shows the famous footage: Big surly Eric Lindros refuses the sweater. He stares off, dark mad eyes and curly hair. A thick neck, a bull. He'll never sign with this team. Maybe they called his name, but that doesn't mean they own him, that doesn't mean he's their *property*. He refuses their blue uniform, their lovely stone city, their scheming owner. In this hexed process, this amateur hour crapshoot, here's what I wish to know, to *divine*: who has the real power and who is the victim? That's what I have to learn, even though I already know the truth.

Wait until Lindros is on the ice, the young man says to Bartender #4. He'll pay. Someone'll stick him good. Get his bad knee.

I say nothing. They shouldn't talk like that. I've seen too many torn up knees. Hurt!? Are you fucking kidding? Unfucking-believable. Anterior cruciate; that's the worst. It digs into my stomach just thinking of ruined knees.

Just how many bartenders are back there? Do they have a bartender pool? There are more bartenders than customers.

Everyone thinks Lindros is a greedy arrogant asshole, but meanwhile the team's owner is mulling over juicy offers of $75 million U.S. for the franchise. The Quebec owner will sell in the night; the owner will hustle the team out of Canada with a tearful press conference. The owner will cry all the way to the bank. Who's the greedy asshole then? What did our pal Peter Pocklington get for selling Gretzky to Los Angeles, for selling a person, a *human being*? $20 million? (For he is an honourable man.) Thanks for destroying the Oilers, *Peter*. And how much money does the crooked meat-packer owe the Alberta government right now? He's in so deep they can't touch his house of cards, his dead pigs and stuffed sausages and offal, his slit-throat palace over the river valley. So the players are greedy? The players are arrogant? Give me a break. Get real.

No one gives me a break. No one gets real. Instead they draft a dead guy. In fact they draft Ryan, my friend from Salmon Arm. His last night on earth we were riding in what journalists would later refer to as the death car. I was passed out in the back seat. Ryan was in the passenger seat. Then I woke up in the ditch, in the rhubarb where the world was utterly different. Green water was pouring out of the upside-down radiator, burning me. The power pole was in three pieces, its line sparking. Ryan's head rolled across the gravel road, his brain still sending messages, questions, trying to find out what's wrong. I took off my wet shirt and hid my friend's head. I was afraid to pick it up so I just covered it with my shirt. What would you do? The car looked like modern sculpture, the driver still curled inside it like a fetus. Not a scratch on me, though my teeth were chattering and my hair was steaming. My friend's head: pebbles and dust stuck on it. And this brain of mine. Then some kind of gleaming milk truck came by and the driver said Jesus.

And the big club must not know he's dead. If Ryan was alive he'd laugh. Here they are throwing away a pick on him before they'll draft me.

I have watched the drunken screen for hours, eating the past, wrapping my head in it, and my eyes complain at the images, at the labour; my eyes are shifting right out of focus. Can't they make a big screen that doesn't kill you?

I am one of God's creatures, but no one is taking me. Not the Lightning in Tampa, not the Panthers. Not the Jets. Not the San Jose Sharks. They're taking hundreds of snipers, killers, muckers, headcases, piranhas, plumbers, pretenders. They call out polyglot Latvian names at the silver microphone. They don't care about my plus-minus, they don't care about my Grade 8 blues records or sensitive feelings or that I move like silt and stick like glue. What about the San Diego Gulls or Las Vegas and that Russian guy named Radek Bonk? This is a great name for a player.

Bonk! Pass me the puck! Hit him Bonk. Bonk him! Marty McSorley was going to sign with Las Vegas, play in the desert. I'd play in the desert. I can't go back to the fucking last-place Cougars. I know I'm *this* close to making it, but the Cougars have dragged me down, they've buried me, made me invisible. In a seething minute you are made to pay for your geography, for being in the snake-bit boonies; the centre doesn't hold for *you*.

I'll have to try my luck as a free agent. Some good players aren't picked but they make it later as a walk on. They force the issue, bull their way in the door. Courtnall, Joey Mullen, Dino Ciccarelli, Adam Oates. It happens. Brett Hull wasn't taken until the 117th pick, and Fleury was 166th his year. Nemchinov didn't go to New York until the 244th pick overall in 1990. Now he has a Stanley Cup ring. Every Cup team has its free agents, its "difficult" players. They made it, crawled out of the ooze. You hear their names: a mantra repeated. There's a free-agent camp somewhere in the States; the scouts look you over, look inside your head, see what you've got. Courtnall has it made in the shade now, big money, owns restaurants and a spiffy log cabin on a cliff over the crashing ocean. Douglas fir and ferns and fishing boats in the harbour where the whales come in to rub. A view. This is Geoff, not Russ. Russ was drafted first round and he married a movie starlet; Russ Courtnall has no idea what it's like to be invisible, to wait all day and be slowly made crazy, to want to punch out a guy named Laszlo. I'm so close, so close to treasure. Is it a litmus test, Russ? No. It's not a litmus test. Just look inside your rolling head, the head and source of all your son's distemper.

I wish the woman with dark eyes hadn't left. Why does one person seem different and necessary? I chose to interpret the angle of her neck, slurred messages the speed of blood inside her unknown neck and uncertain smile, her teeth and her lips with the darkest darkest lipstick. I watched the draft while I watched her eyes move, her brain shift into an uncertain smile, and I knew she was leaving just then to become a bus window or a blur in the rain in the raw city of colours, just as I knew I would not be drafted, as I knew they would take a dead man before they would take a player who clocked a coach.

On the Cougars Geoff punched anyone who touched his little brother Russ. I bet now both brothers bomb around in righteous speedboats, ocean their blue and white freeway while a pretty woman from Hollywood naps down in the V-berth. She is waiting for you and you are waiting for her. You are waiting to catch a big one. You stand wide-legged at the wheel and gaze at the sky over arbutus trees and your hair slides back in the salt breeze. You think your head is attached to your shoulders. Expensive sunglasses protect your eyes, zinc your fair skin, for you cast a shadow, you are the paragon of animals, you have connected the dots. Frantic lawyers and children clamour for your signature, your autograph; children and lawyers shout out your name in the sonic echoing arenas, in Inglewood, in Florida, in United Centre, in General Motors Place.

There is money moving out there, green as antifreeze, green as absinthe, and everyone has a chance at it. Take this from this, if this be otherwise.

That's the *system*. You think they are going to change it just for you?

CALIFORNIA CANCER JOURNEYS

I dwindle ... dynamite no more.
I ask for a natural death,
no teeth on the ground

– Robert Lowell

AT SEA, a whitewater ferry crossing, rocking our way to Port Angeles on the venerable M.V. Coho. The Customs man on the other side looks like my dead father. He drawls an order: "You bring us back some sunshine now."

We drive verdant Highway 101 for a day before sneaking up on Interstate 5 and its oceanless rain and speed blurring county after sandy county. Five heads, five brains, $500 in travellers' cheques: my brand new family entering that ordered thirteen-day hallucination that is the trip to Grandmother's house. Grandmother, Sharon's mother, possesses any number of amiable cancers. We want to visit. She is looking forward to our visit. Our job is to bring sunshine.

At the same moment, in an upstairs room of a half-finished farmhouse in Grande Prairie, my best friend Levi is trying to kill a brain tumour; perhaps this fabled presence in his skull looks like a softball, or perhaps an orchard tangle. Whatever: Levi has lost interest in metaphor. He's taking injections in the thigh. He shuns chemo. He travels to Hawaii instead. R & R. While we travel, Mr. Levi Dronyk's brain is on a parallel journey.

We move and something in his head moves, shakes out tiny reticulate leaves. They cut out as much tumour as they could without making him a vegetable (My vegetable love should grow more slow.) They couldn't yank all its tendrils without cutting his brain. Standing in my sunlit backyard Levi talks to me, he's still himself. He's lost some vocabulary but he's still Levi. How long will this last? The doctors don't like to tell you you're dead. They want you to obey them. Balance and release seems the name of this relentless new dream, disease the new Elizabethan masque.

A first trip for our children; Gabriel is six months, Kelly is two years, and Martin is four. They love dinosaurs and bloodthirsty pirates. They love their parents. We gaze out clear car windows; we take in America the beautiful while something hesitant tries to shut down in my friend's head. Eighteen years I have known Levi. Windows close, a humming human ailment creeping in a joyful conspiracy, an impractical joke blossoming with the same crazy energy he displayed in everything: softball, beat poetry, chicken-skin music, union business, random city travel, wild letters and dubbed tapes mailed to friends in the mountains. Levi wanted us to know the new singers, the obscure voices with their implied eyes and lip-sync violence, their homey versions of winter. Selling his share of the house and blowing the money on records. Levi plays with his one-year-old by my garage. I think, His children will not know him. His records will last longer. He has no estate.

He wanted to play a shining horn, had the Motown moves down like stink; a good dancer, a sharp-dressed man with a hawk-like Slavic face, a good talker and romancer.

Now Levi will be the guy that died years ago. The guy that stood squinting by my garage with his one-year-old. He'll be the guy that worked for the union, giving twenty years to a small TV station, to phantom voices and talk shows and electric lines zipping right through his head all day every day. Levi got zapped, he got a smoked brain as a dowry, a perk from the owners, like a poached smokehouse salmon. Inhaling the room, fuming, fusing, having the company air while having an affair with the woman at work: and then someone slashed the roof of his Mustang in the staff lot, the car he had to sell later, bankrupt, moving from town to town, prowling the boondocks of affordable real estate. Who orders a life wisely?

We try. Sharon and I have borrowed against the house and bought a new car, a white car from a country both our fathers fought against. We drive under huge hydro towers, following the ordered lines of the American Aqueduct, the orchards, this translation of the banquet with bouquets, this demon demonstration of the demand for water, the inalienable right to take over. Los Angeles is thirsty for power, lights, action. California Republic is thirsty; its lines run off the globe, its big metal legs stride the world, a Colossus, a shaking tectonic hangover.

As I drive staring at the wires that lead off the horizon, I wonder, Could you actually run atop this power-line tightrope, run all the way to some East L.A. taco stand? Walk a wire to that lovely infestation of poseurs and confidence men and executive producers? Would it kill you if you're not careful, not articulate? Could you walk to Los Angeles's Crip frijoles or would it fry your brain first? Not unlike TV screens and TV monitors and wires raving all around you in a tiny editing room.

At work Levi was surfing electrical waves, moving his waged brain through a web of invisible beams and hemlines, through bones and border crossings. We force our new car to leap through invisible interstate borders; my three young kids dazed, thirsty, their new blond heads swivelling, leaving home for the first time, miles to go before we weep. New miles go on

293

the new car. That's all right: rack them up, rack up the miles.

At the other end of these thick wires they are jumpstarting a tiny star in the concrete sidewalk, fixing a hole where the rain got in, where they worship the saucers and strangle hookers with their own bra. The quake drops sections of freeway. Hopscotch. It's exciting to arrive at midnight, as if party to a moonlight escape.

Trying to remember the motive, the votive, the fine print, we go through the spiny and naked desert, through the non-woods to Grandmother's house. Breast cancer was her first wolf; bone cancer was next. Her hip. Then her ribs. At least it's not soft tissue. Soft tissue is without hope. Maybe she'll escape. The social contract has changed since our last visit. Now one brings a basket of shark cartilage, cranberry juice, hoping and making small talk: My what big teeth.

Yes well you know they're all using teeth-whitener now, like Tom Cruise.

Oh is that so? one says.

Yes. He's into some cult. They all have personality problems. They have a distorted view of life.

But very distorted is what sells, very distorted is boffo box office.

Yes, that's true enough, I say. This is a nice house you have here, I say.

Hmmph. More like half a house, Gladys complains. (It's bigger than our place and she lives alone.) She painted over the "yella," transplanted small palm trees, she owns it outright, but it's not really her place. She's magic with succulents, blossoms, fruit trees. The avenues are lined with gold and guacamole, but she's depressed about everything.

"I just don't know what's going to come of this," she says. "I don't know what's at the other end of this now."

She's from the treed hills of Pennsylvania. No one here is like her and she's alone most of the year. The barrios are too close. Her oldest daughter, Sharon's big sister, died of a brain tumour. She died when Nixon was President. Her parents voted for George Wallace. I had never before met anyone who voted for Wallace.

"I'm in pretty bad shape. Where's the baby? How did this happen," she wonders.

Mexican workers outside listen to a Spanish version of Blondie's "Call Me." They drive in, work fast on the perfect grass, and get out. Diagonal stripes. The teenage Italian woman across the street bleaches her hair white as cocaine and favours leopardskin and leather. Everyone strives to be blond, to be dark, to be hip, to be ethnic, to be straight, to be crooked, to be something they saw in *Interview* magazine. No one here votes for George Wallace. The pavement glitters. They've never heard of George Wallace. It's a house of straw in a storm, a stop, likely her last in this state.

Neighbours pretend no one else exists, avert their eyes when I try to say hi. Dying is not the in thing. Unless you're beautiful and famous. And how long will she exist? Can she escape this? Gladys has stopped going to the movies or walking at night. Gladys has stopped playing pipe-organ at the church. Soon she'll have to stop driving. Then the rented wheelchair: I can't get to the bathroom at night! Then: I can't get out of bed, I'm choking because I have to eat on my back. I have no garden; I'm going to drown in a teaspoon.

This, you recall, is California. There is always that struggle to keep mobile, to unlearn the unclean past: The frightening sun of a polished asylum, the sum of every plane alive and reflecting its new sheen. Doubt not, though no one will buy an older house, an old shoe or an old story unfolding under an old sun squeezing out too much light over the new house up the cul-de-sac from the giant power lines, the new house in the 24-hour white sun with grass green as paint and grieved with envy beside the spare brittle music of the desert.

In the back of my head I keep hearing the Sons of the Pioneers croon, "Water, cooool clear water." And perhaps this is how tumours begin: something as innocent as an irritating song; that piece of sand that leads to the pearl that leads to the heebie jeebies or the mulberry bush or the river worth gathering at. No one lied to us: the wind rides in from the foggy salt ocean and splits in the scorched valley; the wind heads south and the wind heads north, riding madly in all directions at once. Sea and desert; here are spirited worlds meeting and stripping each other like sex. Birds panic in their guided skyway. Ladders grow into the leather trees, searching for what grows. Like a tumour in a good friend's head. A double helix ladder. The pickers used to be Chinese. They had to go.

Hikers find smashed earthenware in a cavern, broken crockery in a head. Anarchy in a tiny place. Or is sickness a normal state, and health unnatural? Someone slashed the roof of Levi's Mustang; the surgeon slashed the head of Levi's haunted head.

My quiet father died last year in California on Valentine's Day. He had a heart attack while walking out for a copy of the *San Diego Union*. He made it back to the rented condo, but my mother was at the pool above the sandy cliffs, waiting for him. Finally she knew she had to check. She told me later I was lucky not to hear the sounds he made on someone else's chesterfield.

They lost him at the hospital. I'm beginning to associate California with death, with sounds I should not hear. He had been diagnosed with liver cancer, but the heart stepped up first. The squeaky wheel gets the grease, greases you. People said we were lucky not to see him waste away. To nothing. My aunt in England wrote me: "One felt he was the sort of chap who would go on forever quite cheerfully. As in life he was considerate to the end and to me it seems he decided to unfold his wings and just fly away—thoughtful as ever." At the Coroner's he lay in the sliding drawer. My mother kissed him goodbye for all of us.

On the highway we read air's long history, the grasses waiting to bend, willing to wilt, while cattle hang on steep hillsides with black stoic faces; and the white horse lingers, looking for just one tree's shelter. I don't know if my father flew away. The pressed grasses are written on, something in this country stolen or moved and something genuine and fine. The greasers stare at the ground, at the creosote, at the white horse. The Sons of the Pioneers keep singing of water, singing of cool water. This is my three sons' first long trip. They seem so well behaved, benign (as opposed to malignant). We fall from motel beds and drive about three inches and Martin asks if we're looking for a motel yet.

Soon, I say, in about twelve hours.

Why? he asks. How come? How long is twelve hours? I don't know.

He'll forget it after a while. I've forgotten so much. Like reservations. I walk into motel offices covered in baby spit-up and cranberry juice and demand a business discount. I'm in the business of raising blond kids; I'm in the business of going through the non-woods to or from Grandmother's house. I want my discount.

Take Jesus into your heart, they say. Take Jesus into your liver, they don't say. When they're older and my graphic heart or liver has burst will my children remember this earthquake country? This voodoo volcano country? The squashed valleys with such a hard light that all the year's colours have gone dull? Will my young wife become pregnant at my wake? Believe me: I know of this exact event. Remember me? mumbles the ghost bent under the stage in a leather jerkin. Ah forget it, he says after a while. There is no shade, no cover, just saltwhite ground and greasewood scrub, rattlesnakes and Borax muletrain memories. Will my children remember falling between the motel bed and motel wall and screaming, trapped, not knowing where they are? I tried to soothe them. This stripped mezzotint country reminds me of Merle Haggard and the Strangers; Buck Owens and the Buckaroos. These clouds have never seen clover. I remember bits of these trips with my parents. The patched canvas tent and the moose bellowing in the river. The Lethe Motel & Bar-B-Q. The bobcats jumping on tourists and the backseat's play within the play. Will our children remember us? We know so little of where we pass: last week, last decade, last century. Think of the *pobladores*, the lost families in this series of valleys: Alvarado, Castro, Wolfskill, Pico, Duran, Pacifico, de la Guerra y Noriega. The irrigation squabbles, scalps lifted like weeds, night riders and vigilance lynchings, complicated slaughter in the blind canyon. Now: brief moonflowers and insects and cement overpasses with cratered pale masses of swallow nests glued to their side, cells mutating like you know what. Waiting for the airport and the surveyors' ribbons and subdivisions and the all-night Mexican places. We see no people, see no rabble. Just power lines; just the huge Möbius road. What used to seem an escape.

Who lives here other than kingsnakes and sidewinders and swallows and their aboriginal oatmeal nests? Where are they all hiding? The dusty questions as you roll blind and yawning through another squinting crossroads, rattle your fine city bones on another corduroy road, past adobe bungalows and hedgerows that have run out of talent.

Sharon says, "My mother is dying and she still has that ability to drive me crazy." Gladys sprays more chemicals at the spiders in her garage, eats fast food from Jack-in-theBox. She points to the pastel houses: This is what we call a development. Will she be resurrected again? Or is this the last time? It's the last time. It's a development. She has been gathering in death for a decade, learning and turning dying into performance art. I do the dishes every night at 7:20. I am restless, spooked. My children are thrilled by this trip to see their dying grandmother. They bang and clang on her piano and break her sprinkler system and scatter rocks to meet the Mexican's lawnmower. At night, though, my children cry out from their sleeping-bags on the floor, afraid of her Victorian furniture piled high in their room. Their grandfather (divorced and remarried) flies in from Las Vegas to tell war stories, stories I like more than anyone. He apologizes for telling them, apologizes for the divorce.

Gladys's lungs slowly fill with fluid; there is a hole in her hipbone from radiation. She shuffles into the kitchen, zaps her frozen "entree."

"There is a level," she says, "beyond which I won 't allow myself to fall." That doesn't last long. That level is history. History is a bunkbed. Her ribs start killing her. Her doctor quits and the office is bedlam.

After a fortnight of sunny chaos we have lost our heads, lost our sleep, lost our saintly intentions; Sharon and I just want to get the hell out, to escape California Republic, to stop drinking cranberry juice. Gladys wants to die and she cannot; she lives on, mourning doves mumbling from her steep backyard. She hallucinates, believes she is chasing chickens in Pennsylvania, is shopping for bargains at the mall, that she is going to have to sue.

Levi wants to live and yet he dies. The message arrives from Grande Prairie thousands of miles to the north: He's dying, she says, he's checking out. News falls from the buzzing wire, Levi falls from the wire without learning the instrument. Mourning doves have such slim heads. This end has happened so fast I can't believe it. As students Levi and I hopped the ferry to Port Angeles to drink in The Salty Dawg, to thumb up to the glacier at Hurricane Ridge. Suddenly someone is coming to get my friend Levi in a pickup truck, crossing the northern steppes to pick up what's left of him, as if he is a bale of green hay or a dry cord of tamarack to be burned. Not even a purple hearse to Joshua Tree. Not even a drummer or a staggering New Orleans horn.

How to forget that urge to escape somehow? And escape exactly what? Escaping escape? The restless dishes at 7:20? The salt on the ground? The routine blossoms inside your skin and skull? The desert sand that should look different on Valentine's Day? Or is it the displays in all the Encinitas shop windows: those red shiny Valentine hearts everywhere like masks, like masks with lace teeth, and on this day of hearts my father has a heart attack. Going for the newspaper in the morning sunlight by the Pacific Ocean. I flew down and drove his rental car to the mortuary. I was sick of goatees then and I'm sick of them now.

Your lungs with fluid; but your heart with something other. Levi and Gladys and all those in that blind canyon, all those in that last place of scalps and complicated slaughter, have reasons to seek escape, to feel betrayed, reasons to hop in a vintage Mustang or Meteor Rocket and hit the highway. To lose their lost skin beneath the mercury-lit overpass and lingering Northern Lights. To unfold wings and be thought considerate. Escaping escape. Pennsylvania. England. Terra Nova. The rest of us zooming under the prefab trestles are faking it, copping an attitude. Three blond heads chatter like cheerful wrens in the cracker-strewn backseat. (My father never allowed food in his cherished Oldsmobile, the Delta 88 I smashed.) I'm not saying anything to the boys. I am holding a wheel like it's a chisel, but I'm not escaping. I have my father's face, my father's hands, my father's heart. Ocean at my back, I'm going for a morning paper: The noises. A beautiful sweet breeze, sun-hot tiles and tiny reticulate leaves rushing toward me.

BLUEBIRD DRIVER

E's invisible, but we hear the yawl and pitch of his drunken voice. The young waitress explains to the young female bartender that she doesn't want to serve the drunken sailor anymore.

*

A young blond guy in a ball cap hears the voice, mutters, "That's my old man. Navy. Esquimalt. *Get me a beer!* he'd yell when I was a kid. *Get me a beer!* Canadian Navy they teach 'em to drink. The crews are older in the Canadian Navy, guys stay longer. Different than the American ships. Canadian Navy teaches 'em to drink and they don't stop."

*

The young waitress dials a Bluebird taxi for our drunken sailor. The sailor walks up to the bar, leans against my right arm. We're watching Stanley Cup playoffs, Edmonton Oilers and Dallas Stars tied. Great hockey, could go either way, though we know the Oilers are doomed.

The female bartender hands the older man a scalding cup of coffee. It's so hot the sailor can't keep his big hands on the mug.

He looks to be in his fifties or sixties, flat-top haircut, a brown face as if outdoors in the sun a lot. He has battered blackrim glasses like I wore around Grade 3. They're almost stylish again in terms of street-fashion dork cycles.

I feel sorry for the guy, trying to place burning coffee in his mouth to please the young woman behind the bar. The drunken sailor is trying to be good.

"I used to be Golden Gloves," he says to her.

"What's Golden Gloves?"

*

My mother and father were in the Royal Navy because of the war. Portsmouth flattened by bombers, Ceylon like a teardrop shape dangling at the bottom of the Indian subcontinent—that seems so distant, the wrong end of a telescope. But that was the war: my family is not navy. I ask him about Golden Gloves. He turns to me.

*

He tells me that he boxed in the navy, and that he was in Korea, though he doesn't seem old enough for the conflict in '52. This reminds me of drinking in Montana when I was younger. At first no one would admit to being a Vietnam vet, then when it got trendy, people who'd never left Great Falls talked about how rangy-tang it was in the jungle, hoping you'd spring for drinks.

The drunken sailor tells me he was on the Bonnie, which I think is the Bonaventure, a Canadian aircraft carrier. The hull an inverted steel mountain and all that frigid ocean holds it up. Is the Bonnie scrap metal now? I'm ashamed to say I don't know. Does Canada have any aircraft carriers?

He served on other ships, a sailor's life; I wish I could remember the ships' names. He may have been on mine-sweepers or coast guard cutters. No slow boats from China back then, no snakeheads landing pagans off the Queen Charlotte Islands (*Belize, honest, we're looking for Belize!*).

"My wife died of cancer eight years ago," he says. "Quite a woman. I need a woman to calm me down. I get wild you know—need a woman to calm me down."

He says this very calmly.

*

His hands are brown and large, big inflated knuckles, shoved around a bit, as if broken a few times.

How are the hands? I ask.

They used to hurt, he says, as if cut off from them now.

*

You have a family, don't you, he says.

They're at the pool, I say. I dropped them off. Usually I swim with them, but tonight I wanted to watch hockey.

*

I can tell you're happy, he says looking at me with his black glasses.

Surprised, I shrug an *I'm OK* shrug.

I can tell, he explains. I know where you're from, he says.

*

The Bluebird cabdriver climbs the carpeted stairs, looks around. To pluck our sailor from us.

*

I shake hands with the drunken sailor. My hand seems a tiny white flower in his brawny hand. Then that moment when someone has grasped your hand and will not let go his grasp. What do you do with the drunken sailor?

I know where you're from, he says again, still clutching my hand.

He lifts my hand to his mouth and kisses my fingers as if I'm the Pope. He thinks I'm a messenger of some kind, sent to the fake Tudor bar to give him a message from God or the straight world, to show him he can be as boring as me.

*

He moves away obediently with the Bluebird driver, led away like Blanche DuBois—the carpeted stairs, the kindness of strangers.

There is a quiet moment. The athletic students mingle. In the room the women come and go, talking of whatever.

The young blond guy on my left asks, Was he Esquimalt?

Yeah.

Knew it. Just like my old man.

He knew it.

He asks about my pint, local and dark. He likes light beer. The young blond guy won't drink Coors because Coors gave money to Greenpeace and Greenpeace puts loggers out of work and wrecks families. The young guy used to be a logger up island, but the show shut down so now he works construction in Riverside, California. A good tan, curly hair. The California girls like him all right. They keep him calm.

I fail to tell him that I stopped drinking Coors eons ago because back then they were cutting cheques to the John Birch Society instead of Greenpeace. Times change.

*

Dallas scores late in the third period. The American team wins the game and the Oilers are gone from the playoffs and the coach will get the axe, even though they almost beat the team that goes on to win the Stanley Cup.

An NBA game comes on TV, and I leave the bar, go down the carpeted stairs. My car is still outside the Credit Union, though the sign assured me **We Tow Poachers Every Five Minutes!**

Poachers? What—am I jacklighting the King's deer?

I grew to like the drunken sailor's hoarse voice. *I know where you're from.* I'm glad someone does. Maybe I'll join the navy, get big hands, fuck my life up, bonk my brain on bulkheads. *Get me a beer!*

Or maybe I'll turn the tiny key and pick up Sharon and the boys at the swimming pool.

*

When you walk out the pool doors into a breeze, your skin feels clean and the sky is a pretty tangerine colour. My family strolls to the car, sun of early evening strafing them. My boys hold a bag of chips each. None of them understand that I'm a messenger from God. My boys clamber into the car, chatting excitedly about their feet not touching bottom.

THE
HOSPITAL
ISLAND

I would have made a good Pope.

– Richard Nixon, 37th American President

THE AFTERNOON SUN hides a thief in my eye. My cousin Eve hides so little as she sunbathes on my rooftop terrace, hides almost nothing as we read the newspapers or work together on a crossword. She loves gazing at newsprint; I believe if Eve owned a moped here in Rome she'd happily read a rattling paper while buzzing Rome's boulevards. When was the last time I drove!

Eve and I fled like thieves back to Rome via high-speed train, the trip seemed only minutes, cool air and blue seats on the train to Rome and no talk, a train so much quieter than the old train circling the volcano. In Rome I can't believe how comforting it is to be back in our same rooms; we stay inside and lie away the day, eyes shut, but Eve can't sleep after the knifing at the party, Eve can't stop thinking about the knife in the Italian man's leg and why so much blood, she can't stop worrying.

"How does one just go to sleep? It's as if I've never learned."

Yet I sleep soundly, a genius of sleep, which my wife resented greatly. I sleep like a groggy winter bear; what is wrong with me?

I say, "Can't you think about something else, try to not worry?"

Eve looks at me for a moment as if I am a complete moron, but does not say that. She says, "That's like saying, *Why is the sky blue?*" That it is part of her makeup to worry. Her tiny sleeping pills are very bitter on the roof of her mouth.

"It's not the best sleep," she says, "but it's better than none." A green lizard peeks out from a hole in the wall as we start in on a bottle of ferocious red wine.

My mouth tastes of mufflers and conflict (*Rome throat*, says Eve of the exhaust clouds and particulates in the air we breathe, she says it's like smoking a pack of cigarettes, that only Bulgaria is worse), but the moped riders look so beautiful, sleek executives and office workers in silk suits and fluttering dresses and sharp winkle-picker shoes coming at you in formation, a phalanx of Valkyries balanced on tiny toy wheels.

They killed St. Valentine on February 14th outside the Flaminian Gate during the reign of Claudius the Goth. Valentine's skull was crowned with birds and flowers, he gave eyesight to the blind, hope to the bland. They beat him with clubs and stoned him and later severed his head at the gate; they took their time. Christian couples came to the city gate, young couples he had secretly married, they came and left gifts for this martyr as he died slowly for his true faith. Or this saintly man did not exist and was invented by Chaucer, or he worked for a chocolate lobby group, like the Easter bunny. The Church is no longer exactly sure.

But the riders look so beautiful. My admiration for Roman drivers grows and grows. Local drivers seemed crazed at first, but now I see their staggering talent; cars and scooters fly from all sides like jets in a dogfight, but I have yet to witness an accident. Lanes and lines mean little and at each red light hordes of scooters wobble past rows of stopped cars and assemble ahead of their bumpers, a dozen scooters across the real estate of two tiny lanes, scooters ready to roar away at the green. Drivers share such little space without border wars, without crashing, though I did see a woman fly off a moped on a corner by the market, her moving cry the exact pitch of the engine she was leaving behind. The ambulances park right on our street so she was in good hands.

"Look at this photo," says Eve. "Before the war, the German company Hohner gave Pope Pius XI a chromatic."

Eve passes me her book with its colour photo: a gorgeous harmonica with fluttery brass reeds and a gold casing encrusted with jewels and ivory. We both glance over at the imposing Vatican wall; is the harmonica still *there?*

"Can we ask the Pope for a look?"

"The current pontiff doesn't seem very approachable. He is not sympatico, he is not, how do the Italians say it, not *papabile*. They need to clean house."

Eve doesn't like this German Pope, she feels his raccoon eyes speak of bad vibes and red-hatted cardinals stabbing each other in the back, Eve says you could hang pork chops from both his ears and the dogs still wouldn't play with him. She wants a new Pope, she says, "You'd make a better Pope than this Nazi goof."

The green lizard glows in the wall and we punish the bottle of red. Eve becomes more and more certain that I can be the first Canadian pope (I wonder, can we count Louis Riel as a pope of Assiniboia?).

"Yes, the votes are being counted," says Eve, "now I can see the white smoke from the chimney, they've decided!"

What odds would British bookies give on a foreign tourist becoming the new pope? Slim to none. But I am not the worst candidate. Once I was an altar boy serving First Fridays at dawn, I know my way around the rosary beads and confessional and Stations of the Cross, I know some Latin, the Credo and the Confiteor, and as a child I left room for my guardian angel to sit beside me at my school desk and I left room for my guardian angel alongside me in my tiny childhood bed.

"Listen," says Eve. "The Pope is Catholic and you are Catholic, or were once; the Pope has a cool apartment in Rome, you have a cool apartment in Rome; the Pope does not golf, you do not golf; the Pope does not ride a noisy Vespa, you do not ride a noisy Vespa; the Pope likes "Wild Thing" by The Troggs, you like "Wild Thing" by The Troggs."

I can see no flaw in this logic. I am made in God's image while this Pope's raccoon eyes speak of secrets and bad vibes and Machiavellian rooms of red-hatted cardinals. How would I look in a scarlet cassock and beanie cap? My first act will be to free the Pope's butler from his Vatican jail cell and he will kiss my mobster holy-man ring out of gratitude. I'll have a butler! *Ditat Deus*, God enriches.

As a child I wanted to be a priest and I envisioned my guardian angel as blonde and slim and kindly, not unlike the Quebec stewardess who helped me with the taxi, not unlike Natasha who was kind until the moment she left me. Has that childhood religious vision affected my expectations of real women later in life, of those I make room for in my bed?

I say, "I always assumed my guardian angel was blonde. But Jesus was Middle Eastern; would he not be dark-haired?"

"How many angels are there in total?" Eve asks. "Does the Pope know? Do all the angels sleep together in a dorm and have pillow fights?"

There are gaps in dogma, but I love the look and colours of Rome, its lovely hues stuck in my eye, shades of crimson and cinnamon, salmon and sienna, charcoal and blood, black brick touching blond brick touching walls of ashen stone, ochre clay and yellow plaster and tile in startling nebula swirls and slabs of veined green marble.

I could live here where cobblestones lift around the bases of ancient trees and that bridge over the river dates from before Christ. Once they loaded plague victims on barges to float them out of the city to the sea. Laundry on the next building slaps in the breeze, a nautical effect, linen and blouses like mizzen skysails and royal staysails and flying jibs, as if the tenements will also weigh anchor and slip into the Tiber to drift downriver to Ostia and the sea.

"Chin chin," says Eve in a toast, "to a Canuck pope."

Voices drift to us in perfect clarity.

"Tom Hanks just walked right by!"

Tom Hanks is filming some Dan Brown crap in a nearby piazza.

"On the set he made a sour face when someone blew a take, but he just seems so nice!"

Maybe Tom can help me, he's got connections, he's got juice, he knows where the bodies are buried. But what if Tom Hanks also wants to be pope? Maybe that is his real reason to be in Rome and this execrable movie is a foxy diversion. Tom has loads of money: why doesn't he try making a good movie instead of a bad one?

Eve tells me of past popes, reads a list of how many popes were murdered and how many popes were murderers. This is not a happy story. Constantine II: murdered. Stephen VII: strangled in prison. John X: strangled in prison. John XI: died in prison. Benedict VI: strangled in prison.

"Is Pope Joan on the list? What was the life expectancy? This sounds a dangerous job."

"But you'd be famous. The first Canuck pope."

"Louis Riel had a similar idea and I seem to remember that led to Mr. Riel hanging on the end of a rope in Regina."

Fame to me does not seem a good thing. Fame seems like some form of dementia or Alzheimer's where everyone knows you, but you don't know them.

Pope John XIV was killed by Francone, then the brand new Pope Francone was himself murdered, Pope Gelasius was set upon with stones and arrows. Pope Gelato was destroyed by diabetes and Pope George Ringo lost his record deal.

Italian newspapers drift soft as Kleenex outside every station of the Metro. I look at each page for a news article, but the nervous suburb under the distant volcano seems to have absorbed the bloody knifing without comment. They expect it of Napoli.

Eve puts aside the book, says, "See that cloud? It looks like a penis."

I wouldn't have thought that. "Very like a penis."

The clouds are there, but the rain is holding off.

"Or a killer whale."

She says, "I want to see the fresco *The Liberation of Saint Peter from Prison*. I saw the *David* long ago and it looked so lonely."

Eve is scholarly, better at languages and accents than I am; she can mimic any passing tourist voice (*how much is that in real money?*) and she comfortably teaches in French and Italian at her school in the Alps. She skis mountain frontiers and she appreciates fine food more than I can, has made a point to educate herself in French and Italian cooking, likes meat rare where I want it charred black, makes a tasty piece of salmon. When a meal arrives she admires the bright vegetable colours, meals so pretty we don't want to disturb the plates.

"Wait," she says, "wait. The eye must eat before the stomach."

We are deep in a city of millions, but songbirds flit the nearby boughs and a green parrot balances at the tip of the tree; it makes me happy to spy the fabled green parrot in the tree, my eyes, my tree, my parrot's weird chirping as goldfinches zip past my cousin Eve in lines of yellow light, swift radiant birds leaving the imprint of a sunlit laser show on my eyeballs, wild birds asking nothing of me, selling nothing, possessing nothing but beauty and song.

On the sunny terrace above the shaded warehouses my cousin reads to me from her book of Roman history; she knows I am obsessed by Pliny the Elder and she feeds my obsession: here is Pliny battling in northern swamps, Pliny fighting barbarian tribes on horseback, Pliny beating up the Franks, Hungarians, Vandals, Pliny smoking blunts and tossing deadly javelins from horseback.

Pliny rides and our green lizard glows in the wall. The next bottle of wine is reminiscent of cabbage and sardines so we decide it must be way good. My bookish cousin Eve looks nice in that female-who-isn't-yours sort of way: dark glasses, pigtails, Capri pants, Chinese slippers.

St. Valentine is the patron saint of beekeepers and travellers, so I feel close to him (does it really matter whether Valentine existed?). I'm not a beekeeper, but bees seem to like me and I'm a traveller. Pliny travelled the far edges of his Roman world, but he came back to the centre of empire to die under the volcano, asphyxiated near Pompeii, or did Pliny suffer a stroke? The volcanic cloud rose through green sky, a ghost tree hanging over beautiful villas until the shape collapsed and crashed in ash and heavy stones to crush the beautiful villas. I can't stop thinking of Pliny and his last deadly moments in Pompeii, sky gone black as a room with no light, his small apocalypse in the same town as the knife party where the unwanted neighbour fell in the hallway and we ran like spooked goats.

During the day I worry about Eve's pale skin in Italy's powerful sun. My cousin doesn't worry, no, she thrives on sun and heat in scanty summer outfits. Others limp back to their rooms exhausted from our exalted tasks in the world of art and red-faced from our master the sun, but she seems unfazed, Eve thrives.

As the sun fades behind walls I quietly play my new chromatic harmonica, silver flashing as pink Roman stone turns dark, and I gaze at her form, a thief hiding in my eye.

On my rooftop terrace Eve says, "You know you have to get over her. Dwelling on it is not going to magically change things." Eve enjoys lecturing me about my lost Natasha, my girl from the north country. Eve has brought beautiful tart berries from the street market to our rooftop, she passes me a cold lemon drink and reads an André Gide aphorism from her endless heap of used paperbacks: *To be utterly happy, you must refrain from comparing this moment with other moments in the past.*

Yes, but how to *not* compare? How to stop the built-in comparison machinery in your head?

"Well sir, that's another problem," says Eve.

Archimedes worked out problems in the sand. They killed Archimedes in 212 BC as he was drawing his circles in the sand, his colony invaded.

Wait, Archimedes said reasonably as crazed Romans attacked him with swords, wait until I finish my math problem, my circles in the sand.

We must all deal with our problems, the zestless bottled water, the border wars over armrests in dark cinemas, the lost yellow-cake uranium or forgiving the recalcitrant lawn-mower.

But did the Roman soldiers wait for Archimedes to solve his crisis of the lawnmower? No. They put Archimedes to the sword, soldiers invaded the colony, invaded his body. I suppose that is a sort of solution to a problem. Or the problem is swiftly made a lot less relevant.

I am aware of my need to get past this niggling crippling memory, to put to the sword this rash abandonment by Natasha. Don't be a stick in the mud, they say, get out more. LBJ said to me once on his ranch in Texas, "Son, don't let dead cats stand on your porch."

I do thank you, *sage* advice, got it, I hear where you're coming from, I must stop.

But then I realize—I *am* getting out! I'm out skiing the snowy Alps and walking dusty excavations in Pompeii (the fine grit of Pompeii's ruins ruining Father Silas's camera), I'm out for wild-boar sausage in Napoli and good craic in Dubrovnik and dear dirty Dublin (though I loathe the techno maelstrom of Temple Bar) and I stroll sandy strands on Dingle Bay and cheered on pig races in West Cork, I'm drinking wheat beer under the street in Manchester (tiny stellar jukebox hung on the wall), sangria in Madrid, I'm up in planes and I'm jumping out of planes, I'm violating Mayan airspace, I'm moving like an illegal crack- block through the high-stepping June Taylor Dancers, I even snowboarded sand dunes just outside Dubai and man oh man the sand hurts way more than snow when you wipe. No dead cowboy can accuse me of letting dead cats stand on my porch.

Yet my moves and trips don't seem to count in my own head, my jittery journeys on the Adriatic or Irish Sea don't seem *authentic*. I am cowed, I am more awed by any stranger's matrix of travel, real trips with tidy storylines and clear beginnings and madrigal endings and pettifoggers and riot-police Plexiglass and fine hotels in latitudes of lassitude. Why do my own journeys not impress me, why do I have no faith in my blurry couch-surfing pilgrimages to see graves and relatives and breweries and the haughty swans of Sligo. Why do I have no faith in my own life?

The knifing in Napoli may have given me some gruesome perspective. This perspective changes moment to moment, but right now I think I'm weirdly better about Natasha.

It is good to at least *once* be in a relationship with this kind of depth and fervour, to know it, but not to the point of leaping from a bridge. After Natasha abandoned me in a hotel I hit a point where I understood why people leap from bridges, I was on the bridge and fully understood the attraction, but I did not leap from the bridge. I am resilient, I will bounce back, I will be the Superball driven into the pavement and bouncing clear over the roof of my childhood home.

It's a bit of a surprise, but Rome's rouge walls and running water spigots seem familiar and pleasing after Napoli's grey hulks and volcanic dust and volcanic drugs and jackal bedlam and mountains of aromatic refuse and a knife steering its formal way through the air of a kitchen party and a man lying like meat in the hall.

I knew that Rome had a pleasant complexion, but until I left and came back I didn't know that I'd taken it in my head this way, that I was returning to a place that seems an old friend, an open city that seems warm and broad and green— so oddly comforting to be held in Rome's glowing walls again.

As I walk Rome it seems almost a home, as if I know it well and have spent some bright worthy part of my life here, which may not be true, but is a fine feeling since I seem to have lost my sense of home and I don't know if I'll have it back.

In Rome we live inside the beautiful sun; in Rome we live where the ambulances start. The ambulances park on the street below and race away to help the unfortunates, a pleasing musical quality to their sirens, almost mariachi. Where we live in Rome is not far from the river, a 19th-century district that Benito Mussolini expanded while feeling expansive, before things went bad in the 20th century and they hung Benito and his companion Claretta by the heels in Milan, the way the mob cornered Cola di Rienzo with all their sharp knives on the high steps, on the monumental steps leading up to the gods envious of our blades and opinions.

So many blades and invasions—I can't keep track—so much meat and so many martyrs and monsters and gargoyles and gods and I study Eve's face transfixed listening to a woman's high lovely voice singing music of such formality and grief, *And thou true God gave thy only son.* And Croatian daughters on hands and knees scrubbing halls to earn pennies.

Il Signore sia con voi. The Lord be with you.

E con il tuo spirito. And with your spirit.

These Italian church refrains still familiar from childhood Sundays, bells pealing and Sunday memories turning over like those venerable Pontiac Laurentians with straight-six engines that run forever. In Regina the new country hanged Riel by the neck and stole his modest church bell, took it east to Ontario.

Eve hovers near another varnished painting, cracked faces and black shadows, the stone church cool and quiet, mysterious as a suicide on a bridge, and all that sunshine just outside—just a dark chapel bent under endless stone light.

Studying the Immortals makes me feel so very mortal, staring up at shadowy paintings and marble faces speaking of sorrow, staring at the work of murderous turbulent geniuses, at tapestries and crazily amazing ceilings, frescoes in colours like faint laughter from within planets, and angels and saints flying up into the sun, flying from sin and guilt, and collections of gilt Byzantine icons, gorgeous metallic paintings of Madonna in starry blue robes with a tiny child and sober aquiline faces, faces bent into long cubist angles.

These devout Byzantine faces make me want to jump up and tear across an ancient map to know Istanbul's eastern empires and all the Virgin Mary's collection of custard-yellow halos and cobalt gowns.

Pliny the Elder tore around the ancient papyrus maps. I have an image of Pliny when he was much younger, as if I am there on the deck of his wooden boat, part of his crew and Pliny my captain cutting the waves in a speedy Arab felucca, firkins lashed down and sharp sails snapping and swinging around my sunburnt face.

I hang my white shirts in the sun near a lazaretto, the hospital island named after the beggar Lazarus, the island where they sent plague victims on open barges to the sea and I wonder, how does Eve's skin feel and smell, and what is it to cradle her limbs on a high Irish hill and feel her shirt, feel her shadow move over me like a cloud on gold grass.

Mr. Tom Hanks has been zero help in my campaign to be pope, I must now consider Tom Hanks an adversary. Memo:

no more causes. Unlike me, Tom has the money to run a real campaign. And he is well liked. He may well be the next pope instead of me, Tom waving from the balcony. Tell me, is luck a thing you manufacture, like a set of tires?

In my room late at night I can't stop listening to Cat Power's troubled cover of "Moonshiner," listen over and over to her lament, *If drinking do not kill me*. Her voice, ghostly slow, seems to accrue more distant meaning and weight than the song's plain words should ever be able to convey. It's a spooky puzzle and I keep trying to figure it out, at 2 a.m. the matter seems of utmost importance.

Eve downloads music on her laptop; she is a student of Italian opera, but she also likes drone blues and alt-country. Her strange authority.

Eve says she can't stop thinking of the art we've seen, like so much chocolate, too many treasures for one spot. We whisper to each other in the gallery: How was it all collected here in one spot, how many robbed and murdered in its superb suspect provenance?

Eve says, "The big thieves hang the little thieves."

The groaning galleries and museums are too much to take in at once, we stagger as if eating too much, it's staggering. But that rich swag is why we are here.

Our sheets and shirts spread on the bright terrace as we taste apples from Afghanistan and dates from the Euphrates and sip sharp juice from blood oranges. It's so lovely to eat outside with a view of this fabled city. Mangos and blood oranges, mangos her new favourite and Eve waves a tiny knife to demonstrate how to peel the lovely skin.

Eve smiles widely. "Remember we saw that huge fish jump in the Tiber? What timing, just as we walked up. Two or three feet, and fat!"

She seems bright today. Is sleep coming easier at night? Will we ever be reconciled with the knife at the party, will the mind forget the body twitching in the hall and the dead man's daughter weeping? All those body parts worked as a perfect machine until the introduction of the knife into the sensitive wires under the surface. We escaped to the silent train and the town's closed shutters.

"What is Italian for blood oranges? I should know," Eve says.

Later she remembers and e-mails an answer: *Arancia sanguigna. Ci vediamo presto! xxx*

See you soon. In Gaspé the laundry-lines so noisy flapping in the winds off the sea, but in Rome her sheets are silent in sun and heat, no noise or fanfare as moisture exits the cotton, cloth dry in moments.

"Are you peckish? I have some smoked salmon and honeydew apples. We'll eat a bite and then go wander."

When wandering I enjoy happy accidents, enjoy my mind's momentary lapses and I forget where I am. I wandered through Piazza Cavour the other afternoon and found a huge bruised palace fronted by groves of shaggy palm trees, tropical palm trees and erotic statues on stone plinths, this otherworldly palace decorated like a Cuban wedding cake—such long stripes of ornate balcony and porticos and fluttering doves and steroid blossoms pushed toward me from every meaty tree in the piazza. I stand in Rome and walk someone else's fever dream of Latin America. What a dream, what a bewitching chimera city, where they beat the shit out of the patron saint of lovers with clubs and separated him from his head.

In this concussed city Eve cooks a beautiful omelette of market eggs and goat cheese, in my tiny kitchen she chops spinach and green onion and layers a thin membrane of smoked salmon within the eggs. She wields a sharp knife. Does my cousin wish to kill me, leave me twitching? No, she slices her creation so neatly, half for her mouth and half for mine, and on the terrace her tender omelette melts on our tongue, the best I have ever tasted.

Later we will walk fountain to fountain, drift palace to palace, painting to painting, but first we eat and drink at our small table on my sunny terrace. Tomorrow we will go to Cannaregio and dangle our legs in the canal, sit at the canal drinking beautiful chalices of frosty white beer and eating tiny cicchetti from the charming bartender with the shaven skull at Zonan Birreria. I travel so large a world, but my favourite is the tiny world we create when two people are kind to each other.

Mark Anthony Jarman is the author of *Touch Anywhere to Begin, Czech Techno, Knife Party at the Hotel Europa, My White Planet, 19 Knives, New Orleans Is Sinking, Dancing Nightly in the Tavern*, and the travel book *Ireland's Eye*. He was an acquisitions editor for Oberon Press, and introduced many new writers through the *Coming Attractions* series. He is also the editor of *Best Canadian Stories 2023*. His novel *Salvage King Ya!*, is on Amazon. ca's list of 50 Essential Canadian Books and is the number one book on Amazon's list of best hockey fiction. Widely published in Canada, the US, Europe, and Asia, Jarman is a graduate of the Iowa Writers' Workshop, a Yaddo fellow, has taught at the University of Victoria, the Banff Centre for the Arts, and the University of New Brunswick, where he has been fiction editor of *The Fiddlehead* literary journal since 1999. He is also co-editor of literary journal *CAMEL*.

Printed in the USA
CPSIA information can be obtained
at www.ICGtesting.com
JSHW021459050224
56676JS00004B/29